# BORN UNDER PUNCHES

Thatcher's Conservative government in power. The miners on strike. Two Tribes going to war. Blair's Labour government enters its second term. The rail network is collapsing, the Health Service descending into chaos. Things can only get better?
A footballer, a debt collector, a miner, a journalist and his sister... Moving seamlessly between 1984 and the present day, this tautly plotted thriller involves five inhabitants of Coldwell, a former pit town on the Northumberland coast, whose lives are radically changed by the strike – a strike which will have unforeseen and devastating repercussions for those involved, and for future generations.

Please note: *This book contains material which may not be suitable to all our readers.*

# BORN UNDER PUNCHES

# BORN UNDER PUNCHES

*by*

Martyn Waites

**Magna Large Print Books**
Long Preston, North Yorkshire,
BD23 4ND, England.

British Library Cataloguing in Publication Data.

Waites, Martyn
 Born under punches.

 A catalogue record of this book is
 available from the British Library

 ISBN   0-7505-2343-3

First published in Great Britain in 2003 by Simon & Schuster UK Ltd.

Published in Large Print 2005 by arrangement with
Simon & Schuster UK Ltd.

Magna Large Print is an imprint of Library Magna Books Ltd.

Printed and bound in Great Britain by
T.J. (International) Ltd., Cornwall, PL28 8RW

For
Steve Baker,
wherever you are

# Acknowledgements

As the great Norman Lovett once said, No man is an island except when he's in the bath, so with that in mind I have to thank some people for their help with this book. Judith Atkinson of NECA, Hazel Waites, Deb Howe and Alison Taylor for the research assists. Stieve Butler and Dirk Robertson for putting up with my whingeing. David Shelley for your consideration. My agent Caroline Montgomery and my new editor Kate Lyall Grant for knowing when to crack the whip and when to tell me I'm wonderful. And, of course, my wife Linda. For all of the above.

Some publications which were useful: *The Great Strike* by Alex Callinicos and Mike Simons, *Dancing in Mid-Air – People and Drugs in Blyth* edited by Barry Stone, *The Social Impact of Pit Closure* by Dave Waddington, Bella Dicks and Chas Critcher, *Undermined – Oral Testimonies of the Miners' Strike* by Members of South Yorkshire's Mining Communities, *Convicted at Birth* by Jennifer Wynn, and Nick Davies's excellent documentary *Drugs – the Phoney War* plus his accompanying articles.

The town of Coldwell isn't a real place, but that's not to say it doesn't actually exist. As for places that do exist – as usual, I've played fast and loose with them. This is a work of fiction, remember. This is my version of the world. The Ashington Group of Painters also existed. Their work is on display at the Woodhorn Colliery Museum in Ashington, Northumberland.

*Man hands on misery to man.*
*It deepens like a coastal shelf.*

PHILIP LARKIN

# PROLOGUE

## Nowhere Fast

# Now

The music besieged the flat, blaring and thumping, pounding around the walls like a hooligan in a blind rage. The doorbell cut in abruptly, knife-like, demanding immediate attention.

'Fuckin' miserable neighbours.'

Karl buttoned up his jeans, reluctantly made his way to the door.

He violently yanked the door open, mouth ready to spew obscenities at being disturbed. Before he could speak, an arm shot out, catching him by the throat, gripping his neck like an industrial vice. Karl's surprise quickly turned to fear, then desperation. He knew who it was. He knew how small were his chances of walking away unharmed.

The man picked Karl up off the floor and flung him into the living room, upending the sofa, crashing him on to a small table. Karl rolled off and lay on the floor, groaning, blood pooling at the side of his mouth.

The man entered, scoped the room, saw a girl half-standing, half-kneeling. Young, attractive, struggling to pull her clothes around herself. Her eyes quick-flicked between the man and Karl's prone body, fear-gasping down air.

The man glared steel, the girl collapsed on to the floor like her bones had just been removed. Breathing in spasms, she tried to scuttle herself into the corner, through the wall. Brick halted her, and she stopped moving. Trembling, foetally curled, she let out an involuntary, wailing keen.

The man didn't listen. He had heard it all before.

He looked around for others, found only the deafening, pounding dance music emanating from the walls. He couldn't make out where it was coming from; if he had he would have destroyed the CD player. Squinting against the noise, he crossed the floor to reach the girl.

She started to scream.

In the kitchen, Davva and Skegs, heads already fully loaded, garage pushed up to earbleed, heard nothing of this.

Davva looked at Skegs, blasted, jerking his body to the block-rockin' beats. A head full of skunk, a bottle of tequila in his left, Karl's automatic in his right. Davva made a grab for the tequila, got it on the second attempt, Skegs surrendering it easily. He tipped his head back, gulped down big mouthfuls. He stood there rooted, legs numb, waiting for his world to stop spinning, trying to get back on again, swallowing back the bile bubbling up in his throat.

How the fuck do people drink that stuff? he thought. Fuck, I'm shagged.

Skegs just stood there, trying to catch a rhythm, waving the gun above his head. Gone.

Then a noise so loud it topped the music, penetrated their mashed skulls. Crashing, thumping, banging, topped by a real horror movie scream. Davva and Skegs looked at each other, puzzlement forcing itself into their fogged brains.

'Karl must be givin' that bird a real fuckin' seein' to,' Davva slurred, laughing.

'Shall we gan an' watch?' asked Skegs, eyes full of lascivious cruelty.

Davva giggled, nodded. They made their way to the door. Davva put his ear to the wood but couldn't hear anything. He looked at Skegs, shrugged, turned the handle.

It wasn't what they were expecting. It was sheer devastation. Karl's living room had gone from sterile tidiness to post-bombing Chechnya. Glass and ceramics were smashed. Furniture was upended. The fireplace mirror was now just a starburst collection of shards.

The girl cowered in the far corner, a huge sliver of sharpened glass held knife-like in one hand, blood pooling and dripping around her fingers and palms. In the other she clutched the curtains over her naked body in a desperate cloak of protection. On the floor lay Karl, bashed and bruised, mouth pouring blood. His arms flopped slowly and uselessly, his fingers made feeble grasping motions. Between them both stood a man Davva and Skegs had never seen before: compact, powerful-looking, dressed in a light-coloured suit, white shirt, dark tie. The suit splattered with blood. Hair cut short and greying, face twisted, ugly with violence. He was ordering the girl to put the glass-knife down, moving towards her. Then he caught her eyeline, turned, saw Davva and Skegs, stopped. Faced them.

Fear broke inside the two boys as the man pointed towards them, spoke. The words were lost in the beat, but they knew they weren't pleasant. The man began to move towards them, hands outstretched as if about to do damage.

Panic rooted Davva and Skegs. Davva raised his arms in an ineffectual attempt to ward off the blows he knew were coming, whimpering in painful anticipation.

Then a popping sound, not loud but authoritative enough above the din. The man flung himself to his right, spun and crashed down on his right knee as if his leg had been kicked out from under him. He clutched his side, face darkening with surprise and pain, jacket and shirt darkening to black red.

Davva looked at Skegs. He was now sitting behind him on the kitchen floor in sudden, shocked astonishment. In his right hand was Karl's still-smoking gun. Skegs stared at it like he'd never seen it before, as if the gun and the hand belonged to someone else.

Davva looked again at the man, now slid down on to both knees and half-dragging, half-pulling himself along the floor, face caged with agony and anger.

Then Davva heard another noise. At first his clouded-up mind thought it was just extra bass and vibe from the sound system, but it wasn't. Someone was hammering very loudly and very insistently on the front door, holding down the doorbell at the same time.

Oh, fuck, thought Davva. Fuck, fuck, fuck.

Fear ratcheted up several notches, panic rose higher. His head was spinning, sick from more than just weed and booze. He had the sudden

22

overwhelming urge to cry. He fought it unsuccessfully and fell to his knees, sobbing on the kitchen floor.

He gave an inward curse of anger and pity as painful tears ran down his cheeks. Not for the first time in his thirteen years did he wish he wasn't just someone or somewhere else, but that he had never been born in the first place.

# PART ONE

## Dead Man's Town

# 1. Then

Roeder punted the ball into the air and Tony Woodhouse, tracking it, seeing it float over the pitch in seeming slow motion, knew it would be his.

It was a lucky kick, a desperate, scrambled attempt to clear the goalmouth from an Arsenal corner with most of his team back defending. Tony saw the chance for a break and moved. He ran towards it, studs spewing gouts of turf in his wake, ignoring the shouts, focusing on the ball, only the ball. His marker, an Arsenal midfielder, clocked Tony's action and moved in, shadowing, then blocking him.

Tony dropped his left shoulder, making as if to follow the move through with his whole body. The Arsenal player anticipated the movement, took a sudden change in direction. Tony pulled back before his foot hit the ground, kept the course he was on and ran.

'Fucker!' A half-grunt, half-shout from the Arsenal man, now left standing.

A perfect dummy. Tony ran on, the Arsenal man just a receding blur of shirt.

Tony saw the ball arcing down before him and jumped for it. He planned on connecting his head to the ball, knocking it on to someone else – Beardo or the Waddler; they were usually up there mouching – then following in support. But there were no other black and white shirts near him. He went up, grunting, legs compressing then combusting like engine pistons. He was on his own.

He pushed harder, higher, twisting as he went, meeting the ball with his chest rather than his head. He absorbed the impact, deadening the ball in the process, dropping it at his feet. Good. He could work with it now.

He looked up. Two Arsenal defenders were making their way directly towards him. He had no time to think, to look around, scope out other players. He put his head down and ran straight ahead, powering up the centre, the ball never more than inches in front of his toes, held there as if by invisible elastic.

The two defenders converged on him, one either side. Tony kept going, still straight at them, glancing side to side for support. He gave a quick look to his left; Beardo was up shouting, gesturing to a spot past the two defenders, where he would have a clear run at the goal. Tony, thinking on the hoof, calculated the distance, lined up the pass. The left defender saw him telegraph the movement and changed his position, challenging Tony by running straight at him. Tony reacted, thoughts and impulses turning into action with lightning speed. He switched the ball to his other foot, then back, keeping his run going, selling another dummy, sending the defender in the wrong direction.

He reached the penalty box. One defender left, eyes stuck to Tony's feet, trying to follow or anticipate movement. The defender made the first move. He slid forward, coming in fast and low, stretching out his right leg, risking a penalty if the move misconnected, committing himself. Tony skipped the ball over the man's leg, followed it through, and there he was with a clear shot at goal.

His chest was on fire, his legs ached with exertion, his breath ragged. He ignored it all. The rest of the ground, the other players, the crowd tunnelled away into darkness and shadow. There was just him, the ball and the goal. The goal-keeper stood hunched, intense, dancing from side to side in anticipation.

He struck the ball, aimed for the top left-hand corner. The keeper read the action, flung himself at full stretch to cover it. If the ball had gone where Tony intended it to go, it would have been saved. But there was too much spin on it. It sailed to the right, missing the keeper's fingers, gliding just under the bar and smacking comfortably into the back netting.

Two–nil.

The home crowd went wild. The collective pent-up frustration, hopes and faith of a whole city in microcosm were released in a solid block of cheering so loud, so unrestrained, that it became an almost physical thing. The air warmed with the sound, the pitch vibrated, the stands shook. It was like being at the centre of a minor earthquake.

The sonic wave reached Tony, brought him back from his zone, back to the moment. He stuck his arms in the air, fists clenched, added his own roar to the crowd. He turned to the Gallow-gate end, held the gesture, and the roar, if anything, intensified.

Other team members ran up to congratulate

him; jump on him, kiss him, share the victorious euphoria of release. They spoke to him: one-liners, crude encouraging phrases, shared jokes. Tony's lips moved, but it couldn't be called responding. He barely noticed what they said, what he said. Coursing through his veins was a feeling beyond anything he had experienced before: money, sex, drugs, booze, adrenalin. Nothing came close. Thousands of people screaming his name in love and adulation. In worship. This was it. This was life – his life, *the* life – and it was fucking brilliant.

It was a perfect, defining moment, and he held the pose, arms in the air, willing that moment never to end.

Tommy Jobson stood at the far end of the bar in the Trent House in Newcastle, one eye on the room, the other on the door, mentally trying to block out the noise from the jukebox.

He held himself separate from the rest of the bar both by the sharpness of his clothes – smart two-piece, tie, shined shoes and neatly combed hair – and also the dark concentration that enveloped him like an invisible cocoon. The bar was getting crowded, but no one had troubled him or even gone near him. The noise from the jukebox sounded like a guitar being smashed on the floor with a train rumbling past in the background and an emaciated black-clad heroin addict wailing about bats. It just notched up the rage inside him. He would store that, channel it when the time was appropriate. And that time would be very soon.

Tommy had been waiting patiently for over twenty minutes, a barely touched pint of Becks in front of him, alert, enduring all manner of aural rubbish from the jukebox, picking up inane conversational snippets from the self-consciously arty clientele. The noise stopped, replaced by the Smiths and their whiny art school angst. Tommy took a small sip of beer. At least it wasn't Billy Bragg cranking out dirgy protest songs for the miners again.

The punters lapped it all up. Black Levi's, DMs and quiffs for the students, second-hand antique suits and jackets for the local hipsters, Gitanes and black polo necks for the ultimate poseurs. One of the black polo necks was flinging his arms about, monopolizing his table, not letting anyone else speak. Tommy felt irrational anger well up inside. He wanted to go over there and grind his beer glass in the smug cunt's face, shut him up. But he controlled himself because he was here on business. He breathed deeply, holding it down, putting it in reserve. He took another sip of beer. Went back to waiting.

But not for long. The main door opened and in walked a man, quite tall, hair curly, greying and long, wearing a Hawaiian shirt over Levi's, buttons straining over an expanding gut. Over ten years older than the bar's average punter, he looked self-deluded enough to think he was still one of the kids. The man walked through the bar, straight into the gents.

Tommy nodded. From the far end of the room, Nev, Tommy's partner, detached himself from behind a corner table and followed the man in.

31

Nev, one inch short of a behemoth, with a flat-top haircut, was dressed casually in shades of pastel shirt and slacks. He looked like a nightclub bouncer gone golfing.

Tommy straightened his tie, smoothed his hair and, with a careful, measured stride, followed.

Nev stood guard inside, blocking entrance or exit with his massive bulk. The toilet was small, cramped. A stained stainless-steel urinal trough ran the length of one wall. Two cubicles opposite. The walls were plastered with old posters for bands and concerts, scrawled over with graffiti. Two marker pens by the sink had been left by the management to encourage it. One of the cubicles was empty, the other occupied. Tommy knocked on the door. A sniffing, coughing voice replied: 'Someone in 'ere. Not be a minute.'

Tommy swallowed, breathed in fully, exhaled slowly.

'Hello, Neil.' The words clipped, controlled.

The sniffing came to a sudden, tense stop behind the door. Tommy waited.

'Who's that?' asked a shaky voice eventually.

Tommy sighed. 'You know who this is, Neil. Don't play games. Come out. I want to talk to you.' The tone measured, the words sounding carefully chosen and rehearsed.

The bolt was pushed back slowly, the noise reverberating as if in a dungeon. Neil stepped out, nose twitching, swallowing hard. Tommy, gearing himself up, smiled.

'Long time no see, Neil,' he said slowly. 'Where you been hiding?'

Neil's face blanched white, showing up the red-

32

ness in his nose. 'Nowhere, honest. I've just been around, you know.'

Tommy waited, eyes boring into Neil's, breathing increasing.

'Look...' began Neil, 'I know what you're thinkin', but it's not like that, honestly.'

Tommy frowned. 'What am I thinking, Neil?'

Neil sniffed, swallowed hard. 'That I stiffed you. Fucked you over.'

Tommy allowed himself a small smile. Neil's white skin turned almost translucent. 'Let's get this straight, Neil. You're only in business because I allow you to be. Because my bu-bu-boss allows you to be. That's the nuh-nuh-new deal.'

Neil flinched at Tommy's stutter. He knew it wasn't a good sign. He nodded, shrugged. Attempted a smile. 'Aw, c'mon, Tommy, wassa matter, man? I'm playin' straight with yuh...'

Tommy, with razor-sharp speed, grabbed Neil's collar and twisted, pushing him back against the cubicle frame. Neil's eyes bugged out, almost on stalks. When Tommy spoke, he managed to keep his voice low and controlled.

'Really, nuh-nuh-nuh-Neil? You've been heard shouting your mouth off all over town. Saying huh-huh-who do I think I am? About how you're going to ru-ru-rip me off, how I'm only a boy doing a man's job, how I'm there for the t-t-t-taking. Worthless cu-cu-cunt.' He twisted the collar tighter. 'I'm in chuh-charge now, Neil. I'm your new boss. And just because I'm new doesn't give you the right to badm-m-m-outh me, does it?'

Neil shook his head vigorously.

Tommy took a deep breath. He could feel his

face reddening as his control slipped. He exhaled. Kept it together. 'Good. This is what's going to happen. I'm going to give you two days, and in those two days you're either going to come up with my money – all of it – or my product back. And it is my product. OK?'

Relief expelled itself from Neil's body in a huge sigh. He nodded.

'OK. Thank you...'

'But,' continued Tommy, 'I cu-cu-can't let p-p-people take the p-p-p-piss, can I? I've got to remind you who's boss, don't I?' He pulled out a wooden-handled knife from his jacket pocket. The blade glinted and sparkled in the toilet's weak yellow light.

Neil stared at the blade, legs buckling, head shaking. 'Look!' he shouted. 'It wasn't just me.'

Tommy smiled. 'I knu-know that. Let's discuss it.'

Tommy pushed him back into the cubicle, following him in. He cut a strip off the front of Neil's shirt, stuffed it into the man's mouth and, with a smile, went to work.

Nev, standing guard, averted his gaze. Although he was hardened to what was coming next, something about the way Tommy worked disturbed him. Not the muffled screams or the blood. It was the fact that Tommy insisted on whistling, or sometimes singing, Dean Martin songs as he got down to business. With no trace of a stutter.

Now that, thought Nev, was really scary.

Ten minutes later, in the car, Tommy was sitting behind the wheel looking flushed but relaxed and happy. Almost post-coital, Nev would have thought, had the word been in his vocabulary.

'Ah,' Tommy sighed, 'that's amore.' His eyes glinted with malicious glee. He had got what he wanted.

Nev grunted in reply.

'Right,' said Tommy, sprightly once more. 'Fancy a trip to the seaside?'

Rio sat on the seafront at Whitley Bay, a pastel and neon-lit palace of exclusivity, supposedly owned by a member of Duran Duran. Brand-new and notoriously hard to gain admittance to, punters had to show they fulfilled the correct criteria of age, attitude and aspiration before they were allowed in, because it wasn't just a bar they were entering, but a lifestyle, a dream.

Tony Woodhouse had no trouble getting in. The management even bought him free drinks in recognition of his achievements that afternoon. Consequently, he loved everything about the place. The decor, the atmosphere, the music. The girls.

Poised and confident, stylish and sophisticated, they were there for more than just a Saturday-night pull. They were showing what they had, giving glimpses of where they were headed, expressing, but not flaunting, their upward mobility. The boys all loved this and responded accordingly, raising their game too.

Tony was dressed in a double-breasted suit, the dark weave of the material shot through with a silver check that caught the light when he moved the right way. With his sleeves rolled up and his shirt buttoned to the neck, he knew he looked the business. He was with his old school friends from Coldwell, the mining town along the Northumberland coast. They couldn't match Tony financially, being either down the pit, in office jobs or unemployed, but they could match him in their hopes and ambitions. That was why, dressed in their finest smart casual, they came back to Rio week after week. Because once inside it didn't matter what they were the rest of the time. Once inside, they willingly surrendered to their dreams and allowed themselves to be held – like Tony – in Rio's aspirational *Miami Vice*-like grip.

Post-match had been a blur for Tony. He had conducted a short interview for *Match of the Day* while still on a high. The only thing he could remember about it was telling the interviewer he still had a long way to go, a lot of things to prove. Then out of St James' Park and down the coast road to keep his weekly appointment with his old school mates. Although life seemed to be taking him in a different direction, that was no reason to stop seeing them. If the *Match of the Day* interviewer had asked him about that, he would have said that they were still his mates and they still had a laugh together. And that, Tony would have said, looking straight to camera, was the important thing.

If he had been asked what he intended to do with the night he would have answered: Have a few pints with the lads, a few laughs, do a few lines and if I'm lucky pull some skirt. Well, maybe not the bit about doing some lines. Jimmy Hill wouldn't be happy with that.

They had bar-hopped along the seafront, ending up in Rio where they stood drinking beer, scoping the action, telling their stories, having a good time. The music was brilliant. Frankie's 'Two Tribes' segueing into Jeffrey Osbourne's 'Stay with Me Tonight', which in turn became '1984', the Eurythmics needlessly reminding everyone what year it was. Tony, high on the booze, the drugs and the goal, had barely stopped grinning all night. He couldn't have been happier. Time of me fuckin' life, he would have told *Match of the Day* if they had still been listening.

And then he saw her. Standing with a group of friends but, to him, she stood out immediately. Quite tall but given extra height by her spike heels, she was dressed completely in black. Short, flared skirt over tanned legs, tight vest top, short jacket. Her hair was long and dark and her figure curved in all the places he considered important. Make-up used only as and when needed. Tony couldn't help staring. She stared back, their eyes locked and he was in lust.

He looked at his friends, pointed at their glasses. Despite none of them being empty, they all nodded. He pushed his rolled-up jacket sleeves even further up his arms, tossed his gelled-back floppy fringe from his forehead, and walked – like the camera was still on him, the crowd still watching – a circuitous route to the bar. She stared right at him, watching him, letting him approach.

'Hi,' he said.

She smiled back. It seemed brighter than neon. 'Hi.'

Tony, using his charm but playing it safe,

offered to buy her a drink.

She thought for a moment. 'You can, but I'm with friends. We're drinking in rounds.'

Tony stepped up a gear, gave his dazzling smile. If smiles could win games, he thought, this one would get me a hat-trick. 'No problem.' He turned to the other girls. 'What would you like, ladies?'

The girls all giggled, made comments about his generosity and accepted his offer. The girl he had singled out rolled her eyes at such an obvious and tacky gesture, but she smiled when she did it.

Brilliant, he thought. I'm in here.

Tony distributed the drinks, manoeuvring the girl away from her friends, separating her from the main herd as a predator would.

'What's Love Got to Do with It?' Great. He loved that one.

'So what's your name?'

'Louise,' she replied. 'You?'

Not wanting to appear too flash too soon, he gave her only his first name.

Then the question-and-answer session started. Louise was eighteen, down at the coast with her friends for the night. Living in Gateshead, doing business studies at the tech.

Tony told her he had his own flat and – he studied her face for her reaction; this was the bit he loved – he was a professional footballer.

Her first reaction was predictable. She didn't believe him.

'Honestly.' He gave her the winning smile again. 'I play for Newcastle. I played today against Arsenal.'

'Oh yeah?' she said sceptically. 'What was the score?'

'Two-one to us. Beardo got the first.' His grin, if anything, widened. 'I got the second. Then we got sloppy and they got one back. But it didn't matter.'

She screwed her eyes up, scrutinizing him closely. 'Tony Woodsomething.'

'Woodhouse. That's me.'

'Me dad and me brother like football,' she said with polite indifference. 'I'll tell them I met you.'

The smile began to fade from Tony's face. Even if girls weren't interested in football, they were always excited when they found out who he was.

'What?' she asked in response to his hurt expression.

'Nothin',' mumbled Tony.

'Did you expect me to ask for your autograph or something? Fall to the floor and demand a bonk?'

Tony said nothing, just continued to look hurt.

Louise burst out laughing. 'You did! You did, didn't you? You vain bastard!'

Even through the bar's darkness and neon, Tony could feel himself reddening. This wasn't the way it usually turned out.

'You think because you scored a goal and bought me a drink I should be impressed?' Louise asked.

Tony shrugged. 'Well, you know...'

She smiled. 'I can be impressed.' Her eyes dropped. Something came into them that wasn't there before. 'But you'll have to try harder than that.'

The look connected. Tony felt the stirrings of

not only an erection but something else, some-thing deeper flutter inside him. He looked back at her, taking her face in properly for the first time. Louise was beyond pretty. She was really beautiful.

'OK,' he said. 'Listen, why don't we go some-where else?' Louise shrugged, eyes not leaving his. 'Where did you have in mind?'

He was about to ask her back to his place, but something stopped him. It didn't feel right. Not with her. He wanted to get to know her better first.

'Nightclub?' he suggested 'Casino? Indian? Whatever you like.'

While Louise made a show of deciding, Tony glanced through the crowd, catching the approv-ing glances and crude gestures of his friends. He returned their smiles, but not the gestures, hoping Louise hadn't seen the action. As his eyes swept back towards her, he clocked someone and his heart made an immediate flip of sudden fear. Tommy Jobson had entered the bar.

Tony grabbed Louise's arm. 'C'mon, we've got to leave right now.'

Louise turned angrily towards him, trying to shake off his sudden grip. 'What you doing? Get off.'

'I've just remembered ... the car ... I'll get a ticket if I don't move it. Quick. C'mon.' He grabbed her again.

She pulled her arm away, anger in her eyes. 'Tony, I haven't even said goodbye to my friends yet. Or told them where I'm going.'

'Don't worry, you'll be all right.' He looked straight at her, panic in his voice, fear in his eyes.

'Please. We have to leave now.'

Louise sighed. 'Come on, then.'

They said hasty goodbyes, sketched waves to their friends, and Tony dragged Louise towards the side exit.

'You'd better have a fucking good explanation for dragging me round like this.'

'Oh, I have,' said Tony, dashing through the door. 'I have.'

Tommy Jobson had pulled the BMW up directly in front of the vulgar monstrosity that he considered Rio to be, the Chairman of the Board blasting from the sound system. 'Sounds for Swingin' Lovers'. Impossible to top. Nev, monolithic and monosyllabic, sat silently in the passenger seat.

'Just wait here, Nev. This won't take lu-lu-long.'

Nev grunted his assent.

Tommy got out of the car, walked towards the main doors of the bar, palmed a folded twenty to the doorman, walked straight in. The noise, heat and smell hit him. At least the women here looked like they'd made an effort, he thought. Not like the other place. Music's still shit, though.

Tommy scoped the room. This was the place, definitely. Every Saturday after a home game, Tony Woodhouse ended up in here. And it was time for that arrogant little shit to pay. One way or another.

Tommy's eyes locked on the target.

Tony looked around. Tommy tried to hide behind some lagered-up lad, retain the element of surprise, but Tony had seen him.

41

Tommy pushed through the crowded bar, displacing bodies and drinks, ignoring threats and names, shrugging off attempts to grab him. He reached the spot where Tony had stood, but he was too late. The bastard had flown.

Tommy looked around, struggling to keep his welling anger contained. He saw the side exit, the fire door bar down and wide open, and pushed his way quickly towards it, through it, and out on the street, alone but for the usual Saturday-night drunks weaving their way around the pavement. No sign of Tony Woodhouse.

'Fu-fu-fuck!' shouted Tommy aloud and sighed in exasperation. Composing himself, he slowly made his way back to the car.

He had other visits to make, other things to do with the night, other opportunities for fun. He would catch up with Tony Woodhouse eventually.

And that would be worth seeing.

Tony held Louise in his arms, moving his hands slowly over her body. When he strayed too far down or crossed some invisible line, he felt her move, twist away from his grip, shift to a less intrusive position. He didn't mind, though. Holding her was enough.

They were on the dancefloor of the Tuxedo Princess, a floating disco ship moored on the Tyne, moving slowly together to the last few songs of the night. Paul McCartney's 'No More Lonely Nights' had given way to Jeffrey Osbourne's 'On the Wings of Love', ending the session with the Cars' 'Drive'.

After leaving Whitley Bay, Tony had driven as

fast as he dared down the coast road back towards Newcastle, the shock of seeing Tommy Jobson cancelling out the effects of the alcohol. Louise was still seeking an explanation for their sudden departure from Rio.

'Someone came in that I didn't want to see,' Tony explained.

'Who?'

Tony tried for lightness, didn't quite pull it off. 'Oh, just some girl I used to know. Best not to see her. It would have been messy.' At least the last sentence was true. He looked at her, hoping to be believed. 'I'm sorry, OK? It won't happen again. Let's just enjoy ourselves, shall we?'

Louise didn't answer, but Tony could tell from the look on her face that she wasn't happy with the explanation. He decided to change the subject.

'So,' he said, giving her a fragile smile, 'do you fancy a dance?'

They had then made their way to the Tuxedo Princess, where they ate, drank and danced.

The song finished, the lights went up and they found themselves looking at each other, eyes locked.

'So,' said Tony, 'who's going to drive you home tonight?'

Louise smiled. 'The cab driver, I should think.'

'I could. Or I could drive us both back to mine.'

Louise teased the corners of her lips into a smile. 'What for?'

'What d'you think?'

Her smile deepened. 'Tony, I've really enjoyed tonight – really – but I don't sleep with someone as soon as I meet them. Plus, I've already got a boyfriend.'

Tony's head dropped. 'Oh.'

'That's not to say I don't want to see you again. Because I do.'

'What about your boyfriend?'

The smile on her face teased and promised. 'Let's be friends first and take it from there, shall we?'

Tony felt confused. Louise wasn't following the script. This wasn't the way it usually ended, but he felt quite excited by that fact. There was something different about her, something special. They could write a new script as they went along.

'OK,' he said.

'Good.' She reached into her bag, scribbled a note, passed it over. 'This is my number. Call me.'

'I will.'

'We'll see.'

They made their way to the exit, queued at the rank. Louise was about to get into her cab when Tony put a hand on her arm.

'Wait,' he said. 'I don't even know your surname.'

'It's Larkin. Louise Larkin.' She got into the cab. 'Call me.'

And with that she was off, leaving Tony there alone, a gormless grin on his face.

'I will,' he said and sighed. 'What a day,' he said out loud and began walking towards his car.

For the first time that day, he didn't need the cameras or crowds to be with him.

## 2. Now

## The Modern Age: A Prologue

*The modern age, as we know it, began on Monday 28 May 1984. This is not a date plucked at random for its Orwellian connotations, nor is it an officially recognized one. Yet it was on this day that our country changed for ever, the time bomb was primed, the countdown began. And where did this singular event occur? Orgreave coke works outside Rotherham, South Yorkshire.*

*Margaret Thatcher's Conservative government had been returned to power for a second term by an apathetic landslide. People had voted for her because there was no credible alternative. Prior to the election, there had been discontented rumblings over Tory leadership: a distracting opportunity presented itself in the shape of a small conflict in the South Atlantic over the Falkland Islands, a jingoistic adventure which helped assure her a second term. Emboldened by this, she cast around for a suitable domestic target: she found the miners.*

*The NUM, under the leadership of Arthur Scargill, brought the workforce out on strike in protest at the closure of profitable pits. The majority of the general public were behind this action.*

*The government, for all their tough talking, were wavering. They were signalling negotiation, reconciliation. Then came Orgreave.*

*A scab labour force was in operation there; the NUM sent nearly three thousand pickets to stop it. The police, taken by surprise at the sheer number of men, did nothing. The protest was peaceful and productive. By and large, the picket line wasn't crossed. The miners were jubilant. By demonstrating solidarity they scented a real chance of victory.*

*The government, however, felt they had lost face. They wanted something done. They instructed the police to retaliate.*

*The following day, the NUM area representatives handed out the picketing orders: Orgreave had only a couple of hundred men assigned to it. The majority were sent to other collieries. It was a middle-management political decision. There was nothing Scargill at the top or the striking miners at the bottom could do about it.*

*Positions were reversed. Miners in their hundreds, police five thousand strong.*

*They waited until the TV cameras had moved away then charged.*

*Mounted police. Police dogs. Attacking indiscriminately. Anyone connected with the strike – male or female, young or old – was considered a legitimate target. Riot sticks were reintroduced for the first time in ten years. Their previous use had led to the death of an anti-Nazi demonstrator. People were truncheoned, trampled, bitten.*

*The miners fought back with anything they could get their hands on. Bricks. Stones. The long-standing pacifism of the labour movement forcibly abandoned. The jubilation of the previous day forgotten. It was a bloody rout, culminating with the arrest of Arthur Scargill.*

Once released, Scargill wanted the forthcoming talks with the NCB to be conclusive: 'I hope we will be able to lay the foundations of a settlement.'

It wasn't to happen. The government had seen what happened at Orgreave. Dissent quelled by force. Riot police and scab labour to keep production going. And, with the media collusion, no public outcry at the tactics.

NCB chief Ian MacGregor was instructed not to co-operate. To sit out the strike. Starve the miners out if necessary.

The police blueprint for Orgreave became standard operating procedure for dealing with conflicts during the strike. Coldwell was just one in a number of similar battles.

The success of these operations opened the doors in the government's collective mind. Allowed the unthinkable to be thought. If they could get away with this, they reasoned, they could get away with anything. No one else will fight back if the miners lose. They'll be too frightened for their own jobs.

We can get away with anything.

Anything.

So they did.

Then came the wholesale dismantling of the country. Assets stripped, sold off. Public utilities that we already owned were sold back to us–

No. –were sold back to some of us–

No. –were selectively sold back–

No. No good.

Larkin sat back, clicked SAVE. Time for a break.

He closed the lid of the laptop, cracked a can of Stella, put the TV on. News. He watched.

The man walked into Newcastle Crown Court expensively but soberly suited and styled, self-importance fronting his every step, stonewalled by minders and solicitors, leaving cameramen and gawkers scrumming in his wake. His face was drawn and haggard yet arrogant and defiant, like a fading rock star refusing to cede ground to changing fashion or disappearing youth.

The *Ten O'Clock News* voice-overed in news-with-a-capital-N tones:

'Clive Fairbairn, seen here on the first day of his trial, was found guilty on sample charges of supplying class-A narcotics, conspiracy to supply, conspiracy to pervert the course of justice, attempting to bribe a police officer and grievous bodily harm. In his summing-up the judge said–' the screen swirled to a transcripted graphic '– "This is one of the most serious cases I have ever been associated with. Your willingness to exploit the weaknesses of others and callously profit from that is, in my opinion, shockingly unparalleled."'

Cut to the reporter standing outside the Crown Court, brow furrowed, eyes dancing with manic glee. The look said: career-making story means bye-bye regional, hello national. Desk drawers emptied, phone call awaited.

'Now we'll take a look back at the career of Newcastle's Mr Big, one of the most notorious gangland figures ever to come out of the north-east.'

Black and white footage of 1960s-era Newcastle montaged across the screen; old streets, poor people and bad housing morphed into images of bars and clubs awash with ale and martinis, the women beehived and desperate, the men Bryl-creemed and hungry. Soundtrack by the Animals, dancing by Douglas Bader. The report a big production number wobbling between terse moralizing and jocund voyeurism.

Fairbairn's verdict meant media open season, the new palliative of hate, a cloaked music-hall villain drawing the general public's fire, leaving secret empires undisturbed, secret histories untold. Stephen Larkin, watching, took another mouthful of beer and tuned out. He knew a Stalinist exercise in airbrushed history when he saw one.

Once, Larkin himself would have been scrumming outside the court, fighting to be first with the news, his name in print, his by-line in the public's face. Now he was content to watch others run around. Pursue his own agenda.

He had been in the flat for more than two months. Enough time to settle in, not enough to feel at home. The walls held oblong patches of richer colour where the previous tenant had hung pictures now removed. Along with a table, the cheap Lloyd Loom-copy chair he sat on was the only furniture in the room. Boxes and crates dotted the floor like stepping stones, his past compartmentalized, only opened when needed. They contained functional items, books, CDs, a few mementos. Life, for Larkin, was a casting off, not a gathering up. The laptop and printer sat on the table, paper and workbooks piled next to them. In front of a set of bare shelves in the corner sat an unconnected stereo system. He would shelve things, connect things, as he went along. Only when the boxes were empty would he consider calling the flat home.

The one bay window was curtainless; sodium dusk threw shadows against the walls, around the alcoves, where they danced with radiated TV images, filling the room with lonely, flickering wraiths.

Larkin had moved from his old house to his new flat in an attempt to discard the past, exorcise his ghosts.

He took another swig of Stella, stared at the missing picture spaces, tried to imagine what had once been there.

The TV news was finishing with Clive Fairbairn, the reporter's final words wreathed in triumph, mouth twisted with pride, as if he'd put the man away himself.

Back to the studio. And in other news: the countryside cattle pyres still burning. The privatized transport infrastructure dangerous and inoperable. A health service that needed a health warning, an education system no one seemed to learn anything from. The New Labour government begging the electorate to forget all that, vote them in for a second term in the forthcoming election.

Twenty-first century Britain. The legacy.

Larkin turned off the TV, pulled his chair over to the table, powered up the laptop again. The disks, the piles of paper, the well-thumbed books.

More ghosts to exorcise. More work to do.

'So, Mick,' Tony Woodhouse said, leaning forward, shoulders hunched, fingers steepled, left leg awkwardly folded behind, 'how you doin'?'

Mick fidgeted, tried to make himself comfortable, but the old armchair had accommodated so many shapes it was virtually worn out. His mouth moved, his forehead creased, but the words weren't ready to come out.

Tony stayed as he was, body relaxed, mind sharp and attentive. Wanting no further distractions, he put down the file he had been holding and waited. Mick would speak when he was ready.

The office was cheaply but warmly furnished. The morning sunlight made it more so. A desk and chair, an armchair, shelves and filing cabinets, all old when Bobby Robson was a boy, all just about still going. One wall was virtually filled with box folders, textbooks and other items, with no shortage of papers to be filed away. On the walls were posters promoting positive attitudes and embracing inclusive statements, comforting homilies, drawings and poems. The office was a work area but also one of safety and refuge.

Mick looked middle-aged, poorly dressed and unhealthy. Tony was well groomed, his zip-fronted sweatshirt and stone cargoes not quite hiding a developing paunch. The contrast between them skin deep, but not bone deep.

Mick opened his mouth again. 'I kna' you want the truth, Tony...' he managed at length.

Tony nodded.

Mick's lips moved, his brow furrows deepened. He was coming to a conclusion, facing things within himself, finding his voice before speaking the words.

'Not good...' Mick cast his eyes down, shook

his head slowly from side to side. 'It's been bad. I've been ... back on the booze, Tony.'

'Right,' Tony said quietly.

Mick looked up. Tony caught the conflicting emotions bouncing around behind his eyes: guilt, pain, self-disgust. 'I didn't want to. I couldn't stop mesell ... I just...' His fingers flexed and unflexed, a useless gesture, an expression of impotence.

'How much?' asked Tony. His voice held no judgement.

Mick began to pull at the hem of his old, dirty jumper. 'Just ... just the one bottle. Vodka. And ... an' a couple of cans. Special Brew.' He let out a sigh of Atlas-like proportions. 'I just needed somethin'. I've had a rough week.'

Tony nodded empathically. A lot of people in Coldwell had similar problems. Their personal strength dictated the ways they dealt with them.

'How many bottles, Mick? How many cans?' Quietly, drawing the answer out.

Mick shook his head, stared at the floor. 'I cannot remember.'

Tony let out a small sigh, not of exasperation but of sadness. 'Try to, Mick. Be honest with yourself. And me.'

Mick looked up, a sad, imploring light in his eyes. 'I cannot remember. Honest, Tony. I'd just have one, an' then I'd feel all right. An' then before I knew it, it was empty. So I had another. An' another.' He stopped talking, sniffed, composed himself, resumed. 'All this week's dole's gone. An' next week's.' Mick sighed again, continued in a small, broken voice, spiralling down, talking as much to himself as to Tony. 'I've let everyone down. Everyone. Angela, the kids, mesell...' Another Atlas sigh. 'I told them I wouldn't. Not again, I promised...' Mick stopped speaking and fell totally still, a wall of palpable failure surrounding him.

Tony let the silence run its course, then: 'So how are things with Angela?'

'Aw ... she puts up with a lot, that woman. Her jobs, the supermarket, the pub ... they keep us goin'. I tell you, she doesn't deserve this. She doesn't deserve me...'

Tony spotted the signpost pointing down the road of self-pity and expertly changed the route. 'So was it back to the hospital this time?'

Mick nodded absently, eyes averted. 'Aye, but they didn't keep us in for long, though. They say there's nowt they can do with us. If me kidneys or me liver fails one more time, that'll be it.' He looked up, straight at Tony, eyes splattered red like wasted wine. 'That's why they sent us back to you. To stop it happenin' again.'

'Right.' Tony nodded, feeling his own Atlas pressure build. He felt the old familiar throb and ache in his left knee, uncoiled his leg and flexed it. He gave a small, brave smile, hoped Mick caught it. 'So, Mick, what's going to happen next?'

Mick shook his head. 'I don't know...' He cupped his hands in front of him as if holding something awkwardly. 'I've got to stop drinkin' an' never do it again. I've got to get from here–' he moved his hands to the right '–to here...' He shook his head in disbelief, amazed such a huge chasm could exist in such a small place.

Within Mick's eyes was an almost pure

distillation of human suffering. Raw, naked, virtually too painful to look at, to make contact with. But Tony not only looked, he held Mick's gaze. And in doing so showed why he was so good at his job. He understood.

Mick continued.

'Tony, man, sometimes it's just too hard. To keep goin'. To find a reason to get up in the mornin'. To just smile. I kna' I'm a man. I'm expected to just take it an' be strong an' keep goin' ... but...' Another sigh. 'Sometimes it just hits us, you kna'? Apart from me family I've got nothin'. Nothin'. An' I never will have. An' that's not self-pity, that's me bein' honest.' Another sigh, and a smile; a ghost smile full of shadows. 'You kna'... You're the only person I can say this to. Not even Angela.'

'I'm glad you feel comfortable enough to do that.'

Mick nodded, the smile deepening ever so slightly. 'I don't expect you to wave a magic wand an' make everythin' better. But you listen. That's somethin'.'

Tony smiled, hoping it held hope. 'Right, Mick, here's your options. I can put you on a programme...'

Mick scowled. 'Done that. Doesn't work.'

'Well,' Tony shrugged, looked at Mick, waited for a reaction. 'You could join the team.'

Mick's face crumpled up. 'Aw no, Tony, I couldn't do that, man. I've just got out of hospital.'

'Come on, Mick, it might be just the thing you need. Bit of fresh air, do you good.'

Mick's face was still downcast. 'Nah...'

'I'll make a deal with you, Mick. Come to

training on Saturday. Bring your stuff. If you don't feel up to it after that, you needn't play on Sunday. How's that?'

Mick shook his head.

'Come on, Mick, I need all the left-sided players I've got. It'll be a laugh. What d'you say?'

Mick thought about it and eventually his face broke into a full smile. The expression seemed so unfamiliar, Tony thought it was like watching wood bend out of shape.

'You've talked us into it,' Mick said in mock grumble.

'Good man. I'm counting on you.'

A flicker of self-respect passed over Mick's face. 'I'll be there, Tony. You can count on me.'

'I know I can, Mick.'

As they both smiled at each other, the phone rang.

'It's for a book,' Stephen Larkin said a couple of hours later, sitting forward, arms open in gesture, adapting to the old armchair as well as Mick had. Tony sat in the swivel chair, arms folded, legs crossed.

'About the miners' strike and after. Twenty-year anniversary. Or it will be by the time the book's finished and out. Using Coldwell as a kind of microcosm for the country as a whole.'

'But I wasn't here during the strike.'

'I know. But you're from here and you're back here now. Like I said on the phone and in the letter, what I propose is this. I come here for a week, say, sit in on sessions...'

Tony opened his mouth to argue. Larkin

stopped it.

'If you and your clients are OK with that, if not, forget it. I put your work in context with the area, then I do some interviews with you. You know, your playing career, how your life changed, how you ended up as an addiction counsellor. Big profile of you, lots of good things to say about your work.' Larkin sat back in the uneasy chair. 'What d'you think?'

Tony thought. Larkin waited, thinking about the morning.

The day had the colour of smoke and the smell of the coast: sharp salt and decaying fish. Coldwell was along the Northumberland coast just north of Whitley Bay; he remembered it from the miners' strike.

The battle of Coldwell. How could he forget?

It was the first time he had been back to the town since he had started working on the book. The first time away from libraries, documents, dry facts. The first time in the present and not the past. Larkin didn't recognize the place.

He had driven in, parked the Saab in the car park of the new shopping mall. It held the kind of stores that appeared only in poor areas; retailers selling furniture and electrical items on the never-never, stores offering under a pound tat, supermarkets with harsh, guttural names selling discount goods, unfamiliar brands of dubious quality. Staffed by part-timers on short-term, no-benefits contracts, women with families to support, ex-colliers retrained to push trolleys together, beep barcodes on food packaging.

Sadness clung to the small, adjacent bus

station. It seemed the buses never managed to take people far enough away, always brought them mournfully back. On the low wall outside the toilets was a gathering of career alcoholics, crack- and smack-heads, a meeting place for the dispossessed.

The only thing Larkin recognized was the old church, but even that had changed. Its doors looked as if they were hardly opened, its grave-yard now a home to weeds, lichen and discarded hypos. The hope of any salvation long since gone.

The town was now a patched-up thing, dead, just not lying down yet. A town with no industry or future. Post-strike. Post-industrial. Post every-thing.

Tony nodded thoughtfully.

'Do I get paid for this?' asked Tony.

Larkin shrugged. 'I don't have an advance for this yet. But if and when I get paid, although it's not normal practice, I'll make sure some comes to you for contributing.'

'To the Centre.'

'Whatever,' replied Larkin.

Tony thought again. 'OK,' he said at length. 'You've got a deal.'

Larkin found that on first impressions he liked Tony Woodhouse. Most of the footballers and ex-footballers Larkin had met had been arrogant, ignorant bores. Tony seemed different. Articulate, intelligent, instinctively wary, he seemed to Larkin like a decent bloke. Larkin noticed the pronounced limp when he walked. He would get round to asking about that eventually.

They talked a while longer, formalizing the

agreement. Tony agreed to virtually everything Larkin had proposed.

'What made you pick Coldwell, then?' Tony asked.

'I was here during the miners' strike in '84. I saw what happened.'

Tony snapped his fingers. 'That's where I know you from. Why your name was so familiar. You've got a sister called Louise, haven't you?'

'Yeah.'

'I used to go out with her.' He shrugged, smiled. 'Years ago.'

Larkin smiled, nodded. Memory cracked.

'That's right. We met once, didn't we?'

'Briefly, I think.' Tony's expression changed. Larkin couldn't read it. 'Louise... She's married now. How is she?'

'Fine, I think. Haven't seen her for a while. We're not close.'

'Oh, well.' Sadness in the voice. 'If you see her, tell her I said hello.'

'I will.'

Tony nodded, got painfully to his feet, made his way over to the window. 'So what d'you think?' he said loudly. 'Coldwell's changed a bit, wouldn't you say?'

'You could say that.'

'You were here during the miners' strike, eh? Good sense of community then. Everyone pulling together.'

Larkin nodded.

'You see down there? That lot down there?'

Larkin looked. Tony was pointing at the drinkers and druggies sitting outside the bus station toilets.

He nodded.

'They're there virtually every day, the same faces. Always greet each other, always looked pleased to see one another. They talk, they laugh.' He sighed. 'I sometimes think that's the only community we've got left in this town.'

Larkin nodded in reluctant admission. They fell into silence, watching the town square. Eventually, Larkin said: 'You've got a football team too, haven't you?'

Tony turned, eyes suddenly alive. 'Yeah. Great idea. Good therapy – gets the clients to focus on something other than their own problems. Gives them–' he smiled '–something to play for.'

'When's the next match?'

'Sunday. Big bash. Charity affair.' Tony smiled. 'Bring your boots.'

'Oh, no,' said Larkin, arms out in front of him. 'I'm the world's best spectator but the world's worst player. Sorry, I couldn't.'

'D'you want this interview?' Tony's face was smiling, but his eyes were serious.

Larkin sighed. 'All right, then.' He smiled. 'I'll start training this week.'

'That's what I like to hear.'

Larkin took that as his cue to leave. They agreed a time for Larkin to be there the following day. He turned to go.

'If you see Louise,' said Tony, his smile edged with sadness, 'tell her I said hello.'

'I will.'

Larkin left.

Driving back through Whitley Bay, Larkin, thinking over his meeting with Tony, was gripped by a sudden impulse. He pulled the Saab off the main road. He was going to visit his sister.

Behind the links and deserted beaches of the run-down seafront of Whitley Bay was a warren of solid, middle-class semis. It was into this maze that Larkin drove.

He and Louise had never been close; beyond their biology they had little in common. As far as Larkin knew, all Louise had wanted was her husband, her kids and her semi beside the sea. He had wanted different things from life. He hadn't thought of her for ages. He couldn't remember the last time he had seen her.

The house was cut from the same 1930s semi blueprint as the others in the street. They all looked identical; even the small attempts at individuality, such as replacement windows or different-coloured garage doors, seemed uniform. There was an air of comfortable achievement about the street, as if driving a Mondeo and reading the *Daily Mail* were hard-fought-for rights.

Larkin pulled the Saab up in front of number 52, got out, rang the bell before he changed his mind. In the drive was a year-old Ka. Figures, thought Larkin.

The door was opened by a woman a couple of years younger than Larkin but not yet looking her age. Her once-long hair had been cut short but was still dark, perhaps even darker than it used to be, thought Larkin. She had put on weight since the last time he had seen her, but it wasn't much and she carried it well; not fat, just rounded out. She was dressed simply in faded jeans, trainers and a T-shirt, her make-up light and strategically positioned. A middle-class wife and mum who still made time for herself. She looked good.

'Hello, Louise,' said Larkin.

Her jaw actually dropped. 'My God...'

'How you doing?' Larkin smiled. 'I was just passing, thought I'd drop in.'

She opened the door wide. 'Come in.'

Larkin followed her in. The hallway was neat, airy and tasteful.

'Come through.'

Louise led him to the front room, sat him down on a beige Jacquard sofa. She asked if he wanted tea. He did, so she disappeared into the kitchen. He looked around the room. Again neat, airy and tasteful. A touch of classical here, a dash of ethnic there. Nothing forceful or overpowering. Louise soon emerged bearing a tray holding mugs, milk, sugar and biscuits and set it down on the middle table of a nest of three. Larkin picked up his mug. Louise sat in a chair, did likewise. They looked at each other, smiled, felt the gap between them larger than physical space, sought for polite ways to bridge it.

'So ... how are you, then?' she asked.

'Fine,' replied Larkin. 'Still working. Still free-lance.'

'Still at the same address?'

He told her about the move. 'I'll give you my new address. How about you, what are you up to?'

Louise was working part-time in a call centre which brought in a little extra, gave her something to do and allowed her to be home in time to cook the tea. He enquired about the kids. Ben was fourteen and doing very well at school, Suzanne was fifteen and would soon be sitting her GCSEs.

Larkin smiled. 'Good...' He was drying up. They had never had much in common, but this wasn't just small talk, it was practically microscopic. He imagined Louise was finding it equally painful and awkward.

'So how's–' fuck, what was his name again? '–your other half?'

'Oh, fine,' replied Louise.

Larkin thought he caught something, a ripple of disturbance pass over her face, but it was over so quickly he wasn't sure.

'Still working hard?' he asked.

'Oh yes. He's area sales manager now,' she answered with pride. Larkin remembered she put stock in such things.

Larkin had no idea what he was actually area sales manager of, but from Louise's tone felt he should. He skated over it. 'Oh, good.'

The conversation then ground to a dead halt. Larkin looked at his tea, willing it to cool down so he could drink it and leave.

'So,' said Louise, equally grasping, 'what brings you round here?'

'Work,' replied Larkin, pleased at last to be on familiar territory. 'I'm doing a job down the road in Coldwell. Profile. Actually, you know the guy.'

Louise's face suddenly tightened. 'Who?'

'Old boyfriend of yours. Tony Woodhouse.'

A glob of tea fell from Louise's mug on to the patterned mustard-coloured rug. She ignored it.

'Tony Woodhouse? You've spoken to him?' A sudden, barked laugh. 'Haven't seen him in years.'

'Yeah?' said Larkin. 'That's where I've been this afternoon.' He noted her reaction then continued. 'He asked after you, by the way.'

'What did he say?' she asked too quickly.

Larkin shrugged. 'Just hello.'

'And that's all?'

'Yea. I'll be seeing him again, though, if you want me to pass on a message.'

'A message?' Louise's eyes darted around the room, as if checking for eavesdroppers. 'No, no message. Well, hello. Just tell him I said hello back.'

'OK, then.' Larkin said nothing. His tea had cooled. He began sipping it.

She smiled, barked a sudden, hollow laugh. 'Tony Woodhouse. Feels like yesterday I was with him. You were with Charlotte.' She gasped. 'I'm sorry, I didn't...'

'That's OK. All done with now. All in the past.'

She smiled. It was shaky. Then the subject changed, the small talk started up again. They were both grateful for it. They sketched in the blanks, filled in the years. Larkin kept his accounts deliberately oblique. Louise admitted she read his journalism, admired his angry, political pieces.

'It's not my thing, as you know,' she said, 'but I was very proud of you.' She smiled.

Larkin returned it. 'Thank you.'

His mug now drained, it was time for him to leave. The meeting hadn't been unpleasant, he thought, just awkward. Two people without much in common, talking as if they should. Louise seemed equally relieved that he was leaving.

She walked down the hall with him, showing him to the door. As she opened it, a car something sleek, shiny and Japanese – pulled up just behind the Saab, music pounding out loud enough to damage the subframe, crack the tarmac beneath. A girl emerged from the passenger side and headed for the house. Tall, attractive, carrying an air of experience her youth couldn't match, a mesmeric swing in her hips. She had the teenage pout down to textbook perfection and the lips to carry it off. She looked, thought Larkin, just like Louise at that age.

'Oh, here's Suzanne,' said Louise with a cheeriness so sudden it had to be false. 'Hello, Suzanne.'

Suzanne swept into the house offering a grunted greeting but no eye contact to Louise.

'This is your uncle Stephen...' Louise began, but Suzanne wasn't listening. She swept up the stairs, ignoring him.

'Oh to be a teenager again,' said Larkin, aiming for lightness.

The car outside sped noisily away. From upstairs came a door slam and the sudden, rhythmic thump of garage.

Louise gave a smile, but it didn't reach her eyes. 'Yes,' she said, and gave a small, dry laugh.

Larkin decided it was time to leave. He made his way to the car and, with a final wave, drove off.

So Louise has got her middle-class dream, he thought to himself, and there seemed to be cracks in it. He sighed. But it's not my problem, he thought. It's not my problem.

There are few things, thought Larkin, more depressing than seaside towns out of season, and Whitley Bay was no exception. The seafront seemed a world away from Louise's tidy little area. As he drove along, the spring sky was muddying with dusk, holding not promise but threat, pointing up a tawdry strip of cheap amusement arcades, their fronts in terminal repair, their interiors deserted, interspersed with germ warfare labs masquerading as burger bars, boarded-up seafood stands that probably glowed in the dark, and dangerous pubs. The Spanish City, with its yellow stucco peeling, its domes and minarets crumbling and its roller-coaster looking as if it wouldn't last another ride, hadn't just seen better days; it had waved them off at the station, knowing they would never be back.

Stretching further on was a row of bars and nightclubs, biding time until the night when, gauded up with neon, they would become magnetic north for cheap possibilities, first base for one-night stands, guilt-ridden sexual affairs or emergency trips to the A & E.

In this stretch stood Rio. Larkin remembered it from the 1980s when it had been in its aspirational glory, a pastel and neon shrine to Thatcherism. Now it looked almost as bad as the Spanish City. Scrolled ironwork, pitted and flaking, seeped rust down peeling walls, paintwork having gone one makeover too far. Still, thought Larkin wryly, the perfect shrine to Thatcherism.

He slipped a tape in the deck. The Go-Betweens:

*Sixteen Lover's Lane.* Something else from the 1980s. 'Streets of Our Town' started up, the beautiful, simple melody brimming with feel-good nostalgia, fatally punctured when Grant McLennan started singing about butchers sharpening their knives in a town full of battered wives.

Larkin sighed. It's not my problem, he thought. It's not my problem.

## 3. Then

Ponteland golf course looked like a colour sup photoshoot for the *Mail on Sunday.* Stereotypical Sunday-morning suburban golfers, all pastel and Pringle, dotted the fairway, their pre-lunch clubhouse drinks beckoning, their voices a veneer of moneyed bonhomie, their wives invisible. The grass immaculately manicured, the club fees well spent. The surrounding trees kept out unwanted sounds, sights and people, kept members cosseted and enclosed. Newcastle, sprawling and unacknowledged, was just down the road.

The breeze was sharpening and the temperature sliding, but the golfers ignored this. They played on, wringing the last drops from a disappearing summer, not surrendering to the coming autumn.

Tommy Jobson parked the BMW, cut the engine. The car park was chocked with other Beamers and Mercs, smattered with GTIs and Subarus, tolerant to a couple of imposter

66

Acclaims. He got out, checked his hair, suit and tie in the car's reflection, strode towards the fairway. He hated golf but knew that one day he would be expected to join a club like this. Still, Dino and Frank loved the sport, so it couldn't be that bad.

Although not a member and clearly not there to play, no one questioned him or looked directly at him. Tommy's pores secreted strength and violence. Internally, Tommy felt something different. Fear. Given who he was meeting, it was well justified.

On the sixth hole he found who he was looking for standing with another man who looked vaguely familiar to Tommy. Clive Fairbairn was tall, lean and tanned, hair swept back from his forehead, slightly greying temples. His clothes matching and complementing pastel yellows and pinks, his shoes gleaming white. He carried himself with poise and assurance. He looked more like he belonged on the deck of a yacht moored on the Riviera or a Marbella marina rather than just north of Newcastle. The other man, by comparison, looked like the ugly best friend, only there to make the handsome one more handsome. He was short, rounding, with a Bobby Charlton combover. His clothes were similar to Fairbairn's, but where the former's fitted and complemented him the latter's just appeared mismatched and ridiculous.

As Tommy approached, Fairbairn swung. The ball sliced straight down the fairway, as the other man looked on admiringly, making an attempt at a hearty one-liner which Fairbairn ignored. The other man, reddening slightly, silently tee-ed up and stood over the ball, ready to swing.

'Tommy! Over here!'

The man swung and mis-hit, sending his ball into a clump of trees.

'Bad luck,' said Fairbairn heartily but insincerely. 'I think you'd better go and look for it.'

The man, glancing at Tommy and knowing an exit line when he heard one, sloped off into the trees with his bag dragging, taking random swings at the grass with his club.

Fairbairn kept the smile in place until the man was out of view. 'Tedious little fucker, but still,' he shrugged, 'a local councillor is a local councillor. Handy when you need one.' Fairbairn's voice was used to being listened to and not argued with.

Tommy nodded in agreement.

'Let's walk.' Fairbairn set off down the fairway. Tommy matched his stride, not speaking until spoken to.

'Been hearing good things about you, Tommy,' said Fairbairn, 'very good things. You're taking care of our little problem.'

'Th-thank you, Mr Fairbairn.' Tommy felt his cheeks flush, his butterflies subside a little.

Fairbairn stopped walking and looked about, filling his lungs with air. To anyone watching he was just another Sunday golfer. 'Like your style. Very positive. Sends out a strong signal. Reinforces the chain of command. Keeps them in line.'

'Thank you, M-Mr Fairbairn.'

They reached the spot where Fairbairn's ball

had landed.

'But,' he said quietly, eyes seemingly engrossed with choosing his next club from his wheeled bag.

Tommy swallowed, tried to quell his sudden shakes.

'But, Tommy, you slipped up. No money back, no product.'

The butterflies returned. 'I gu-gave him a time limit, Mr Fairbairn.' His voice trailed off as his mouth dried up. 'I scared him. I'll get it.'

Fairbairn smiled. His teeth were shark-sharp. 'You did scare him, you're right. Unfortunately our friend Neil's still in the General after a week. Maybe staying longer than we anticipated.'

'S-sorry, Mr Fairbairn.'

Fairbairn moved his face close to Tommy, his voice dropping. 'Never apologize, Tommy. Never. Sorry is for wimps.'

Tommy nodded. Fairbairn gave him a thoughtful appraisal.

'I like you, Tommy. A lot.'

Fairbairn smiled, assumed an air of avuncularity. Tommy wasn't fooled.

'Now, you know me, Tommy. I'm a businessman. And so are you. Now, selling the stuff you sell's a young man's game. That's why I've got you doing it. You do what you do in the way you do it, it brings the money in and that's all I care about. But it's still business.' The avuncularity faded. 'Lucrative business. My business. And if you're working for me, you need to find your limit. Keep control.'

Tommy nodded. 'What d'you want me to do? Wait until he's out? Pay him a visit?'

Fairbairn flung his arms wide in an expansive gesture. 'Maggie would say to write it off as misplaced venture capital.' Fairbairn screwed up his eyes, looked down the fairway, saw something there no one else could see. 'But much as I admire the bitch, I couldn't do that.'

Tommy swallowed. 'Duh-don't worry, Mr Fairbairn. I'll get the money.'

Fairbairn smiled. Everyone's favourite uncle. 'I know you will, Tommy.' His eyes hardened. 'Our friend had a partner, didn't he?'

'Hu-he did.'

'Have you spoken to him yet?'

A sharp crack of anger ran through Tommy as he thought of the previous Saturday, the way Woodhouse had dodged him at Rio. 'He mu-moves in different circles now. More high-profile ones. Difficult to reach. But I'll get him.'

Fairbairn looked interested. 'Useful circles?'

Tommy nodded. 'I think so, Mr Fairbairn.'

Fairbairn nodded, his eyes harder than granite. At that moment Tommy knew why he was so feared. 'Get to him. But don't let him or anyone else take the piss out of you. Make sure they give you respect. Make sure they know who's boss.'

Tommy nodded. Fairbairn smiled again.

'But be subtle, eh?'

Tommy felt himself reddening.

'Well, Tommy, thanks for coming.' They shook hands. 'Oh, by the way, call into the clubhouse on the way back. Something for you. Take the rest of the day off.'

Fairbairn turned away, Tommy was dismissed. As if on cue the councillor emerged from the

70

trees looking disgruntled and humiliated. Fairbairn walked towards him, greeting him like a long-lost friend. Tommy walked away, at first wondering why the councillor put up with that treatment then, with a smile, speculating on what kind of dirt Fairbairn had on him.

Louise's body moved rhythmically, hips forward then back. Her arms stretched out, hands clutching either side of the headboard, head tipped back, eyes closed in pain and ecstasy. Tony Woodhouse above her, matched her hip movement with his own; grinding, pushing. He took in everything about her: the way her underarm muscles clenched, the way her breasts moved backwards and forwards with her body's rhythm, the way her lips pulled back, baring her teeth. He saw all this, and loved her for it.

He could hold back no longer. Louise, sensing this, wrapped her arms around him, fingernails digging into his back, pulling his body further into hers. He came, exploding inside her, almost shouting with release. She rode it with him then, still holding his body to hers with one hand, slid the other hand down between them, finding the spot, working her own orgasm up to join his.

She came violently, screaming, each spasming wave the thrust of a beautiful knife. She ground against him, nails clawing, gasping like she was finding air after drowning under water.

They kissed and their bodies, spent on each other, relaxed. Tony, his arm round Louise, gently stroked her shoulder. She looked at him, smiled. He smiled back.

'Is that better than scoring against Arsenal?' asked Louise.

'Yeah. But it was Everton yesterday. And we lost three–two. Beardo and Wharton got them. I didn't score.'

Her fingers trailed down his body. 'Well, you've just made up for it.'

They lapsed into a comfortable silence.

Tony looked around the room. It had all the trappings of a teenage girl's first flat away from home. The music centre and small stacks of LPs and tapes, the bookcase with a smattering of bestsellers, the dressing table and the posters on the wall: Bryan Ferry, the Police. Magnolia walls. White window frames. Just looking around her room drew Tony closer to her.

Louise leaned over to the bedside table, lit up a Silk Cut. 'So,' she said, 'what shall we do today?'

Tony's hand moved over her nipple, squeezed. 'More of the same?'

She took a drag. 'After that.'

'Well...'

'Shit!' Louise sat suddenly upright. 'What time is it?'

'Uh ... twenty to eleven. Why?'

She jumped out of bed and made for the wardrobe. 'I need to ask you a really big favour,' she said, pulling underwear from a drawer, a jumper from a shelf.

'What?'

'I need you to disappear.'

Tony looked at her.

'Just for an hour or so.' She turned to face him, pulling her pants on at the same time. She looked apprehensive. 'Please. Just for an hour. Then you've got me for the rest of the day. Please?'

Tony's eyes took in her full breasts, trailed down to her flattened waist, wandered down over her slightly rounded tummy, imagined her soft, dark pubic hair now covered by the stretch cotton of her briefs. The rest of the day, he thought. 'Yeah. Why?'

'I'll tell you later. I wouldn't ask, but this is important. You'll have to go.'

Tony got reluctantly out of bed and began to dress.

'Thanks, Tony. Go for a walk round Saltwell Park or something. I'll make it up. I promise.'

Tommy entered the clubhouse, scoped the room. He saw moneyed, middle-aged straights, abandoned wives martinied up, no one he knew. In the far corner a group of men and women, about the same age as himself, sat drinking, smoking and talking. Their conversation was animated, their circle closed. A girl in the group detached her attention from the others, made eye contact with him. She was brown-haired, very attractive. Tommy returned the look just as someone spoke to her, pulling her attention back into the group.

'I Just Called to Say I Love You'. Still number one. Still playing.

He looked away, walked to the bar, pointed to the whisky optic, paid, sat and began to drink. Suddenly he wasn't alone. As if on cue, a blonde girl took the stool next to him. Stylishly dressed, well made up, she looked as out of place as Tommy did.

'Tommy?' she asked, her voice elocuted Geordie. Tommy nodded.

'Mr Fairbairn says you're doing a good job.' She smiled. 'I've got a reward for you.'

Tommy smiled. He downed his drink in one, got up and left with the blonde, knowing that the girl from the group in the corner was watching him go.

Outside, both the BMW and the sun were still shining as they drove away. As the blonde's hand began to snake around his thigh, Tommy smiled. He was going to enjoy his day off.

The same sharp, autumn sunlight stretched from Ponteland golf course to Saltwell Park in Gateshead. Tony walked slowly through the park. Children enjoyed the playground next to disconsolate bunches of sneering adolescents. Families and couples alongside Sunday fathers with their kids. Sparrows and squirrels in front of the caged birds in the aviary. Everywhere was contrasts, choices. He thought of his own.

He had left school with two things: a passion for football and a determination to get out of Coldwell as quickly, and by whatever means, as possible. There were two traditional industries in Coldwell: the mine and the docks. Not wanting to spend his life in darkness, discomfort and disease, Tony had taken a job on one of the piers. The number of working piers, few to start with, had become fewer and fewer, the cargoes smaller and smaller. He had begun to realize there was no such thing as a job for life any more and that something had to happen.

It did.

A talent scout for Newcastle United spotted him playing in a local Sunday-league side and asked if he would be interested in a trial. He took it, impressed them and, through hard work and perseverance, jumped from the under-seventeen team, to the reserves, to the first team bench. The goal against Arsenal had been his first at the top level. He didn't intend it to be his last.

However, yesterday's defeat away to Everton was a different matter. Newcastle were two–nil down by the time Tony was sent on. He had been completely ineffectual, even personally contributing to Everton's third goal.

Big Jack's bollocking came soon afterwards: his concentration and focus were lacking; his skill nowhere to be seen; if he wanted a career as a top-flight footballer, he would have to do much better than that. Tony had listened, shrugged, said he'd sort it out during the week.

But Tony had been living in terror all week. The business with Neil and Tommy Jobson had scared the shit out of him, got him looking over his shoulder, staying out of the shadows, keeping in company. He had to think, find a way to square things and walk away without getting hurt. Let his past die.

Then there was Louise. She scared him too, but in a different way, a good way. He had thought about her all week, talked to her on the phone, was impatient to be with her again. She was starting to mean something to him. He didn't want to screw things up with her. If he could sort the thing out with Tommy, then concentrate on his football and Louise, things would be fine.

Coach back to Newcastle, couple of lines to calm and sharpen him, off to meet Louise in the Barley Mow on the quayside. Not the sort of place Tony normally went to, but not one that Tommy Jobson would be looking for him in either.

Louise had been standing with her friends, knocking back drinks and unwanted advances. He felt a sudden rush of warmth knowing she was waiting for him. She saw him, her eyes lit up and virtually all his fear evaporated.

They began to talk and it seemed that the rest of the bar was gradually disappearing. At closing time, Louise's friends moved on Madisons.

'So where d'you want to go?' Tony had asked her.

Louise had smiled. 'How about Gateshead?'

Tony swallowed. 'Are you sure? You don't think you're rushing things?'

'I'm sure.'

Tony glanced at his watch. His hour was up, so he turned round and made his way back to Louise's.

As he rounded the corner of Coatsworth Road he saw Louise standing on the doorstep outside her flat. By her was a small, sandy-haired young man and parked at the kerb an aged but well-maintained pale green Ford Escort Mark One. Tony felt a sharp stab of jealousy, but Louise's posture – folded arms, erect back – helped dispel that. The other man, shoulders slumped, spine – or at least spirit – bent, stuck his hands out as if imploring her. Louise shook her head. The man climbed into the Escort, slammed the door, over-revved the engine and drove away.

Tony approached Louise and, although he had a fair idea of what had been going on, asked her about it.

'Remember when we met I told you I was seeing someone?' Louise was staring down the street after the departing car.

Tony nodded.

'Well, I'm not any more. Keith's gone.' She turned to face him. 'Sorry about earlier.' She sighed. 'But you've got me all to yourself now.'

Tony placed his arms around her. 'Good.'

Louise smiled. 'Let's go inside.'

Tony smiled back. That was one less thing they had to discuss.

Tommy came, lying flat on his back on the bed in his spartan flat in Wallsend with the blonde girl, who had given her name as Cathy, naked and straddling him.

When she had milked the last spasm from his body, she smiled and dismounted. She hadn't come. Tommy hadn't offered. They both knew the rules.

Cathy made her way to the bathroom. Tommy heard the sound of the shower and sighed. It had been difficult getting aroused at first, despite Cathy's efforts. It wasn't until he imagined her as Kim Novak and him as smooth, suave Dino putting one over on that blind, black Jew Sammy that he let the mood take him.

All those years in care homes, foster homes, lashing out at anyone and everything with undirected

77

anger, no control. Then, by chance, he heard the voice. Sinatra. 'In the Wee Small Hours of the Morning'. And something spoke to him, directly. It summed up the pain, the loss, the melancholy he had kept locked up inside since he was little. He bought the record and anything else he could find. That led him to Dino. Even better, the total epitome of couldn't-give-a-fuck cool. And then there were the suits. Ratpack-sharp, but with such style, such attitude. From that moment on, he knew what he wanted to be. He sighed. Dino and Frank. They had always been there for him. Better parents than his real ones had been. Wherever they were.

Then there was Clive Fairbairn. Everyone knew Clive Fairbairn. On the surface an Empire-loving, old-school, likeable rogue, only hurting his own sort, kind to his old mum, do anything for kids' charities. Just a dodgily honest businessman dealing in casinos and gaming machines. Underneath, a different story. Fairbairn was hard. Hardware, hardcore porn. He dealt with it all. Apart from the prostitution and protection rackets, he imported decommissioned military hardware from the Soviet Union and pornography of all kinds, even snuff and kiddie porn. He had the north-east sewn up.

Although much more intelligent than his children's home contemporaries, Tommy had enjoyed the same games, especially twoccing. He had been working for a chop shop in Gateshead, picking up and delivering cars to order. Although the money was good and he had done over two hundred, he was starting to find the work boring.

He had gone as far as he could. He needed to move up. He needed Clive Fairbairn.

Fairbairn had a sociopathic ability to generate money for himself and his associates, unhindered by morality or ethics. A perfect, feral capitalist. But there was one area Fairbairn knew nothing about but still wanted a cut of: hard drugs. It was becoming a booming market but he just couldn't get to grips with it. He had supply routes sorted but severe distribution problems. That fact Chinese-whispered its way to Tommy. He needed a plan, something to get Fairbairn's attention.

So Tommy stole his Jag. From the car park of a casino owned by Fairbairn. Fairbairn went ballistic – a huge cash reward for whoever found it, a slow, torturous death for whoever had taken it. No one owned up.

Three days later it turned up outside Fairbairn's house in Ponteland, cleaned, valeted, with a full tank of petrol and a note in the glove box reading 'You can use a man like me' followed by a phone number.

Fairbairn had phoned the number. Give me one good reason why I don't break your fucking back, he had said.

Tommy, letting the spirit of Dino control his stutter, had told him: 'You need someone like me on your side.'

They arranged to meet, and Fairbairn had found himself being impressed by the sharp-suited seventeen-year-old. Tommy talked about the streets, about drugs. He talked himself up as the perfect man to run distribution. Fairbairn had checked him out, taken him on. But I'm not going to forget what you did to my car, Mr Fairbairn said. Don't make me remind you.

That was six months ago. Tommy was working his way up Fairbairn's organization. Almost to the top of the pyramid and only eighteen. And doing it with such style.

Cathy came out of the bathroom, bent to slip on her shoes. She stood up.

'D'you want me to hang around?' she asked. 'You've got me for the day, if you want.'

Tommy shook his head. He didn't like other people staying in his flat for too long.

Cathy smiled. 'Mind, you don't say much, do you?' She reached into her bag, took out a card, laid it on the bed. 'It's been fun,' she said, her voice brittle-bright. 'If you want to see me again–' she dropped her eyes in a well-practised gesture of fake seduction '–call that number.' She walked out, closing the door behind her.

Tommy lay on the bed, staring out of the window at the blue sky.

It won't be dark for hours yet, he thought.

Tony drove, Louise sat beside him, Aztec Camera provided the laid-back Sunday-afternoon sound-track and they talked and talked.

Louise was from Grimley, a small town on the way to Chester-le-Street. 'Well, a street with houses behind it, actually,' she explained. Her family were working class, she was at college doing business studies, she shared a flat with Rachel, another student, her older brother Stephen was trying to make a name for himself as a journalist.

Tony's turn, and he told her that he too was

from a working-class background; his father had been a miner until he was invalided out. 'One lungful of dust too many,' he said. He had a brother still at school who hopefully wouldn't have to. 'Mind, with the strike and everything, it looks like he's not even going to get the chance.' He told her he had just bought himself a flat in a new development in Ponteland.

'Is that where we're headed now?' she asked.

Tony smiled. After making love on his return from Saltwell Park they had decided to go for a drive. 'Not yet,' he said with a smile. 'I thought I'd show you round a bit first.'

'Where?'

'Start with my old home town. Coldwell.'

They drove down the main street. The town looked deserted.

'You'd think they'd dropped the bomb and evacuated the place,' said Louise.

'It's always like this,' replied Tony. 'No one here goes out on a Sunday. Day of rest.'

Louise thought of Sunday afternoons back at her parents' house. Harry Secombe's *Highway*, Jim Bowen's *Bullseye*. 'I've always found that kind of thing depressing.'

Tony nodded in agreement.

Louise put Coldwell at about the same size as Gateshead. Although clearly not a prosperous town, it seemed tidy enough, civically well maintained. Lampposts, walls, boarded-up shop windows and advertising hoardings bore the familiar legend, 'Coal, Not Dole'. She had seen the posters often enough, the miners and their supporters rattling their buckets by Grey's Monument in Newcastle, people walking around with stickers on their lapels, but this was the first time she had ever visited an area directly affected by the strike. She kept looking at the streets. Coldwell didn't just seem quiet, she decided; it felt like the town was holding its breath, waiting for something to happen. Like a medieval fortress under siege, waiting for some robber-baron's armies to attack.

'What do you think about the strike?' Tony asked her.

'I think they've got a point,' she replied. 'But I think they have to be honest. The coal's not going to last for ever. It has to run out sometime.'

'I know what you mean,' said Tony, not taking his eyes off the road, the streets. 'This was one of the mines the government wanted closed. But my dad said it was making a profit.'

'So why close it?'

Tony gave a bitter smile. 'Politics. Them down there don't like us up here.'

Louise smiled uncertainly. 'D'you really believe that?'

Tony shrugged. 'Dunno. Probably. I just wish my dad had had somewhere else to work, that's all.'

They drove without speaking. Roddy Frame singing about the knife whose twists were cruel and hopeless, how neglect had worn it thin.

'Hey,' said Tony. 'You hungry? D'you fancy a drink?'

Louise did.

'Come on, then.'

They drove to a pub in Seaton Sluice with a view of the coastline stretching from St Mary's lighthouse to the Cambois power station. They just made the lunchtime deadline, Tony ordering fish and chips for both of them, since the pub was famous for that. As they settled into their booth, Louise looked around. She stopped dead, drink frozen on the way to her mouth, eyes locked.

'What's up?' asked Tony.

'There's our Stephen,' she replied. 'Me brother.'

Tony looked around to where she was pointing. He saw three men sitting at a table; one older, two younger. One of the younger ones was wearing a faded Levi jacket and matching 501s, a black T-shirt and brown DMs. His dark hair was short at the back and the sides with sideburns and a gelled quiff. He was talking animatedly in an intense, serious manner. He looked, to Tony, like that dickhead from the Smiths.

'Him there?' asked Tony.

'Yeah. Let's say hello,' said Louise.

She led him by the hand across the pub to where the three men were sitting, deep in discussion. As they approached, the older man looked up and Tony knew he'd been recognized.

'Hiya, stranger,' said Louise, her face beaming.

Stephen Larkin looked up, clearly annoyed at being interrupted. When he saw who it was, his annoyance gave way to surprise. 'Louise. What you doin' here?'

'Just having some lunch,' she replied. She linked her arm around Tony's. 'This is Tony.' She looked at him. 'He's me new boyfriend.'

The smile and the look she gave him, the words she said, gave Tony a good feeling inside.

'Hello, Tony,' said Larkin. He gestured to the two men with him. 'This is Dougie an' this is Mick. They're leadin' the strike in Coldwell. I'm writin' about it. Helpin' where I can.' He spoke with the kind of intensity Tony expected.

They all nodded to each other. An embarrassed silence descended on them. The older man broke it.

'Are you Pat's lad?' he said to Tony. 'Ian's young 'un?'

'Aye,' said Tony, 'that's me.'

'You're doin' a grand job. Keep gannin', son. You're bringin' a bit o' pride to us.' The man smiled. 'Howay the lads.'

Tony laughed, blushed slightly. 'Thanks. I'll try to. Well,' he said, 'they'll be bringin' our dinners over soon. We'll leave you in peace. Nice to meet you.'

They said their relieved goodbyes, Tony and Louise retreating to their table.

'Nice, isn't he?' Louise asked.

Tony looked across to where her brother had resumed his conversation with the two men. The one who had spoken looked over and smiled. Tony smiled back. Louise's brother was talking as if he'd forgotten he had ever been interrupted.

'Yeah,' said Tony.

Their fish and chips arrived and they ate, talking and laughing their way through the meal.

'So,' said Tony once they had finished their meals and had another drink, 'what d'you want to do now?'

84

Louise smiled. 'How far's your flat from here?'

Tommy Jobson had worked out with his weights, been running and had a session of sit-ups and press-ups. He had showered, his body feeling toned and powerful, then sat in an armchair, Coke in hand. He didn't drink alcohol. He knew Frank and Dino did – famously so – but he didn't. It kept him sharp, honed. On guard.

He turned the TV on but could find nothing of stimulation or solace. He switched it off again and looked out of the window. It was nearly dark now. He looked around. His flat was minimally furnished, not because of any fashion statement, but because he had hardly anything to put in there. Furniture was functional, the weights were necessary, what LPs and books there were were all Frank and Dino. There was one picture on the wall – a framed black and white print of the Ratpack in front of the Sands in Vegas circa 1959. Tommy looked at that a lot. It helped him focus. Ignore Joey, Peter, Sammy and the rest, concentrate on Frank and Dino. Keep the deadwood out of his life, concentrate on what was important.

But it wasn't working tonight. He wasn't in the mood. There was something he wanted, some hole to be filled, some need to be catered for. But he didn't know what.

He thought of the girl who had given him the glad eye in the bar at the golf club. Only on the other side of the room, may as well have been on a different planet.

'I Just Called to Say I Love You'.

He sighed, went into the bedroom, found the

85

card Cathy had left. He checked his wallet for cash, picked up the phone and dialled.

It wasn't what he wanted, but it would fill the need. For now.

## 4. Now

Davva and Skegs ran as fast as they could, haul clutched in their arms and jackets, shedding bits as they flew out of the newsagent, the Paki owner swearing, screaming and giving chase, down the street, smacking arms, legs and shopping, skipping over a pushchair, getting told to fuck off by the teenager pushing it, into the road laughing, shouting and screaming, drivers swearing, brakes screeching, hearing the Paki give up the chase, then on to the other side and into the mall, knowing the fat old security guard would have a heart attack before he could catch them, dodging and weaving the shoppers, giving V-signs and obscenities to the CCTV cameras as they passed, then banging through the double glass doors, into the car park out back, making straight for the far corner, squeezing between two parked cars, then up and over the wall, trampling flowers as they landed, making for the CCTV blind spot, a wall by the bushes, which they flopped down behind on the grass, flat out, and choked down air.

Chests burning, legs aching, heads light and tingling, they were both exhausted and on a giggly, adrenalin-pumped high. Skegs reached into his jacket to retrieve his haul: two packets of Embassy Regal, one Silk Cut, three Bensons. It looked like beating Davva's haul: two large bars of Cadbury's Fruit and Nut, four chunky Kit-Kats, but when Davva reached into his jacket and pulled out the bottle of Bacardi and the can of lighter fuel, Skegs knew he'd been trumped again.

It pissed him off a bit because even with the booze, Davva's haul had been easier to come by. Skegs's had involved skill, risk, reaching round the counter to make a grab, timing it so he didn't get his arm grabbed and twisted. The Paki had known what they were after the minute they'd walked into his shop, but there was that doubt, that small piece of suspicion that they might be legit customers, so he had played along. But when he turned his back, the fun had started.

Davva halved a bar of Fruit and Nut, handed it to Skegs who was pulling the wrapper from a packet of Bensons, throwing it to the breeze and uncapping the Bacardi. They were getting their breath back, reliving bits of the run to each other. Their haul would keep them going, keep things at bay for a bit.

Skegs, the smaller, more thoughtful and nervous of the two, lit two fags and handed one to Davva. Although the same age, Davva had the street wrapped around him like a filthy blanket; he tried to wear it as a shell. They drew the fags down to the filters, alternating with mouthfuls of chocolate and swigs of burning, bile-inducing Bacardi until the first bar had gone. They looked at each other.

'What now?' asked Skegs.

Davva shrugged. 'Dunno.'

Davva reached for another bar of chocolate, halved it. Skegs lit two more fags. They passed the bottle. As they did so, the comedown started, real life folding in on them again, and they lapsed into fidgety silence, smoking, chewing, swigging. Just filling in the day, killing time.

The front door thudded shut like a coffin lid and Louise automatically checked the kitchen clock. Six thirty-five. Bang on time.

The ritual began:

'Hello, love,' she shouted into the hall. There was a grunted reply, then the sound of her husband making his way into the living room, flopping into an armchair. The TV started up, the local world according to Mike Neville.

Louise walked to the foot of the stairs and shouted up: 'Dinner's ready, Ben, Suzy.' She walked into the front room, looked at her husband. It was hard to believe he had just walked through the front door, the armchair seeming to have osmotically absorbed him.

'What's for dinner?' he asked, not removing his eyes from the screen.

'Pot roast.'

'With what?'

'Vegetables.'

Her husband turned to look at her. Louise was struck once again by how tired he looked. His sandy hair now absent from the top of his head, his eyes sunken and dark-rimmed, his mouth – always weak and pinched – now ineffectually disguised by a moustache. Whereas most men spread out as they got older, thought Louise, he seemed to have contracted, hardened.

'What kind?' he asked. 'Parsnips?'

Louise sighed, swatting something away from her eye with a finger. 'Yes, Keith. I've made parsnips.'

'Good,' he said, his eyes returning to the TV.

They sat around the dining room table, Louise, Keith and Ben. A place was set for Suzanne, but she hadn't shown. It wasn't unusual.

The meal commenced in silence.

'I had a visitor today,' said Louise between mouthfuls.

Keith made a non-committal sound.

'My brother Stephen.'

Keith looked up. Something unpleasant flitted across his face before settling back into pinched repose. 'What did he want?'

'Doing some work in the area. Popped in to see me.'

Keith let out a sound that managed to be both sneer and snort. 'What now? Whingeing on about how dole scroungers can't get jobs because they were all abused as children?' He gave a short, hard laugh.

Ben gave a skittery glance from his dinner, like a tortoise peeking nervously out of its shell, ready to withdraw at any time.

Louise felt herself redden. 'He's writing a piece on Coldwell.'

Another hard snort of laughter. 'Well, he won't be short of material. They're all on the dole there.'

Louise took a deep breath, blinked rapidly. Her

chest was suddenly fluttering. 'He'd just been to see someone about it.'

'Some other moaning liberal, no doubt.'

Louise swallowed. 'Tony Woodhouse.'

A sudden fear appeared in Keith's eyes. He stopped chewing, his fork and knife limp in his grasp.

'Yes,' said Louise calmly, a small triumphant smile pulling at the corners of her lips. 'Tony Woodhouse.' Her voice became louder, more confident. 'And Stephen's going to be spending quite some time with him, so I wouldn't be surprised if we see him again.'

Ben, looking from one to the other, pulled his head right back into his tortoise shell, trying to make himself invisible.

Keith's eyes dropped to his plate, his breath quickening. 'Not in this house, we won't.'

'Yes, we will.'

When Keith spoke there was anger rising in his voice. 'He's not welcome in this house.'

Louise stared at him. 'He'll be welcome as long as I live here, Keith.'

Keith tried to hold her stare, but his eyes flashed with fear, his weak mouth dropped. 'Well, I'll make sure I'm out, then,' he mumbled.

'Fine.'

They lapsed into silence. Louise ate, her dinner tasting of bitter, petty victory. Keith's hands and mouth were idle. Ben, head down, looked in fascination at the way his knife cut, his fork transported food to his mouth.

'Finish your dinner,' said Louise.

Keith jumped, began to obey the command,

automatically forking food into his mouth, staring at Louise, eyes like witch-hunt torches.

Suddenly, cutting through the silence, from the front street came the noise of a car being sonically pulverized, sound system blaring out garage. In response, a door upstairs slammed, followed by feet running downstairs.

'Suzanne,' called Louise, 'your dinner's getting cold.'

Suzanne put her head round the dining room door. She was dressed and made up well beyond her years. 'I'm going out,' she said.

'Well, eat first,' said Louise. 'And where are you going, looking like that, anyway?'

But she was speaking to thin air. Suzanne was already on her way to the front door. 'Got to go. Bye.'

The door slammed, followed by the car door, then the decreasing thump as the mobile sound system receded into the distance. It left the silence in the family dining room even louder and heavier than before.

Louise sighed. 'That girl,' she said, almost unaware she was thinking aloud. 'I don't know what to do with her.'

Another hard snort from the other side of the table. Louise looked across. Keith was chewing his lips, eyes shining in malicious triumph. He waited until he had her full attention before he spoke.

'Well, Louise,' he said. 'She is your daughter.'

He sat back, pleased to have had the last word.

Louise picked up her glass of red wine, knuckles clenched and white around the stem, lifted it to her mouth and, hand trembling, drained it. She quickly refilled it, drained it again, then spoke.

'Are you finished?'

Keith sat back, nodded.

'Then I'll fetch the pudding.'

She got up, gathered the plates together and went into the kitchen. Once alone inside, she put the dishes down, pushed her back hard against the units and, her breathing ragged and trembling, willed the tears that were gathering at the corners of her eyes not to fall.

'Oh, God, oh, God,' she whispered to herself, a plea and a prayer. For her life, her loss, her love.

'Oh, God.'

With an effort she willed the tears away, the turbulence from her heart. She picked up the pudding dish and walked back into the dining room wishing, not for the first time, that her husband was dead.

Davva and Skegs were bored. The chocolate was long gone, they had smoked as much as they could without throwing up, the Bacardi bottle was empty. Even the can of gas they had saved until last as a treat was used up. They had relived their dash through Coldwell in minute comic and heroic detail, but now the moment could be postponed no longer: they had nothing to do.

Dusk was settling, what workers there were returning home. Davva and Skegs stared at them as they poured from the buses, walking past in their suits and working clothes, tired and unemotional. Some cast glances down at the two boys as they sat by the wall with the debris of their day around them, and the boys returned the looks with hard, flinty ones of their own; a two-way passage of non-comprehension and fear of others. But not hatred as such. Not specifically.

Heads fogged and stomachs swimming from what they had consumed, they listed the possibilities for the night ahead. They could go home. For various reasons, neither wanted to do that. They could wander around, try to score some weed or speed, twoc a car. Maybe later. They could go to Davva's sister Tanya's flat.

'I'm starvin',' Skegs said. The booze, fags and chocolate had given him an appetite.

'We'll go round our Tanya's then,' Davva replied. He stood up, reeled and steadied himself. The matter was settled.

As they walked off, Davva picked up the empty Bacardi bottle and threw it as hard as he could at a lamppost. It connected and shattered, showering the now-empty pavement and road with small, glistening shards that caught the street-light and, glinting like tiny prisms, fell into the gutter, tinkling gently as they went. In the boys' fogged minds, the whole thing was in blurred, cinematic slo-mo. Beautiful, like diamonds. Streetlight like gold. Skegs smiled, Davva wanted to but wouldn't allow himself. They turned and walked away.

Past the red-brick council semis and three-storey blocks of flats lay the T. Dan Smith Estate. Entry was marked by the Magpie pub and the strip of shops with the gunmetal siege fronts. Police, ambulances or pizza deliverers rarely ventured there. Cut off, it was starving, dying.

When Tanya had discovered she was pregnant, her mother wanted nothing more to do with her. Her name was not even to be mentioned in the house. Alone and unsupported, she had gone to the council and found herself housed with amazing speed. Once in her new flat, she found out why. Wyn Davies House was a concrete-plated high-rise. The block was damp and mouldering, the lift stank of piss, the stairs of shit, the walkways crunched with underfoot hypodermics. It was no place for a seventeen-year-old, with or without a baby. Tanya was on the sixth floor. At first she hated it deeply. After a while she accepted it. Now she didn't even notice. Sometimes she even contributed.

Tanya was sitting on the second-hand settee watching *Coronation Street*, Carly asleep in her cot, when there was a knock at the door. She jumped up, eager to answer it. She knew who it would be. She had been waiting for him.

She opened the door. There stood her little brother Davva and his weird mate Skegs. She tried not to let her disappointment show.

'What the fuck d'yays want?'

'Howay, Tanya, let wuh in, man.'

She sighed, took her hand off the door and walked back to the sitting room. Davva and Skegs walked in, Skegs closing the door after him. She flopped back on to the settee, trying to look interested as Ken and Deirdre went tiredly around the houses again. Davva and Skegs stood.

'Have yuh got owt to eat?'

'There's a chip shop down the bottom. Gan

94

there.' Tanya tried not to smile at her own wit.

'Howay, man, Tanya, we're starvin'.'

Tanya turned to look at the two boys, their vacant, blurred expressions. 'Are yous two on somethin'?'

'Aye, we're pissed,' said Skegs with his irritating giggle.

'Aye,' said Davva, puffing himself up, 'we raided the Paki shop. Gorrway wi' loads, didn' wuh?'

Skegs nodded. Davva reached into his pocket, pulled out twenty Silk Cut, tossed them on the settee. 'Got you these.'

Tanya looked at the cigarettes and smiled. 'You're not a bad lad, are you, Davva?'

'So, can we have somethin' to eat now?' Davva asked.

'There's some beans in the kitchen. Help yerself.' Tanya ripped the cellophane from the cigarettes, opened them, lit up. Suddenly, there came another knock at the door, different from the last one, sharp, businesslike. Tanya jumped up to answer. This was the one.

She opened the door and there he stood. Tall, good-looking, clothes all street and rightly labelled, flashes of gold, wearing arrogance as aftershave.

'Hello, Karl,' Tanya said. 'Come in.'

Karl had already swept past her. He walked into the room, stopped dead when he saw the two wasted boys standing there, spooning cold beans out of a tin.

'Who's this?' he asked.

'Me brother and his mate. Don't worry about them.' She started to walk towards the bedroom.

'Come on in here. It's private.' Karl followed her in. The bedroom smelled of mildew, sweat, dirt and guilty, unsatisfying sex. In the corner the baby, Carly, slept in her cot. Tanya walked over to the dressing table, opened a drawer, took out a roll of notes and counted them out. She handed them to Karl. He checked and pocketed them.

Karl sat on the edge of the bed, looking at his watch. 'Come on, I'm in a hurry.'

She took a last, long draw on the cigarette, stubbed it out in an ashtray on the dresser. She sat next to him, unzipped his trousers, reached inside and began squeezing his cock to erection. Once it was at a workable size, she dropped to her knees in front of him, placed it between her lips and began to pump it into her mouth.

It wasn't long before he came, Tanya holding on, pulling the last drops from him, fighting the bile rising in her throat, swallowing down hard. She looked up at him, smiled. He returned the smile, his own cruel and cocky.

He fastened himself up, got to his feet. He reached inside his jacket, brought out a plastic wrap, handed it to her. Tanya took it, wanting it there and then.

'This might be the last time I'm around here for a while,' he said.

'Why?' asked Tanya, a sudden, stabbing sound.

Karl shrugged. 'Getting too dangerous to come in here.'

Tanya spoke as if her lover was leaving her. 'But you can't stop coming here. What'll I do?'

The baby stirred, moaned in her sleep. Karl ignored it. 'Find someone else.'

She rushed over to him, grabbed his jacket. 'Please, Karl, you can't stop comin'. Get someone else to do it if you don't want to come here any more.'

'Who?' he asked.

Suddenly there came the sound of arguing from the front room. Davva and Skegs were apparently fighting over who was going to have the last of the baked beans.

'What about them?' asked Tanya.

Karl smiled.

'Come on, Karl, they'll do it. They're good lads.'

Karl looked thoughtful, then walked back to the living room.

Davva and Skegs stopped their tug of war when he entered.

'Hey, lads,' Karl said, reaching into his jacket, 'got a present in here for you. And if you like it, got a job for you too. What d'you say?'

Tanya stood behind him, eagerness, relief and amusement all over her face.

Suzy waited. The car was freezing, and he said he'd only be a minute. Over twenty of them had passed and she was still here, really pissed off. Suddenly she saw him emerge from the tower block and make his way over to the car. He got in, shut the door.

'You took your time,' she said huffily.

'Business, pet. Took longer than I expected.' He put the key in the ignition. 'One more stop, then we can go and have some fun.'

'What kind of fun?' Suzy asked, tongue teasing out between her smiling lips.

He flashed his special smile, the one she could never stay mad with for too long. 'Anything you like,' he said.

He started the car up and they drove off, garage blaring as they went.

It was nearly one o'clock when Louise heard the noise. Like a hand grenade tossed up the quiet close, the car drummed 'n' bassed its way up the street and stopped to disgorge its passenger in front of Louise's house.

She was awake. She had tried to sleep, but couldn't.

The front door opened and closed quietly, the footsteps light on the stairs. Suzanne wasn't doing that out of consideration for the rest of the household, Louise knew from bitter experience; she was trying to avoid a fight.

Louise heard the car pull away, the soft click of Suzanne's bedroom door, then silence. She lay in the dark, flat on her back, staring at the ceiling. Beside her, Keith was snoring lightly, his back to her.

Something would have to be done, she thought. Things can't go on like this.

Louise sighed, kept staring at the ceiling. It was going to be another long night.

# 5. Then

*because, make no mistake, this is not just a labour dispute. What we are witnessing in the mining towns and villages around the country is the premeditated, systematic destruction of working-class communities and the deliberate silencing of the right to any legitimate voice of dissent or protest. This is being done by a cruel and oppressive government who only seek to plunder the country and line the pockets of themselves and their cronies, led by a dictatorial dominatrix who will use all the powers of government to destroy opposition, from changing or ignoring laws to removing rights and civil liberties as it suits her.*

The typewriter clacked, the argument grew: thoughts to fingers to keys to ribbon to letters to words to sentences to paragraphs. Larkin wrote speedily: fingers punching, mouth forming and following words, forehead creased, eyes slitted behind National Health tortoiseshells. Energy fizzed, focused down his arms. Fingers fed the machine. Black Uhuru on the stereo: 'What Is Life?' This is life, thought Larkin. Life like it should be. Like it shouldn't be. Like it is.

*Thatcher and her boot boys are trying to change today into tomorrow using hatred and fear. And we have to fight back. Or we'll lose more than a strike.*

Ping. Paragraph over. He batted the carriage to the next line, stretched, looked out of the window.

Argument halted.

He was on the first floor, his table/desk in the bay affording him a view of the street. Down below, the inhabitants of Fenham were going about their day, their lives. An ordinary, urban street in Newcastle. Real lives, real people. The view energized Larkin.

He had it and he knew it. The heat of an impassioned, subjective heart wrapped around an objective, chip-of-ice core. A writer's heart. And he knew how to use it.

He sighed, flexed his fingers. His mind and gaze returned to the work in front of him. His fingers soon followed.

Argument resumed.

The record ended; he didn't get up to change it. The room was alive with the angry staccato of the typewriter, backgrounded by the electrostatic hum of the stereo.

Sound of a door opening and closing downstairs. Footsteps on the stairs. The flat door opened. Larkin raised his arm in greeting, kept typing with the other.

''Lo,' he shouted distractedly, not turning round.

A sigh behind him, a bag being placed down, someone moving towards him.

Charlotte swung her head round in front of his, coming between Larkin and the typewriter, her hair falling, covering the words.

'Kiss, please,' she demanded poutily. 'Attention, please. Charlotte's had a busy day.'

Larkin tried to hide his irritation at being interrupted, bent forward and kissed her on the lips. She opened her mouth, sliding her tongue into his. Larkin tried not to respond but, work or no work, he had to kiss her back.

Her mouth was warm, soft and yielding. Her tongue insistent. She smelt of Poison. He began to feel a heat slowly building inside him. Charlotte sensed this and pulled away. She smiled. There was a note of triumph in the smile: *I've managed to come between Stephen Larkin and his precious work.*

'Don't want you too distracted,' she said, straightening up. 'We're going out tonight, remember?'

'I've got this to finish,' Larkin replied, slightly annoyed at allowing himself to be interrupted, piqued that Charlotte had scored a pyrrhic point. 'Then I've got to drop it off with Bob tonight.'

Her voice rose a little. 'But we're meeting Claire and David. Francesca's at eight, remember?'

Larkin had remembered. Claire and David. She, a pretty, vacant airhead from a gormlessly moneyed family, he a maliciously snide Thatcherite whom Larkin had often threatened to deck after a few pints. He dismissed her, he hated him. Law students, trainee barristers. No wonder the country was so fucked up, he thought.

'Yeah, I know,' he said.

Charlotte looked at him. 'Look, I know you don't get on with David. He just likes to wind people up. Take no notice. It's just his way.'

'Yeah.'

'Try to like them, please, Stephen. They are my friends.'

'Yeah.' The typewriter began to clack again. 'Well, I've got this to finish first, then I've got to drop it off. Then we'll meet them.'

'But that'll make us late!'

Larkin stopped writing, turned to face her. 'This is my work, Charlotte. This is what I do for a living.'

'This piece isn't even going to be published.'

'No, but if they like this then I'm in. I've got a mainstream audience.' He looked at her straight in the eye. 'And they're paying me for it.'

She held his gaze for a second, then exited to the kitchen.

Argument resumed.

*They have allies too, influential ones: media magnates suck up to Thatcher. She lets them build their expansionist empires in return for free publicity. Same with big businesses. If there's one thing she loves more than the subjugation of the populace it's naked, aggressive capitalism. Which also leads to the subjugation of the populace. All enforced by the police. Oh, yes, after Orgreave we can be in no doubt about whose side the police are on.*

*And where's the Labour Party in all this? Defeated. Humiliated. Demoralized and fighting among themselves. They're supposed to be leading the opposition, fighting against her, but they've let us down. They've got too many problems of their own. They're scared to challenge her.*

*So against this evil bunch, the miners must find new allies in this struggle. And we must help them because they can't fight alone.*

A glass of wine appeared on the desk.

He looked up. 'Thanks.'

She looked back at him. Her eyes held unreadable emotions, but her tone had softened slightly.

'Please, Stephen. I hate being late. And this dinner's important to me.'

Larkin looked at her. Blonde hair kept long and fringed, subtly but well made up, stylish clothes making only a passing concession to her current student status: long black pleated skirt, white silk blouse, brocaded waistcoat, boots. beautiful face, eyes of startling arctic-blue sky. Larkin again felt something stir inside him. He knew what.

'I'll be as quick as I can,' he said.

Argument suspended.

'Good. And take those ridiculous glasses off.'

'They're for writing,' Larkin replied.

'They've got plain glass in them,' She spoke as if explaining this to a four-year-old.

'So?' Larkin sounded hurt and defensive. 'They focus my mind. Elevate my work. Sharpen my thinking.'

'Bollocks. You wear them so you can look like Morrissey.'

'Oh, fuck off. No, I don't,' said Larkin, hurt. 'It's because...'

'Stephen? I was joking.'

She smiled. He sighed.

'Ha fuckin' ha.'

She turned away with another unreadable look on her face, crossed to the stereo and changed the record. The needle dropped to the vinyl, hisses and scratches, then 'Perfect Skin' by Lloyd Cole and the Commotions kicked in. Charlotte crossed to the sofa, took a textbook from her bag and began to read. Larkin took a hefty mouthful of wine, resumed his argument.

*Take, for instance, Coldwell colliery, just outside*

103

*Newcastle in Northumberland. The pit itself is one of the most profitable in the region, if not the country. It's got a strong workforce and a good history of productivity. But it's been earmarked for closure. Naturally, the workers are fighting back. So why is it being closed down? Simple. Politics. They're taking power away from the regions, centralizing it in Whitehall, taking it back themselves. If we've got no job or nothing to hold them to ransom with, we've got no voice. Plus we're Geordies. We're working class. We've got a strong local tradition of socialism and union membership. We've got our own opinions. So that makes us a threat. That makes us the enemy. The enemy within. So we have to be disposed of.*

Both Larkin and Charlotte loved the *Rattlesnakes* album. Their taste in music was one of the few things they had in common. Charlotte, middle class, star pupil at her private school, was in the middle of the third year of a law degree at Newcastle University. Great things were expected of her. Larkin, on the other hand, was the son of a bus mechanic and defiantly working class. He had attended university for two terms before deciding it could teach him nothing he didn't already know. He had dropped out, becoming first a face about town then a chronicler of the faces about town. Journalism followed, and his polemical articles in left-field, underground magazines mixing fiercely left-wing politics with his love of indie bands attracted a loyal readership among the young and the disenfranchised and, lately, the attention of the mainstream. The piece he was writing on the miners' strike was going to be his first for a mainstream newspaper. His AOR/FM piece as he liked to regard it.

The fact that Charlotte and Larkin had stayed together so long surprised everyone, not least Charlotte and Larkin. There was a deep, tempestuous love between them, a primally intense attraction of opposites, that bound them tight. A relationship that held no half measures, that was, like everything else in their lives, all or nothing.

*The people of Coldwell, and indeed all the communities under threat, desperately need not just our help but our compassion and our anger at what is being done. We need – all of us – to be made aware of what the stakes are in this conflict, and we must be prepared to fight alongside them if need be. Like the prophet said, if you're not part of the solution, you're part of the problem. If you're not with us, you're against us.*

*Think about it. If we let them defeat the miners, who is going to be next?*

Larkin pulled the paper from the typewriter, took his glasses off, stretched, rubbed his eyes. Argument concluded.

'Finished,' he said.

A non-committal grunt came from the sofa.

'Wanna read it?'

Charlotte took it from him, eye-scanned the pages. 'Is this your mainstream piece?' There was faint humour in Charlotte's voice.

Larkin felt himself redden slightly. 'Yeah.'

'I don't think many will agree with you.' She put it down. 'I'd love to read it now, but we're not going to have time. I'll read it when it's published. Just make sure they pay you for it.'

Larkin felt his anger rising, the kind of heat only Charlotte knew how to kindle. They both knew which buttons to press with each other.

'Is that all that matters to you? Who's paying?'

Charlotte looked up. It was her turn to redden. 'Money's important, Stephen. You don't do this for love.'

'My work's about more than just money, Charlotte, you know it is!'

Charlotte stood up, glass in hand, face so close that once again Larkin could smell her Poison. Between them, Lloyd Cole sang about how he would believe in anything that would get him what he wanted, get him off his knees.

'Save the world, Stephen, by all means. Just make sure you get paid for it.'

Before he could open his mouth to argue, she put the glass to her lips, tipped her head back, drank the wine down. Larkin watched as her tiny Adam's apple moved delicately back and forth, up and down with each mouthful.

Once the glass had been drained, she removed it from her lips, eyes remaining locked with Larkin's. A small amount of red wine trickled slowly from the side of her mouth towards her chin. She caught it with her thumb, moved the trail back towards her mouth and slowly licked the juice from it with her tongue.

Larkin felt the anger of moments earlier being displaced by a different kind of heat.

Charlotte was aware of the change in him. She smiled, her blue eyes alive with cold heat. 'I'm going to take a bath,' she said, her voice still low. 'That's where I'll be if you want me.'

She turned, walked towards the bathroom.

Larkin, his erection rising, watched her go. He drained his wineglass and followed.

'Forest Fire' faded out and side one of the record came to an end with a soft click as the needle returned to its original position. From the bathroom could be heard the sound of running water, splashing. In the front room, the insistent electromagnetic hum of the stereo charged the air.

'Aw, fuck,' said Dougie Howden. 'That's aall we need.'

Beside him, Mick Hutton sighed, shook his head, worried. The faint clatter of pots and pans being washed, dried and put away came from downstairs accompanied by female voices. The soup kitchen was closing down for the night.

'Are you sure about this?' asked Dougie.

'Aye, I'm sure,' the man at the other end of the table said. 'Our Iris's cousin works for Northumbria police. He telt 'er.'

Dougie sat back, letting the information sink in. He was a big man, muscle flirting with fat, wearing an old, dark suit, an open-necked shirt and a frown. His hair, grey and grizzly, was unsuccessfully slicked back from his forehead, his moustache nicotine-yellow. He looked at least ten years older than his fifty-two years.

Next to him, Mick Hutton was both younger and smaller. Wearing a knitted tank top over a short-sleeved polo shirt and chinos, with hair cut into a fledgling mullet, he wore his worry on the surface. His eyes looked hunted and haunted,

107

while his wiry frame contained a nervous energy that suggested either a life of intravenous coffee intake or coping with too many responsibilities while living hand to mouth.

The other striking miners sat around the table in the upstairs room in the Miners' Welfare Hall. They drank with stoic intensity from mugs of tea and fugged the room up with cigarette smoke, using it as a smokescreen to hide their fear from each other. They were hard men, solid men. Scared men.

'Well,' said one of the men, his throat tightened from something more than nicotine, 'we knew it was ganna happen. Just a question of when.'

The others nodded grimly, grunted their assent.

'What we ganna do?' asked Mick, his voice untempered fear.

Dougie sighed, shook his head. He knew the men were waiting for him to speak to them. For them.

'I kna' what we should do.'

They all turned to the source of the voice. Dean Plessey, twenty years old. Extreme left-winger, extremely angry. The rest of the table groaned inwardly, bracing themselves for assault.

'And what's that, Dean?' asked Dougie patiently.

'Fight the bastards! Take it to them. The scabs an' the cops. We fight them when they try to bus them in, then we find out who they are an' where they're from, an' take it to them.' Dean rose from his chair. 'Same with the cops. Those smug cunts are laughin' at us. Tauntin' us. Well, we'll show them. We'll find out who they are, where they live. They won't look so smug when we torch

108

their cars an' houses, will they?'

'Dean, man, yer talkin' shite...'

'Naw, he's not, man. Listen to 'im...'

The room descended into chaos as voices were raised, passionate opinions vented. The debate was hectic and heated, the fear in the room carrying the men beyond the boundaries of what would normally be suggested.

Order had to return, thought Dougie. A sense of perspective be restored. Someone has to hold them together. He stood up.

'All right, all right...' He spoke loudly, firmly, the natural authority in his voice moving like a knife through the men's raised voices, cutting their arguments down to silence.

'Come on,' he said. 'This is ganna get us nowhere.' He turned to Dean. 'Yes, Dean, we need to fight. But we've got to be clear what we're fightin' for. We're not ganna go round torchin' them, even if they are coppers.'

He looked around the table. Dean was silent, eyes glaring, but he backed down. From the looks Dougie got from some of the other men, it seemed as if they shared Dean's opinions.

'Look, lads, let's be reasonable about this,' said Dougie, placating but firm. 'Let's study wor options, talk them through.'

He waited until he had the men's full attention, then continued: 'Now, we've known the scabs were comin'. For ages we've known that. An' I know that doesn't make it any easier. But what we have to do now is organize. We get in touch with the local executive. Get them to bus in pickets from Yorkshire, Lancashire and Nott'n'hamshire.

We helped them, they'll help us. They'll wanna show solidarity. Then we get Terry Collier, our MP, to make a fuss. He's no problem, he'll make his mouth go.'

'Aye, he'll talk, but there'll be nee action,' said one disgruntled voice from the table. Others agreed.

'Aye, well,' said Dougie. 'He does what he can. He's a good Labour man.' He gave a small smile. 'But he's also a politician. So don't expect too much.'

There were a few half-hearted laughs. Dougie continued: 'Get the people who are on our side to do what they can. Any other unions who might.' He knew they wouldn't get much support there – most of the other unions had been told that if they helped the miners, their jobs would be next to go. 'We'll get that journalist laddie an' all, he'll make a fuss for us.' Dougie leaned forward, eyes roving around all the men in the room. 'Now, look, you're aall doin' a grand job collectin' an' your wives an' lasses runnin' the kitchens an' takin' care of the food parcels an' that, but we've got to keep goin'. We've got to get on that picket line, stand in front of those gates an' not let them pass. Not let them in.' He hammered his fist into his hand. 'We. Do. Not. Let. Them. Pass. You got that?'

The men nodded, murmuring their assent. Their voices, their intentions seemed stronger, more resolute, their faces and postures hardened.

'Right, good,' said Dougie, something of a spark back in his eyes. 'I'm gonna hand you over to Mick.'

Mick rose hesitantly to his feet. Glancing at a sheet of paper in front of him, he spoke, in halting tones, of how much money had been collected through donations, what the food parcel situation was and how the soup kitchen was going. With the NCB and the government refusing to pay strike pay, and local councils refusing to pay benefits, the miners were relying on savings, charity, donations and a stoical optimism.

Mick reached his summing-up, unable to keep the fear and diminishing self-belief from his voice, face or frame. To the men around the table, watching Mick was like looking into a soul mirror, listening to their hearts. Dougie was the ideal – how they wanted to appear. Mick was how they feared they really were.

He finished speaking, sat down. At his words, a pall had fallen on the room, the optimism and solidarity of Dougie's words replaced by the reality and hopelessness of Mick's. Dougie sighed. They needed something. A lift. He stood up.

'Look,' he began, 'I kna' things are bad. We all kna' that. We've got to keep it together, not give in. It's not time for quittin' yet.'

He talked to the men. Of mining and community. Of comradeship, bravery, laughter. He gave them history, he gave them passion, he gave them anger. With the voice of a street-corner orator and in words of a common dignity. He fed them self-respect. They took it in, they ate it up. When he finished speaking, their fears were assuaged, their bellies full with pride.

The meeting was at an end. The men stood up, began making their way out, hearts slightly lighter than when they had entered, bodies ready to keep up the fight. Where once they would have gone to a pub or a club, shared pints and stories with friends, now they just made their ways home, back to their families.

Alone with Mick in the empty hall, Dougie began tidying up, Mick helping him. Dougie avoided the other man's eyes. It was one thing to inspire a roomful of people, another to be asked point-blank if everything would work out fine in the end. And Mick would ask. He was a good man, a sound organizer, thought Dougie, but he had no strength. Soon he would ask for reassurance, and it was something that, looking straight into Mick's frightened eyes, Dougie couldn't give.

Mick, his chair stacking complete, crossed over to Dougie, mouth open to speak.

Dougie smiled. 'Right, Mick, we've still got work to do. Who's ganna make the first phone call?'

Larkin was pressed up against the wall, legs bent, shower water bouncing off his naked body. He was oblivious to the cold of the tiles against his back, unheeding of the discomfort in his leg muscles, untouched by the water as it hit him. He was aware only of Charlotte, her legs stretched, wrapped around his thighs, her arms braced against the wall as she pushed her hips backwards and forwards with increasing, rhythmic urgency. Her mouth was locked on to his, tongues entwined, his hands roamed all over her body, caressing, alternately gentle and rough; stroking her breasts then pinching her nipples, running

112

first fingers then nails down the skin of her back, each movement eliciting a moan or a sigh from Charlotte.

They were both lost somewhere between love and lust, sweetly oblivious to everything but each other.

Then the phone rang.

Larkin was lost, didn't let it register. Charlotte heard the noise, opened her eyes.

'Phone,' she said, reluctantly untangling her mouth from Larkin's, her body's rhythm unconsciously slowing.

'Ignore it,' replied Larkin breathlessly.

The phone kept ringing.

'Might be important,' Charlotte said, her body grinding slowly to a halt. She gave a half-smile. 'Could be someone offering me a job.'

Larkin sighed. 'Go and get it, then.'

She swung her legs off him, picked up a towel, made her way to the front room, dripping.

Larkin, alone, began to feel the coldness of the tiles, the discomfort in his legs, the irritation of the water. He stood slowly, willing the circulation back into his limbs and switched off the shower, just as Charlotte re-entered the bathroom.

'For you,' she said, less than happy.

Larkin stepped out of the bath, moved towards the door naked, his erection tall and proud.

'Hey,' said Charlotte.

Larkin turned.

'Don't be long.' She let the towel drop to the floor. 'I'll be waiting for you.'

Larkin stared at her body, smiled. 'Stay hot,' he said, and exited to the front room.

Charlotte sat on the edge of the bath, smiled. Her mind flicked on to their earlier argument, the one that the shower had solved. She sighed.

Sometimes I wonder what keeps us together, she thought. What keeps me with him. We're complete opposites, almost enemies at times. But there's something...

They were sexual twins; sex with Larkin was electrifying, despite the fact that they seemed to have settled into a conventional relationship.

She heard Larkin replace the receiver and moved her hands between her legs, to regain her previous ecstasy. He entered the room and she turned to face him, parting her legs to give him a better view of what her hands were doing, where her fingers were. She saw his semi-deflated erection, smiled.

'Looks like you've got some catching up to do,' she said. 'Come here.'

Larkin stayed where he was. 'That was Dougie Howden, the strike leader over in Coldwell. He's got a date for them busing in scabs.'

'So? Deal with it in the morning.'

Larkin's eyes were lit by another kind of passion. 'I can't. I have to do it tonight. Write it up straight away, get as many people alerted as possible, steal the lead on the others. This is what we in the trade call a scoop. Sorry.'

Charlotte stood up, walked towards him. Suddenly she felt exposed, angry at revealing her previous intimacy before him, and clutched the towel to her body.

'Sorry? Right, well, you just do that! You just run off and save the world! Who do you think you are? Fucking Superman?'

Larkin felt his earlier anger resurfacing. 'Listen, this is my job! If it was something to do with your career, you'd have been out of that door already!' He moved directly in front of her, finger pointing. 'And anyway, if your needs are so important, you shouldn't have answered the fucking phone!'

Charlotte's eyes narrowed to tiny, blazing embers.

'Fuck you.' Her voice was small, controlled and dangerous. 'I'm going out now to see my friends. Not because my career depends on it, but because I enjoy their company. You can do what the fuck you want.'

She swept past him out of the bathroom. Larkin sighed and sat on the edge of the bath. He heard Charlotte angrily make her way to the bedroom, heard the door slam shut. He stared at his reflection in the mirror for a moment, his mind not articulating his thoughts clearly.

Eventually he sighed again, pushed his wet quaff back from his forehead, stood up, wrapped a towel around his waist and walked towards the front room.

The flat was then gripped by silence, the electronic burr of the still-live stereo humming with tension.

The silence was soon broken by the sound of the front door slamming followed by the clacking of Larkin's typewriter.

Argument resumed.

## 6. Now

Larkin, carrying a notepad, pen, dictaphone and the mildest of hangovers, knocked on the front door of the Coldwell Addictions Treatment Centre. The door was opened by a woman with vibrantly dyed red hair, a black T-shirt, baggy, blue Carhartts and trainers. Mid-twenties, Larkin reckoned.

'Hi, I'm Stephen Larkin. Here to see Tony Woodhouse?'

The girl frowned for a moment before her eyes came alight. 'The journalist?'

'That's me.'

She smiled slightly, noticeably wrinkling the skin around her mouth and eyes. Either she had laughed a lot or cried a lot in her life. Larkin didn't know which, mentally revised her age upwards.

'Come in,' she said.

Larkin followed her up the stairs.

'Have you had a look around?'

'Not yet.'

She smiled again. 'I'll do the honours, then.'

The woman, who gave her name as Claire Duffy, showed him round, then sat him in her office with a mug of coffee.

'You don't mind if I start work, do you? Tony won't be long.'

'Fine by me.' Larkin sipped his coffee, looked

around. 'The centre. It's a lot better provided for than I thought it would be.'

Claire smiled. 'One of the perks of having an ex-football hero as a boss.'

'Yeah?'

'Opens doors us mere mortals never could.' There was an edge of amiable sarcasm to her voice.

Larkin nodded. Football hero? A handful of appearances for Newcastle, not even a regular first-team place, and then a career-stopping injury? Did that make him a hero? Larkin said nothing. But filed the information away.

He stood up, crossed to the window, looked down. The small town was struggling to wake: buses taking straggling commuters to Whitley Bay and Newcastle, shops opening to meagre trade, keen shoppers and aimless human flotsam spilling on to the pavement. On the low wall outside the public toilets sat a lone man, age indeterminate, bottle of economy cider at his side. He stared straight ahead, either at nothing, or something only he could see. Just waiting. An early riser or a late nighter, thought Larkin. He wondered if the man was still aware of the difference. One of Tony Woodhouse's last surviving community members. The man became animated, started talking, addressing an invisible audience. Perhaps he carried his community around with him, thought Larkin.

He glimpsed a red car rounding the corner. A gleaming Puma with a disabled badge on the windscreen. It pulled up directly outside the building. Larkin watched as Tony Woodhouse hauled himself painfully from the car, wincing slightly with every step.

'Here he comes,' Larkin said.

Tony Woodhouse locked the car door, straightened up. His left leg was aching more than normal, dull throb sparking to painful, attention-sapping stabs. He knew, without looking at the sky, that it would rain soon.

He gave a grim smile to himself. Tony Woodhouse and his amazing gammy leg. Psychic weatherman.

He looked at the man sitting by toilets. 'Mornin', Jerry.'

The man looked at him, a smile split his broken face. 'Mornin', Mr Woodhouse.'

Tony nodded, then looked up towards the front windows of the CAT Centre and saw an unfamiliar face looking down at him. The face smiled. Tony frowned in response. Then he remembered. The journalist. Louise's brother.

Tony smiled back, threw the vague arc of a wave, thought: How am I going to play this? Answered: The standard story, complete with liftable quotes and handy soundbites. Give him that, send him home happy.

And see if he has a hidden agenda.

Persona in place, Tony made his way painfully to the door.

'So,' said Tony with a pleasant, open smile, 'what d'you want to do next?'

The centre was getting busy. Larkin was beginning to get some sense of the need for the place.

118

People had been in and out all morning, some stopping to talk, some just wanting somewhere to go.

Larkin was in the same uncomfortable armchair he had occupied on his previous visit. He had asked Tony about his life and work, made notes, taped the whole thing. There was nothing there he hadn't heard already. A sketched-in life story.

It was clear to Larkin, even in the short time he had been there, that Tony Woodhouse was popular with both staff and clients. He had an easy, amiable charisma people responded to.

Larkin shrugged. 'Up to you.'

Tony thought for a moment. 'Let's go for a drive,' he said.

Larkin stood up immediately, trying not to show his relief at being freed from the chair. He grabbed the dictaphone, followed Tony out.

'Here,' said Tony, looking through the windscreen, 'is where most of our clients come from.'

As soon as Tony and Larkin had climbed into the Puma, the heavens had opened, washing people from the streets, grime from the buildings. Tony had made a comment about his leg forecasting the weather, then driven to the T. Dan Smith Estate. There they now sat, looking out.

Larkin followed Tony's eyeline. Here, the rain wasn't washing the estate clean; it was just giving the discoloured concrete and brick a dark, oil-like sheen.

'T. Dan Smith?' asked Larkin. 'Is that some kind of town planner's joke?'

Tony smiled. 'Apparently not. They decided that the estate – and all the blocks and streets on it – should be named after prominent north-easterners.' He gestured. 'There's Catherine Cookson House, of course, and those bungalows next to it are in Jimmy Nail Walk. There's also Jackie Milburn House, Paul Gascoigne House–'

'Tony Woodhouse House?'

Tony's expression changed, darkened slightly. 'No,' he said, looking through the side window, eyes beyond the rain. 'Only the heroes. Not the ones who never made it.'

Larkin nodded.

'So most of your clients...'

'Yes,' said Tony, jumping on the subject change, 'most of them come from here. Most of the people on the estate are on something or other.'

'What's the worst?'

Tony gave a bitter laugh. 'There isn't a worst. There are just differences. Degrees. Booze, heroin, crack. Different strokes for different folks. Same end result.'

'They all visit you?'

'Not all of them. Only the ones who think we can help them. Who want to be helped.'

'And do you?'

Tony sighed. 'We've had some successes, but mostly it's a question of slapping a Band-Aid on and sending them out again. There's only so much we can do with what we've got.'

Larkin followed Tony's eyes. Through the windscreen-bleaching rain, the estate looked almost derelict. Broken fences spilled wild-growing grasses and weeds on to pavements. Rotting furniture, rusting appliances and burned-out cars were dotted around like parts of a dismantled barricade. The flats and houses, boarded and burned out, decayed and uninhabitable, sat side by side with lived-in ones. A darkness more than rainclouds hung over the place.

'The estate's always been rough. I should know, I come from around here,' Tony said, 'but it's never been this bad. When the mine went, the town died with it.' He gave an angry sigh, air hissing through his teeth. 'You take away the work, you take away the pride, what have you got left? This.'

'Were you around for the miners' strike?'

Tony's face clouded, his thoughts suddenly unreadable. 'Not ... really. My dad was, though. And my brother. It was the pit that killed my dad. His lungs.'

'What about your brother?'

Tony stared away from Larkin, avoiding eye contact. 'Moved away. Got a job in Chester. Works with computers now. I don't see much of him. Suppose he did the right thing, getting out when he could. The only growth industry around here now is—'

'Drug dealing?'

Tony gave a grim smile. 'Got it in one. And I'll tell you what, some of the kids are good at it. Fuckin' good. Under different circumstances they could be running ICI or something like that.' His Geordie accent was becoming stronger.

They lapsed into silence again. 'D'you hate them?' Larkin asked eventually.

'I hate what they do, but...' He paused. 'Comin' from around here, I understand why they feel they

121

want to escape. Both the dealers and the punters.'
He nodded, more to himself than to Larkin.

'Can you see anything improving?'

'Not really,' Tony replied. 'At the end of the day, we just treat the symptoms, not the causes. It would take a hell of a lot to get rid of them.'

'Like what?'

Tony smiled. 'You'd have to take away the boredom. Give them jobs. Stop what they were trying to escape from in the first place.'

'That's a tall order.'

'Right. You're talkin' a massive injection of cash and a huge redevelopment programme. But that's not gonna happen. Still, there is one thing you could do.'

'What?'

'Legalize heroin for a start.'

'What?'

'Legalize it. Not just decriminalize it, legalize it. Legalize the lot. Do that and street crime'll disappear virtually overnight.'

'How?'

'You break the chain.'

Larkin stared at Tony, frowned. Tony turned to him, explaining. 'OK. Think about it. Does heroin kill?'

'Yes,' said Larkin.

'No,' said Tony. 'Heroin has never killed anyone. Fact. It's a painkiller. Admittedly a highly addictive one, but a painkiller. Full stop. Overdose on it and all you'll get is a bit of a headache. Maybe an upset stomach. An overdose of paracetamol will do you more harm. No, it's the stuff it's cut with that kills you. Drug dealers are gangsters. For them the profit motive is everything. They'll cut it with anything. Talcum powder, brick dust, cement dust, face powder, curry powder, drain cleaner. Anything. Some of this stuff is toxic, obviously. Some gets in the body and clots. Causes gangrene. Leads to amputation.'

Tony was getting into his argument.

'It's like America during prohibition. You know why so many blues musicians in the 1920s were blind? Because of the prohibition alcohol they drank. Moonshine. Bathtub gin. Gangsters. Same with drugs now. You legalize them, get addicts to register with their doctors. Given clean supplies, you take the gangsters out of the equation.'

He gestured at the estate.

'Like around here. People think addicts just sit around all day getting out of it. They don't. They're a hard-workin' bunch. They're always on the go, looking for money to get their next fix, stealin', muggin', sellin' their bodies even. Anythin'. You take that away and they could get on with their lives. Sort themselves out. Drugs aren't the problem. Criminalize water or air and you'll be sold dodgy stuff by gangsters. No, heroin doesn't fuck you up. You could take it for years, a clean supply, and your best friend wouldn't be able to tell.'

He smiled. 'Honestly.'

Larkin smiled also. 'Pretty persuasive argument.'

'All absolutely true.'

'Can you see that happening?'

Tony laughed. 'Not immediately. Especially not with an election comin' up. They don't want to say anythin' that would upset the *Daily Mail*. But

123

it has to be done. I firmly believe that. But until they do that–' he looked around again, gestured '– they'll keep comin' to me. And I'll patch them up and send them home again. And that's where the demons are.'

'So why d'you keep doing it, then?'

Tony opened his mouth to reply but stopped himself. His face broke into shadow before opting for a smile. 'Someone has to... You got plenty of quotes there?'

Larkin clicked the tape off. 'Yep.'

'Then come on,' said Tony. 'Let's go somewhere else.'

They drove away, leaving the rain to hammer away at the T. Dan Smith Estate.

The Garden of Eden the pub was called. If there was a prize for most inappropriate and misleading pub name, thought Larkin, then this would win it.

It was perched on the edge of a particularly unpicturesque stretch of the Blyth River on the borders of a red-brick housing estate. Upriver to the left stood the tall, belching chimneys of the Cambois power station. Downriver to the right were what remained of the docks and piers, with the tall, white wind turbines rotating slowly in the distance. On the opposite bank bordered by flat, open space were six rows of terraced housing, looking peculiarly bleak and out of place.

The pub, which had an incongruous new conservatory backing on to an old wooden jetty, was exactly as Larkin had expected it to be. Scarred, wooden tables and chairs, carpet worn

124

down by use, too expensive to replace. However, the landlord gave them a hearty welcome, which surprised Larkin, but as he and Tony were the only two customers he was probably glad of the trade. Larkin sat in the conservatory waiting for Tony to finish his conversation with the barman and bring two pints of lager to the table. Thankfully, the rain on the conservatory roof drowned out the Tina Turner tape.

'Cheers,' said Tony, sitting down.

'Nice place,' said Larkin, looking around.

'They do their best.'

They both sipped.

'I used to work down here,' said Tony.

'What, this pub?'

'No, there.' Tony pointed to the docks. 'When I left school. It was either that or the pit. After seein' what happened to me dad, I thought me chances were better in the open air.'

'And the football?'

'Thank God it came along when it did.' He looked at the docks. 'Yeah...'

'D'you miss it?' Larkin asked quietly.

Tony frowned, sighed. 'Ended before it started, really. If I'd been in it a bit longer ... I don't know.' He smiled. 'Don't miss the training, though.'

'D'you miss the docks, then?'

'No,' said Tony quickly. 'That's what I was usin' the football to escape from.'

'Know what you mean,' said Larkin, but Tony wasn't listening. He was staring at the docks, drifting away, seeing something Larkin couldn't.

'Clive Fairbairn,' said Larkin suddenly.

Tony came back into focus with a jolt. 'What?'

'Clive Fairbairn,' Larkin repeated. 'That's where I'd heard it before. His trial. Something about him using Coldwell docks as one of the main inlets for hard drugs from Europe.'

'I wouldn't know,' said Tony. 'But I wouldn't be surprised.'

'Yeah, that's right. There were a number of raids a few years ago. Hard drugs and decommissioned guns from Russia. On the way to the IRA, they reckoned.'

'Oh, that's right,' said Tony, putting on a show of remembering. He took a hefty mouthful of beer. 'Glad they got all that off the streets. Makes my life that bit easier.'

'Anything like that going on when you were there?' asked Larkin.

'I wasn't there long,' said Tony, not keeping eye contact, 'and I wasn't looking.'

Larkin held the look, then nodded. There was something there, something in Tony's answers that didn't ring true, but he was going to get no further. At the moment. Time for a change of subject, he thought.

'So, anyway,' he said, 'what happened after the football?'

Tony smiled, back in control. 'I did a degree in sociology...'

Back to the familiar biography. How he had accidentally come to attend university after his football career came to an end. How he ended up running the CAT Centre– 'Just lucky. Right man in the right place at the right time.' How he gets donations– 'Do a Bob Geldof. If they say no, threaten to name an' shame. Always does the trick. Always opens the chequebook.' He went on to talk about the structure of the centre, the qualifications of the staff, the success stories they'd had. Larkin had heard all the stories before. It was like Tony was giving a chat show performance. But Larkin nodded along, his dictaphone on the table capturing it all.

Tony finished talking. Larkin picked up the dictaphone.

'Got everything you need?' Tony asked.

Larkin smiled. 'For now.'

Tony nodded, stood up, popped a breath mint into his mouth. 'Won't do for me to counsel alcoholics smelling of booze.'

They both laughed.

They headed for the door. Outside, the rain had stopped, leaving Coldwell temporarily glistening.

Larkin waited until Tony had the car key in his hand and said: 'Oh, by the way, I called in to see Louise the other day.'

Tony stopped dead, the key frozen on its way to the lock.

'Oh, yeah,' he said, his voice a little thin. 'How was she?'

'Fine,' replied Larkin. 'She asked after you.'

'That's nice,' said Tony, his face pleasantly impassive. 'Well, if you see her again, give her my–' he paused '–regards.'

'I will do.'

Tony opened the car door, swung his left leg painfully in. Larkin didn't move.

'You don't mind if I walk?' he asked. 'Take in

127

some local colour.'

'Not at all.'

They made arrangements for Larkin to return the following day and Tony drove off, but not before reminding Larkin of the football match on Sunday. Larkin reluctantly agreed to be there. Tony sped off, leaving Larkin standing alone on the pavement.

He began to walk back towards the town centre, slowly, taking it all in. It had changed. And not for the better.

He walked past a grim, low-lying council estate, past terraced streets, the red-brick rain-purged of grime. Past an old Victorian ex-pub turned community centre, one wall covered by a mural, the paint now faded, chipped and tagged, the door locked, the windows caged up. Past a hole-in-the-wall pub, the interior dark and uninviting, human misshapes silhouetted by fruit machine glow sat hunched on bar stools, threat pooled and lurking in its shadows. Next down, a used furniture and appliance store, offering 'not unreasonable' rates of credit. Through the window, Larkin saw a fat man in a stained polo shirt laughing down the phone. Probably at the not unreasonably small amounts of rubbish he was getting desperate customers to buy.

He reached the main shopping area, started to walk towards the car park. Past some girls pushing pushchairs, kids trudging miserably behind them. The girls, seventeen or eighteen, saw someone they knew on the other side of the street; another girl with a pushchair. They started a shouted conversation, the first girl bellowing,

'Aw, man, ahm a single mother now, man,' then looking around, smiling as if expecting a round of applause, as if that fact should get her noticed. She didn't look very bright. The two kids with her tried to wander away into a shop.

He reached the bus station. The lone wino still occupied the low wall in front of the toilets. He looked wet through, as if he hadn't moved during the rain. His matted mohican and ratty ponytail were damp but still worn proudly, as if they had just come into fashion. None of his friends had joined him. He had given up talking to himself now, and just nodded, as if listening.

Larkin headed for the car park, moving among the pedestrians. They were all poorly and cheaply dressed, looking for the most part either over-weight or undernourished, some of them both. Bad skin, greasy hair. The plentiful fast foods and bakeries selling cheap hot pies offered tempting quick fixes, food for a hungry heart. People fed as they walked, giving their bodies the illusion of satisfaction, leaving their emptinesses unfilled.

He reached the car park, got his keys out, looked around. Suddenly the air was filled with the rhythmic throb of drum 'n' bass. He turned, saw a flash Japanese car go past, heading in the direction of the T. Dan Smith Estate. One of Tony Woodhouses's ICI directors, thought Larkin wryly. Then a second thought: the car that had dropped Suzanne off at Louise's house the other night.

He sighed. There must be plenty of boy racers driving overpowered cars with tinnitus-inducing sound systems built in. So what?

He took one last look around the town. The sun was now shining but it still felt cold. He got in the car. Yeah, he thought, I've got the measure of you, Coldwell. Where you were then, where you are now. Then he thought of Tony Woodhouse.

But I haven't got the measure of *you* at all.

He started the car up, drove away.

Karl drove the way he did everything else: cockily. He swung round parked cars, paid only the barest lip service to traffic lights and road markings, showed other drivers that, no matter who they were or where they were going, he had right of way. He came first. He had never been in an accident, would never be in an accident. That was other people. Lesser people. On the road, as in all other aspects of his life, Karl was bulletproof. His immortality was assured.

He smiled as he drove, head nodding unconsciously to the music as he planned his day: distribution run to the T. Dan, gather up the cash from his delivery boys, maybe take a couple of freebie blow jobs. Then later, pick up Suzy, take her back to his place. His smile widened as he felt the first throbbing of an erection.

He had a surprise for her later. She was going to love it.

Davva and Skegs were having the time of their lives. Davva piloted his brand-new mountain bike down the concrete ramp of the old skateboard park on the outskirts of the T. Dan. He pedalled faster, furiously plummeting, before letting the momentum carry him up the opposing slope. He hit the top and turned, jackknifing the bike in midair, twisting like the pros on TV, to make a return journey down.

The front wheel hit the slope dead on, but the back one, still at an angle, juddered. Davva wrestled with the handlebars, trying desperately to keep his balance, but it was no good. The bike slid away beneath him and Davva smacked on to the concrete, bruising his limbs, his new jeans and sweatshirt getting friction-scuffed in the process. The bike scraped down the slope, coming to rest at the bottom.

Skegs couldn't stop laughing. 'Stupid fucker!' he shouted before laughing again. 'You shoulda seen yersel'...'

Davva got to his feet and, face reddening, walked over to where Skegs stood by his bike, arms draped over the handlebars, and smacked him in the head. The laughter stopped immediately. Skegs looked at Davva, his face showing more than just physical hurt.

'Fuck d'ya do that for?' Skegs rubbed his head.

'If you can do better, fuckin' do it.' Davva righted his bike.

Skegs reddened, lip trembling. 'Ah'll right.'

He straddled his mountain bike and walked it, with difficulty, to the top of the slope, then began the descent. He pedalled as hard as he could, mouth twisted with exertion. He followed Davva's trajectory, down then up, but on reaching the summit found he didn't have enough speed to take off. He tried the same manoeuvre Davva had tried, with even less success. The bike

131

began to fall backwards on to him. His legs buckled as the weight of the bike pressed down on him and he began to stumble. He fell, the bike came with him, and he rolled and twisted his way down the ramp, landing in a contorted heap at the bottom.

Skegs extricated himself from his bike and stood up, cheeks burning with humiliation. He looked across at Davva. The boy wasn't laughing; he was just smiling. Somehow it made it worse.

Skegs walked his battered new bike over to where Davva was standing and took his place, wordlessly, by his side. Davva was still smiling. Skegs was close enough to see the mix of contentment and cruel pleasure.

Skegs idly spun his pedal with his foot, said nothing. Waited.

They stood like that for what seemed a long time. Eventually, Skegs took a battered joint from his back pocket, lit it, sucked it down and, stifling coughs, offered it to Davva.

Davva looked at the boy, nodded and took a toke. They relaxed a little after that.

Soon the spliff was gone and they were deciding what to do next. Their minds were made up for them by the approaching thump of drum 'n' bass. Karl's car pulled up to the kerb. The boys ran over to it. He wound down the window but not the music.

'Afternoon, boys,' Karl said, leaning out of the window. 'Got anythin' for me?'

Davva and Skegs found it difficult to hear Karl over the incessant thump from the speakers but they didn't mind. It was all part of the whole scene to them. Flash. Bling bling. Besides, they knew what he wanted. They reached down into their pockets and turned over bills and coins to Karl.

Karl counted it, shrugged. 'Not much for a mornin's work.' Something sharp and glittering came into his eyes. 'You boys not holdin' out on me, are you?'

The boys shook their heads, quickly, fear bulging in their eyes. Karl smiled.

'Good,' he said. 'Make sure you don't. Now, you got enough stuff for the rest of the day?'

They both nodded.

'Good. Remember, if you get caught, you're on your own. Now get a fuckin' move on. You didn't get those bikes just to fuckin' play on. Fuckin' shift.'

The two boys pedalled away quickly, not daring to look back.

Karl watched them go, smiled to himself, then drove off.

Claire Duffy shut down her computer, checked the contents of her shoulder bag and moved towards the door. She paused, wondering whether to put her face round the door to Tony's office. She did. He sat at his desk, playing with his pen, staring off beyond the four walls. She shook her head, concerned. He hadn't been the same since getting back from meeting that journalist. She gave a tentative knock on the doorframe.

'Tony?'

He looked up, startled to find her there.

'I'm just off.'

He nodded. 'OK. Goodnight, Claire.' He went

back to his pen.

Claire nodded, didn't move. 'Um...'

He looked up again.

'You OK?' she asked.

'Yeah, I'm fine.'

She moved into the room. When she spoke, her voice was deliberately airy. 'Look, I'm not in a hurry tonight. Fancy a drink or something?'

'Not tonight. Sorry. We'll do it another time.' He didn't meet her eyes.

Claire nodded, understanding. 'OK,' she said. 'See you tomorrow.'

She left.

Tony waited until the front door closed and he was alone in the centre. He picked up the phone and dialled a number from memory. It was answered eventually. He told the person who answered who he was and who he wanted to speak to. After what seemed like a long wait, they picked up.

'Hello, Tommy,' Tony said. 'It's me. We need to talk.'

Tony listened to the reply, made arrangements for the meeting, put the phone down and sighed. His eyes wandered around the office. He didn't see the surroundings, the furniture, files and posters. He saw the achievements, the results. The successes the centre had had, the failures. The people who had come through the door, the lives he had become involved with. To him, that was – they were – the centre. That was what mattered to him. That was what was important.

Outside, the day was fading, the dark taking hold. He knew it was time to leave, to go home.

He had that familiar feeling, the craving upon him, but still he didn't get up.

Just sat there, staring at the walls, the door.

'So, I'm finally getting to see where you live?' asked Suzy with a giggle in her voice. 'I should feel flattered.'

She stepped through the doorway straight into the living room. The Wills Building, the old cigarette factory on the coast road, had been recently refurbished and turned into minimalist, modernist designer flats, aimed at young aspiring professionals. Karl thought he fitted this description right down to the ground.

It looked like a show flat: white leather sofas, pale walls, blond wood, straight lines and unostentatious, shining precious metal. A huge wide-screen TV and DVD sat in one corner, expensive midi system next to it.

'This is lovely...' said Suzy, wide-eyed.

Karl closed the door behind her. It locked with a soft, yet forceful, click.

'All mine,' he said.

She turned to face him. 'Can I have a guided tour?'

Karl placed his hands on her hips, thumbs moving slowly inside the waistband of her jeans.

'Oh, yeah,' he said, eyes locking on to her, 'we're gonna go exploring.'

They ended up in the bedroom where, without a word being spoken, Karl had undressed Suzy and, not ungently, but firmly, pushed her down on to the bed. She lay there flat on her back, knees clenched together in nervous anticipation, arms wrapped tightly around her breasts. Her heart was beating like a jungle clubbing rhythm. She was sure he could hear it. She sighed, her breath juddering out. Yes, she was unclothed, but lying there in that room, looking at Karl, she suddenly felt somehow more than naked.

She watched Karl undress, neatly fold his clothes on a dressing table. She gasped as she saw his erect cock spring loose from his jeans. It excited yet frightened her at the same time. Like Karl himself.

He stood there, looking down at her. He took in her firm, high breasts, slim waist, dark pubic hair and smooth, long legs. She looked clean, unsullied. His cock stiffened more at that thought.

He knelt beside her and began to move his hand slowly up her body.

She felt his fingers tracing their way up her calves, her thighs... She tingled where he had touched. Her heart palpitated.

'Karl.' Her voice came out hesitant and breathy, her throat suddenly dry. He looked at her, didn't answer, kept his hands moving.

'I know we've done things...' she said, 'in the car and that, but I've never gone all the way with anyone before. You're the first one.'

'I know.' There was no hesitancy in Karl's reply, no breathiness. Just calm, authoritative words.

'I wanted it to be you.'

Karl moved his body on top of her, put his hands between her legs. She gasped, jumped.

'Tell me what you want me to do,' he said, smiling.

She swallowed. Her throat was dry. 'Fuck me,' she whispered. 'Fuck me, Karl.'

Karl obliged.

Larkin walked up the flight of stairs, into the flat's front room. It was still a mess: unpacked boxes just raided when needed and CDs piled around. The one chair. He couldn't call it *his* flat yet; he doubted if he ever would. It was just where he lived. He doubted it would ever look lived in.

He went to the fridge in the kitchen, removed a Stella, popped it, slumped himself down in the chair. He looked around. He sighed.

The flat. His life. The mess. He didn't want to see. He didn't want to think. He was tired. He kept the light off. He swigged hard at the can.

Tony Woodhouse. Louise. Other people's lives. Another swig. It was easier to go into other people's lives. Make judgements. Sort them out. Easier than doing it in his own.

Another swig. He looked around the room, saw the shadows. Hiding in the shadows, the shapes of the ghosts. Standing on the edges. This world and the next. Hunched, black against black. Looking at him with sightless eyes. Reminding him.

Their names: Sophie. Joe. Charlotte.

Dead.

And the missing: Andy. Henry. Faye.

Alive, but gone.

And the others. All the others.

He stood up, turned the light on. The ghosts fled, the shadows disappeared. The naked bulb hunted them down, threw them out. He crossed to the TV, turned it on, sat back down, picked up the can.

The TV washed over him. He didn't even know what he was watching.

He just sat there, thinking, but trying not to.

Just ghosts left. Just shadows. Just the past.

Later, they lay side by side on the bed. Karl had drifted off to sleep but Suzy was still wide awake. She lay on her side, watching the gentle rise and fall of his shoulder as he dozed. She smiled, relived their lovemaking.

Because that's what it had been, she decided: lovemaking. At first it had been painful for her; she had been unprepared for the sheer depth of Karl's cock and contracted her body, her legs, together. But Karl had been patient. He had gently eased it into her, stroked her and talked to her. Gradually she had given in to the feeling of pleasure spreading through her and eventually abandoned herself, ceding control to Karl, opened her legs as wide as they would go, letting him all the way in.

He had pulled out of her before he came, and when she saw him kneeling above her, panting and sweating, that was when she told him she loved him. And he said he loved her too, then came all over her breasts.

She was fascinated. She had never seen a man come before. She touched her fingers to the sticky white stuff, picked it up. Karl saw this and slowly moved her hand to her mouth, smiling, until she had licked it all off. Although she didn't like the taste, she tried not to show it, so as not to upset Karl. She smiled.

'Now your turn,' he said, and knelt down between her legs. He brought her to orgasm with his tongue. She had honestly never felt anything like it before. When she had regained her breath, she told him again that she loved him.

The whole thing was perfect. Just like she had imagined her first time would be.

And now she was watching her lover sleep. Her lover. She smiled. It felt good saying that. Grown up at last.

Suzy was bright; she knew what Karl was, what he did. Yes, it bothered her, but not too much. It was his work, what he did to make money. She could box off that bit of him and have the rest. The thing was, he was so much more interesting than all the boys at school. Yes, she was both brainy and good-looking, but it was a combination that either scared boys off or only attracted the real losers. What she wanted was excitement, danger. Anything but her boring school life, her depressing home life. And with Karl she had it. And she was so grateful for it.

She reached out her hand, began to tenderly stroke him. Her fingers trailed down his body until they came to rest on his semi-deflated cock. She began to explore it, felt the soft ridges that had so recently been hard, the rough bits, the smooth bits. Slowly, she felt it begin to harden again.

Karl's eyes opened and he jumped up, turning quickly to face Suzy, grabbing her by the wrist. Suzy jumped back from him, shocked by his sudden reaction, but he held her hard.

'What you doin'?' Karl asked, voice sharp but sleepily edged.

'Ow, you're hurting me...'

'What you doin'?'

'Just ... just touching you...' she said.

'Don't do that unless I ask you to, yeah?'

Suzy nodded. 'Sorry, Karl.'

'Good.' He sighed, looked at her, the sudden fear in her face. He smiled. 'Sorry,' he said. 'I just woke up too quickly.'

Suzy smiled in return, relief at having the old Karl back evident on her face. 'That's all right. Would you like me to keep going?'

He smiled again. 'Why not?'

She smiled again and began enthusiastically to resume stroking him.

'Suzy...' Karl said after a while.

'Yeah?'

'Use your mouth.'

'OK,' she said, and did as she was told.

And the more she sucked him, the more relaxed and responsive he became, and the more she enjoyed pleasing him.

And when his body bucked and he held her mouth over his cock, she didn't complain or pull away. And even though she didn't like the taste, she swallowed his semen, happy and content to have a part of him inside her.

And she loved him all the more for it.

# 7. Then

Tony Woodhouse drove east out of the city centre of Newcastle, the sky darkening the further he went. He drove past Tyne Tees Television, City Road becoming Walker Road, then took a right down Glasshouse Street, in among the industrial estate and reclamation plant. Almost at the river's edge. He slowed the car to a prowl, his neck craning left and right. He breathed heavily. His stomach was doing backflips. His hands made the steering wheel wet and slippy.

Then he saw it. Squat, ugly, dilapidated. Paint flaked away, the blue star out front no longer lit. The Ropemakers Arms. Silhouetted starkly against the Tyne, it should have spoken of the city's faded maritime history – a ropery, a chandler – but it just brought to Tony's mind another use for a rope – a noose. Something you walked towards but never away from.

He had been planning this moment all day, and building up to it for longer than that. The dread was knotted inside him. He had had a terrible morning in training; no concentration or application. In the end he had complained of a stomach upset, which wasn't far from the truth, and begged off. They had sent him home. He hadn't gone home, however.

Neil Moley had been released from hospital. He wouldn't talk about what had happened to him in the toilets of the Trent that night. In fact, due to the knife wounds that Tommy Jobson had inflicted on his face, he couldn't talk at all.

Tony pulled up outside Neil's Benwell flat. Crumbling red brick, roads chicaned with debris, feral dogs and children roamed. He knocked at the door. Neil answered, his face Michelin-Manned with bandages and gauze, his eyes shot through with fear. Neil pulled Tony inside, checked up and down the street, followed him in.

'Fuck me, Neil...' said Tony, inside.

Neil picked up a pad and pen.

*There after you next.*

'I know,' said Tony. He looked at Neil again, shook his head. 'Shit...'

*What you gonna do?*

Tony looked at Neil. And made up his mind.

'I'm goin' to see Tommy. Talk to him. Straighten it out.'

Neil's hand shook when he wrote.

*Be careful.*

'I'll be careful.'

He sighed, shook his head again. He put his hand into his jeans pocket, drew out his wallet, handed over the notes that were in there.

'Here, Neil. Take this.'

Neil took it. No arguments. He held up a finger, then disappeared from the room. There came the sound of rummaging from somewhere else in the flat, then Neil returned with a bundle wrapped in an old Fenwick's carrier bag. He handed it to Tony.

'Should have just given it back in the first place,' Tony said.

What was showing of Neil's face reddened.

'Hell's bells,' said Tony. 'What a fuck-up, eh?'

Neil nodded.

'I'll get it straightened out. Leave it to me.'

Neil nodded. He didn't have to write down that it was too late for him. They both knew it anyway.

Tony left, before the weight in his chest could get any heavier.

Now, he found the brightest streetlamp, took his chance with the broken glass that littered the road like cat's eyes and parked the car. He cut the engine, cut the headlights, took a deep breath, held it and let it out in a controlled stream. He tried to leave the car, but his body wouldn't budge.

*Aw, fuck it, just do it.*

With a sense of dislocation, he felt his body get out of the car, lock it and walk towards the pub as if someone else was pulling the strings. He patted the parcel in his pocket, opened the front door and entered.

The interior more than lived up to the exterior's cheerless promise. Men who either had something to prove or nothing left to prove were dotted around the drab room, either seated at old Formica-topped tables or standing against an old, solid-looking bar. There was no music, no TV. There was no sound at all as the men stopped what they were doing and stared at Tony.

Tony, with nearly no expression on his face, walked up to the bar. He cleared his throat.

'Lager, please.'

The barman's muscles were wrapped in years

143

of fat, but it looked like they still received regular exercise. He moved slowly down the bar and, with visible reluctance, began to pour. He slopped the pint down on the counter, waited for Tony to hand over his money.

'Tommy in tonight?' asked Tony quietly, handing over a couple of pounds.

The barman's face was like a stone wall. Hard, chipped and blank. 'Who?'

'Tommy. Tommy Jobson.'

Stone wall.

Tony sighed. His chest shook as the air expelled. 'Just tell him Tony Woodhouse is here. He'll want to see me.'

The barman didn't move, but from the corner of Tony's eye he saw a small, ratty-looking man detach himself from the bar and slip out of the room. The barman kept on ignoring Tony. Tony stared into the depths of his lager. Soon the ratty man returned, gave a slight nod to the barman.

'Through there,' the barman said to Tony, thumb gesturing to the doorway ratty had just emerged from. Tony, who hadn't touched his drink, didn't thank the man. He just turned round and walked through the doorway.

There he found a flight of plain wooden steps and began to climb, trying to steady himself on the loose banister. At the top of the stairs were several doors, all closed bar one, slightly ajar. Gasping and groaning came from inside. Swallowing deeply, Tony entered.

'Hello, Tuh-Tuh-Tony,' said a voice he immediately recognized. 'Come in. Huh-huh-have a seat.'

Tony looked around. The room was dark, curtained. The nicotine-flocked wall a dull, dingy background pattern. Dark seating encircled the walls, a small bar in the far corner. The function room. No lights bar the glow from a TV pumping out hard-core porn. A blonde hid grimaces behind faked joy as two well-built men roughly penetrated her. Big Nev sat in front of the TV along with two other men. The men watched. Big Nev checked the racing form. At the back of the room, behind an anglepoise-lit desk, sat the boy who would be king. Immaculately suited, smelling of Arrogance for Men. He smiled, gestured to the TV.

'Like her? She's a luh-local girl. You might have cuh-cuh-come across her before. Eh-eh-everyone else has.'

The two men by the TV laughed. Nev didn't need to. He went on reading the paper. Tommy gestured Tony forward. Tony moved slowly, planting his weight firmly, keeping his legs from shaking.

'This is a suh-surprise,' said Tommy. 'What brings you here?'

Tony cleared his throat, hoping the cracks in his voice wouldn't show. 'I think you know why I'm here.'

Tommy raised his eyebrows.

Tony moved his hand towards the package sticking out of his pocket. Nev was immediately on his feet, paper flung to the floor. Tony stopped, looked around, startled and scared. Tommy made a placatory gesture with his hand. Nev sat down, still staring. The other two men

145

divided their attention between the porn and Tony.

'Nuh-nice and slow,' said Tommy.

Tony slowly eased the package out of his pocket, laid it on the desk. Tommy picked it up, opened it.

'Well, well, Cuh-Christmas come early.'

Inside were two piles of notes, bundled together with elastic bands.

'It's exactly as Neil gave it to me. I haven't counted it, I haven't looked at it.'

Tommy looked at it, did a quick mental calculation. 'Seems about right.' He smiled. 'Don't think Neil would try an' stiff me now.' He looked up. 'Thuh-thuh-thank you, Tony.'

Tony swallowed again, launched into his prepared speech. 'Look, Tommy, that's my part done. I don't work on the docks any more, so I'm no good to you there. And I've never been any good at dealin' or distributin'.' Tony stopped and waited.

Tommy looked at him. Hard.

'So that's it. You just walk away.'

Tony nodded. The room was cold but he was sweating. 'I just want to forget about it. You know what I'm doing now. I've got all that to lose. I won't say a word.'

Tommy continued to stare at him. The only sound in the room was a badly faked orgasm. This was abruptly silenced as Nev, with a sigh, leaned forward and flicked the video off. The room was filled with the sounds of Leslie Crowther imploring people to come on down. Nev put his paper away, settled down to watch.

146

The other two men didn't look pleased, but they said nothing.

Eventually Tommy spoke. His voice was slow, calm and modulated. His words almost singsong. 'You started off by lookin' the other way on Coldwell docks. But you wanted more.' He pointed a finger. 'It was you who asked me if you could start dealin'. Remember that.'

'I've got the football now. I've got somethin' to lose. I can't do this any more.'

Tommy stared long and hard at him. Like a cobra coiled to strike, all muscle and force.

'No.'

Tony almost fell to the floor.

'But Tommy, I can't–'

Tommy smiled. 'Juh-juh-juh-juh-joke.' He laughed. The other two men laughed. Even Nev pulled himself away from the screen for a second and smiled.

Tony gave a nervous smile. 'What?'

'You're fuh-free to go.'

A round of applause from the TV.

Tony couldn't believe what he was hearing. 'And that's that?'

'That's thuh-that.'

Tony smiled. It was for real this time. 'Thank you, Tommy. I appreciate this.'

Tommy shrugged. 'Off you go. We cuh-can't stop you.'

Tony turned. 'Thank you.'

'But.'

Tony reached the door. He froze, turned slowly.

'Buh-but. Just ruh-remember where you are now. Footballers. Like a bit of chuh-charlie.

Maybe a market we'll want to exploit in the future. When we do, wuh-we'll let you know.'

Tony shivered. 'But–'

'Or maybe not.' Tommy shrugged. 'Who knows? Guh-goodbye, Tony.'

Tony left the room, made his way down the stairs, through the desolate bar and into the dark street as fast as his shaking legs would move him.

He walked slowly back to his car, feet crunching on loose gravel and broken glass, feeling cautiously pleased. He thought of Tommy's last words. Just a threat. That's all. Something for me to walk away with. No, he was out of it, he decided. That was that.

He sighed, noisily, gratefully sucking in air, fear leaving his body.

He reached his car, pleased to see it still in one piece, took out his keys, leaned against the door and vomited into the gutter.

Past ten thirty and chucking out time.

The dowdy pubs and half-lit working men's clubs of Shipcote in Gateshead were sweeping the last of the stragglers through the doors and on to the streets. Beer-bloated men, lagered lads and Bacardied women made their way home, the streets alive with the drunken symphony of laughter, fighting, singing and shouting.

One such group meandered down Coatsworth Road, arm in arm, rivalries and differences put aside, filled with the temporary solace found in the bonhomie of the bottle. As they walked past a side street, one of them entertaining the rest by singing 'Jump', doing his David Lee Roth impression to accompany it, none of them looked down the backstreet. None of them registered the green Mark One Escort sitting there. None of them saw the man behind the steering wheel, slumped in shadow, staring at the flats opposite.

Keith had turned up earlier to talk to Louise. Reason with her, make her see sense. What she had done was wrong. They were meant to be together. If he could just talk to her, tell her his side of the story, she would see that.

But it hadn't happened that way. He had driven to her flat straight from work. The door had been answered by her flatmate Rachel, who seemed surprised and embarrassed to see him. She told him Louise had gone straight to town, was meeting someone and wouldn't be back till late, before closing the door.

He stood in the street, shaking with anger. Louise with someone else? He couldn't believe it. That settled it. He had to talk to her. Urgently.

Keith had driven around aimlessly for over an hour with no recollection of where he had been, only the conversations in his head with Louise. Then he had driven back to Coatsworth Road, parked up a backstreet, waited. All night if necessary.

Rachel had gone out, surrounding house lights had come on, the street changed from white sky and red brick to cat-grey dark patched with sodium orange. Keith sat in shadow. Around nine thirty he began to feel hungry. He ignored it. He wanted to piss. He ignored it. Keith stayed in shadow.

The drunks passed, the street was quiet again.

149

Keith kept watching. No radio, no tape player, just his own silence. Lips moving to imaginary conversations. Watching. Time passed.

Then movement. A car pulled up in front of Louise's flat, smooth soul/funk blaring. Keith didn't recognize the tune or the car. The music cut out with the car's lights. The passenger door opened and out stepped Louise. Keith checked his watch: nearly half-past eleven.

He was out of the car and crossing the street. Hunger gone, need to piss gone. Louise moved around the car, waited for the driver to emerge. The man was well dressed, good-looking. He said something to Louise as he was locking the car that made her laugh. Keith's stomach filled with sour, angry acid.

'Louise!' It came out shakier than intended.

She turned and saw him. The smile froze on her face, the laugh died in her mouth. 'Keith? What are you doing here?'

He reached the pavement, opened his mouth to speak.

'I...I...–'

He couldn't find the words. Hours of imaginary conversations with her and he couldn't find the words.

Louise looked at him. Anger tinged with sympathy. 'Look, Keith, it's over. You and me are finished. I'm seeing someone else now. It's what you should do too.'

Keith's eyes began to well with tears. 'But ... I love you...' As he spoke, he realized how pathetic the words sounded. He hated himself for saying them.

Louise sighed, 'Keith, it's over. Go home.'

She turned to enter her flat. He made one last, desperate attempt to grab her, caught her arm. The man she was with interceded, grabbed his wrist with speed and force.

'I think you should go now,' the man said.

Keith felt his cheeks redden. He dropped his arm and looked at the pair of them. There was nothing more he could do, nothing more he could say. He turned and walked back to his car, ignoring the goodbye Louise gave him.

He climbed back in the driving seat and watched, through tears of humiliation and self-loathing, Louise and her new man enter her flat. He started the engine and drove away.

But he was soon lost. He didn't want to go home. He didn't want to get anything to eat. He wanted to piss, though. He drove the car in a huge circle, returned to the same spot in the backstreet. He got out, unzipped his trousers and let fly a stream of piss against the brick wall. It came out fast and hard, steaming, acrid. Seemingly endless. He cried all the while, body convulsing with big, racking sobs.

Then, eventually, empty and spent, he got back into the car and sat. He sighed, looked up at the flat. The front room light was on. It stayed on until twenty to one. Then darkness.

In the shadows of the backstreet, Keith watched the darkness.

Larkin woke up to find himself alone in bed. No Charlotte. No surprise there. Since their row the other night, they had been spending as little time

151

together as they could. Even by their tempestuous standards this was dragging on.

He threw back the duvet, stretched himself on to his feet, made his way to the bathroom. He entered the front room to discover Charlotte in her terrycloth bathrobe, sitting in the swivel chair by his desk, staring out of the window.

'Mornin'.'

She slowly spun the chair to face him.

'Hello.' Her voice was small, quiet.

'Shouldn't you ... have gone by now?' Larkin hoped the words bridged more than just the physical space between them.

'I'm not in till this afternoon.' She looked up, seeming to see him properly for the first time then. 'What about you? Are you just going to walk around the flat naked all day?'

Larkin sat down in an armchair.

'There was a time when you would have liked that.'

The ghost of a smile haunted Charlotte's face. 'Yes, there was a time...' She sighed. 'What's happened to us, Stephen? Why can't we get along any more?'

'I don't know, Charlotte. I don't know.'

'I still love you.'

'I still love you.'

He smiled, opened his arms slightly.

'C'mere.'

'You come here.'

'Compromise,' he said. 'We'll meet on the sofa.'

Smiling, they both moved towards the sofa, sat down. Larkin put his arm round Charlotte, pulled her to him. The weight of her body felt good against his. Her arms moved around him, stroking. They sat like that for a while.

'I'm naked under this dressing gown, you know.'

'I know. Look.'

Her eyes took in his growing erection.

'Oh, yes.'

They both looked at each other, smiled. Larkin saw pleasure in her eyes, but something else. Loss? Dissatisfaction? He didn't know. At that moment he didn't want to know.

He didn't know what she could see in his eyes.

'So,' he said, 'is this the bit where we kiss and make up?'

'Kiss?' All mock-effrontery. 'We're just going to kiss?'

'Oh, no,' said Larkin, pulling open her robe and easing her down on to the sofa. 'We're not just going to kiss.'

Tony felt lighter than air, as if he could fly to training rather than drive. He could just rise above the opposition, win the ball and score every time.

On the radio: Bruce Springsteen – 'Dancin' in the Dark'.

Last night had gone better than he had expected. The meeting with Tommy had been like a dream. There was a little niggle of doubt at the back of his mind, but he chose to ignore it. It would be OK.

Then there was Louise. It wasn't just the sex – although that was something special in itself – it was her. She made him feel like he was in love.

153

That glitch with her ex had been nothing. They wouldn't see him again.

He sighed contentedly as he pulled into the training ground. Dancin' in the dark? No mate, I'm dancin' in the light.

Lighter than air. As if he could fly.

He was going to win the ball and score every time.

'Keith!'

Keith's head snapped up, eyes sprang open. No idea where he was. Completely disorientated.

'What the hell's the matter with you?'

He looked around. He was at his desk at work. Gavin, his boss, was thrusting a handful of paper at him.

'Sorry. I must have ... nodded off a second.'

'You must have nodded off all fucking morning judging by this.'

He threw the papers at Keith's desk. They scattered with an angry flap, then gently floated down. Keith just looked at them.

'We've just had one of our buyers on the phone...'

Gavin began to talk, ranting at Keith until his face had turned crimson. Keith heard nothing of it. His eyes stared at the floor, head back in the car, in the alley. The street had lightened. People had left for work. She still hadn't come out when he'd left.

'...the fuck's wrong with you?'

Keith sighed, knew some response was called for. He rubbed his eyes.

'I'm sorry. I'm having a few ... problems.'

154

Gavin sighed, perched on the edge of his desk. 'I can't seem to think straight at the moment.'

'Can't think straight, eh?'

Keith shook his head. She still hadn't come out when he'd left.

'Well, you'd better fucking start thinking straight or I'll find some other fucker who can.' Gavin stood up. 'Got that?'

Keith's face flushed. He nodded.

'Good. Get on with it, then.'

Gavin walked away.

Keith waited until he'd gone then, trembling, rose and made his way down the hall in the direction of the toilet. The rest of the office were staring at him. He knew that. He tried to pretend they weren't there.

The men's room. He laughed. I'm being treated like anything but.

He looked at himself in the mirror. Skin and hair dirty and greasy, suit creased, tie askew. His shirt: black-rimmed collar, sour armpits. Stinking breath.

He felt tears begin to well behind his eyes. Loss, anger, self-pity. He was damned if he was going to cry.

He gripped the porcelain, making it vibrate, struggling to control himself. But he was defeated. The tears bubbled up inside him, came out.

He spun away from the mirror then, with a howl of pain, turned back and struck the glass. It didn't break. But the pain in his hand was sudden and excruciating.

He turned away. Loss, anger, self-pity. Now pain. Keith looked for an outlet. The cubicle door swung open. Someone came out. He didn't know who. The man hurried out, wanting to avoid him. He looked at the cubicle door. And kicked it. And kicked it. And kicked and kicked and kicked and kicked.

And screamed as he did it. Screamed her name as loud as he could.


Larkin walked into the Groat Bar on the Groat Market, the darkened interior causing his eyes to squint after the bright Newcastle city-centre sunlight.

He had spent the morning on the phone. First to Dougie Howden. The scabs were being bused in the following Monday. Larkin was alerting friends and comrades in the press, sorting out a photographer, going to Coldwell to document the event. Tell the truth. Dougie's last words: 'I know you mean well, lad, but tempers are runnin' high. Remember Orgreave. Be prepared.'

While he was doing this, Charlotte had kissed him goodbye and left the flat. He remembered their lovemaking following their making up. When he entered her she cried out, when she came she cried tears. Afterwards they lay on the living room floor, naked, entwined.

'Why do we do this?'

Charlotte's voice was quiet, like she didn't want to break the spell.

'This fighting, then this making up?'

'I don't know.' Larkin sighed. 'Maybe we like it.'

'It's not good, you know. It's not good for us.'

Larkin nodded. He said nothing.

'I love you, Stephen.'

Larkin turned his head, looked at her. She was perfect. Beauty itself.

'I love you too, Charlotte.'

She gave a fragile smile, turned her head away.

'That's all right, then.'

Soon afterwards she had left for college and Larkin had begun to work.

He had received a call from Bob Carr, an editor down at Thomson House. Local newspaper publishers. He was Larkin's contact there, the one he'd sent his latest article to. Bob liked the article, wanted to give him more work. More than that, Bob wanted him to meet someone, had invited him down to lunch at the Groat Bar.

Bob, middle-aged, bespectacled, with too much life lived the wrong way and nothing to show for it, sat in a booth with another man. The other man, well suited, groomed, looked the opposite to Bob. Larkin knew what he was: the metropolitan success story next to the regional burnout.

'Stephen.' Bob waved him over. 'Great article. We loved it. Well done. Looking forward to the next one.'

Larkin smiled. 'Thank you.'

'Oh, this is Mike Pears. An old mate from years back.'

They shook. Bob went to the bar to get Larkin a drink.

'So you're Stephen Larkin?' asked Pears. 'Heard a lot about you.'

Larkin was taken aback. 'Really?'

Pears nodded, smiled. He had teeth like a shark.

'Really. All good.'

Bob returned with Larkin's pint, joined them.

'Gettin' on all right, yeah? Mike used to work up here. Down south now, aren't you?'

'That's right.'

Pears smoothly angled his shoulder, subtly excluding Bob from the conversation.

'Who for?' asked Larkin.

'The *Daily Mirror*.'

Larkin smiled. 'Thought all the journalists, the proper ones, left when Maxwell took over.'

Pears laughed. 'You said he wasn't afraid to be confrontational, Bob. I like that.'

Bob shrugged, about to speak. Pears ignored him, kept going, face businesslike again.

'Mr Maxwell hasn't been in charge long. I think you'll find if you give him a chance he'll surprise everyone. Turn that paper into something truly remarkable.'

'If you say so.'

'I do. That's what I wanted to talk to you about.'

'Oh, yeah.'

'Mmm.'

Pears took a sip of his drink. It was either Perrier or gin and tonic.

Bob smiled, nodded.

'And this is where you come in.' Pears put his glass carefully down. 'I was having a chat with my old mate Bob here, about how we'd lost Foot and Pilger and how we were looking for someone, a bright young investigative journalist, to take their place. Bob thought of you.' He held his hands out, smiled a faux-innocent smile. 'And here I am.'

'Really?'

Larkin had to admit, after that little speech, he was impressed. Flattered to be compared with two of his heroes. But he tried not to let it show.

Pears continued: 'We looked at your work and liked what we saw. We liked your anger. Your passion.'

Larkin nodded, flattered.

'So what do I get out of this?'

'Job satisfaction, prestige.' Pears leaned in closer. 'And a lot of money, of course.'

'And I can just write anything I like? Keep on doin' what I'm doin'.'

Pears looked slightly pained. 'Well, yes, to an extent. Keep it broadly anti-Thatcherite, of course. We would have some ideas that we would want you to cover, but we can discuss them later.'

'Such as?'

'We'll discuss them later.'

'We'll discuss them now.'

Pears shifted uneasily in his seat. 'Well, what we had in mind – initially, after which you'd probably be on your own – would be an exposé of the yuppies in the City. You know the kind of thing. Too much money, not enough sense. Stick it to Thatcher's darlings. That kind of thing.'

'And you want me to come all the way down from Newcastle to do that?'

Pears smiled his shark smile again. 'Why, yes. I shouldn't think you have yuppies up here.'

Larkin reddened, took a large gulp of his drink, stared at the other man.

'No, we have miners. We have strikes. You interested in that?'

Pears floundered.

159

'Well … I … I mean, of course, eventually. But at the moment, I mean it's not a priority.'

Larkin drained his pint, stood up.

'And it's not a priority for me to sit here and be patronized by one of Maxwell's arselickers.'

Pears stood also.

'Wait.' He reached into his jacket, pulled out a card. 'Just think about it. Here's my card.'

He handed it over. Larkin took it.

'Catch you later, Bob,' said Larkin. 'I'll have a cracking piece for you in a couple of days.'

'Glad to hear it.'

Bob didn't look glad. Larkin wondered how much Bob stood to gain or lose from a finder's fee.

Larkin walked straight out of the pub and turned left towards Grainger Street. As he reached the corner, he realized he still had Pears's card in his hand. He looked at it, about to toss it into a nearby litter bin. He saw the name, the address, the phone number. He flicked it over, ready to throw. And realized there was some writing on the back.

In longhand, it said *Stephen Larkin: starting salary*.

There followed a figure.

Larkin stared at the number a long time, jaw open.

Traffic went by, people walked around him.

He looked up, snapped out of it, pocketed the card. He began to walk home.

As he walked, he began, quite unconsciously, to pat the pocket that held the card.

He shook his head.

And then he smiled.

# 8. Now

His chest was aching, lungs aflame. Every inhaled breath fanned the fire. His legs moved slowly, laboriously; like the ground was coagulating and his knees couldn't bend. His thighs, calves and arches threatened pain if he continued, cramp if he stopped. His arms moved slowly, feebly punching air. The air was winning. His breath came in jagged shudders, facial muscles contracted with exertion, mouth open and gasping. A lumbering bipedal on a coronary countdown.

Larkin was jogging.

Over the unevenly grassed surface of the Town Moor, ignoring the stares of passers-by, ignoring the cold, grey drizzle.

Not because he wanted to, but because he felt he must.

Old trainers, old tracksuit bottoms, positively prehistoric Elvis Costello and the Attractions' 1986 Blood and Chocolate Tour T-shirt. The clothes disused and damp, his body misused and cramping.

It was the dead man's hair that had done it.

The morning after the night after the visit to Coldwell with Tony Woodhouse. Alone, drinking, thinking: 1984/seventeen years ago/the miners' strike/Charlotte.

Charlotte.

The empty cans had multiplied, the memories

161

had kept up. The CDs had come out: Lloyd Cole, the Smiths, Elvis Costello and the Attractions. Bought consciously to replace vinyl, unconsciously to keep his memories pristine and laser-accessed. Bad move. When the laser hit, the ghosts came out, got up and danced with the sounds.

'How Soon Is Now?', 'I Wanna Be Loved', 'Are You Ready to Be Heartbroken?'

Mournful, slow dances. The empty cans multiplied.

And in the morning, the mirror. He had not wanted to look, but he had, and for once had looked honestly, seeing what was there, rather than what he deluded himself into believing was there: eyes black-rimmed, creased at the sides, heavy with the weight of what they had seen. The beginnings of a broken vein collection at either side of his nose. His chin being joined by another underneath. His skin showing the seasons of the years.

He scrutinized his body with the same honesty: ridges of excess flesh, surplus folds around his chest and waist. The years of junk food and alcohol had made territorial gains, settled into parts of his body, claimed squatters' rights with no plans to move. Not fat, but not fit any more.

Twenty-one to thirty-eight. Seventeen years. He could see it.

So Larkin, hungover, tired, had resolved to do something. He would get a haircut.

Down to Scotts, in the chair, looking down at the nylon paisley covering his body. The barber started, the hair fell. Not black, but grey: old man's hair. Dead man's hair.

So now he was running, sweating back time, hoping thirty minutes could roll back seventeen years.

And then his body declared its limitations: legs aching, left knee locking, ribs burning, chest cramping and tightening. He had to stop, or at least slow down. He reduced his speed to a trudge and a shuffle.

He looked around: to his left, Spital Tongues, the dental hospital, the BBC. To his right, Grandstand Road curving out and away from the city.

To his left. Beyond what he could see was Fenham. Where he used to live. With Charlotte. He tried to see beyond the moor, tried to see seventeen years into the past, his old flat, him in the bay window typing, her coming in from college, them on the floor making love. He tried to see how happy they were then, tried to see the future they would have had together. Tried. But couldn't.

All that belonged to another life, another person.

Dead now, just ghosts. Just pristine, laser-accessed memories.

He stopped, got his breath back, turned round.

He ran away from Fenham, away from his memories. Back to the flat where, knees creaking, chest aching, he would reward himself with a long bath and a cup of coffee.

Or perhaps a cold beer.


'There, watch.'

They watched the screen. A man stood at a roulette table, watching the wheel spin, the metal ball glinting, dancing within. He stood next to other men wearing chinos, polo shirts, sports jackets. Blending in. Blanding in.

'Now he loses this one...'

The ball stopped on a red number, the croupier raked in the chips, including the bland man's.

'Now watch what happens.'

An almost imperceptible nod passed between the croupier and the man.

'There, see it? There.' The voice quietened, became studied, concentrated. 'Now there'll be the bit with the hand.'

The croupier began to call for bets, moving her hand beneath the table as if to scratch her knee.

'That's it there. Now the look.'

The croupier looked at the man, nodded slightly.

'Now the bet.'

The bland man appeared to hesitate then slid most of his chips on to a red square.

The voice sighed. 'Now we know what'll happen next.'

The wheel was spun, the ball did its dance, came to land on the man's square. The man faked amazement and delight, raked in his winnings.

'So, boss, what d'you reckon?'

Tommy Jobson sat back in his chair, fingers across his stomach, and stretched his legs. One polished shoe crossed the other. He uncurled his fingers, picked at the crease in his trousers, keeping it sharp.

'What do I think?'

His words were well modulated, voiced slow

and dark.

'I think there's a croupier who's soon going to be unemployed. I think there's a man who's about to be taught a lesson.'

'You want me to deal with him? Or d'you want to talk to him?'

The man speaking, Jason, was sharp-suited, well dressed. Nasty, brutal and short. Lethal, Tommy knew, like thin electric cable fizzing in water. Tommy's second-in-command.

'I don't know. What d'you reckon, Davy?'

The man at the other side of the table, drinking twenty-four-year-old malt, smiled. Detective Inspector 'Davy' Jones. A big man who didn't like struggling for the good things in life but certainly enjoyed fighting for them. He smiled. 'You want me to have a word?'

'Yeah. You and Jason sort it out.'

Jason's eyes were lit with a sudden, cruel light. 'You want to come?'

'I'll watch from here.'

The two men stood up, left the room. Left Tommy alone.

The mini-Vegas on Tyne, the Ratpack dream made real. Tommy sat behind the desk, drinking twenty-four-year-old malt, at the heart of it.

One wall all screens, showing his kingdom, his empire's cornerstone, from all angles and distances. Tommy watched. Tommy liked to watch.

He watched them move through the casino, turning their money into chips, turning chips into his money. Faces telling stories: furrows and frowns, joy and self-confidence, arrogance and loss, dejection to elation. Faces telling stories. Usually the same one.

And the body language: from the rigid tension of the lucky streaker struggling not to betray himself, to the desperate slump of the last-chance loser, and everything in between.

And the hands: holding, folding, dealing, feeling. The smooth plastic coating on the razor-edged cards, the heavy, tactile beauty of the chips. The chips being stroked, caressed, stroking and caressing in return, asking to be used, to be spent. The punters obliging.

Sometimes a sensuously choreographed ballet of charm and fortune, sometimes a rough, struggling threesome between punter, luck and money. Natural theatre. CCTV soap opera. Life.

Tommy watched it all. Apart from it, above it. No matter who won on the floor, Tommy won in the end. Because the house always won. And Tommy was the house.

On the wall behind him, framed certificates and photos. Financial certificates, charity certificates. Photos: Tommy with celebrities. Footballers, rock stars, actors, politicians. Pride of place: Tony Bennett. No Frank and Dino, just Tony Bennett.

He flicked a switch on the desk, the screens changed. Now they showed a basement, colour, but lit starkly in black and white. The bland man was pushed into a pool of light by Jason. Davy, taking his jacket off, folding it neatly over a chair, stepped into view.

Tommy pressed another button on the desk. A hidden VCR began to record.

166

Jason was talking to the man.

'So, Mr Blacklock, it seems you and your girlfriend have been abusing our hospitality here.'

The bland man made protestations of innocence.

Tommy muted the sound, poured himself another drink. Watched. He didn't need to hear. He knew what was coming next.

Davy talked to the man, produced his warrant card. The man still protested his innocence, hands raised.

Then Davy hit him. A punch in the kidneys. The man went down, face opened with surprise. Then a kick in the ribs. Then another. Then Jason, leaning down, squatting, talking to him. The man nodding. Jason looking at Davy, disappointed, giving another kick just for fun.

Jason opened his jacket, took out a contract and a pen, handed it to the man. The man, hands shaking, sighed. Tommy knew what it was: a legal document allowing the house to reclaim the money they thought he had stolen, plus any interest they deemed necessary, plus a waiver saying the house was not responsible for any injury to his person. All legal, signed and co-signed by a high-ranking police officer.

Jason then took the man's debit and credit cards, pulled him to his feet.

Tommy switched off, emptied his whisky glass.

The house always won. And Tommy was the house.

He put his whisky glass down on the desk, looked around, sighed.

No Frank and Dino, just Tony Bennett.

167

The Chuckle Brothers went through their routine: one thick, one thicker because he thinks he's clever. They were being chased around a deserted car park by a security guard.

Davva and Skegs stared at the TV, watched the antics, a spliff between them. Skegs wanted to laugh but felt he couldn't. Davva just looked annoyed.

'Why don't they just fuckin' hit 'im, man? Stab 'im or shoot 'im or somethin'? Then they can just walk off.' Davva shook his head. 'That's what I'd do.'

"S funny, man,' said Skegs. 'Just a laugh.'

Davva turned to face him.

'It fuckin' isn't funny. They wanna knife 'im. That'll stop 'im.'

Skegs was going to tell him it was just for kids, just a laugh, but he decided not to. He looked around the room. He didn't think Davva would appreciate it. Tanya hadn't tidied it since the last time they'd been there. The big colour TV was gone, a portable black and white replacing it. There were other things missing too. The room had less in it, but seemed much messier.

The baby was sleeping in the other room. It had been complaining noisily when they had turned up with Tanya's stuff, but after she had given them their money and retreated to the bedroom it had stopped. Must've fed it or something, Skegs had decided.

Tanya sat in the armchair staring in the direction of the TV, slack-mouthed, slack-eyed. Skegs looked at her. He didn't know what she was seeing, but he didn't think it was the same thing he saw. A smile played at the edges of her lips, small and distant.

The security guard had caught up with the Chuckle Brothers, had them both by their collars. He was huffing and puffing, throwing out threats.

'He ain't gonna do nothin',' said Davva. 'Listen to him. If he was gonna do somethin' he'da done it by now, steada just shoutin' about it.'

Another, suited, man turned up to explain things and the Chuckle Brothers were free to go. Davva stood up.

'This is shit. C'mon.'

Davva stubbed the spliff out in an overflowing ashtray.

Skegs stood also.

'Where we goin'?'

'We've got work to do, haven't wuh?'

Skegs followed him out. He was glad to leave. Tanya's flat didn't seem like the comfortable shelter it used to be.

'See ya, Tanya, we're gannin' noo,' said Davva from the door.

Tanya partially inclined her head. 'See yas, lads...'

They left, slamming the door.

Tanya sat still, staring ahead. The Chuckle Brothers finished, Badger and Bodger started.

Then from the bedroom, the familiar cry: the baby.

Tanya didn't move. Just stared straight ahead, slackjawed, slack-eyed. Unsmiling.

The baby cried.

A single tear rolled over her blank features.

The baby cried.

The tear moved slowly down her chin, dropped and was gone.

The baby cried.

Tanya didn't hear.

With Billie Holiday on CD, Tommy Jobson piloted the Daimler east out of the city centre, past Yorkshire Tyne Tees TV, City Road becoming Walker Road. He took a right down Glasshouse Street, past the industrial estate and reclamation plant down to the river's edge.

The old warehouses and pubs had been swept away, replaced by St Peter's Basin: a marina, townhouses, apartments, penthouses. Docklands on Tyne in miniature. He drove through the strangely deserted streets, the mournful, lost voice of Billie not totally at odds with the surroundings.

'I Cover the Waterfront'.

He turned into the gated car park of Chandler's Quay, switched off the engine, sighed. Took a minute to sit, think, then took the lift up to the penthouse.

From the Chandler's Arms to Chandler's Quay.

Same place, different view.

Same place, different world.

The view stretched from the city all the way down the Tyne past Riverside Park. Quite beautiful, surprisingly so. At first it had excited him, thrilled him to see how far he had risen, until he realized the people in the council flats up the embankment in Walker had the same view.

That leached the pleasure from it, killed it for him.

Same place, different world.

But somehow not so different.

From Chandler's Quay to the Chandler's Arms.

Memory was becoming increasingly important to Tommy. He would sometimes do little tests, take himself down streets that were no longer there, into pubs or restaurants that no longer existed, relived conversations with people either dead, gone or lost, re-dressed a person in a fashion they used to wear. This, for Tommy, was history. The history that mattered. And he felt it his duty to remember the past in order to understand the present, otherwise the present would just be a collection of actions in a vacuum, not the consequences of previous actions.

He had to keep the past, his past, alive. And he did. Sometimes, he thought, too alive.

He poured himself a hefty whisky, looked at it, added some more. He sat down on his white leather sofa and waited.

'Just checking some other interests,' he had told Jason, as he had left the casino.

Jason had given a leering smile in return. That was fine with Tommy. Let him think what he liked.

The wait was soon over. The entryphone buzzed. He opened the door without checking. He knew who it would be. She walked in a few minutes later, gave him a faint smile. Tommy opened his wallet, counted out the bills.

'You can get changed in there,' he said, pointing to the bathroom.

She trotted off, heels clacking on tiles.

Tommy drained his glass, went into the bedroom. The frame was already in place. He stripped off slowly, folded his clothes neatly on the bed. He stood there, naked, face showing no emotion.

She re-entered. Black PVC basque, spike-heeled boots, blonde hair pulled into a severe ponytail, razor-gash red lipstick.

'Hello, Cathy,' he said.

It wasn't her name. She was just the latest in a long line of them.

She ignored him.

'Get over there.' She pointed to the frame.

Tommy crossed, stood, legs apart, as she lashed him to the X-frame using strong leather restraints. The frame stood against the bedroom's glass wall. Tommy stood gazing out over the Tyne.

Behind him he heard Cathy give the first experimental crack of the whip. He waited, expecting the sting across his back at any second.

It came. Not a sting, a buzz.

'I didn't feel it.'

'I'm just warming up.' Cathy's voice was harsh.

He waited. The next blow came. Harder, but not hard enough.

The third. Still not hard enough.

'Harder.'

Cathy obliged.

'Harder. Harder.'

She whipped him. And again. And again.

Thirty minutes later, Cathy's time was up. Her hair had slipped from the ponytail and hung loose over her shoulders, plastered to her face and body by sweat. Red lines ran round her body and legs where the basque and boots had chafed against her slick, salty skin. Her armpits stank of exertion, her arms trembled from work.

In front of her, Tommy leaned against the frame, his back and buttocks a mass of red welts, stripes, bleeding and broken skin. Cathy, panting and shaking, began to undo Tommy's restraints. Once undone he didn't move, just stood as if still restrained, staring out over the Tyne.

'So what d'you feel like?'

Cathy snaked her arm round to touch his penis.

'Nothing.' Tommy spoke quietly.

She squeezed his penis. It hung flaccid, limp. She began rubbing it.

'How d'you feel?'

'Nothing.'

Tommy felt her remove her hand, turn, heard her clack-clack into the bathroom, heard the shower run.

He didn't move.

Eventually she finished, got changed and left quietly.

He stayed where he was, ignoring the pins and needles in his arms and legs, watching the sun go down, spread-eagled before the Tyne.

'I feel nothing,' he said to the river, the glass, his reflection. 'I feel nothing.'

Night had fallen completely and with the darkness came the thrill of expectation, flipping Suzanne's stomach over and over.

She lay naked under the thin, cool sheet, the aromatic candle she had brought and lit providing

173

the room's only light, the smell chasing away the faint lingerings of antiseptic and bleach. The room – the whole flat – always smelled of that. Karl was fastidious in his cleanliness.

He had promised her a night she wouldn't forget: the candle had been her idea, an attempt to introduce sensuous romance to the room's clinical minimalism. Karl had reluctantly agreed.

The bedroom door opened. Karl stood there, naked, erect, face red, breath heavy, eyes like dots.

Her breath caught, she smiled at him, began to edge the sheet down slowly, thrilled by his body.

'D'you wanna see what I've got down here?' Coyly.

Karl walked straight over to the bed, ripped the sheet off her body. He stared at her nakedness, chest heaving, breath escaping in laboured gasps. His cock, his body, looked ready to explode.

Then he was on her, straddling her, pinning her wrists down. Breathing hard, harsh breaths into her face.

'You trust me, yeah?' Gasping.

'You know I do, Karl.' Suzanne's voice was small, unsure. This seemed like a different Karl.

'Good.'

He moved both hands to her right wrist. Something cold and tight on her skin, a soft click, then she couldn't move her arm. Same with the other arm. Quickly, he moved to her legs, restraining each ankle until she was spread, starred and naked, on the bed. He straddled her again, smiled.

'Trust me.'

Part of her was scared, part of her was excited. A small part, the part that liked the forbidden, the taboo. The part that had drawn her to Karl in the first place.

'I love you,' she said.

'You'll love this.'

From behind the pillow, Karl produced a wide strip of black cloth. He blindfolded her, eliciting a gasp.

'Relax. Let me do the work.'

She felt his hands over her body, stroking, pinching, tickling, scratching. Her breasts, ribs, arms, thighs. She began to ease into it, enjoy it, muscles releasing, body relaxing. It felt like pleasure in space: she was floating, drifting through black clouds of bliss, smelling the candle, hearing Karl's breathing.

His hand slowly snaked between her thighs, fingers gently tugging on her clitoris, rolling the hard knob of flesh slowly between them. She moaned slightly, pushing her pelvis towards his hand. She was hot and wet and ready for him.

Suzanne felt him then, between her legs as he slowly slid into her body, one hand still stimulating her clitoris.

But it felt different. It wasn't his cock – even in a condom it didn't feel like that. This was cold and hard and with every thrust something caught her. It didn't hurt, it didn't make her panic, but it unnerved her slightly.

A vibrator, or something. A sex toy. That would be it. She relaxed, tried to enjoy it.

'D'you like that?'

'Yuh-yes,' she said. The sharp bit had just

175

caught her, made her jump.

'Wanna see what it is?'

She didn't answer at first.

'OK...'

Leaving the thing inside her, he leaned over, untied the blindfold. She blinked: even the candlelight seemed strong after total darkness.

Still blinking, she looked down. And froze.

There was Karl, erect, red-faced, smiling. And in his hand was a gun. An automatic. The grip in his hand, the trigger beneath his finger. The barrel inside her body

She tried to pull back, buck her body away from the gun. She screamed, pulling her wrists and ankles against the cuffs, straining, pain shooting up her arms and legs, panic coursing round her body.

'Get that thing out of me! Please!'

She started to cry, big, juddering sobs. For the first time in years she wanted to go home.

Karl slowly pulled the gun out of her. She calmed down. He smiled at her.

'It's OK,' he said. He looked at the barrel of the gun, caressing it with his eyes, slowly licked his tongue down the length of it.

'Mmm. The taste of you. Your love. Your fear.'

'Let me go, please, Karl.' Her voice was small, frightened. 'I want to go home now.'

'Just a minute.'

He moved up the bed until he was lying next to her. One hand gently stroking her clitoris, one hand holding the gun. He looked into her eyes. They were wide with terror, like a veal calf on an abattoir killing floor.

'We're different, you and me.'

His voice was whispered, his words warm.

'We're not like ordinary people. We're not boring.'

He smiled again.

'Wuh-what are we, then?'

Karl seemed to give the question some thought.

'We're ... freethinking. We're liberated. Don't you think?'

Suzanne didn't answer.

'We're nonconformist. We're *exciting*.'

The final word was half-whispered, half-shouted.

'Aren't we?'

Suzanne dumbly nodded.

'D'you like that?'

She looked at him, his smiling face, his muscular body, his erect cock. She allowed herself to feel what he was doing to her.

'Yes.'

'Good.'

He smiled, began trailing the gun over her flesh, cold metal stroking warm flesh. She tensed, tried to pull away.

'Sshh. Don't. It's OK. Just listen. Just listen.'

His words calmed her down slightly.

'Good.'

His mouth was right against her ear, whispering. 'We're different, you and me. We see things differently. We see the world differently. We see sex differently.'

The gun continued to stroke her. She listened.

'Sex for us isn't like sex was for your mam and dad. It was just something they did, something

177

they felt embarrassed about. A job they had to do. A function.

'But not for us. We know what it does, what it can do for us. It frees your mind, your body, it unlocks your inhibitions, your fantasies...'

His voice was soothing yet exciting, sensual and mesmeric.

The pressure on her clitoris increased. Her body responded accordingly. He saw the change, smiled.

'Yeah... There's only one thing as powerful as sex, one thing in the world.'

'What?' She was gasping.

He held the gun up, watched it glint in the candlelight.

'Death. Sex and death. The most powerful things in the world. One gives life, one takes it away.'

He reapplied the gun to her skin, moved it downwards, over her stomach. She tensed again.

'Sshh, it's all right, it's all right.'

His voice was soothing. The gun touched her clitoris.

'Sshh...'

The gun trailed over her clitoris, slowly moved back inside her again.

'Sshh...'

The gun was inside her, his fingers moving over her clitoris.

'Some people love to be strangled when they come. They say it's the ultimate orgasm...'

The gun moved, caressed. His fingers moved, caressed.

'The French call orgasms la petite mort. The

178

little death. They know the score...'

Her breathing intensified, her hips thrust forward to meet the gun, to pull it in further, to press herself harder against his fingers.

'That's it... Come on, feel it... Let yourself go... Give yourself up to it...'

And it built up inside her until she had to find release. Screaming, thigh muscles tensed to cramping, fingernails digging blood from her palms, hips pressed forward to devour his hand, his gun, she came.

Love, fear and hate, all finding release from her body. The orgasm was the most shattering thing her fifteen-year-old body had yet experienced. It was something she didn't understand but fully acknowledged.

She lay there, restrained, body riding out the final waves.

She eventually opened her eyes, looked up.

Karl was smiling at her. She smiled back.

He kept smiling. It went past warmth, became a thing of triumph, of encapsulation.

'I love you.'

Her voice trembled, seeking assurance.

'I know.'

That night:

Louise lies wide awake in bed, staring at the ceiling, wondering what time the front door will open this time. Wondering if the front door will open this time.

Keith lies next to her snoring noisily. He grinds his teeth. He dreams of getting even.

Larkin lies down with ghosts and dreams about

the past. Rewrites the past.

Mick dreams of white beaches and blue skies. Permanent holiday.

Davva dreams of clowns, comics and comedians. It's safe to laugh in his dreams.

Suzanne lies awake on Karl's bed. Something has changed, but she isn't sure of what.

Karl lies next to her, dreaming of gladiators, of swords and knives, blood and victory.

Skegs dreams of pastoral scenes, of woodlands and warmth, of welcoming, happy, talking creatures, of a realm where he feels safe and loved.

Tanya dreams about a lost jigsaw she once had, but every time she tries to complete it, more pieces appear, and the right ones are missing. The harder she tries, the more she feels like ripping it up.

Tony dreams away the pain in his leg. He dreams away the past. He dreams of the future.

Tommy lies there. He dreams about everything. He dreams about nothing.

# PART TWO

## Two Tribes

# 9. Now and Then

The way Dougie Howden saw it:

The call had gone out and from over the hills and far away it had been answered.

They were coming. He knew it, could feel it.

They were coming from similar places to Coldwell, villages grown around work, towns built on tunnels. Home to men who had once proudly fuelled the country, now left angry, fearful and bitter. From places now under martial law, where the police had laid siege in an effort to contain them, to stop them fighting back against an arbitrary erosion of a way of life.

They were the great escapees, eluding police checkpoints, stop and searches and roadblocks. Gone by the time armoured woodentops had dawn-raided their way into homes, kicked in front doors, pulled lives apart; finding nothing but manless families, feeling the curses of miners' wives ring in their ears, fists on their chests, and fleeing, leaving behind a blueprint to turn sobbing children into next-generation police-haters.

They were coming despite intimidation, personal hardship, weariness and physical threat to themselves and their families. They were coming because it was the right thing to do.

Dawn at the Miners' Welfare Park. Grass and trees leisurely stretched around a lake, swings and slides off to one side. A picnic area. Land gifted to the miners, for them and their families to enjoy open space and clean air, to cherish the surface.

The prearranged time, the prearranged place. The day shift.

They had arrived.

Vans, cars and minibuses were unloading. Men were greeting each other, some veterans of picket action who knew what to expect, some first-timers. They were smiling, fixing on brave faces: the laughter in the dark of the mine replaced by the steely humour of adversity against authority.

They were dressed for work: flannel shirts, denims, jumpers, boots, donkey jackets.

Banners were unfurled, laid out on the ground, poles screwed together, leather carrying belts strapped on. The painting and embroidering had been done with obvious care and love, the depictions of mines or trade unionist heroes rendered with pride. Dougie read the names and locations: Yorkshire. Nottinghamshire. Derbyshire. Northumberland. Even one from South Wales. His heart seemed to grow inside his chest.

Loud-hailers were given batteries, tested with chants. Stones and half-bricks were held in carrier bags just in case.

Emotion lodged in Dougie's throat. He smiled.

He looked up, saw clear blue sky.

Yes, he thought, it's going to be a good day.

That was the way he saw it.

Mick Hutton saw things differently.

It was a fight, a struggle. Everything was a struggle. Either confrontation or avoiding it.

He crept around the, house quietly, as if the slightest noise or touch would undermine the foundations, set it shaking. He flitted ghostlike between rooms, finding his clothes, making breakfast, washing, brushing his teeth. Everything was too loud: the corn flakes, the running water, the strokes of the toothbrush. He cursed himself and aimed for yet more silence, willed himself, cloaked, invisible, absent.

Angela was asleep in bed. Or appeared to be asleep in bed. She had had a bad night, the restless baby in her belly giving her uncomfortable insomnia. He was trying to let her sleep, to rest. He didn't want her to wake up without being fully rested. He didn't want her to wake up and be reminded of where he was going. He didn't want her to wake up to confrontation.

He prepared a bowl of corn flakes, put them on a tray, added a jug of milk and a spoon and carried it up to her bedside. He backed carefully out of the room and made his way downstairs. He put on his jacket, let himself out, and closed the door with a silent click.

On hearing that, Angela opened her eyes. She checked the bedside clock, saw the corn flakes.

She moved on to her side, sighed.

She closed her eyes again. Willed the day away.

'Listen, lads.'

Dougie looked around the hall, knocked on the table a couple of times, waited until he had the men's attention. Mick Hutton stood next to him, fidgeting, all suppressed anxiety.

'Thanks.'

185

They were in the Miners' Welfare Hall, once, Dougie always thought, the hub of socializing and socialism back when the town was a village, now the headquarters for the strike action, where the soup kitchen, clothing and food distribution took place. All the pickets were there along with miners' support groups, miners' wives. Dougie looked at their faces, saw optimism. Abraded by reality and hopelessness, but not completely removed.

Today was going to be a good day. He knew it.

'Thanks for comin' here. I know some of you have come a long way and put up with a lot of unfairness. But if everythin' was fair you wouldn't have to be here in the first place.

'Now, I don't wanna go on for long.'

'Makes a change,' someone mumbled loudly.

Heads turned to the voice. Dougie looked too. Dean Plessey.

'Thank you, Dean.' Dougie looked at his watch. 'Now, as you know, the local executive don't want this march to happen. They want to negotiate. Well, we've seen what happens when they negotiate, haven't we? Right. Nothing. You can't negotiate with these people. You have to stand up to them. So that's what we'll do. We'll show them.'

He looked again at his watch. 'Right. They'll be comin' soon. So let's go down there. Let's stop them comin' in. If we stick together, we can beat them.' His voice rose. 'And beat them with pride. Come on.'

He walked towards the door, the men following.

The grey clouds had berthed.

The drizzle started as Larkin turned off the roundabout into Coldwell, the final leg of the journey. Football kit in a rucksack on the passenger seat, ache in his bones from exercising, ache in his head from drinking, Wilco on the stereo.

'When You Wake Up Feeling Old'.

Tell me about it, he thought.

Last night had been memory lane, trip two. He had powered up his laptop, intending to work on his book.

The Miners' Strike and After: One Community's Legacy.

Provisional title.

He had opened a bottle of Spanish Rioja to keep him company as he wrote. But once he'd uncorked the bottle, the genie had come out again dancing, dismantling the order of his thoughts, imposing chaos on his memories. The journalistic arguments became personal ones. He lost the battle, went to the aftermath. The battle for Coldwell became the battle for Charlotte. And beyond. Back there again, word for word, blow for blow. Alcohol sharpening rather than deadening his memories. Mouthing the words, dodging the fists. No perspective: individual strands mashed together, knotted, inextricably linked.

He drove through the streets, pavements filling with Saturday-lunchtime crowds. It looked unreal, the windscreen a TV screen, black and white and badly tuned, the buildings a dark, hazy grey, the people indistinct forms. Ghosts. Rain-wraiths. The previous night's memories seemed more real than what was around him.

He shook his head, tried to pull himself back to the present, will colour into the world. He drove away from the shops and past the Miners' Welfare Park, the grass now yellow and threadbare, the brown-black trees gnarled and leafless, the playground barren with neglect. His head continued to pound. He drove through residential streets, houses too small to contain their occupants' dreams, just big enough to kill them. A house like he had grown up in. He drove to the edge of the town.

The colliery was now gone, the big gates missing, the wheel and tower razed, the tunnels filled. Dismantling had begun the day after it had closed for the last time in 1986. In its place was a leisure centre complete with swimming pool, tennis courts, squash courts, gyms, five-a-side pitches and a full-sized football pitch.

He looked at the building, tried to look into the past, see the wheel tower against the sky, see the outline of what was once there.

And he did.

Grey and indistinct, like the earlier phantom streets, but there. Hanging over the town, its ghost, its shadow, haunting it still.

Larkin parked the Saab in the car park, grabbed his bag and, feeling his knees creak as he walked, went to find Tony Woodhouse.

He didn't have to look far. Rounding the corner of the main building, he saw a crowd gathering before the football pitch. Tony Woodhouse, Claire and what he presumed were the team. The Coldwell CAT Centre Crew, Tony had said, named after the centre. In addition there was a TV crew, a flash-suited man, leisure centre staff and spectators. Families, friends. None of them seemingly bothered by the damp. Larkin, jolted into the present, made his way over to Tony Woodhouse.

Tony Woodhouse saw him, smiled. 'Not a bad turnout, is it?'

'It's not. So who's the opposition?'

Tony smiled again. 'The police.'

'What?'

'The local drug liaison team. Community policing. Gives them good PR, gives us someone to play against. They do a lot of this kind of thing.'

Larkin nodded. 'Right.'

'I can see those journalistic cogs whirring away. The irony of the situation. Playing the police on this ground. Where the pit used to be.'

It was Larkin's turn to smile. 'Something like that.'

'That's what the local paper were saying. Well, it's all changed here. There's not many people think that way any more. There's not many can remember the strike.'

'You reckon?'

'I reckon. Anyway.'

He drew out a sheet of paper.

'This is who we've got to start the match. He'll be auctioning a few things at half-time.'

The man was a hugely famous TV actor.

Larkin, although not a fan, was impressed. 'How did you manage that?'

Tony shrugged. 'Lots of celebs like to do stuff for charity. Or be seen to be doing something.

Besides, everybody owes somebody something. C'mon and have a cup of tea.'

He walked Larkin over to a portable tea urn where Claire Duffy was busy buttoning up her coat. She saw Larkin, smiled.

'Roped you in an' all? Very persuasive, our Tony.'

She looked at Tony Woodhouse, holding her smile as if waiting for a response. None came. She looked back at Larkin. 'Nice to have you here.'

'Thank you. Nice to be here.'

Tea in hand, Larkin watched the local TV news crew interview an immaculately suited and groomed man. He was answering questions in an earnest, self-important manner.

'Who's that?'

'Dean Plessey,' said Tony. 'Our local MP. Electioneering.'

Larkin thought. The name meant something to him. Dean Plessey. He shook his head, the context out of reach. 'I know that name,' he said. 'Is he from round here?'

'Yeah, local lad. Started off as a miner.'

It clicked.

'He was involved in the strike. Yeah, Dean Plessey. He was a right dick.'

Tony smiled. 'He still is. C'mon, I'll introduce you.'

Tony limped over to where the TV crew were concluding their interview.

'Dean,' Tony said when they had moved away. 'Got someone I'd like you to meet. This is Stephen Larkin. He's a journalist.'

The politician stuck out his hand.

'Dean Plessey. Pleasure to meet you.'

He had the smile and look of an expert flesh-presser.

'Don't try too hard to impress him, Dean,' said Tony, smiling. 'He doesn't live round here so he can't vote for you.'

Dean Plessey laughed as if it was the funniest joke he'd heard in ages.

Larkin politely joined in, looked at him. The years had treated him well. Everything about Plessey was smooth: smooth skin, smooth hair, smooth suit, smooth manner. Only the eyes gave him away. Jagged, hard.

'So you're here with Tony, are you? Who are you reporting for?'

'Actually, I'm playing. He's roped me in.'

'Very good at getting people involved, is Tony. Just look at all this. And he does wonders for Coldwell. For the community. Wonders. We support him to the hilt. And we need more like him.'

Tony said nothing.

'Well, good to meet you,' said Plessey, turning to go.

'Oh, Dean...'

The politician stopped, looked at Larkin.

'I'm writing a book on the miners' strike. Using Coldwell as a study. You were involved in that, weren't you?'

Something passed over Dean Plessey's eyes, like a breeze ruffling a peacock's feathers.

'I did my part.'

'Yeah, I remember. I was here then as well.'

Dean Plessey's Blairite grin remained fixed while the rest of his face changed around it.

'Different era.'

'Not so different, I don't think.'

Dean Plessey waved his hand dismissively. 'I disagree. It's the future we have to look to.'

'Isn't it always?'

'Well,' Dean Plessey said, 'pleasure to meet you. Again.'

He shook hands. It had built up quite a sweat in a short space of time, Larkin noted.

Larkin smiled. 'I might come and have a word with you about the strike, some time.'

'Whenever.'

Plessey gave Larkin a brittle smile, Tony a nod and hurried off to vote-pester someone else. The two men watched him go.

'Well, he's changed.'

'For better or worse?' asked Tony.

'Hard to say, really.'

They laughed.

'Come and meet your team-mates. See if we can get a bit of practice in.'

The Coldwell CAT Centre Crew were in the dressing room changing, talking. Some were older, bearing ravaged faces and bodies, eyes like burned-out fires waiting to be relit, veins in their arms hard, dark and prominent, like lines on a tube map. Some were younger, lads seen in any pub in any city on any Saturday night. No stereotypical addicts.

'This is Stephen Larkin,' said Tony Woodhouse. 'He's that journalist I was telling you about. He's all yours, lads. Be kind to him.' With a grin he was gone.

A few of the men looked up, nodded. Larkin

nodded in return. The men all continued to get changed. Keyed up, tense. Serious. He joined them in changing.

Tony entered with tops and positions – Larkin was fourteen, on the bench – then outside for practice and warm-up: bending and stretching, short runs, ball skills.

Tony came alive: animated, encouraging, his leg ignored.

Frailty slowly peeled from the CAT Centre Crew; steeliness, determination took its place. They worked with each other, read each other. They became a team.

Larkin tried to join in. He ran, dribbled, moved. Felt booze sweat on his skin, wished he hadn't drunk so much the previous night. His timing was out, he couldn't read them. They were good-natured about it, let things go with him.

Then back to the changing room.

'Fine pair of legs,' said Claire Duffy as Larkin walked past. She was laughing. 'You hanging around after the game?'

Larkin shrugged. 'Yeah.'

'I'll see you then.'

She held the moment a beat longer than necessary, then went.

Larkin, taken aback but happily so, went to join the others.


'Well, it's all about empowerment, really. Showing people that yes, they do have the choice. Yes, they can turn things around. This–' he gestured to the football pitch '–is just one way of doing that.'

He smiled. Gave them what they wanted to hear.

The interviewer smiled also. Practised sincerity. Knowing collusion.

'And the score?'

Another smile. 'I couldn't say.'

'Think you'll win?'

Tony smiled. Self-effacingly, the way the camera liked it. 'I hope so.'

The interviewer thanked him, the camera stopped taping.

He was pleased with the interview, how he'd come across. Strong, committed, knowledgeable about the centre, pleasant and confident about his work. The only glitch had concerned his footballing career.

'Do you miss it? Do you not wish it had gone on?'

*Every fucking day.* 'Not really. Some footballers are destined to be all-time greats. Some are destined to be remembered for one goal.'

'It was a great goal.'

'Yeah, it was. But it was a long time ago.' The smile. The mask. 'And I doubt it would be as rewarding as this job.'

The hesitation had given him away. There to see for anybody who wanted to look.

A man came towards him: mid-thirties, neat and trim, wearing jogging bottoms, sweatshirt and trainers, carrying a sports holdall. Tony smiled.

'Hi, Dave.'

They shook hands. Dave Wilkinson: the local drugs liaison officer for Northumbria police. So neatly dressed, thought Tony, that even out of uniform he still looks in uniform.

They chatted. Small talk, work issues. They often worked closely together and, despite their differences, had a mutual respect for each other.

'Your boys here?'

'All here,' said Tony. 'Just waiting to thrash the life out of you.'

Wilkinson smiled. 'Got a couple of ex-pros in our line-up. Used to play for Newcastle and Sunderland. So that'll make it interesting.'

'But they're not managed and coached by an ex-pro. The CAT Centre Crew are. And that makes all the difference.'

'We'll see. Tenner says you're wrong.'

'Just give it straight to the centre when you lose.'

Dave Wilkinson smiled, shook hands, went inside.

Tony smiled after him, then turned to the main gate where a car, expensive, fast, was pulling up.

The celebrity auctioneer had arrived.

Once people saw who the car belonged to, who was driving, it was engulfed. Word of mouth spread, and soon there was a waiting mass, whooping, cheering, wanting something, anything, signed. The actor stepped from the car. The crowd made surprised remarks to each other about how unexpectedly small he was. Smile in place, he affected not to hear anything disparaging and patiently signed autographs, chatted.

Tony moved forward to greet him, his own smile in place.

The actor wasn't anyone special, thought Tony.

Not really. Just a mask-wearer *in extremis*.

Everyone wore masks every day. A celebrity's mask was an image, carefully selected, controlled and filtered, then presented as real. A persona simultaneously public and private; one that showed themselves but revealed nothing.

Something Tony could empathize with.

He separated the actor from the crowd. 'Bit of a crush out there.'

The actor shrugged. 'You get used to it. Just part of the job. Better than being ignored, I suppose.'

Tony nodded.

He walked him in, settled him with Claire, then went to see his team in the changing room.

'So let's recap. Four four two, OK?'

Tony talked tactics and formations. The men listened, enrapt. This was more important than football.

Tony had gone round everyone, explaining what their role was, how their own individual qualities shaped that role, how important their contribution was to the team. It built them up all the more. Man management and therapeutic self-esteem building all in one.

'Now, you know who you're up against. And I know what a lot of you think of them. So if anyone's got a point to prove, the best way to do that is by winning. So let's see what you've got. Passion. Commitment. Heart. Let's go out there and show them.'

The men stood up, made for the door. Tony held up a hand, stopped them.

'But remember, lads, it's just a game. Enjoy

196

yourselves, Now, come on.'

The men filed out of the room and on to the pitch. Larkin and Mick took their seats on the bench.

The opposition emerged, took their positions.

The TV actor said a few words, the crowd applauded. He took the whistle from the ref, blew it, handed it back, and ran off the pitch. Game on.

The procession marched through the town, Dougie leading, Mick next to him. Men got behind their banners, marched with pride. The loud-hailers were chanting, calls and responses with simplicity, directness and familiarity:

Maggie, Maggie, Maggie.

Out, out, out.

Maggie, Maggie, Maggie.

Out, out, out.

What do we want?

Coal, not dole.

When do we want it?

Now.

No less powerful for their familiarity. No less heartfelt in their simplicity.

People came to watch, opening their doors, standing in their gardens. They cheered, clapped and chanted. Children ran alongside them. Dougie noticed a few people turn away as they passed, muttering, but they were in the minority. The majority were with them.

Dougie smiled. He couldn't help himself.

'Gonna be a good day, Mick. I can feel it.'

Mick nodded but didn't reply.

They rounded the corner, began the final stretch that would take them to the colliery gates. There was a small picketing contingent outside the gates. Red-eyed, tired-looking, they had been there most of the night. Shift work continued above ground. Days and nights measured by stubbled faces and bloodshot eyes. They began to applaud when they saw the procession.

The police were there too. A small contingent, uniformed, not body armoured. Watching.

Observing.

Dougie was surprised; he thought there would have been more.

TV cameras turned, pointed at the men, recorded their approach. The men's voices got louder, the chants stronger, the pace quicker.

A TV reporter moved alongside Dougie, mic in hand, camera in her wake.

'D'you mind if I ask you a few questions, Dougie?' she asked.

Dougie smiled. He recognized her from the local news.

'No, pet. Fire away.'

She turned to check that the camera was with her, took the thumbs up from the cameraman and said: 'So what d'you hope to achieve here today, Dougie?'

'Well, Wendy, we're here today to make a point. This strike is all about the future. Remember, this strike started because they wanted to close Cortonwood down in Yorkshire, despite sayin' they were goin' to keep it open. The NCB said it was uneconomic. That didn't mean there wasn't coal in it, that didn't mean it wasn't making a profit.

Just uneconomic. For who? Not for the miners.

'See, we're here today to show that there's more to work than just a few bosses makin' a profit. This is about whole families, whole communities gettin' their work taken away from then just on the whim of the NCB or whoever's in charge of where they work. We've got to make a stand. 'Cos you never know who'll be next.'

'And how would you respond to accusations of pickets intimidating people who want to work? Stopping them going to work with threats of violence or violence itself?'

'Wendy look around you. D'you see anyone here bein' violent? No. And you won't today. That's a lie. A media myth. It's what the government want people to believe. And I'm tellin' you, it's not true.'

'Dougie Howden, thank you.'

He thanked her, kept walking.

They reached the gates, joined the men already waiting there. Greetings went round, introductions were made, old friendships reaffirmed. They talked and acted like soldiers, veterans bound together by adversity and experience.

They waited. Dougie looked around, made a rough head count.

'Reckon there's about five hundred pickets here, Mick.'

'Aye, I reckon.'

'Hello, Dougie.'

He looked in the direction of the voice. The journalist lad, Stephen Larkin. A blond lad with him, holding a camera.

'Aye, aye, Stephen. Good to see you.'

'And you.' Larkin looked around. 'Good turnout.'

'Aye. Makes you proud. Gives you hope.'

'It does. Oh, this is Dave. Dave Bolland.'

The young blond man shook hands with both Dougie and Mick.

'He's a photographer. Here to capture the event.'

'You've missed the procession.'

'No, we didn't. We saw it happening, so we got alongside. Got some good shots too,' said Bolland.

'Good.'

They chatted a little more, then the whisper stream started. There was a bus on the way in. A local private charter.

They listened. Heard it. They looked. Saw it. Gears crunching, diesel fumes belching. Revving up and down as if hesitant to approach.

Word spread through the pickets. They steeled themselves, stood firmer. Loud-hailers were raised, they chanted louder.

Maggie, Maggie, Maggie–

Coal, not dole–

The bus came nearer.

The watching police tensed themselves but didn't move.

Maggie, Maggie–

Coal, not–

Maggie–

Dole–

Out, out, out–

Larkin and Bolland moved to the side of the road, observing, camera poised.

The pickets stood their ground in front of the closed gates, four and five deep. Voices raised, fists clenched, held downwards.

The bus approached, driving slowly.

The pickets didn't move.

The bus pulled up in front of them, air brakes bringing it to an explosive halt.

No one moved.

Behind the wheel, the bus driver shrugged.

Dougie looked around to see he wouldn't be stopped, moved to the bus door, knocked on it. It opened with another air-hiss.

'Right,' said Dougie into the bus. 'This is an official picket. This colliery is closed. We will not move out of the way of the gates, but if anyone wants to continue their journey on foot we won't stop them.'

'You hear that, lads?' the bus driver shouted down the length of his coach. 'I'm goin' no further. The rest's up to you.'

Dougie looked down the coach. The scabs sat huddled, scarves, hoods and balaclavas hiding their faces, obscuring their identities, failing to shelter the fear lodging in their eyes.

No one moved. No one spoke. The bus driver looked at Dougie.

'I think that's your answer.'

Dougie stepped back into the road.

'Fair enough.'

The doors closed and the bus began to reverse up the street.

A cheer went up from the pickets as the bus receded. Dougie looked at Mick. The young man was cheering along with the rest of them. Dougie had never seen him look so happy.

'We won, we won...'

Dougie had been right. So far, it was a good day.

The opposition had been taken by surprise.

They had come expecting a runabout, a jolly; some positive PR from allying themselves with a good cause and, by extension, some good grace in the day job. What they got was a game.

A fight.

The CAT Centre Crew started aggressively, taking the fight to the opposition, pushing the ball up front, passing, shooting to score. Intentions clear from the get go. They wanted to win.

The visitors were on the backfoot, bending but still defending. They all looked fit, or relatively fit: years on the beer and curry diet, fast-food breaks snatched on patrol, propping the bar up after work, all had eaten into their muscle tone. Games like this were both an attempt to keep themselves in shape and a justification to keep the same eating and drinking habits. To buy off their gut guilt with sweat.

The professional sportsmen were trying to keep some shape to the team, those who had harboured footballing aspirations were rediscovering them, the ones who were just there to sweat out beer were lost.

The Crew were running hard, chasing something more than the ball. All shapes and sizes, all various stages of fitness, all giving it five–nil, running away from something, running towards something better.

Tony Woodhouse watched from the bench. Sidelined yet still in motion. Eyes darting, lips moving; the match being mirrored, live on his face.

He couldn't sit for long.

'Ged, get up there!'

He made his way to the touchline and stood, arms wind-milling, one palm flat, one fist clenched. Mouthing words. Football sign language.

'Mark 'im!'

Larkin watched him. Tony Woodhouse was more alive than he had previously seen him. He was back there, playing his game through the team.

Larkin looked along to the opposition. A neat man in a tracksuit sat blank-faced, arms folded, watching the game. Tony Woodhouse's opposite number. He caught Larkin's eye, nodded, went back to watching the game.

Next to Larkin on the bench was another CAT Centre Crew player.

The man kept staring at Larkin. Larkin ignored him, looked straight ahead.

'I know you. Don't I?' the man said eventually.

Larkin looked at him. Hair thinning and grey, face puffed and patchworked, red blotches, deep-purple broken veins. Thin body, skin gooseflesh-pallid.

'Where do I know you from? You from round here?'

'No,' said Larkin. 'Haven't been here since the miners' strike.'

The man's face darkened. He looked away.

'You're that journalist that Dougie Howden was workin' with.'

Larkin looked again. 'Mick Hutton?'

The man nodded.

Seventeen years. Mick seemed to have aged double that. At least.

'Sorry–' *I didn't recognize you there.* Larkin stopped himself saying it.

Mick still seemed to hear it. 'We've all changed.'

Larkin nodded. He took a small camera from his bag, focused, waited for action to happen near him. He didn't wait long.

A crunching tackle on a copper. The copper loudly remonstrating. Tony's player smiling, shrugging.

Click.

'This for that thing you're writin'?'

'Yeah.' Larkin nodded.

'What is it? Somethin' about the strike?'

'Yeah. Looking at the legacy, concentrating on the effects on one community. Then and now kind of thing.'

Mick nodded as if confirming something to himself.

'Good luck to you,' he said.

They watched the game. One of the ex-footballers lost the ball in a tackle with one of Tony's players. Standing up, he petulantly tripped the other player. The ref saw it. Yellow card.

Click.

Larkin and Mick laughed.

'Never liked him much anyway,' said Mick.

They kept watching.

'I bet you notice the changes round here,' said Mick after a while.

'Aye.'

Mick's focus shifted. He was looking at something other than the game.

Larkin didn't press him.

A sliding tackle on a younger copper caused the ball to bounce on to the bench.

Click.

Larkin moved to pick the ball up, but Tony Woodhouse was there before him. It was grabbed and thrown back in the time it took Larkin to straighten up.

The game resumed.

'So where've you been, then?'

Larkin looked at Mick, surprised he had spoken.

'When?'

'Since. . . you know.'

'Oh. I went to London.'

Mick rolled some phlegm around in his throat. 'Rather you than me.'

Larkin nodded.

'So...'

'What am I here for? What's me addiction?'

Larkin felt his face redden. 'Well...'

Mick shrugged. 'I can't handle me drink. Long story.'

'Oh.'

Mick nodded, eyes hidden. 'So, you back up here for good, then?'

'Yeah.'

Tony's players were moving forward. One touch, pass. One touch, pass. They played well.

Poised and confident. Energetic and inventive.

Larkin and Mick watched, drawn. The movement was magnetic, the opposition rendered ineffectual. The result inevitable.

Goal.

One–nil to the CAT Centre Crew.

Larkin and Mick were on their feet cheering. Tony and Claire gave each other a spontaneous hug. Claire, hugging harder than Tony, held on a little more tightly.

Larkin noticed. Tony didn't.

The two subs sat back down, smiling.

'That's Ged who scored,' said Mick. 'Good lad. Bit of a gobshite. Crack was his problem. Mind you–' Mick pointed at Tony '–he's a good bloke. Done a lot for this town. Helped me a lot. Might be dead without him. And Angie.'

The opposition manager was on his feet, calling to his players, attempting to re-form them. He shook his head, sat down again.

Tony Woodhouse, hands stabbing the air, mouth open, trying to get the players' attention, hurling words like stones.

Click.

Larkin nodded, looked at Mick. 'I bet you wish the pit was still here, then?' he said.

Mick's throat rattled again. He rolled his mouth, grimacing, as if it were full of bitterness, then spat. 'Naw. Hated the place.'

'Yeah?'

'You surprised?' Mick gave a harsh laugh. 'Livin' in the dark under ground, breakin' your back an' coughin' your guts up. It's a shit job, minin'. Should have pulled the place down years before.'

'Yeah?'

'Aye. An' all that bollocks about comrades an' socialism...' He pointed in front of him, gestured to the opposition. 'An' what those bastards did an' all...'

The ref blew his whistle.

Half-time.

The teams walked off the pitch: the opposition to a changing room post-mortem, the look on their coach's face saying they weren't in for an easy ride.

The CAT Centre Crew to enjoy the quiet, contented glow of confidence, self-respect and pride.

Larkin and Mick went to join them.

The Miners' Welfare Hall hadn't seen anything like it for ages.

Drink, donated by a local brewery and stored by the miners until they had something to celebrate, was cracked open. Food was supplied by twinned companies and charities and channelled through the miners' wives and support groups. A group of local musicians, traditional instruments, Northumbrian pipes were playing. It seemed like the whole town – men, women, children, miners and non-miners – were there. All wanting to share, to be a part of, to write themselves into the history of the small victory. To be there on the day Coldwell won.

The hall smelled of alcohol and cigarettes, reverberated with laughter and music, felt of abandonment and release.

Mick stood by the bar, sipping his Coke,

207

watching. Couples were flinging each other round to the music, time being kept by the clapping circle around them. Those in the middle, those in the circle, him not a part of it.

That just about sums it up, he thought.

Mick had never wanted to be there, had never felt part of the close-knit mining community, but had never had the courage to leave. Until recently. But that had all changed now.

'You not joinin' in? Howay, man.'

It was Dougie.

'No, I'm ... a bit tired.'

Dougie nodded, then noticed Mick's glass.

'What's that?'

'Coke.'

'Have a proper drink, man.'

Dougie reached over the bar, found a can of lager, popped it open.

'There you go. Get that down you.'

'I don't–'

'I know, but it's a party. One won't hurt you.'

Mick looked at Dougie: swaying, eyes red, smiling. He was drunk. Better just to do as he said. He put the can to his lips, took a mouthful. The fizz made him grimace, the taste made him gag.

'That's better,' said Dougie. 'Where's Angie?'

'At home. She's feelin' a bit tired.'

Dougie nodded.

Mick took another drink from the can. It didn't taste as bad this time.

'Look,' said Mick. 'Tomorrow. I dunno–'

'Don't worry, lad. It's ganna be great. Some of the lads are stayin' over so we'll have their support again. Aye, we'll do it all again, don't you worry.'

Mick nodded. That wasn't what he had wanted to say. The moment was gone. He couldn't say it now.

He took another drink, found he didn't mind the taste at all this time. He looked at his watch.

'I'd better go. I told Angie I'd be back.'

Dougie smiled. 'Aye. You got any names for that baby yet?'

'Aye. If it's a boy, David. If it's a girl, Tanya.'

'Smashin'. Go on then, son.' Dougie shook his hand. 'We've had a great day. Tomorrow'll be better. The tide has turned. The tide has turned.'

Mick nodded and left. But not before draining his can.

Dougie swayed a little, then smiled to himself. He reached over the bar, found another can, opened it. He looked around the room, happy to see people happy. His family, his friends all in the one place. Dougie found strength in the whole thing. The music, the dancing, even the drinking and laughing. Decades old but still fun, still exciting. Enjoyable because it had always been done this way and it had always been done this way because it worked.

He could see some of them, the younger ones mostly, Dean Plessey and his mates, sending the whole thing up, taking the piss. He didn't mind, though. He had been like that at their age, before he had come to realize that the old ways were the best ways.

He saw himself, quite unapologetically, as a traditionalist. He stood for things, believed in things, that he thought were important. Comradeship.

Fairness. Family. Community. Decency. Respect. All the things he saw the strike being in favour of, all the things he saw the government being against. He would stand for them, and he would stay standing, until he drew his last breath.

He smiled again, took a mouthful of beer. He was happier than he had been for a long while. Happy to be at an event that celebrated the community.

He went to rejoin the party.

Home for Mick was a new housing development on the outskirts of the town centre. Built the previous year for young, professional couples with their eye on commuting down the coast road to Newcastle, it was at least three-quarters occupied. Mick and Angela had moved into a starter home on the estate the previous autumn, believing themselves and the estate to complement each other's aspirations. Now Mick found it a confusing warren of cul-de-sacs and dead ends, a conformist orange- and red-brick maze.

Mick walked. He had to. He had sold the car to pay off his strike debts. To go on living.

He stuck his key in the front door and entered. It slammed shut behind him like the seal on an airless tomb.

'Hello, love,' he said.

He heard the TV being turned off, variety show laughter being silenced.

He entered the front room. It was sparsely furnished, the decorating money ended when the strike started. Mick kissed Angela, who was uncomfortably contorted into an armchair, then sat on the sofa. The house was small, but there seemed acres of space between them.

'How are you?' he asked.

'OK.'

'Good.' Mick sat forward, hands together, elbows on knees. 'Good. Did you see the news?'

'Yes. You were on.'

Mick nodded.

'But they said some cruel things. Really hurtful.'

Mick said nothing.

'They want people to hate you, you know.'

Mick nodded again. 'I know.'

Angela sighed, redistributed her weight from one buttock to the other. 'I don't know how much longer I can go on like this.'

Mick looked at her. Her face was red, her eyes sore-looking. He said nothing.

'Did you talk to Dougie? Did you tell him about tomorrow?'

Mick sighed. 'I tried to. I started to, but...'

'But you didn't. So he's expecting you tomorrow morning.'

Mick gave a small nod.

Angela let out a long breath. Pure exasperation. 'Why can't you do one simple thing? Ay? Mick, he's using you. He knows that some of the others won't get involved unless you're there. He knows that. And you let him get away with it.'

Mick said nothing. He knew she was right. Mick wasn't political; he didn't even vote. When the strike started, Dougie had asked him to get involved, knowing he was more representative of the majority of miners. Sold him it as a question of right and wrong. Mick had agreed despite Angela's loudly expressed misgivings.

Another exasperated sigh from Angela.

'I wish you'd left when you'd had the chance. Then we wouldn't be going through all this.'

Again he said nothing. He didn't need to. It was a familiar argument. They had had it so often they knew which words filled which spaces.

Mick, with Angela's pushing, had been planning on going to college. Evening classes in business studies, accountancy, computers. That was the way things were going, she said. The pit couldn't go on for ever, she said. It'll be gone sooner or later. Get out before it goes. Besides, he wasn't suited for it. It was too physical. He was better off in an office job, she said. Think of the future. We're a family now, she said.

Mick had listened and agreed with her. Angela was right. And he had planned on going to college, saved for it. Reserved a place.

But then the strike started. And the money he'd saved became money to live on. And the car had to go, to pay the mortgage. And bit by bit, their lives became sparser, smaller.

Until September. Now. The month Mick should have been starting college.

Mick sighed again. 'Look,' he said, 'I'll go with Dougie tomorrow. Then that'll be it. I promise.'

'Don't do it, Mick, please. I don't like you doing it.'

Angela's eyes were becoming redder, wetter.

'I hate turning on the telly and seeing the miners. Hearing the things you're being called. Opening a paper and reading hate. I can't stand it. I can't stand it.'

She took two shuddering breaths.

'And what have you got to show for it?'

She made a helpless shrugging gesture, held emptiness in her hands.

Mick said nothing.

'Please, Mick, don't go. Tell them I'm sick. Tell them you can't go. Tell them anything. Please, Mick.'

Mick sighed, face contorted. 'I'm sorry, Angela, I promised...'

Angela pulled herself awkwardly from her chair, made it to the door before the tears started.

Mick put his hand out.

'Angela...'

She batted it away.

'Leave me alone...'

He heard her go upstairs, heard the bedroom door slam, then nothing but the faint sound of muffled tears.

Mick sat silently on the sofa, thinking nothing, looking at nothing. Then he stood up, went into the kitchen, opened the fridge. There stood four cans of Guinness. Bought to keep Angela's iron levels up, but she hadn't liked the taste so they had left them there. He took one out, popped the ring pull, drank.

It tasted cold and bitter.

Good.

He carried the can back to the front room, flicked the TV back on, sat back on the sofa.

A toupeed, dicky-bowed comedian was turning easy targets into vapid jokes. The unemployed. Arthur Scargill. The miners.

Canned laughter answered his punchlines, distorted and cruel.

Mick watched.

And drank.

While Mick drank alone, Angela cried and Dougie and the rest of the town drank together, the police arrived.

Erecting barricades, checkpoints, deploying barriers and cones. Implementing a well-drawn, well-practised operation. Working through the night, remaking Coldwell, reordering it in a new image, to a new plan.

Their plan.

Leave cancelled, overtime doubled. Reinforcements called in on mutual aid. Stocking up on helmets, body armour, shields and batons. Given roles to play. Strategies to act out. Horses groomed and ready.

A silent, night-time invasion. Ready for the morning.

Their briefing:

'They'll be expecting confrontation. Make sure we're ready for war.'

Tea and oranges: Tony was treating half-time seriously.

'Come on, tracksuits on.' Tony clapped his hands twice. 'Keep those muscles warm.'

Larkin, who hadn't yet taken his tracksuit off, helped himself to a cup of tea.

The mood was happy, buoyant: the men reliving their first-half heroism, building their contributions up to legendary status, honing and perfecting experiences into future treasurable anecdotes. Larkin smiled too. Although not really a part of the group, the enthusiasm of their achievement was infectious.

Tony came over to Larkin.

'Good first half,' Larkin said.

Tony nodded. 'Could have been better from a professional point of view, but the lads did a great job. Turning ordinary men into heroes. Even on their own heads. That's what it's about.' Tony smiled. 'There's a quote for you.'

Larkin nodded, looked at the team. The inner fire that they had seemed to be lacking before the game was well and truly lit. They were kindled by something no external ravages could touch.

'Your opposite number didn't look too pleased.'

'Dave Wilkinson? Tries to pretend it's no big deal, but he takes it very seriously. Very competitive bloke.' Tony leaned in closer, his voice low. 'And I know that him and his lot'll hate the fact that they're one–nil down to a bunch of ex-addicts. Hate it.' He gave a conspirational smile. Pride in his eyes.

Larkin smiled back.

'Right.' Tony turned to the team. 'Listen up, lads. You did a smashing job out there. Pace, commitment, the lot. I was very proud of you all. Now, a couple of things...'

Tony gave notes. Detailed, descriptive ones assessing each player's performance in turn, praising their strengths, addressing their short-comings. He didn't sugar-coat the pill; he spoke to them like professionals and they responded in kind. He gave them respect. They returned it.

'Right.'

He told them he had to pop out but would be back before the second half and left the room.

Larkin looked at the men. They were talking, bonded, happy. They didn't need him there. He put his plastic cup down. The tea had gone straight through him.

He wanted to look for the toilet and made his way into the corridor. Dave Wilkinson's voice was audible through the closed door of his team's changing room, all along the hall. He was giving less a half-time talk, more of a team character assassination.

Larkin glanced both ways, looking for a sign. As he looked left, he saw Tony standing at the end of the corridor, talking. The man he was talking to was in his mid-thirties with cropped hair and a well-tailored suit which showed highly defined muscles. He stood with authority.

He looked familiar. Larkin knew him from somewhere. He spun the face through his mental rolodex. There was something...

'You all right?'

Larkin turned. There stood Claire Duffy.

'Oh, yeah. Just looking for the toilets.'

She gave him directions. They were the opposite way to Tony and his friend.

'Thanks. Oh, Claire?'

She looked him square in the eyes. 'Yes?'

'Who's that guy talking to Tony up there?' He gestured along the corridor.

'Oh.' She seemed slightly disappointed. It didn't look like that was the question she had been expecting. She followed his gaze.

'Him? That's Tommy Jobson.'

Click. That was it.

'Tommy Jobson? Is he a friend of Tony's?'

'Yeah. Local businessman. Owns casinos or something. Gives loads to charity. Well, loads to us, anyway.'

Larkin nodded, said nothing. That description didn't match the Tommy Jobson he was aware of.

'Why d'you want to know?'

Larkin shrugged. 'Just ... thought I recognized him, that's all. Must be someone else. Well, I'd better be off to the loo.'

Larkin turned to walk away.

'Hope you see some action in the second half,' Claire shouted after him.

'Me too,' he said without turning around.

By the time Larkin returned to the changing room, Tony was there. His rallying speech was in full flow.

Agincourt in Coldwell.

Henry V inspiring his army of recovering addicts.

It worked. They were ready to run back on and play their hearts out.

Larkin joined them.

Dougie had never seen anything like it.

At fifty-two he was too young to remember what occupied France looked like during World War Two. But he could imagine. It would have looked like Coldwell did now.

The town had joined the list of those under

siege, martial law.

The gates to the colliery were locked shut, ringed by tooled-up, visored woodentops. They stood impassively, waiting. It looked like a border checkpoint between warring neighbour states. Keeping one side out, one side in.

Word had gone round late at night, early in the morning. Homeward-bound partygoers leaving the Miners' Welfare Hall had seen the police operation but were too physically depleted to take action against it. The news had spread, angrily at first, then with a contemplative sense of inevitability: the gains of the previous day couldn't go unpunished.

There was no procession today. Word had gone out: pack the gates with bodies. Yesterday's remaining flying pickets were there, as were neighbouring miners, plus the near-acronyms: RCP, SWP, WRP. Their numbers were much depleted from the previous day, the organization haphazard. The chants had no rhythm, the shouts were random: scatter-gun targeting. The banners were absent.

The men were dressed for work again; boots and denim, plus a smattering of Frankie Says Coal Not Dole T-shirts.

Tension choked. Tension stifled. Tension ate up the air between the two tribes.

Dougie hadn't had much sleep. The elation of the previous day, the previous night had drained completely away. He had watched through bleary eyes and an aching head as convoys of police buses, vans and support units had rolled up and disgorged officers, riot visors rendering them

218

faceless, identities as blank and unaccountable as their numberless epaulets.

As the police buses had passed, coppers had waved money out of the windows, tenners and twenties, shouted taunts about how much overtime they were making, the holidays in Majorca they were taking. Some of the older ones had looked embarrassed at this, had looked at Dougie and shrugged apologetically: *This isn't what I wanted from my job.* Dougie could empathize with them. This wasn't what he wanted from his, either.

The roads and walkways had been reshaped. With bollards, cones and barriers, the only way round was the way the police wanted. Junctions were manned, routes enforced, entry scrutinized. Anyone intending to enter the town was stopped, questioned and sometimes searched. Pickets and sympathizers or suspected pickets or sympathizers were turned away with as much force as individual officers felt like inflicting. Anyone granted entry was directed to a designated parking area. The police had everyone where they wanted them.

Dougie looked around at the townspeople, the locals. They watched helplessly as, piece by piece, their town was taken away from them. And with that, their dignity, their pride. Even neutrals, people who had no connection with the mine or the strike, were drawn in. With each decision, each section of Coldwell claimed by the police, lines were drawn. Divisions made. Sides, out of unconscious necessity, were taken.

The people's faces reflected anger hardening

into hatred. Complacency turning into resolve. But above all, fear. Fear of the future. Fear of the present.

Fear of the immediate future.

The mini was travelling towards Coldwell, the Redskins on the tape player. Larkin nodded along to the beat, sang snatches of lyric. Bolland unconsciously kept time on the steering wheel. Larkin, buoyed by the events of the previous day, was allowing the music to carry him further up.

'X. Moore wrote these songs on a picket line, you know,' said Larkin.

'Is that supposed to make them sound better?'

'Yeah. Thinks they have more honesty and heart because of it.'

Bolland smiled. 'Some catchy tunes might be a better idea.'

Bolland was a friend of Larkin's, a journalism student at Newcastle Poly. He had an eye for a dramatic picture, marking him out as an excellent photojournalist of the future. They had worked together before and were good friends, although Larkin suspected Bolland's George Michael-style coif extended further than his hair roots.

Larkin was about to argue back when they saw it. The roadblock.

Stretching the width of the road, manned by over a dozen policemen flagging down cars indiscriminately. The smell of testosterone was almost corporeal.

'Shit,' said Bolland. 'That wasn't there yesterday. What're we going to do?'

'Don't worry. Leave it to me,' said Larkin.

'We'll be fine.'

A policeman flagged them down, pointed to the side of the road.

Bolland pulled over, waited.

'Better turn the tape off,' said Larkin.

'Morning, gentlemen,' said the copper. Only school age but already swaggering, as if natural authority came woven into the uniform. 'Tell me where you're headed?'

Bolland swallowed. 'Coldwell.'

The policeman tensed, a hard, anticipatory smile developing on his lips.

''And can I ask what for?'

'We're journalists,' said Larkin.

'Really.' The copper scoped them: Levi's, DMs. Larkin wearing his Meat Is Murder T-shirt. 'Working for who?'

'The *Daily Mirror.*'

'Oh, yeah?' The copper looked over to his comrades, readying them for some fun.

'Yes,' said Larkin. He opened his jacket, took out the card Pears had given him, held it up. 'This is our boss. Call him if you don't believe me. The name's Stephen Larkin.'

The policeman looked at the card, hesitated. A blip in his cockiness. Larkin held his gaze.

'Are you going to call him?' asked Larkin. 'If you are, could you do it quickly? I don't mean to be rude, but we've got a job to do. Deadline to meet.'

The policeman was confused. His instinct was not to let them through, but Larkin's insistence, his calm, unblinking gaze, seemed genuine. He decided to take the chance.

'Go on then, off you go.'

221

'Thank you, constable,' said Larkin, smiling.

They drove off, Bolland putting his foot down. Bolland sighed with relief. Larkin laughed.

'Fucking fascist bastard,' he shouted, looking back at the retreating figure of the policeman as he watched them go.

'Cunt,' he said.

Larkin turned the tape back on.

'Do we have to?'

'What's the alternative? Your stuff? Wham?' said Larkin.

Bolland said nothing.

'We've got through the first stage. Let the lyrics inspire you.'

Larkin settled back in his seat, mouthing the words.

'Bring it Down.'

Dougie entered the Miners' Welfare Hall.

Last night's party was a distant memory. Formica-topped tables were pushed together, newspapers, mugs and notebooks scattering the tops. Mick was just putting the phone down.

'How's it goin'?'

Mick sighed. 'Not good. The Yorkshire pickets got through all right. Most of them stayed here last night. But the Notts lads and the Lancashire men haven't. They've got roadblocks all the way down the Al. There's coaches and vans blockin' the lanes... It's chaos everywhere.'

Mick rubbed his face with his hands while Dougie digested the news.

'Aw, shite...' said Dougie.

'Listen,' said Mick, his voice hesitant.

Dougie looked at him.

'I need to go home.' His voice was small, distant. 'Angie... She needs us there. She's not...'

Dougie sighed. Mick saw strain and worry etched into the lines on his face.

'It's all right, I'll stay.'

'No,' said Dougie. 'If she needs you, she needs you. You'd best be off. We'll manage here.'

'Are you sure?'

Dougie nodded.

'Thanks.'

Mick stood up, made his way to the door.

'Tell her I'm askin' after her.'

Mick nodded and left. Dougie sat alone, thinking.

'Fuck me, it's like Eastern Europe,' said Larkin, looking at the gates to the colliery.

'You ever been to Eastern Europe, then?' asked Bolland.

Larkin reddened slightly. 'No, but it's what I'd imagine it to be like. Why, have you?'

'Just the once. East Berlin. Very bleak. But a kind of strange ... chromatic beauty about it.'

'Spoken like a true poncy photographer.'

Bolland smiled. 'Piss off.'

They had had to park in a designated area, directed there by the police. Even then they had been scrutinized for signs of miner sympathy, not allowed through another cordon of police until they could convince them who they were and what they were doing there.

They looked around, breathing in the tension like an airborne virus.

The strikers stood against the gates and the chain-link fence, sticks, dustbin lids and other makeshift noisemakers in hand. The police stood opposite them in lines with shields, batons and anonymous visors in place. They looked to Larkin like something out of a sci-fi film, a faceless, merciless invasion force.

'Imperial storm troopers,' said Bolland, echoing his thoughts.

The TV crews were there; hungry-eyed, beige-jacketed reporters there to capture the news, hoping to make some.

'Let's find Dougie,' said Larkin.

They found him outside the Miners' Welfare Hall, talking to some pickets who had made it through the roadblocks.

'Hello, lads,' he said. 'It's gonna be bad today. I think the best you can do is get some shots that'll tell the truth. That's all, just tell the truth.'

Larkin nodded. 'We will.'

There was no more time for talk. A rumour began to move through the crowd, a Mexican wave of apprehension and adrenalin.

A voice cried out: 'The bus is comin'. This is it.'

'Right, lads,' shouted Dougie through a loud-hailer to the assembled miners. 'Get ready.'

The men surged towards the gates.

'But remember the TV crews are here. Watch what you're doin'. Don't play into their hands...'

Dougie's words were lost in the air as men moved all around him.

The mood was different, thought Larkin. More angry than the previous day, more ready for a fight.

Dougie could feel the rasping shake of his breath, the thump of his own heart. Within that heartbeat he felt the beat of all the men there.

Coldwell waited.

But not for long. The bus, the same one as the previous day, made its way towards the colliery, revving and crunching as it negotiated the new road system, the route created specially for it.

It turned the corner, progress slow but inexorable. At either side walked lines of armoured police.

The strikers were waiting.

'Come on, lads!' Dougie shouted.

He was a general giving an unnecessary order.

The men swarmed forward, chanting, shouting, sticks and bin lids held aloft, clanged together. They surrounded the bus, were pushed back by police shields. They were yelling, lungs venting, football terrace training used against different opposition.

The bus jerked, halted, grey clouds bursting from its rear, enveloping police and miners alike. Despite the police escort, the driver was more scared than on the previous day.

The miners kept pushing.

Scab! Scab! Scab!

Bastards!

Ya scab bastards!

Words overlapping, fired out sharp. Sticks and lids clattering against the shields. Rhythm in free fall, a ferocious beat.

Inside the bus the scabs sat, again scarved and huddled, even more fearful than on the previous day.

The strikers were still chanting, rage feeding their energy, taking their arms beyond tiredness, their voices beyond hoarseness.

The miners pushed, the police pushed back. The bus stopped moving.

Dean Plessey found an opening in the police ranks. He jumped at the bus, trying to prise open the door with his fingers. Words hurled with spittle-flecked fury, eyes alight with mob-fuelled hatred, narrowing the gap between legitimate anger and the legitimization of violence.

He was pulled off and hurled back into the crowd.

The bus started moving again, moved, centimetre by centimetre.

The strikers didn't move.

The driver put his foot down, revved again. The bus moved and kept moving.

The colliery gates were pulled open, a solid wall of police admitting the bus, keeping out the miners, shields pushing back bodies.

The miners, outnumbered, had no choice but to give way. The bus moved inside, the gates closed. The police regrouped in front of the colliery.

The pickets fell back, spent. The chanting died down, replaced by a bitter silence.

'Dougie Howden. You've just watched–'

A microphone thrust in his face.

'Get out me way, woman.'

Dougie knocked the microphone to one side, kept walking.

'Bloody reporters...'

The men stood there looking at each other.

Dougie looked at the police. Even behind the visors he could see them smirking.

'Bastards...'

Chants started up again as miners ringed the fence.

Maggie, Maggie, Maggie.

Out, out, out.

Scab, scab, scab.

Dougie joined them, adding his voice.

'If you don't stop throwing stones, my men will move in.'

The voice, amplified by the buzz of a loud-hailer, rained over the top of the strikers. Gradually the chants stopped, their voices trailing off.

The strikers looked at each other, confused. None of them had been throwing stones.

The voice again.

'This is your second warning. If you do not stop throwing stones, my men will move in.'

Confusion became bemusement. The strikers began to laugh.

Again: 'Since you have not complied with the orders given, I am left with no alternative.'

Before the words had echoed and died, the riot police in front of the gates ran towards the men. Shields up, batons drawn. It was like an advancing, offensive wall moving towards them.

The men stood for a few seconds, rooted in shock and disbelief, then turned and ran.

From the other end of the street the sound of hooves began to tear up the air. Mounted police, charging.

The strikers looked around, stunned. They dispersed: running right and left, pell-mell, into each other, anywhere to get away. The riot police kept moving towards them.

They looked around, trying to find anything that could be used as a weapon.

Stones started to fly. Batons engaged.

The battle of Coldwell had begun.

They ran. Through streets, past shops, through gardens, round houses. No plan, no tactics, just to get away.

The police had planned. They had tactics. Men deployed to get the miners running, men deployed to be there when they stopped. And the rerouted, reordered Coldwell would ensure they stopped exactly where they wanted them.

Some uniforms felt nothing: this was just part of their job, another way to earn overtime. To others with family and friends in the pits it was difficult, a conflict of loyalties. But to most of them it was the Falklands War they never had. They weren't the army, they were the next best thing: police behaving as army. But this time it wasn't the Argies; it was the miners who were the enemy.

The enemy within.

They lay in wait: tooled up, ready.

Here they come.

Hidden and braced, coiled and bated.

Here they–

Waiting for the enemy to come to them.

Here–

The sound of running feet, the huff of men unused to exercise, forced into action. Scared. Confused. Voices shouting, overlapping.

Waiting for the signal—

And then they were on them: shouting whooping, batons raised, armoured bodies rushing forward, a blue serge tsunami.

Batons slowly up, straining back, quickly down. Connect. And again. Connect. And again.

Unguarded bodies twisting, crumpling and falling. Fighting back: some fists thrown, some lucky punches landed, some desperate kicks connected.

On the police: opportunistic injuries, lessened by the armour.

On the miners: plenty of injuries. No armour.

Batons slowly up, straining back, quickly down. Connect. And again. Connect. And again.

Connecting with flesh, punching through and breaking bone. Kickback from the impact: reverberations felt all the way through to collarbones.

Pain raining down, soaking through skin, reaching bones, organs.

Bodies, not heads. Bodies, not heads. The chief constable's words. The official policy. Hard to implement every time. Sometimes the necessity of winning every battle overrode that command. Sometimes like had to be answered with like. And sometimes you just needed to see, feel and hear the skull crack like an egg hatching blood.

One by one, the enemy went down. A pile of bloodied plaid and denim. A broken mass.

Some ran off, escaped. They would be caught, dealt with, by other patrols hidden elsewhere. Taken down by another wall of batons.

The defeated bodies of the enemy were hauled away, sealed in armoured police vans, transported to police cells. The batons and boots of the frontline soldiers had done their work.

Now they tended their wounded, regrouped and re-prepared. They were laughing, self-mythologizing their baton work, perfecting later legends. Laughing up the body count. They were high on testosterone and blood: even those with initial misgivings, now they had had a taste, they too had a hard-on for hatred.

They reassumed positions, waited for the signal.

Waited to attack again.

Dougie couldn't move. He just watched, rooted by horror.

He was a veteran of picket lines and no stranger to confrontation, but he had never seen anything like this before. He had thought he never would. Not in his own country. His own town. His own street.

He thought again of his national service. Germany in the 1950s. There as friends, not foes. The German people happy to see them. He remembered bar-room conversations he had had with German ex-soldiers. Their English better than his German. One man, Florian, attempting to explain the temporary insanity that had gripped the country two decades previously. The rise of Hitler. Nazis and Germans, he explained, were two different things. The National Socialists were elected on the promise to reunite a divided country. They ruled by propaganda and brutality, rewarding a few, persecuting those who didn't share their vision. People, he said, would watch

230

Nazi soldiers abuse and beat other people in the street. And no one would stop them. Not because they didn't think it was a terrible thing that was happening, but because if they did thcy knew they would be next.

Above all, Florian told him, it was something that could happen anywhere. At any time.

Dougie hadn't believed him at the time, had thought he had just been apologizing, self-justifying.

But he did now.

All the police were lacking, he thought, was a swastika on their arms.

His mind couldn't find a rational vocabulary to process what his eyes were seeing.

A miner on his knees, a mounted policeman encircling him, two foot officers beside him, taking turns with their batons, the horse keeping him in place, dissuading him from running.

Dougie knew the man, had worked with him for several years. He was a big man, wife and three children, came in the club on a Friday night and drank with his friends. He was no coward, but no angel, and could settle an argument with his fists as he had done on several occasions. But not a bully. Not a man who went looking for trouble. A man unafraid to stand up for himself.

That man was now crying, his right arm hanging uselessly at his side, his body twisting ineffectually in a futile attempt to dodge the blows.

The policemen were taking it in turns, their arms showing little sign of tiring.

The man's sobbing increased. Dougie saw a

dark stain spread over the front of his jeans, the ground dampen beneath him. The man had pissed himself.

Dougie heard the two policemen laugh and continue the beating, their enthusiasm intensified.

The man gave a final howl of rage, fear, humiliation. Then silence. He slumped on to the ground, broken.

The policemen carried him away.

That wasn't an isolated incident. All around him, Dougie could see the same scene being repeated. With variations, but the same result.

Florian's words again.

It was something that could happen anywhere. Any time.

His body began to move. Slowly at first, as if in a dream, then with increasing speed once the danger of his situation became apparent.

I've got to keep moving, he thought. I can't stop. Because if I do, I'll be next.

Larkin, like everyone around him, ran.

Pelting through the streets with the rest of the pickets, up blind alleys, around corners, past shops, it was like the Pamplona bull stampede: for black-coated bulls read bodyarmoured coppers, for goring horns read batons.

They rounded a corner and found another police unit waiting for them. They charged, batons waving, screaming.

Chaos reigned. The miners ran down alleyways, through doorways, into each other.

Batons rained, stopping escapes, breaking limbs.

Larkin ran. Oblivious of who was with him, not risking the time to look. Just powering on.

Bolland ran too, aware of the camera's weight in his hands, aware of the job he had to do.

He stopped running, found a doorway and aimed.

He saw:

A teenager running in terror, an armoured policeman pulling his T-shirt, ripping it off, beating him down over the bonnet of a Montego.

Click.

A man lying beneath the hooves of a police horse, his cardboard Socialist Worker banner held up to ward off the hooves.

Click.

A policeman holding a middle-aged miner round the neck in an arm lock while another truncheoned his stomach.

Click.

Click. Again and again. Click.

The images were diamond-hard, precious and real.

But not rare.

When he had what he thought were enough, he ran. Holding his camera in his jacket, protecting it like a fragile bird.

Larkin's surroundings changed. Council estates gave way to older, bigger houses. Concrete-panelled boxes and mugger-maze walkways became high hedges bordering substantial front gardens and Edwardian stone frontage on tree-dotted pavements. He had reached the edge of Coldwell, where the inhabitants didn't need to work down a mine.

All he saw was shelter. He was exhausted, his body reduced to just elements and minerals: his legs were sand, his feet were water, his chest a burned-out lump of old, rusted iron. Shaken and shaking from fear and exertion, he could go no further. He jumped into a garden, flopping down behind a hedge. All around him, other runners were doing the same.

They lay, chests heaving, faces reddened, long-unused muscles stiffening and cramping. Exhausted, ordered by exhilaration. Despite the fear and the threat, it was the most excitement some of them had had in years.

Larkin, his breath returning, propped himself up on his elbows, opened his eyes. His body was crushing a flowerbed, his legs stretched out on a rockery. There were two pickets with him.

Then a crash as another body joined them: Dave Bolland.

'You all right?' he asked Bolland.

'Just about,' Bolland said through ragged breaths. He opened his jacket, exposing the camera cradled inside. 'Got some good shots, I think. If they come out.'

Larkin smiled. 'Ever the pro.'

Bolland changed films, putting the used roll in his jacket pocket, fitting a new one. Larkin looked at the other two men, smiled.

'Reckon I made better time than Steve Cram,' said the older one with a short laugh. He looked at the camera. 'What are you, journalists or somethin'?'

'Yeah,' said Larkin. 'Trying to balance up the

coverage a bit.'

'Best o'luck to you, lad,' said the other miner. He had a broad Yorkshire accent. 'I were at Orgreave. Saw some stuff that never made it into papers. Reckon strike would be over now if it 'ad done. We'd a' had a bloody revolt against this lot.'

Larkin nodded. 'Well, we'll do what we can.'

'What d'you think you're doing?'

The men turned to the source of the voice. The front door of the house had opened and there stood the owner. The man sat sharply upright.

'Just look what you've done to my flowers.'

'We're sorry, pet,' said the older man. He stood up, not without effort, and crossed to the woman.

Larkin made her age as early fifties. Wearing a three-quarter-length skirt and a long-sleeved round-necked jumper with the collar of a frilled blouse ruffing her neck. Hair a mature ash blonde, probably naturally grey. She didn't look happy.

'We're very sorry,' the older man said again, 'but we had no choice.'

'We're being chased,' said Larkin.

'Chased?'

'Police.'

The woman's anger subsided, replaced by a fear of involvement.

'Now, look–'

'As I said, we're very sorry, pet. But if you could just let us stay here till it's safe, we'll be on our way.'

The woman thought. She nodded.

'Thanks, hinny.'

'You're miners, aren't you?'

The two men nodded.

'What's happened at the colliery now?'

The older man told her.

'Oh, dear,' said the woman, after he'd finished talking. 'Well, I must say I'm very sympathetic to your aims, but I don't like the way you go about it.'

'How d'you mean?' asked the Orgreave veteran.

'You know. Throwing stones. Violence. A lot more people would be on your side if you weren't so aggressive towards the police.'

A look of weary incredulity passed between the four men. They had heard that sentiment voiced so often that they had a stock reply.

'It's not aggression, it's retaliation,' said the older miner. 'If you found you and yours bein' threatened, what would you do? You'd fight back, wouldn't you?'

'Well, yes.'

'That's all we're doin'. Fightin' for what's ours.'

'But you see so many injured policemen in the papers.'

'And how many injured miners do you see?' asked Larkin.

'Not many.'

'That's right. Because they never make it to the papers.'

The woman looked at them. 'I'm just saying you shouldn't be so violent, that's all.'

Conversation was abruptly cut short. They heard noises from further up the street. Voices. Violence. And something else.

The ground around them trembled and the

hedge began to shake.

They moved out of the way. They knew what was coming next.

Police horses.

Running through the row of gardens, their riders taking them over hedges and fences as if it were the Grand National, flushing out or trampling on hidden miners as they went.

The men didn't wait. They fled before the woman's hedge was forcibly shredded, her garden ground to mulch and clay.

Larkin ran.

'Bastards! Bastard coppers!'

He risked turning, wanting to see who was shouting.

The woman was standing in the remains of her garden, throwing chunks of her dismantled rockery after the retreating riders. Her face angry, her voice venomous.

'Bastards! Police bastards!'

'Another convert,' the old miner shouted, running.

Larkin nodded but didn't reply. He ran.

And kept on running.

Click.

Mick was halfway home. He quickstepped, confident he had made the right decision, happy to be returning home to Angela, looking forward to seeing the expression on her face when he walked in, told her of his decision, demonstrated where his loyalties lay. Slightly guilty about leaving Dougie but, as Angela said, he had done his bit. Let someone else take over now.

And then he heard it. He heard it before he saw it. A stampede.

Behind him. Bearing down on him.

He turned, saw pickets running, pursued by uniformed police. They were running away from the town, towards the streets and estates, their home territories. The same route he was taking.

Every so often they stopped, turned, hurled missiles.

Sometimes they connected; missiles hit shields, sent jarring shock waves up arms. Hit heads. Slowed their pursuers down.

The crowd moved towards Mick. He began running, trying to outpace them.

They started to gain on him, he ran faster. Head down, powering towards home as fast as he could.

Soon both sides were after him, the miners and the police. He ran harder, trying to put more distance between himself and them, not wanting to get involved with either of them.

But it was unavoidable. Gradually he tired and the crowd of runners caught up with him. He was no longer the pacemaker, the front man. He was overtaken, overwhelmed. Sucked back into the ranks once more, a component of a group he had never truly felt part of.

The turn-off to his estate was coming up. He tried running towards it, tried to break free of the press of bodies around him. He collided with other miners, got into the paths of other runners, was knocked out of the way, hit, rebounded back into his place. The press of bodies and the speed of the men held him tight. The gap between

238

himself and his house became smaller yet further away.

He thought about Angie, sitting at home waiting for him. Saw the entrance to his estate recede behind him. Felt an ache in his chest from more than exertion.

He was part of the mass, powerless to break away, powerless to change direction.

He ran on with them, down streets, around corners. The men began to tire, the mass loosen. The chasing police began to slow. One by one, men stopped, hands on knees, heads down, gasping. Mick started to edge his way out.

He reached the pavement, began to walk backwards, retracing his route, going home.

He didn't get far.

From either side of the road, from in front of him, behind buildings, through alleyways, hidden riot squads charged. Helmets in place, batons raised.

The miners looked around, off guard, tried to find escape routes, legs to run on, breath to put in bodies. They reached for weapons – bricks, anything – fitted them into weak grasps, hefted them with trembling arms.

The police were on them.

Batons slowly up, straining back, quickly down. Connect. And again. Connect. And again.

Mick tried to run, back the way he had come, back home. There were too many bodies around him. He pushed, elbowed, kicked. Tried to force an opening, a gap to squeeze through. A hand grabbed his shoulder, swung him round. He tried to shrug it off, saw the uniform above it, pulled harder. The grip didn't loosen.

He knew what was coming next, threw his arm up to protect himself. Pulling frantically away, flinching all the time.

The baton cracked across his forearm, the pain as sudden as it was indescribable. He instinctively moved his free hand to his injured arm.

Another baton crack on his shoulder and Mick went down. There was no thought of escape now, just protection.

He attempted to fling his arms over his head, hoping the blows would hit knuckle rather than skull, but his arms wouldn't respond. They hung, hurting and useless, at his sides.

He looked up, tried to speak, to tell his assailant he'd made a mistake. He wasn't meant to be here. He was on his way home to be with his wife. His pregnant wife.

He saw a face behind a spittle-flecked visor, eyes twisted with rage, mouth hurling hatred. At Mick. A man he'd never seen before in his life. No communication, no reasoning there.

He thought again of Angie, at home.

Baton slowly up, straining back.

He wished he was with her now.

Quickly down. Connect.

She had been right all along.

And again. Connect.

He should have listened to her.

And again.

*I'm not meant to be here.*

The day wore down. The fights ran on. Police trying to impose a structure, a control, pickets

240

forcing them back, shrugging them off.

Territory became liquid: gains and losses tided forward, rushed back, ebbed and flowed, constantly moved, never still. The map redrawn by the minute.

The police were well drilled, well ordered. The miners were fighting back with whatever they could find. Anything they could get their hands on. Bricks, stones, bottles. The debris of the streets. Makeshift barricades were hastily built, missiles launched from behind them. A true working-class resistance, thought Dougie. Symbolism made corporeal, as that journalist lad would have said.

But he knew the miners would tire. There were only so many of them. The police could draft in reinforcements. And they would.

Dougie stood at the window of the Miners' Welfare Hall, mug of tea in hand. He didn't know whether it was hot or cold, full or empty. He didn't care. He had seen the carnage in the streets, now he stared at the aftermath. Broken placards. Destroyed banners. An overturned oil drum that had been used as a brazier for the pickets at the gate. He looked around the room, saw beaten men. Broken men. Still moving, but they had given in. Given up.

Earlier, from the window, he had watched as the police had taken full control of the gates. Laughing with each other, making jokes at the pickets' expense. He had watched them talk to the news crews, the chief constable shaking hands with the journalists, joking as if they were old friends, asking which shots they had got of the battle, explaining tactics, suggesting camera angles and vantage points to capture the best of the action. Inviting the crews to position their cameras behind police lines for a better view.

'Bastards...'

It was an epiphany: the moment Dougie realized what the miners were up against. Why they wouldn't win. He had allowed the previous day's victory to carry his heart away, to make him believe they had a chance. They had no chance. They were going to lose.

He sat down, the sound of his spirit breaking almost audible to himself.

Someone came over to him, asked a question. He didn't hear the words, was vaguely aware of some of the words. End of the shift. Busing the scabs out. Picket line.

Outside the window the chief constable was shaking hands with the news crew, walking down the street towards the Miners' Welfare.

'What should we do?'

Dougie sighed. 'Nothing.'

He looked up, saw a surprised face.

'There's nothing we can do. They've won.'

There was a knock at the door.

Men were losing the will to fight. The faceless, uniformed horde didn't seem to stop. Break one, another sprang up in its place. Fight them off, they kept coming back. They saw their numbers fall, saw their friends and workmates injured and arrested. Some men began to drift off home. Others to the pub, pretending they'd been there all day.

The remaining ones got together on a square of grass in the T. Dan Smith Estate. They knew what time it was, knew the scabs would be bused out soon. Dean Plessey was there. He addressed them.

'Time for one last push. Get yourselves armed with anything you can find and we'll rush the gates. Take them by surprise. We know what they can do. Let's show them how we can fight back. They'll be waiting for us. Let's show we can be ready for them. Let's show them we can win.'

The men went about gathering weapons. Stones, bricks, bottles. Chair legs, clothesline poles, discarded batons, lengths of metal. Dustbin lid-shields. Anything. Resistance had to be registered. Disapproval demonstrated.

They marched towards the pit. They were tooled up, bristling. They chanted. Angry as before, but now edged with hatred.

Maggie, Maggie, Maggie.

Out, out, out.

Coal, not dole. Coal, not dole. Coal, not dole.

Kill the pigs. Kill the pigs. Kill the pigs.

Marching as one, chanting as one. They drew strength from each other, let the crowd subsume personal fear. Collectively, they dismantled their individuality, created a new mass identity. One forged from terror into hatred.

Maggie.

Out.

Kill.

*Kill.*

As they walked, they were joined by others. Gangs of men, bands of brothers.

Larkin and Bolland joined them.

They all traded news: who was injured, who had been taken. This strengthened their resolve, made their walk, their gait more purposeful.

They reached the gates and stopped.

Armoured woodentops all in a row In front of them, some high-ranking policemen. And Dougie Howden with a loud-hailer. He raised it to his lips.

'Listen. I've talked to the local executive. And they believe a negotiated settlement can be reached. They've asked me to ask you to put down whatever you're carrying and go home. The chief constable has assured me that if you all comply with this, no more arrests will be made. If you go in peace, they'll go in peace.'

He put the loud-hailer down. He grimaced, like he had just swallowed something unpleasant.

'Sellout bastard!' It was Dean Plessey.

Dougie raised the loud-hailer again, spoke with no conviction. 'It's not sellin' out.' He sighed. 'It's the only way forward. What's your answer?'

The men looked around. They looked at the police, immobile, poised. Batons ready. They looked at each other. Saw tired men, used men, prematurely old men. The previous bloodlust was receding, replaced by a more honest assessment of the situation. One by one, they dropped the weapons they were carrying and turned away, avoiding eye contact with each other.

Dean Plessey pointed an accusing finger at Dougie.

'Bastard! Bastard! You've sold us out!'

Men moved around him, drowned out his words.

The chief constable offered his hand for Dougie to shake. Dougie turned and walked away.

The battle of Coldwell was, officially, over.

The uneasy, bitter peace had begun.

Larkin and Bolland drove home.

No music on the stereo. No conversation between them.

They were both exhausted; tired, filthy, dirty.

Bolland had cradled his camera under his jacket until they'd got into the car, transferring it to the back seat. He had managed to take four rolls of film. Ninety-six shots of police inflicting pain and humiliation on striking miners.

Larkin had more images to turn into words than he needed.

They drove out of Coldwell. The streets seemed eerily quiet: what faces they did see looked defeated and bitter.

As they approached the outskirts, they saw the police checkpoint.

Bolland sighed.

They were flagged down. They pulled over. Seven policemen stood at the side of the road. Larkin recognized the one they had spoken to that morning. He recognized them. He had words with the officer who had asked them to stop. Took over from him. He indicated Bolland to wind down his window.

Bolland did so with weary compliance.

The copper leaned in.

'Evening, lads. How's life at the *Daily Mirror?*'

'Fine,' said Larkin.

'Interesting. 'Cos I phoned them and they said

they'd never heard of you. Descriptions, names, nothing. Could you step out of the car, please?'

The copper's eyes had a cruel glint to them.

'Look, it's late and we've—'

'Get out of the car, you fuckers.' The copper had his baton in his hand.

Bolland stepped out of the car. Larkin did likewise.

'You were with them, weren't you? Fuckin' communists, eh? Deserve all you get.'

'I told you,' said Larkin. 'We're journalists. I work for—'

'Hey, look at this.'

Another copper had lifted Bolland's camera from the back seat.

'Put that back, please,' said Bolland.

The copper ignored him. 'Always fancied one of these.' He opened the back, pulled out a roll of film. 'Oh, dear. Holiday snaps, were they?'

Bolland's face reddened.

'Hey, there's more here.'

The copper reached in, found the other roll of film, began opening their canisters, unwinding them.

'You fucking cunts,' Bolland said. He began to shake.

The first copper rounded on them.

'What did you say? What did you call me?'

He was right in Bolland's face. Bolland could smell his bad breath.

'You heard.'

A sharp movement from the copper, Bolland went down.

'That's the fuckin' thanks we get from

protectin' decent people from scum.'

He kicked him as he lay. Bolland groaned.

Larkin grabbed the copper's arm. "I've had enough of your fuckin' lot today.'

He swung at him, catching the copper on the cheekbone with his left fist. The copper went down. His colleagues were there. One grabbed Larkin, half-nelsoned him round the neck, held his arms out of the way. Larkin struggled but couldn't break free. The copper he had hit was getting up off the ground.

'Right, you bastard.'

He swung at Larkin's stomach. Right, then left. Right, then left.

Larkin's legs buckled. He would have collapsed if not for being held upright.

'That's enough,' said another watching copper. 'Unless you're going to charge him.'

The first copper was out of breath. 'Naw, not worth it.'

'OK.'

Larkin was let go. He crumpled to the ground, joining Bolland.

From where they lay they watched as the coppers systematically destroyed Bolland's car. The headlights went first, then the back lights. Then the side windows and finally the windscreen. They watched, unable to intervene, as the coppers rifled the tapes in the glove compartment, pocketing ones they wanted, grinding out the ones they didn't with their boot heels, ransacking the boot and walking off with Bolland's camera. When they had finished, the first copper came up to them, knelt down.

'You're free to go now, sir,' he said, gave them a final kick each, and left.

Larkin and Bolland, broken glass around them like spilled diamonds on the tarmac, just lay there.

Mick lay on his right side in the police cell, his body curled, his shoulder and arm throbbing. Another striker lay on the floor next to him, unmoving. Mick hadn't spoken to him since he had been put in there. The man hadn't moved. Mick didn't know whether the man was alive or dead.

Mick closed his eyes, tried to blot out the naked bulb, the graffitied walls, the huge, studded metal door. The pain, the confinement.

But he couldn't blot out the sounds. The screams he heard from other cells. They had stopped now, replaced by a silence leaden with tension and fear.

The man on the floor groaned, turned over.

'You all right?' asked Mick. His throat was harsh and dry. The words came out sandpapered.

The man groaned, then answered. 'Aye...'

Mick rolled over, looked at him.

The man looked as if he had been dropped from a great height. His arms and legs moved as if they were not correctly joined to his torso. He didn't look too bruised, but his skin was stretched and shiny, like a plastic bag carrying offal and blood. He clutched his stomach, rolled.

'Shall I push the button? Call someone?'

The man shook his head, kept on clutching his stomach.

248

Mick sighed, lay back, closed his eyes. His memory was like the night sky, black with small, shining pockets of white brilliance. He had collapsed in the street, knocked down by a hail of blows. He had come round briefly in what he presumed was the back of a police van: the feel of rough metal walls, the smell of diesel, sweat and blood, the sound of injury and laughter. Then someone in uniform asking him questions: he couldn't remember answering, could remember someone answering for him. He remembered a form being signed. Then the cell.

He had no idea what time it was. He had no idea how long he'd been there. He just knew it was too long. Any time was too long.

And all this time Angie was at home, waiting, wondering what time he would come back, putting another brick in the wall between them with each passing minute.

Fear and rage, tears and bile began to well up inside him. He fought them down, kept them back.

Then: keys in the lock.

The door swung open.

'Sorry about the delay, lads. Shift change.'

Mick heard baton slap against palm. Smelled sweat, fag smoke, bad breath. Smelled blood and testosterone.

He closed his eyes, curled foetally.

Then it started.

He thought of Angie at home, the wall around her. He imagined himself at home with her, stepping towards her, entering the wall, closing it up behind him.

He stayed inside, let his and Angie's wall come between him and the rest of the world.

Auction concluded and money raised, the ref's whistle blew the second half under way.

The Coldwell CAT Centre Crew picked up where they'd left off, firing forward.

The opposition were sullen, Dave Wilkinson's interval bollocking having lowered their collective spirit rather than raised it.

Larkin thought of Tony's comments. *Him and his lot'll hate the fact that they're one–nil down to a bunch of ex-addicts.* Larkin smiled. It was informing every move the team made.

The CAT Centre Crew made a good team but not because of their footballing brilliance. The opposition were better players. They were a good team because they worked with each other, supported each other. Helped each other.

As before: Larkin and Mick on the bench. Dave Wilkinson and his subs sitting on the opposing bench. Tony animated on the sidelines. Claire watching.

A former professional footballer slid in behind a CAT Centre Crew player, taking his legs away, making no attempt to connect with the ball. The player – Larkin noticed it was the first-half scorer, Ged – went down painfully. A bad tackle. A professional foul. The crowd oohed and aahed in response.

Click.

The footballer held out his hand to help the man up. Ged slapped it away, got up himself and advanced on the other player.

'Oh, shit,' said Mick. He stood up.

Larkin did likewise. 'What's up?'

'Ged. He's a bit volatile.'

Tony looked at the two of them. 'Get warmed up.'

'Me?' asked Larkin.

'No, not you. Mick.'

Mick began peeling his tracksuit off, running on the spot. Tony had his fingers in his mouth, whistling, attracting the referee's attention, looking to make a substitution.

The angry player stomped off.

Mick looked at the opposition, tuned himself in to the game. A dark shadow fell across his face.

'Good luck,' said Larkin.

Mick turned to him, the shadow gone, thanked him, took a deep breath and ran on.

The first-half scorer came to the sideline. He opened his mouth to blast Tony.

'Don't start on me,' Tony replied, finger pointing. 'You got yourself brought off. What did I say before the game?'

'But he was—'

'I don't care. Yes, he took you down. But that doesn't mean you have to react, does it? Now, we had a deal. And you were ready to break it. I did it to protect him. And you. Now, sit down. Calm down.'

The man looked ready to argue again but, not without obvious effort, managed to contain himself. He said nothing, sat down next to Larkin.

Tension crackled from Ged's body like electricity. Larkin could feel it.

The man was solidly built, skin bulked with

muscle. Cropped hair, broken nose. He looked more like a nightclub bouncer than a footballer. He shook his head.

'Fuckin' cunt,' he murmured under his breath.

Larkin turned to look at him, wondering if the words were meant for him.

'I wouldn'ta done anythin'. Just had a bit of a row. Fucker.'

Larkin said nothing.

Ged sighed.

They watched the game.

Mick was a different kind of player from Ged. Where Ged had been forceful and bullish, running headlong at the other team, Mick tried to slip in, dance around them. It was as if he didn't want to go near them. Like he wanted to avoid confrontation.

'Tackle 'im! Tackle 'im!' shouted Tony Woodhouse.

But Mick wouldn't.

He ran quite well, worked hard for a man in his bad physical condition, but he wouldn't tackle. Wouldn't confront.

The dynamics of the game changed as the opposition sensed his weaknesses, began to pass balls around him.

The CAT Centre Crew noticed it too and adjusted their game play accordingly. They compensated, let him use the skills that he considered his strengths, let someone else step in when he couldn't cope.

Working with each other, supporting each other. Helping each other.

Teamwork.

'You're that journalist bloke, aren't you?'

Larkin turned, surprised to hear Ged's voice.

'Yeah. Yeah, that's me.'

'I'm Ged.'

'Stephen Larkin.'

They shook hands.

'Bastard pulled me off. I wouldn'ta hurt 'im.' He shook his head. 'Just 'cos he's a copper. Thinks I'd have a go.'

'Would you?'

Ged smiled. 'I wouldn't mind. But we've got better ways of teachin' them a lesson.'

'Like how?'

Ged gestured to the pitch. When he spoke, there was pride in his voice. 'Like that. Beatin' them.' He sat back. 'That'll show them.'

They went back to watching the match.

The CAT Centre Crew were still playing well but some of their aggression, their edge, was gone. Larkin thought it was because Ged had been subbed, but there were other reasons; no matter how focused they were, how much they wanted to succeed, they were still physically ravaged men. Most of the fighting and pushing wasn't done on the pitch, it was done within themselves.

Larkin had surprised himself by becoming completely involved in the game. He didn't think he would have been, not to this extent. He wanted the CAT Centre Crew to win, willed them to succeed. He was watching the game through Tony's eyes, through Ged's. Sitting on the bench, he was on the team.

The game wore on. Both teams were tiring. The

physical condition of both sets of players was beginning to show.

The police made a substitution.

Larkin stood up, crossed to Tony.

'D'you want some fresh legs up there?'

Tony didn't take his eyes off the game.

'No, thanks.'

'When am I going on, then?'

'You're not.'

'What d'you mean?'

Tony turned round, faced him.

'Sorry, Stephen, but you won't be playing.'

'Why not?'

He gestured to the pitch, to the CAT Centre Crew. 'Because they're the ones who need to play, not you.'

Larkin was confused and a little annoyed. 'So why get me over here? Why get me dressed up and sat on the bench?'

Tony sensed Larkin's annoyance. His face softened, became kinder. 'Because I wanted you to experience what the lads were going through, see it from their point of view. I didn't want you to be just a spectator.'

Larkin nodded, thin-lipped. 'Right.'

'I'm sorry if that's upset you, I didn't mean it to. I just wanted this game to mean the same to you as it does to the lads.'

'OK.'

Their conversation came to an abrupt end. Some of the crowd started cheering, some complaining. Dave Wilkinson was on his feet, loudly remonstrating with the referee.

They turned to see what had happened. The

referee was ignoring protests from the opposition, pointing to the spot.

Penalty.

Larkin and Tony weren't quite sure what had happened, but Mick was on the ground near the opposition goal, being pulled to his feet and congratulated by his team-mates.

Ged was on his feet, shouting, telling them which player should take it.

One of the younger lads placed the ball, stepped back.

Larkin, Tony, Claire and Ged watched, not daring to speak, hardly daring to breathe.

The younger lad stood looking at the ball. He took a couple of deep breaths, rubbed his hands together. He looked at the goal, saw the keeper, calculated his angle. He ran at the ball. Kicked it.

Top left corner: straight in, keeper diving to the right.

Two–nil to the Coldwell CAT Centre Crew.

Cheers and hugging from the sideline. Dave Wilkinson spat on the grass, sat down again, folded his arms.

'That's what this means! You see?'

'I do.'

Tony nodded, smiled. 'Good.'

Larkin sat back down on the bench to watch the remainder of the game.

He felt good about the goal, enjoying it as much as the rest of the team, feeling a part of the success, the celebration.

Once the elation had died down, he thought of Tony's words. He took them deeper, applied them on other levels.

I suppose he's right. I suppose this is what I am, he thought. An observer. A watcher. Someone who's involved but doesn't directly take part. A recorder. A chronicler. Like an actor watching a friend's performance from a house seat in the stalls. In the audience but not of the audience. Not passive, but not really active, either.

I used to be an active participant. It wasn't always this way, but this is what I've become.

Maybe it's better this way.

Maybe it's safer.

He took the camera from his bag, held it to his eye, focused.

Nothing was happening in front of him, so he dropped it to his lap, waited.

Waited for something to happen in front of him, something he could record.

Click.


'Well, thank you for coming here.' Tony sipped his Coke, smiled. 'All of you. You've helped us have a great afternoon.'

He scoped the room. The Coldwell leisure centre bar: strip lights, tubular-framed furniture, beige walls, oatmeal carpet. So little atmosphere they should provide spacesuits, he thought.

A buffet ran down one wall. The food unreconstructed northern working class: pork pies, sausages, white bread sandwiches. The drinks soft. No alcohol.

The guests: The Coldwell CAT Centre Crew plus friends and families, the opposition plus same, the centre staff, the famous actor, Stephen Larkin, Dean Plessey and other assorted councillors. Colleagues to be congratulated, clients to be encouraged, friends to be thanked, councillors to be cajoled. A gathering to be enjoyed, a room to be worked.

He talked on, thanking each in turn for their contributions, offering weak jokes, accepting weak laughter in return. Glancing surreptitiously at his watch.

Larkin drank his Coke, half-listening. Claire caught his eye, smiled. He smiled back.

Final whistle: two–nil to the Coldwell CAT Centre Crew. The team had been ecstatic, cheering, shouting, hugging each other. It was their Cup Final, their Champions League. The fact that they had beaten the police sweetened the victory.

The opposition were gracious in defeat. They swapped shirts, shook hands, applauded the crowds, applauded the victors. The last time they had seen these people was when they had arrested them. Now these people had bested them. The respect was reluctant, begrudged, but it was shown.

Then back to the changing rooms, the showers, then up to the bar for the reception. Larkin missed Tony's congratulatory post-mortem talk in the changing room. He didn't feel he'd contributed enough to warrant being there.

He had arrived first and watched as the room had gradually filled. Dean Plessey and his councillors, making straight for the buffet, chattering vapidly, hoping for a photo in the paper. Plessey avoiding eye contact with Larkin. They had surrounded the actor, ringfenced him up the stairs, telling him how good he was in his TV films, hoping some of his charisma would wear off on them. He managed to extricate himself, moved away. He stood now, looking out of the window at the damp town. He seemed lost without an audience. Larkin moved alongside him.

'Enjoying yourself?' asked Larkin, nodding towards the councillors.

The actor smiled diplomatically. 'Part of the job.'

He twinkled when he spoke. Larkin could see how he had become a star.

They talked. Larkin introduced himself, explained why he was there. 'D'you do many of these things?' he asked.

'A few,' said the actor. 'If they're for a good cause, like this. Plus some of my family are from here. It reminds me of home.'

His Geordie accent returned the more he spoke.

'And those lads on the pitch, you know? I mean, I went straight into the shipyards from school. Then they closed. And if I hadn't had a talent for acting and been lucky with it, I might have ended up like one of them. There but for the grace of God, y'know?'

Larkin nodded.

The room had begun to fill. The actor went to talk to Tony. Larkin went to the buffet, saw Mick standing with a woman, piling his plate up. It didn't matter how much Mick ate, Larkin thought, it would never fill him, never round him out. The years had pared too much of him away, sliced portions off him, like a knife to a ripe pear, leaving only the core, the seeds.

The woman beside him, however, made up for it. Whatever had been removed from Mick had been placed on her. She was big but uncomfortably so: her body bulked, her hands, wrists, feet and ankles small. She was piling food from the table on to her plate. The expression on her face said it was more of a duty than a pleasure.

'Good game, Mick. Well done.'

Mick smiled. The sides of his face crinkled like paper.

'Thanks.' He turned to the woman next to him. 'This is Angela. Me wife. This is Stephen Larkin. He's a journalist. He worked with Dougie Howden during the miners' strike. Now he's writin' a book about it.'

Angela, her face expressionless, said, 'Hello.'

'Did you see the game?' asked Larkin.

She nodded only, pushed food into her mouth.

'Yeah,' said Larkin, turning to Mick. 'What happened to Dougie Howden? Any chance of an interview?'

'Only through a clairvoyant,' said Angela through mouthfuls of food.

'Oh, I'm sorry,' said Larkin. 'Was it recent? He couldn't have been all that old.'

'Nine months after the strike finished. Cancer of the lung, they said. Blamed workin' down the pit. But I reckon it was the strike that killed him. He just seemed to lose the will, didn't he?'

Angela nodded, took a bite from her pork pie.

Mick sighed. 'Either way, it was minin' killed him. Told you we were better off without the pit, didn't I?'

There was something dry and joyless about the couple, thought Larkin. Mick, grey and insubstantial as a ghost, Angela mechanically cramming food into her mouth, taking neither pleasure nor nutrition from it. One trying to disappear from the world, one fighting to remain substantial.

Tony finished his speech. Applause, then conversation again.

The gathering was reaching its peak. The CAT Centre Crew had brought their own atmosphere into the room, replacing the earlier muted sterility with a temporary warmth and bonhomie. Temporary because the bar would revert to normal once they had gone, temporary because they would have to wake up in the morning and get on with their lives. No longer heroes.

But not yet.

The evening was still for enjoying. All around the room tribal demarcations were breaking down. Crew players chatted with policemen and, in some instances, councillors. Tony was talking to Dean Plessey. Claire, standing between the two, nodding. Tony giving his watch surreptitious glances.

No sign of Tommy Jobson.

Larkin, finding himself refilling his Coke glass next to Dave Wilkinson, introduced himself. They talked. The game. Small things. Introductory stuff.

'So what are you doing here exactly?' asked Wilkinson. 'I know you're not local.'

'Writing a book. About Coldwell. The miners' strike and after.'

Wilkinson nodded.

'Actually,' said Larkin, 'I wonder if I could come and have a chat with you some time?'

Wilkinson's eyes narrowed. 'Why?'

'Find out about the role of the police now. How it's changed from during the strike.'

'I wasn't here during the strike.'

'No, but you're here now.'

Wilkinson said nothing.

'I won't stitch you up.'

He smiled. 'Why do I feel suspicious when a journalist tells me that?'

Larkin smiled also. 'Check me out with Tony if you like.'

'All right, then.'

They walked over to Tony. Plessey saw them coming and excused himself.

'Tony,' said Wilkinson, smiling, 'this journalist says I can trust him. Should I?'

They talked with good humour. Wilkinson gave Larkin a card, then excused himself.

Tony looked again at his watch.

'Well, I think I'd better be off.'

'You're not coming for a drink?' asked Claire. 'I thought we could all go for a drink after this.'

'Sorry,' said Tony. 'I've got to go home. Expecting an important phone call.'

Claire looked disappointed. 'OK.' She turned to Larkin. 'What about you?'

Larkin looked at her. Drink in one hand, shoulders back, breasts pushed forward against her shirt, one leg straight, one leg open.

Signals, he thought, and felt something stir inside himself. The signal had connected. Now a response.

261

'Fine by me. I'm up for it.'

She smiled. 'Good.'

Tony made his goodbyes around the room and left.

Larkin looked around. The party was wearing down. Tribal units were being re-established, numbers were dwindling. Time to leave.

Claire pulled her coat on. 'So where d'you fancy, then?'

Larkin shrugged. 'I'm easy.'

'How easy?'

He smiled. Her eyes locked on to his. So big he could have fallen into them.

'Let's go.'

They left.


Tony sat at home. Curtains drawn, lights off. In an armchair in the front room.

By the phone. Ready if it rang.

His house was old, Edwardian. On the outskirts of Coldwell. No wife, no significant other. No one in the house to come home to.

He felt no pain in his leg. He had taken something for it. Wearing off now, leaving him comfortably numb. Pleasant pins and needles.

He looked at his watch.

Time.

The phone rang.

He picked up the cordless receiver, allowed three rings, pressed the button.

Signal answered, he was connected.

All he could hear was atmospherics. The whistle in the wire. Breathing at the other end.

He said nothing. He just listened, eyes closed.

'I'm here,' said a voice eventually.

He said nothing.

'I know you're there. I can hear your breathing. Makes me feel near when I hear that. Like you're with me. Beside me.'

He said nothing.

A sigh. 'That last time we were together I never wanted it to end. I know you didn't either. When I'm with you it just feels good. Time flies. When you're gone and I'm back here ... it's like I've never been away. The good feeling wears off so quickly.' A laugh. 'I'm like one of your clients. I need a fix. More and more often.

'But it's not getting any easier. In fact I think it's getting worse. The days build up. And they mean nothing. They just crowd into your memory, take up space. Take up the space of the good times. And I need the good times. I need to remember them. I need to know there'll be more of them. They'll be back again. They will be back again, won't they?'

He said nothing.

'Sorry. I know. No questions. It's better this way. I know. But it's not easy. It's not for ever. I keep telling myself it's not for ever. Just a few more months at the most. Then we'll be together properly. Perhaps all of us.'

A choke.

'Sorry. It just gets to me. I look at him and think ... it should be you here. I wish he was dead.'

Silence on the line. Only breathing.

'Sometimes I can't believe it's like this. It's come to this. I wonder how we got here. The mistakes

263

you make, the path you're forced to take.

'I can talk to you. I always could. I could talk to you about day-to-day things. I used to save, them up to tell you, going over in my mind what I would say. But I don't need to now. I don't want to talk about the small things. I need to talk about the big things. Love. And loss. There's a broken heart here. Two broken hearts here. But it's funny, don't you think? Something broken can be whole at the same time. Like this. There's distance, physical distance, between us. But at the same time I feel close to you. I feel like I do when we're together. We're here but we're not here. Is it a paradox, is that right? I don't know.'

He said nothing.

'I suppose it's time to go. You phone me next time. You know when.'

Another sigh.

'I can't wait to hear your voice. You've still got my heart. You still turn me on.

'I love you.

'Speak to me soon. Good night. I'll be with you.'

The phone went dead in his hands.

'Goodnight,' he said.

'I love you too, Louise.'

# PART THREE

## Secret Lovers

# 10. Now

Larkin sat at his desk, laptop open, trying to work on the book.

But it was no good. He couldn't concentrate. His mind would skip back to the previous night, on to parallel lines of thought. He sat upright, stretched his arms above his head. Two people kept coming into his mind: Claire and Tommy Jobson. He had replayed the previous night with Claire and the events leading up to that while he worked. But he couldn't stop thinking about them. Either of them.

Especially Tommy Jobson.

It was no good. He had to do something about it.

He saved the work he had done, shut down the laptop. He wondered for a moment whether he was just using Tommy Jobson as an excuse for avoiding work. No: he had that tingle, that journalistic intuition that announced itself when he was on the verge of something interesting.

He grabbed his jacket, shut the door, made his way into town.

As he walked, the previous night came back to him.

Fragments. Flashbacks. He smiled at the memories, let them keep him company as he walked.

Down Osborne Road.

'Sorry about the mess,' Claire Duffy said, opening the door of her flat and letting Larkin in.

It was what he had imagined it to be. IKEA and budget-end Habitat. Comfortable, lived-in. Candles and shelved books. Framed prints and posters.

'It's not a mess,' he said.

He looked at her, smiled.

She returned it. It was a nervous smile, frayed at the edges. The earlier layer of sexual bravado peeled off like the skin of an onion.

'Have a seat. Would you like some coffee or something?'

'Yeah,' he said. 'Whatever.'

The bottom of Osborne Road, right on to Jesmond Road.

'Here.'

She handed him a mug. Brown with blue spirals.

'Thanks.'

He hadn't sat down. He had been looking around the room, reading the spines of books, the spines of CDs, checking ornaments. Taking in the visible accessories of another person's life. Subconsciously searching for compatibility, for differences. The music belonged to someone a decade younger but there was common ground: Macy Gray, Massive Attack, Moby. All the Ms. On the bookshelves, along with the latest literary bestsellers, were plenty of large-format art books, serious studies of technique alongside vast colour reproductions. He stopped at a framed drawing hanging above the mantelpiece. It was an original, the paper slightly yellowed. On it were broad, sweeping curving strokes, charcoal or heavy B pencil. The lines formed a reclining, naked figure, white against dark. Viewed from the back, lying on one arm, legs lightly crossed. The picture was mounted in a clipframe with no backing paper, just bare brown hardboard.

'This is good,' he said. 'What is it?'

She lit a candle.

'What does it look like?'

'A naked woman.'

Claire smiled.

'I studied fine art. That was my breakthrough piece.'

She came and stood next to him. Larkin was aware of his breathing changing.

'The first one you sold?'

'No. The first one I drew. Properly. With my hand and mind connected, free enough to put down what I wanted the way I saw it. I was so excited then I felt like I could do anything. I mean, I've done better since than that, but I keep that up there so I never forget what it feels like. That "whoo" feeling. Y'know what I mean?'

'Yeah,' said Larkin, 'I know.'

She moved over to the sofa. Another nervous smile.

'Why don't we sit down?'

Her voice sounded dry, breathy.

Larkin sat down.

Jesmond Road West. Down Barras Bridge.

The coffee sat cooling, barely touched. Larkin and Claire were on the sofa, lip-joined. Hands touching, exploring. Hearts quickening, blood singing. New skin on new skin.

'Shall we go into the bedroom?'

Claire directed the breathily phrased question at his chest.

'Yeah.'

She stood up, took his hand, led him across the room.

Once there, they stepped up a gear, stripping each other with an urgency that had no regard for fabrics or aesthetics.

Claire sat down on the bed, chest heaving, back against the pillows, the headboard. Larkin moved to join her. She put up a hand, stopped him.

'Not yet.' Another breathy whisper. 'Don't touch me. Just look at me.'

Larkin stopped suddenly as if physically restrained. He knelt at the bottom of the bed, coiled, ready to move.

The room was dark, faint, second-hand candle-light from the living room and a muted gold glow of a streetlight through the curtains the only illumination. She was shadow-lit, darkness high-lighting the curves of her hips, her breasts, her legs. It brought contrasts: the white of her breasts against the shading of her nipples, her milk-plaster thighs, the ebony-rendered pubic hair.

Etched in charcoal, white against dark.

Her hands rested on her thighs, one bent down, one bent up. Both open. Relaxed.

'Look at me. All of me.'

Larkin looked.

She was breathing hard, eyes wide, locked on his. She moved her legs. He followed the movement.

'What d'you want me to do?'

Larkin was breathing heavily too. He was surprised: Claire was now different, a sexually emboldened girl. Another layer of the onion. He liked that, the element of surprise. He moved towards her.

'Don't. Don't touch me. Just tell me what you want me to do.'

He told her.

Down to the Haymarket.

'Was that OK for you?'

Afterwards, under the duvet. Bodies spent, entwined.

Larkin smiled. 'More than OK. So. What's a nice girl like you—'

'Doing in a place like this? Oh, please.'

He smiled.

'D'you mean why am I in Coldwell, the CAT Centre or in bed with you? Are we talking geography or philosophy?'

'Whatever. In Coldwell. Working with addicts. Seems a long step for an artist.'

Claire sighed. 'Well, I finished my degree at Edinburgh and came back down here. I didn't know what to do. I didn't want to go back to Rowlands Gill and my family and I wanted to paint, so I came to the coast for inspiration. But it wasn't like I thought it would be.'

'How come?'

'I remembered the Northumberland coast as being bleak but beautiful. But I think that's further up. This town is just bleak. Like a big lump of old machinery that's broken down and no one's bothered to fix it. Just left it to rust in the street. Anyway, long story short, I'd found my subject. I just need some models. Faces that would match the landscape.'

'So you got a job at the CAT Centre?'

'Volunteered at first. Then Tony gave me a regular job. I paint there, help the clients to work through their situations, express themselves through art. Kind of ad hoc art therapy, I suppose. Anyway, it helps me pay off my student loan. Gives me a worthwhile job to do. And provides plenty of models.'

'Good arrangement. So can I see your pictures?'

She smiled. 'No. Well, not yet, anyway.'

'Not finished?'

'Don't know you well enough.' She smiled again Differently, this time. 'Yet.'

Larkin returned the smile. It held promise in it.

'Right. So that's two out of three answers. How come I'm here?'

'We fancied each other. We decided to do something about it.'

'What about Tony?'

He felt her body tense against his.

'What about him?'

'I might be wrong, and I might be out of order for asking, but isn't there something between you two?'

She waited a while before answering. When she

spoke, the words sounded like they had been carefully rehearsed. 'There was once. But it didn't last. There's nothing now. We're better off as friends.'

She nodded, confirming it to herself. 'Yeah.'

He held her. They lay in silence.

Northumberland Street. Nearly there.

'Morning's coming.'

The room was lightening, candlelight gradually replaced by dawn.

They had drifted into sleep, woken at the unfamiliarity of the other's body, touched, drifted again.

It felt, to Larkin, like the dawn had made the world over, made things new.

That 'whoo' feeling.

'You in work today?' he asked.

'Yeah. You?'

'Back home. Working on the book.'

'All right for some.'

They looked at each other. Face to face. The morning light a new light. In it, they saw each other differently. Intimate strangers.

'I'd better get ready.'

Claire got out of bed, quickly pulled on a dressing gown as if embarrassed by her nakedness, by the previous night's need.

Larkin lay there, heard noise from the bathroom, the kitchen. He scoped the bedroom. It looked different in the light. Less homely, more impersonal. Touches of comfort were dotted around, but as a whole the décor stopped short of total

273

ownership. As if she didn't feel at home.

He thought of his own flat. And how things were relative.

She returned, carrying two mugs of coffee.

'Waitress service, thank you.'

She placed Larkin's mug by his bedside, hers on the dressing table.

'Come back to bed.'

'Got to get ready for work.'

'Five minutes. Go on.'

Claire gave an exasperated sigh, climbed back beneath the duvet. She didn't remove her dressing gown. They lay side by side. Not touching.

'So,' Larkin said, 'was last night just a one-off?'

'Don't know. That's up to you.'

'And you.'

She paused before answering.

'You know where I live. Where I work. I won't stop you if you want to call.'

'OK. I'll call.'

'Good.'

Claire's body relaxed, softened. They moved together.

John Dobson Street. Into the concrete precinct.

They finished their coffee, played around a little, dressed, went their separate ways.

The day looked like being a good one: bright, sunny.

Larkin dropped Claire off at the CAT Centre and made his way home. He replaced Wilco on the stereo with Jim White. Tapped the steering

274

wheel, sang along.

About being handcuffed to a fence in Mississippi but things being always better than they seem.

He found the music curiously uplifting.

The Central Library. Reference department. His destination.

Tommy Jobson. Born 1968, brought up in a succession of children's homes and foster homes. Mother alcoholic, depressive, unable to cope. Father absent, violent and abusive when there.

Public records. Time-consuming but easy to trace if you knew where to look. And he did. Piecing together the next few years took some educated guesswork.

He sat in Newcastle Central Library, poring over rolls of old microfilm looking for names, links, clues. Joining the dots in reverse. Following the river back to its source. Like a psychic investigation, a forensic meditation.

A court appearance in the early 1980s for twoccing. First offence, suspended sentence, community service. Then nothing. He either wised up or went straight.

Larkin could guess which.

He decided to widen his search, take in Clive Fairbairn. That proved easier. Hardly a month went by without Fairbairn's picture in the paper. A boys' club. A hospital wing. An art gallery. Charitable donations. Philanthropic gestures.

And there, in most of the photos, was Tommy Jobson.

That tingle, that journalistic intuition. Proven.

Standing at the back, to the side, the smiles and handshakes circumventing him. Bypassing him. Unsmiling, ill at ease. Never identified, never named. Dark-suited, a sullen shadow Slicked-back, light-refracting hair. An eminence greased.

Larkin kept searching.

The years rolled forward. Fairbairn inching towards legitimacy: talk of retiring coincided with rumours of a police investigation against him. He was quoted as wanting to hand on the baton, groom his successor. No mention of Tommy Jobson by name.

Then the next phase: Tommy striking out on his own. No mention of Fairbairn, just the shadow, centre stage. Now billed as local casino owner. Posing with celebrities, from footballers and boxers to actors and Tony Bennett. Making charitable donations of his own, holding up oversized cheques for good causes. Throughout all, the same expression: mouth turned up, eyes turned down. Masking more than uneasiness. Larkin looked closer, detecting even through the newsprint a sadness, a definite emptiness.

Then Fairbairn's fall: the court case, the verdict, the profiles. Vilification upon vilification. Recast from lovable rogue with an open chequebook to devil in human form. A tabloid bogeyman. Taking the fall on his own. Associates no more than hinted at, a lawyer-shaped hole where there should have been portraits.

Consequently, no mention of Tommy Jobson.

Then up to the present day.

Larkin sat back, rubbed his eyes. He turned the

276

viewing machine off, began to gather his things. He boxed up spools, handed them back. The exercise had been helpful but not conclusive. All he had were facts. Hard little cogs. What he needed was a lubricant, something to make them go round, mesh together. Turn the bones of fact into the flesh of substance.

And he knew just the person to talk to.

'Steve, long time no see. Wonderful! Come in.'

Dave Bolland opened the door to his office, showed Larkin to a chair. He resumed his position behind his desk, smiled.

Bolland ran an independent news agency, the News Agents, out of an office beside Newcastle University's old Lit and Phil Building. It was home to a rotating team of journalists, all selling local stories to the local and national press. Larkin had worked there himself for a while.

Larkin looked at Bolland. His old friend was looking tired. Trim and fit, purple shirt tucked into suit trousers, showing no fat, only squash muscles. Hair cropped short, receding at the temples, and a slightly more artificial shade of blond than it used to be. His face showed lines but wasn't overly creased. He was wearing his years well.

Larkin knew Bolland would be similarly appraising him. He wondered what he saw. And whether he'd be too polite to say it. He was:

'You're looking well, Steve,' said Bolland politely.

Larkin smiled. 'And you, Dave.'

'So. What do I owe the pleasure? I presume this

isn't just social.'

'You presume right.' Larkin told him he was looking for information on Tommy Jobson. He didn't tell him why. He wasn't sure himself.

'Teflon Tom?' said Bolland.

'So called because nothing sticks to him?'

'Exactly.'

'Like what, for instance?'

'Like his connection to Clive Fairbairn. Like the fact that whenever the law line up someone to testify to his nefarious deeds, that witness has a sudden change of heart.'

'Why can't you find anything?'

'Because he's too good. Because he's got the right people working for him who know how to respond to different threats. The Fairbairn connection, for instance, is hidden under so many paper trails and payoffs you can't find it. I know. We've tried.'

'So what is the connection?'

'Well, Fairbairn regarded him as the son he never had. That's an open secret. Spent the last decade grooming him to take over. And now due to the extended holiday forced on the charming Clive, Tommy runs the show.'

Larkin smiled again. 'Is that the word on the street? That he's Mr Big?'

'That's the word on the street.' Bolland laughed. 'Well, listen to us. Aren't we just a couple of hard-boiled private eyes?'

'Private dicks, don't you mean?'

'Speak for yourself.' Bolland leaned back in his chair. 'So, what's this about, anyway?'

'I'm not sure, really. I'm writing a book on the

278

miners' strike. Using Coldwell as a case study. Britain in microcosm.'

Bolland shuddered. 'Can't you leave all that alone, Steve? It's all in the past. Ancient history.'

'Well, I disagree, Dave. I'm looking at the actions then, the consequences now. Reaping what you sow. It's not just in the past.'

Bolland sighed. 'Doesn't being so angry all the time wear you out?'

Larkin sighed. 'Yeah. Well, wears me out and keeps me going.'

Bolland laughed. 'Let it go, Steve. Enjoy yourself. Live a little. You've earned it.'

Larkin shrugged.

Bolland waited, realized Larkin wasn't going to speak further. 'So, why all the interest in Tommy Jobson? D'you think he was behind the strike? Was it all a massive conspiracy?'

'I was at a charity football match. So was he.'

Bolland rolled his eyes. 'Definitely worth investigating.'

Larkin leaned forward. 'You don't happen to know if he contributes to that charity, do you? The CAT Centre?'

''Course I don't.'

'D'you know anyone who would know?'

Bolland smiled. 'I usually charge for this, you know.'

'I'll give you a cut of the fee.'

Bolland sighed. 'I've got someone here who's good with numbers. It's his forte. Knows where to find them, knows how to read them. He'll give you as much as he can find.'

'Thanks, Dave.'

'But you'll have to pay him, though. He doesn't do favours.'

'OK.'

'Anything else? Would you like me to solve who murdered Princess Di?'

Larkin shrugged. 'Up to you. Don't put yourself out on my account, though.'

Bolland laughed. 'Good to see you again, Steve.'

'And you, Dave.'

They talked a while longer, filling in gaps, reminiscing. The more they chatted, the more Larkin realized how little they had in common any more. Bolland had gone his merry New Labour way, Larkin was Larkin. But they were still friends.

It was time to go. Larkin stood up, thanked Bolland for his help.

'No problem. I'll let you know what I come up with.'

''Preciate it.'

'You know, we should go out for a drink some time. Play catch up properly.'

'Yeah, that'd be good.'

'Let's do that, then.'

They shook hands, the physical act bridging a gap that stretched further than years. They parted without making arrangements. There was very little chance of them getting together for a drink. They both knew that. But they were old friends.

It was something else that was said out of politeness.

Larkin saw himself out of the building, stood on the pavement, looked around.

Rush hour. Because he didn't have a nine-to-five job, Larkin liked this time of day. It would have been different otherwise.

All around, commuters and traffic were hurrying to leave the city before nightfall. Like virgins fleeing vampires, werewolves fearing full-moon lycanthropies.

Larkin began to walk. He had a lot to think about. The book. Tommy Jobson. Tony Woodhouse. The past. The present. Claire Duffy.

Claire Duffy. That had taken him by surprise. But pleasantly so.

He had to go somewhere, order his thoughts. Decide what to do next. About everything.

He couldn't face going home, so he checked his pockets for money, found he had enough for what he wanted without visiting an ATM. He looked around, pub radar on high. Settled on the Forth, headed for Pink Lane, and his invaluable aid to the thought process.

He could taste the first pint already, imagine it keeping him company as the day faded totally and the dark took over. The one constant to set against change and uncertainty. The one thing that would help him reach decisions.

He couldn't get there quickly enough.

Suzanne was nervous. Nervous and, if she was honest with herself, more than a little scared.

She stepped out of the concrete bus shelter, swapping the smell of stale piss for cold night air. She looked up and down the street. Nothing. She checked her watch. Seven minutes. No pedestrians during that time. Only the occasional

281

passing car, headlights picked her out, throwing her sharp relief shadow against the concrete, bleeding slowly away to nothing as it passed.

She looked at her watch again. Eight minutes. Just gone.

She was about five miles out of Newcastle in an anonymous satellite town she didn't know the name of. All she knew was that it was Tuesday night. The dullest, most depressing night of the week, according to Karl. Monday was optimistic, Wednesday was halfway, Thursday was tolerable because it was almost Friday, and Friday was the end of the week. But Tuesday, Tuesday was nothing. You've got to get into their mindset, he'd said. You've got to think like them. You have to have a special reason to be out on a Tuesday night, especially in a dump like this. Either that or you're lost. Whichever, he'd said, it's perfect for us.

She shivered, zipped her collarless burgundy-leather jacket up to her neck, shifted her weight from foot to trainered foot, flapped her arms about her body. Her teeth were beginning to chatter, but she preferred the street to the stink of the bus shelter.

She was shivering from more than cold. She felt dirty, like her body was covered from head to foot in greasy black grime. It was only imaginary dirt, she knew, but strange imaginary dirt. Made her skin tingle to think about it. She didn't know whether to luxuriate in the sensation or stand under a hot shower, attempt to wash it away, only turning the water off when her skin was red and sore. Purged.

She checked her watch, flapped her arms. Nine

282

minutes. Nearly ten.

The only people she had seen were a couple in their mid-twenties leaving the pub opposite. As soon as the door swung closed behind them, they were on each other, pulling themselves into a shop doorway, performing lingual tonsillectomies and febrile body cavity searches. Their passion eventually consumed them and they hurried off to consummate in private.

Suzanne watched, fascinated. They looked like boring, ordinary people. What Karl would call lesser people. But their passion had a depth that was anything but ordinary and boring. It seemed in no way a lesser thing. It excited her. It confused her. What she and Karl had was great, she knew that, but he'd never done anything like that to her. Never been spontaneous with his love. Never dragged her into a doorway because he couldn't wait to be alone with her.

She checked her watch again. Ten minutes became eleven.

Then she saw someone walking towards her.

A man: medium height, medium build. Black curly hair, black-framed glasses. Mid-thirties: young enough to still have dreams, old enough to realize they would never now come true.

Perfect.

She stood, miming a bored traveller waiting for her bus, watching him surreptitiously. She knew he had been eyeing her up as he approached, probably without consciously realizing it. It was what men did. She was often eyed up, tooted at. Especially when she was dressed for school.

He drew level.

'E-excuse me,' she said. It came out croaking, almost a whisper.

Her heart was beating overtime, body trembling. She swallowed. Her throat was dry, empty.

The man stopped walking, looked at her.

'Huh-have you got the time, please?'

The man looked swiftly at his wrist. Eager to please.

'Nearly half-ten.'

'Thanks.' Suzanne forced a tight smile.

The man returned the smile for a hesitant yet expectant beat, then made to resume his walk.

'Well?' Suzanne raised her voice slightly.

The man stopped, turned. Eyes widened in expectation.

'Well, what?'

Suzanne smiled. Put more effort into it this time. 'What d'you think?'

Even under the streetlights she could tell the man was reddening. It was his turn to dry swallow.

'I don't know,' he said, thinking he knew what she meant but not quite believing his luck.

Suzanne forced another smile, tried to remember the script they'd agreed on. Or rather, Karl had agreed on.

'Well...' she said, 'I really wanna fuck. I haven't had a fuck for three weeks and I really want one.'

She stretched her arms behind her back, sticking her small breasts out as she did so. Even through the leather her erect, cold nipples could be seen.

The man's face lit up, mouth fell open. It looked like Christmas and his birthday had come at once.

'Wh-what?'

Suzanne was surprised at how quickly, how well, the line had worked. Emboldened, she tried the next one.

'I'm really feeling kinky tonight, so...'

She took a step towards him. God, he was ugly. 'Why don't we go somewhere where we can get started?' She was right up close to him now. The stale beer on his breath couldn't mask the halitosis. Abruptly she turned, began to walk. The man meekly followed.

She was amazed at how much power she had over him. What a few well-chosen yet badly spoken words had done to him. Karl had said to her, Tell a man you'll fuck him and you can lead him around by his cock. She hadn't believed him. She did now. His imagination will be fuelled by dull, unimaginative pornography, Karl had said. It'll be simple for you.

He had been right, it was. But he hadn't realized how powerful it would make her feel.

And it did. This was beginning to give her a real thrill.

Then the man stopped.

She turned, suddenly scared, fearing it was all going to go wrong.

'What?' she said quickly.

'How much is this ganna cost us?'

She gave a laugh of relief so hard it seemed almost spontaneous. She recovered, quickly remembering the script.

'You wanna pay me as well? How much?'

The man was taken aback. 'Naw, naw, if it's free ... y'knaw, well...' He shrugged, smiled like a child with a new expensive toy he had never expected to receive. 'Howay, then.'

She walked, he followed. She was aware of him fidgeting as he moved and turned back to see what he was doing. He was trying to remove his wedding ring without her seeing.

She was touched. The act made her feel a pang of pity for him, but it was too late to stop now. There was no turning back.

She led him off the main road to an unlit backstreet absent of life. She flattened herself against a back yard brick wall and smiled at him.

'What's your name?'

The man fumbled to find any name other than his own.

'Bruce,' he lied. 'What's yours?'

'Louise,' she said.

'How old are you?'

Suzanne paused, wondering what age he would like her to be.

'Twenty.'

It seemed to be the right answer. Bruce nodded.

'C'mere,' she said, and spread her arms.

The man moved towards her, landing his mouth on hers.

And then he started. He touched her hungrily, as if it wasn't just a long time since he had been with a woman but an even longer one since his hands had been usefully employed. He poked, squeezed, prodded as if he were searching for something or roughly checking she was real. All the time his mouth was working at her face, like some alien life form, sucking the air out of her, leaving her skin covered in drool.

He shoved his hands down the front of her jeans, kneaded her between the legs. His other hand forced its way up her zippered leather jacket, squeezing her breasts and pinching her nipples so hard she would have bruises in the morning.

It was a struggle to act as if she was enjoying it. She ran her hand over his front, fingers coming to rest on his erect penis. The feel of it through his jeans made her gag. She quickly swallowed back the bile so he wouldn't taste it. She kept her hand on his penis. With a feral grunt, he stepped up his exploring, as if he was running out of time.

He grabbed the front of her jeans, tried to open them.

Suzanne was scared now. All previous thoughts of power were long gone. This wasn't supposed to happen. It should have ended before this.

She tried to scream but no sound would come out.

He opened the button of her jeans, worked the zip down. His fingers still probing her. She was hurting. He undid his own jeans, put his hand on his penis, attempted to shove it roughly inside her.

Suzanne couldn't bear any more. She screwed her eyes tight shut. Froze, rigid with terror.

Please, oh, please...

She had never been so relieved to hear a voice in her life. She breathed deeply; felt that relief travel all over her body.

Bruce turned towards the sound, saw only a blond-haired young man, well dressed, well muscled, walking towards him. He looked furious.

'What the fuck d'you think you're doin'?'

'Oh, shit,' said Suzanne, remembering the script.

Bruce's face was clouded by terror and confusion.

'Who's that?'

'My brother.'

'Oh, shit, oh, fuck...' Bruce looked ready to dissolve on the spot.

'What the fuck d'you think you're playin' at, eh?'

'I met her at the bus stop... She said she wanted sex...'

'He's lying, Duke, honest...' said Suzanne. She could barely get the rehearsed words out. 'He grabbed me. He saw me at the bus stop waiting for you and he dragged me down here.'

Duke looked at Bruce, standing with his trousers undone and his rapidly retracting penis hanging pathetically. His gaze was rage-filled.

'You filthy fuckin' rapist. You bastard.'

Duke got up close to Bruce, stuck his face into his.

'You know how old she is, eh? Fifteen. Aye, fifteen, that's all. An' you were tryin' to fuck 'er.'

Duke sighed in angry exasperation.

'Fuckin' fifteen.' He grabbed Bruce's jacket. 'Put your cock away, you're comin' with me.'

'Where?' Bruce croaked. He was almost too terrified to speak.

'The coppers. They know how to deal with you. Fuckin' rapist paedophiles. Fuckin' scum.'

Bruce's legs gave way. The only thing holding him up was Duke. Bruce began to cry.

Now that her ordeal with him was over, Suzanne felt pity for the man. Daring to believe dreams come true. This was where it had got him. She pulled her clothing back together, said nothing. Her part was over.

'Come on,' said Duke and started walking.

'No, please … please…' wailed Bruce as he was dragged stumbling along, trousers falling down, flaccid penis hanging out. 'I don't … I don't … please…'

'Why not? You got any better ideas?'

'I've got money, I'll give you money…'

Duke stopped walking.

'How much?'

Bruce scrambled for his wallet, shaking as he opened it.

'Look, I've got … I've got … thirty quid! Thirty quid!' He held the notes out.

The fire was reignited in Duke's eyes.

'Thirty quid?'

He slapped the notes from Bruce's trembling hand. He pointed to Suzanne.

'You think that's all she's worth, eh? Thirty quid?'

Bruce looked at Suzanne. She couldn't meet his eyes.

'No,' said Bruce. 'I can get more…'

He fumbled his Switch card from his wallet, held it up as if it was a ticket to paradise.

Duke snatched it from him.

'Let's get goin'.'

He gave Bruce a look of total contempt.

'An' tuck yourself in, you fuckin' nonce.'

'Duke? Where the fuck did Duke come from?'

Karl laughed, kept looking straight ahead. The car ate up the coast road as they travelled back to

289

Whitley Bay.

Suzanne stared out of the window. Away from him. Watched the night go past.

'It was all I could think of,' she said, not looking around. 'You didn't want me to say your real name, did you?'

Karl laughed.

They had got over three hundred pounds out of Bruce, whose real name had been James. Suzanne had seen the look on his face when he'd handed it over. It wasn't just money. He was handing over holidays in Majorca, new cars, presents for the kids, clothes for the wife. The look: pure hatred for her, pure loathing for himself.

'Don't you feel bad about taking his money?' she said.

'No. If he's stupid enough to be led around by his dick, he deserves all he gets.'

She could feel Karl looking at her. His eyes boring into the back of her neck. He was waiting for her to agree with him, to fall into line with his way of thinking.

She said nothing, kept staring out of the window.

Karl sighed.

'People are thick, Suzanne. They're not like us. Don't get upset about them or their sordid little lives or their sordid little dreams. Think of us instead. We're higher beings than they are.'

Still no response from Suzanne.

'It's like nature. When lions pounce on them ... what are they called? ... wildebeests and devour them. Survival of the fittest. That's all. We're lions. And you want to stay with the lions. Not the wildebeests.'

She didn't reply.

'The money tonight? It's all for you. Have it. Buy yourself something pretty with it. Something I'll like.'

She sighed. 'OK.'

They drove in silence for a while. Eventually Karl spoke.

'Didn't it make you feel powerful? Having that bloke there? Knowing you could tell him to do anything and he would do it?'

She remembered the *frisson* of power it had given her. Then the feeling of powerlessness. The fear. She shivered.

'You left it a bit late. You could have stopped him earlier.'

Karl's voice became edged with steel.

'I stopped him just at the right time.' He took his hand from the wheel, finger pointing accusingly at her. 'Don't question me. I know what I'm doing. I know what's best.'

She didn't look around.

He sat back, in control again.

'Don't worry, it'll get easier. Next time we do it.'

She didn't look around.

'And anyway, turned me on seein' that bloke with you. When we get back to mine, we'll fuck.'

Suzanne sighed. She replayed the night's events in her mind, rapid speed. Made a decision.

'I'm not coming back to yours tonight. I'm going home.'

Karl laughed.

'Why? You missin' Mummy and Daddy?'

'No,' she said. 'I want a shower.'

291

# 11. Then

'So? I don't see how that stopped you coming home.'

Charlotte's voice, her words wrapped in a metallic carapace by a zinging phone wire, sounded hard and instant: at the other side of the world rather than the other side of Newcastle.

'Well, we–' Larkin winced. The pain in his side stabbed at him. 'It was late when we got back and we were–' another stab '–were tired. I didn't want to wake you.'

'You wouldn't have. I was awake. Waiting for you.'

He tried to move his position on the sofa, gasped in pain.

'What's the matter with you? Are you all right?'

'Nothing, I'm just ... sitting uncomfortably.'

The wire hummed, sent static tension through the air.

'Can I expect you tonight, then?'

Larkin felt his side again. Perhaps a rib was broken. Cracked, at least. He remembered his face in the mirror from earlier. Bruised and bloodied.

'Might not. I'm working with Dave on this article. Got to get it done.'

Another static silence.

'I'll see how I get on.' He sighed. 'Sorry.'

'Well, at least you weren't out with another woman.'

'No, I was in with Dave.'

Charlotte sighed. It seemed like one of relief rather than exasperation.

'We need to have a talk, Stephen.'

The earlier harsh tone was lessening by several degrees.

'I know.'

'It might be better if you stay there tonight. Give us both a bit of thinking space.'

'Yeah, suppose you're right.' Larkin winced again. 'Look, I'll see you tomorrow. Where we arranged. We'll sort everything out then.'

Another static sigh from Charlotte. 'Yes.'

Hum.

'Aren't you going to ask me what it was like?' he asked. 'What happened?'

'I don't need to. I saw it on the news. Look, I've got to go. I'll see you tomorrow.'

And she was gone. He replaced the receiver, sighed.

'Shit.'

'Giving you a hard time?'

Bolland moved slowly, painfully, into the living room, handed Larkin a mug of coffee, lowered himself carefully into an armchair, like an arthritic pensioner into a hot bath.

Bolland's flat was in Jesmond, his student grant supplemented by parents much wealthier than Larkin's. And by Bolland selling some of his pictures.

Athena bought most of them. He took artful landscapes, classic cars, anything he happened to see that he thought they would go for. He never used models, never used studio shots, developed them himself, kept his overheads down, his profit up.

Examples of his work adorned the walls of his flat. Framed and mounted, they were the opposite of his greeting card work. Toiling manual labourers, pickaxes glinting in the sun, captured not in a romanticized glow but in a harsh, stark light, the pain clearly seen on their bodies and faces, the tarmac and concrete cracked and splintering beneath their steel toe-capped feet. Pub-life: dusty boozers, sunlight streaming in through grimy windows, anointing solitary old drinkers, caught with roll-ups and pints, mouths open, caught between past memory and present inertia. Gangs of youths clutching pints of lager, heads thrown back in laughter, mouths stretched wide over teeth: the feral baying of the hunting pack. There was a professional objectification of the subjects. It was clear Bolland knew where he was going.

Larkin hadn't noticed it before but, as he looked around the room, with its second-hand furniture and first-class TV and hi-fi, he was struck by the thought that Bolland was just playing at being a student, adopting protective camouflage for this period in his life. Waiting to change – evolve – into whatever the next phase of his life would be. A natural chameleon.

But for all that, still a good friend.

Larkin sipped his coffee. It was hot. Another sliver of pain to slip into his body. It was bitter. Good. So was he.

'Yeah,' he said. 'Charlotte's not happy because I didn't go home last night.'

'She'd be even more unhappy if you had,' said Bolland, 'state you're in.'

Larkin nodded. 'I know.'

'So what d'you want to do, then?'

Larkin thought. His clothes were currently in Bolland's washing machine. He had borrowed a pair of tracksuit bottoms and a sweatshirt. He didn't feel like venturing outside with Thompson Twins 1982 Tour on his chest.

'D'you mind if I stay here? Work on the article?'

'No problem. You can use my electric typewriter.'

Electric. Of course.

'Thanks.'

'I take it you'll be wanting to crash here tonight?'

'If that's OK.'

'No problem.'

They sipped their coffee.

Arriving back the previous night, they had compared injuries. Stomachs and ribs bashed and bruised. Severe gravel rash on their hands and faces. Larkin had found out with panic that he was pissing blood. Bolland had assured him it was nothing to worry about. Said it used to happen to him quite regularly when he played rugger at school. Larkin, disquieted by the revelation but reassured by the fact, made no comment.

'So fucked off about those photos,' Bolland said eventually. 'So fucked off.'

'Me an' all.' Larkin sipped his coffee. 'We've still got the words, though. If I write up everything that happened just as I saw it, that should be enough.'

Bolland nodded, stood slowly up.

'OK. I've got to go in today. Explain where I was yesterday. You know where everything is. Just help yourself.'

'Cheers, Dave.'

Bolland got ready, slowly, painfully, and left.

Larkin was alone. He finished his coffee, crossed to Bolland's desk, moved the clutter, replaced it with the electric typewriter, plugged it in, switched it on. He thumbed through the record collection, selected something suitable to work to.

Talking Heads: *Remain in Light.*

He placed the vinyl on the turntable, let the arm fall slowly on to side one, track one.

'Born under Punches'. Perfect.

Feeding a sheet of paper into the typewriter, he focused in, concentrated on the previous day. He brought forth all the anger, pain and inflicted suffering. He let it percolate inside him. Then, when he felt it about to explode, he began to write.

Four hours later, he had finished.

A speed-written fever dream: his own wounds opened on the page.

He had recalled specifically the events of the previous day. Personal experience mixed with anecdotal evidence wrapped in fact-heavy reportage. Nothing omitted, nothing glossed over or exaggerated. Just truth. Pure, filthy truth.

He read it over.

It breathed, it lived. It pulled the readers in, forced them to stand on a picket line, introduced them to their comrades, made them understand what was so important about the conflict.

Showed in both personal and political terms why the miners had to win. Why losing was unthinkable. It hummed with power. It was a weapon.

It was undoubtedly the best piece of work he had ever done. He stood up. Adrenalin pumped around his body. He felt alive, his injuries all but forgotten. He picked up the typewritten pages. Shuffled them. Straightened them. Felt the pages in his hand, ran his fingers over the typeface.

He smiled. Proud.

Then he phoned Bob.

'So, what d'you think?'

Larkin sat on the corner of Bob's desk. Bob held Larkin's article in his hands, was leafing through it. 'I'm sure it'll be fine.'

'Are you going to read it now? It really needs to be read now.'

Bob looked up. He couldn't hide his shock and distaste at Larkin's appearance. The cuts and bruises, the bad, mismatched clothes. As he had led Larkin to his desk, he had been aware of the whole office staring at him.

'Have they just let you out of St George's on day release or something?' he had asked.

Larkin had ignored him. He had begun to view his injuries and even his clothes as badges of honour.

Bob stapled the pages together, placed them on his desk.

'Have you phoned Mike Pears yet? He won't wait around for ever, you know.'

Larkin stood up, thrust his hands into the pockets of his tracksuit bottoms.

'No, Bob, I haven't phoned him. And I'm not going to either.'

'Why not?'

'Because I don't need to, that's why not. I don't need him or his money. Not when I can do stuff like this.'

Bob sat back, crossed his ankles, gave a quick glance around the room. People seemed to have stopped staring.

'I think you should, you know.'

'I know you do. Because you'll be getting a nice fat finder's fee if I do.'

Bob reddened.

'That's not the point and you know it. You're a talented lad. What future have you got up here?' He pointed to Larkin's article. 'You going to do stuff like this for ever?' He waved his hand at Larkin's appearance. 'You going to get into this state every time you have to cover a story?'

'I only want to do work I believe in.'

'Then you'll starve.'

'No, I won't.'

'Look around.'

Bob gestured round the office. Larkin followed his gaze, looked through Bob's eyes. All he saw were burned-out people, ambitions traded for hackery. Staffers who didn't have the nerve or talent to follow their dreams.

Bob's voice was barely above a whisper. 'This is where you'll end up. Maybe not here but somewhere like here. And you'll hate it.'

Larkin shrugged. 'I'll think about it.'

Bob nodded, thinking he had won that round. He looked down at Larkin's article again. 'Where

298

are the photos?'

'Tells you in there. Read it.'

'Tell me now.'

Larkin told him.

'Great story,' Bob said at the conclusion of it.

'And it's all in there.'

'Good.'

Bob stood up. 'Right,' he said. 'Well, this should be in tomorrow's edition. I can see a big spread on this. Pity about the photos, though. We'll have to see if we can get some replacements.'

They shook hands.

'Well done,' said Bob. 'I look forward to reading it.'

'Me too,' said Larkin.

'But think about what I said. Give Mike a call. Even if it's just to discuss—'

'Yeah, all right, Bob, all right. I'll talk to you tomorrow, OK?'

Larkin left the building.

The euphoria of writing the article was beginning to wear off, like a painkiller dissipating and dissolving away. His injuries began to hurt once more. They no longer felt like badges of honour. He became aware of the fact that he was walking round in a Thompson Twins tour sweatshirt, DM shoes and tracksuit bottoms.

He hurried back to Bolland's flat, hoping his clothes were dry.

The mother walked on thin stick legs, her body enervated beyond expectation, weary beyond hope. She held out a metal pan into which was poured two plastic scoops of rice. She then turned round and trudged away, letting the next defeated woman receive her share.

What marked her as a human being had all but disappeared. Clothed in rags and dust, eyes deadened beyond horror, she was no more than a frail wraith haunting a scorched earth, no longer living in this world, not ready to pass to any other.

Then the children: skin shrunken back to bone, distended stomachs barely supported by legs like used matches. Flies buzzed, landed on their mucus-masked faces. They didn't have the strength to knock them off. And their eyes: fear, pain, incomprehension. Surely life wasn't meant to be like this.

A BBC reporter appeared, talking to the camera. The words background, the images foreground, all contextualized by the children's wailing. He strove for impartiality, non-emotive reporting. He failed. The words stuck out:

Ethiopia. Famine. Hopelessness. Death.

Dougie watched. The images were horrific, made more so by being seen in his comfortable, familiar living room. Phrases came to him:

Years of civil war, decades of conflict.

A humanitarian disaster of monumental proportions.

The outside world doesn't understand, doesn't care.

Dougie nodded, sympathizing.

The outside world doesn't understand, doesn't care.

Then back to the studio. The anchorwoman, usually thin-lipped and hard-faced, was visibly moved by the report. She took a second to compose herself, turned to another camera, began to read from an autocue. It was a progress report on the strike. Coldwell in Northumberland was mentioned, scene of much recent violence by striking miners, pickets and other political agitators.

But now, her eyes glinting, her lips creeping up in a semi-smile, all vestiges of the concerned, shocked woman of a minute ago gone, police have restored order to the streets.

Coldwell on the screen, a press of bodies round the colliery gates. Then close-ups, mouths chanting:

Out, out, out.

Coal, not dole.

When do we want it?

Now.

Voices not trained, not used to shouting. Raw with passion. Coarse and distorted by amplification. The effect less honest passion, more raging hatred.

Then the camera being jostled, scuffles breaking out. Cut to the bus coming through, Dean Plessey clawing at the doors. The scabs caught on camera turning away. The voiceover lending them heroic status, bravery in the face of aggressive picket line intimidation.

Then noise, clamour.

A posed and framed shot of an injured PC, head bleeding, being led away.

The chief constable, whose hand Dougie had refused, soundbitten:

'There has been an element here today whose

301

only goal has been to cause as much damage and violence as possible. These people are not here in support of a labour dispute. They are destructive and anti-democratic. My men have now rounded up and removed them. Decent citizens of Coldwell can now go about their business without fear of attack or molestation.'

The voiceover continued in triumphalist tones.

A shot of the gates, of scab convoys being driven out.

Then a long shot of the town. Peaceful. Quiet. Empty. A couple of people shopping.

Order has been restored. The troublemakers have been removed. We are safe in our own homes again.

Dougie watched. He was beyond anger, beyond pain. He was broken. Beyond repair.

The outside world doesn't understand, doesn't care.

And until it experiences it first-hand or has it sympathetically explained to it, he thought, it never will.

The doorbell rang.

Dougie didn't move. He heard Jean go to answer it. She spoke in surprised tones to the caller, closed the door, ushered them in. The living room door opened.

'Dougie...'

He heard the concern in Jean's voice, turned. There stood Mick, his face red, blue and purple, his clothes torn and soiled with dirt and blood. His body damaged and roughly bandaged. His eyes lost, defeated.

Dougie got quickly to his feet, crossed to him.

302

'Bloody hell, Mick... What happened?'

Mick looked at him, opened his mouth.

'Can I sit down?'

'Course you can,' said Dougie.

Mick sat on the sofa, Dougie back in his chair.

'I'll make some tea,' said Jean.

She left the room, soundlessly closing the door behind her. The two men looked at each other. One unsure how to explain, the other not knowing how to ask. Both grasping for their voices.

'How... Who did this?'

'I got arrested.'

'Wha'?'

Mick started to talk. Haltingly, fractions of information coming at a time, stopping to reorder his thoughts, careful to keep the chronology, stick to the truth.

He told Dougie everything. Walking back home. Being swept up in the middle of a fight. Being beaten into submission. The van. The police station. Further beatings.

'I couldn't move... Just lay on the floor...'

His voice sounded dislocated, as if someone else was telling the story, or Dougie and Mick were watching a news report. Human rights abuses in a Third World country.

'On the floor of this cell. An' there was another bloke there. He couldn't move at all. They had a button in there. To press, like, if you were in trouble. This other bloke started moanin', changin' colour. I managed to get up an' press it. They took their time, but when they got there they hauled him straight out. They didn't look too pleased about it.

'Then they went out again. I heard them havin' words, like. I couldn't hear what they said. Then they came back, hauled me on to the bed, sat me down. One of them sat next to me.'

Mick was back there. Dougie's sofa was gone. He felt the thin mattress beneath him, the hard, profanity-inscribed wall at his back. The naked bulb overhead. The cold. The fear.

The policeman to his right smiling at him. Calm. Controlled.

Let's see if we can come to some sort of an arrangement, he said.

He handed a clipboarded form and pen to Mick.

You're free to go. Just sign this. Then you can walk out of here.

What is it?

A waiver. Says that all your injuries were inflicted prior to you getting here. As a result of your unlawful picket line activities.

He uncapped the pen, held it out.

Mick shook his head. I'm not signin' that. It's not true.

The policeman sighed, re-capped the pen. Then in that case I'm afraid we're going to have to charge you.

With what?

He shrugged. Violent conduct. Incitement to violence. Grievous bodily harm. Actual bodily harm. Criminal damage. Wanton destruction of property. Shall I go on?

Mick sat there, stunned. But I didn't... I didn't.

The policeman held out the form.

Sign this and you walk out now. A free man. No

charges against you.

He uncapped the pen.

'You did what?'

'I signed.'

Mick was back in Dougie's warm, homely living room. Back, but still carrying the cell with him.

Dougie shook his head.

'Mick, man, you shouldn't have done that. You could have had them. Done them for this. You might've got thousands.'

'An' I might not, an' all. I might've got sent to prison. D'you think I'd've got a fair trial, eh? D'you think they'd've listened to a word I said?'

A knock at the door. Jean entered with a tray bearing a pot of tea, milk, sugar and two cups and saucers. She placed it on an occasional table between the two men. She looked at them.

'Can I get you anything to eat, Mick?'

'No, thanks.'

'A sandwich, even?'

'No, thanks.'

'Right.'

She retreated, closing the door behind her.

The two men sat in silence. Eventually Dougie sighed.

'Well, Mick, I can't be angry with you. It's not for me to tell you what you should have done. I sold everybody out.'

'What d'you mean?'

Dougie told him. About the final march on the gates. About the chief constable telling him that if he didn't get the pickets to disperse, his men would move in on them with so much force they would probably never work or walk again. How he had stood at the gates telling the men lies, saying the police would drop back and negotiate if action was halted. How Dougie had probably saved their lives, and possibly destroyed their futures.

How he hated himself for it.

Mick nodded.

'You shouldn't hate yourself for it, man, Dougie. You did what you thought was best. If the men knew that, they'd understand.'

'I know,' he said. His voice sounded so hollow he expected it to bounce off the walls, echo. 'I know.'

They poured tea. Drank. The TV continued in the background. A chat show came on. Celebrities lined up to sell their book, their film, their play. Themselves. Free advertising. Human beings as commodities.

All alike, thought Dougie. All we have to sell is ourselves.

'There's something else,' said Mick.

Dougie looked at him.

'I went home. Angela's not there.'

'Have you tried the hospital?'

'I haven't tried anywhere. I was scared to in case she'd... Y' know.'

Dougie nodded, stood up. He crossed to the phone, picked up the Yellow Pages.

'Which hospital was she due to go in?'

Mick told him. Dougie found the number, dialled. He told them who he was, who he was calling on behalf of, who he wanted. He repeated his litany three times before he was finally put through to someone who could help him.

Mick watched. He couldn't hear the words Dougie spoke, didn't want to listen. His emotions were so churned up, he didn't know what to think or feel.

Dougie put the phone down, smiled at him.

'Congratulations. You're a dad.'

Mick looked at him, speechless.

'Baby girl. They told us the weight an' that, but I'm not good at rememberin' things like that.'

Dougie looked at Mick's face. It was completely open, like a raw wound.

'Still,' said Dougie, attempting to widen his smile, 'somethin' to be happy about, eh?'

Mick burst into tears. He cried for everything. For the last few days, the last few months, for his marriage and his future. For his daughter. He cried for his life.

Dougie watched, helpless. He felt for Mick but he couldn't intervene. He wasn't a man who cried, but he didn't think anything less of Mick for doing it. If Dougie was honest, he had felt like doing the same thing himself for the last few days. And if he did, he probably wouldn't stop.

Mick searched through his pockets, found a handkerchief, blew his nose.

'You goin' to visit her?'

Mick nodded. 'I'd better.'

'If you leave now, you'll just catch visitin' time.'

Mick nodded again, stood up, checked his pockets.

'I'd better just...'

'Have you got any money?'

Mick reddened, shook his head.

Dougie delved into his pocket, brought out a

five-pound note, handed it over.

'Here.'

'Dougie, I–'

'It's all right. Just take it.'

Mick slipped the note slowly into his pocket.

'Thank you, Dougie.'

Dougie nodded. 'Now, go on. Your family needs you.'

'Awe. Thanks Dougie. You're–'

'Go now. Or they'll not let you in.'

Mick nodded, gave a slight smile. Then he left.

Dougie resumed his seat in front of the TV.

Game shows. Soaps. Chat shows. Sitcoms. Anything and everything.

He tried to let them wash over him, act as narcotic rather than stimulant.

It didn't work. His mind was too active. He thought of Mick. He thought of himself. He thought of the strike. He thought of the future.

And one phrase kept coming back, taking up residency inside his skull:

The outside world doesn't understand, doesn't care.


Mick checked his watch, pulled his jacket closer.

Twenty minutes he had stood at the bus stop. No sign of a bus. Hardly any traffic at all.

The previous two days played over and over in his mind in a continuous loop. He would pause, pick out a particular scene, examine it closely, trying to find meaning in it, purpose, but all he could find was pain.

He checked his watch again, stamped foot to foot.

A new baby daughter. He couldn't believe it, didn't know how to let the feeling sink in. He was a father. Elation crept up on him.

A father.

In his mind the elation took form: a shiny new coin rose in the air. Landed heads up.

He smiled to himself.

But with fatherhood came responsibilities. Things were expected of you. Money.

The coin flipped. Tails. Elation became instant depression.

He had nothing. Nothing to offer her. No job. No hope of a job.

The coin kept spinning: a downward spiral.

He thought of the way he looked. What Angela would say when he walked in.

Look at the state of you. Coming to greet your daughter looking like that. I'm ashamed. None of the other fathers look like that.

She was right. He couldn't go looking like this. But he had to go. He had to see them.

The coin disappeared.

He had to see them. But if that was the case, then he needed something to bolster him.

He looked around. There was a pub just beside him. The blue star shone. The windows emanated warmth.

Dougie's fiver was in his pocket.

Just the one, he thought. A pick-me-up.

He checked his watch, looked around.

The blue star shone.

Dougie's fiver was in his pocket.

Just the one.

He checked the road one last time. Nothing.

He turned and entered the pub. The air was thick and warm. The barmaid didn't recoil at his battered face. She greeted him, smiled.

He ordered a drink, tasted it. It felt good.

He found a seat, got comfortable, took another mouthful. Already the pressure of the last few days was beginning to ease. He began to relax.

Outside, the bus he had wanted drew near.

It didn't stop.

He had missed it.

Skewered spicy pork. Brown rice. Gado gado sauce. Red wine. Bistro fare, but classy.

The decor: soft lighting, stripped-pine floors, bentwood Windsor chairs. Retro prints on the walls: James Dean's cheekbones, Ronald Reagan selling Chesterfields.

And the music: Sade. Working Week. The New Jazz. Smooth.

Tony looked across the table at Louise. Forking rice into her mouth. Hair tied up, dress cut down.

Beautiful. She caught him looking at her, stopped chewing.

'What?'

'Nothing,' he said. 'Just looking at you.'

He smiled. She joined him.

Berwicks on Old George Yard off the Cloth Market. The perfect little bistro, thought Tony. Intimate and comfortable yet sleek and fashionable. The kind of place our parents would never have gone to. This was the third time Tony and Louise had eaten there. It was rapidly becoming their favourite restaurant. They didn't even notice the other diners. It was a special place reserved just for them.

They finished their meal, Tony paid, they stepped outside. Began walking along High Bridge. The autumn air was carrying on it the first ice notes of winter. Louise shivered slightly, pulled her coat around her body. Tony placed his arm round her. She snuggled into him. They were a perfect fit.

'Cold?'

'Yes,' she said. 'I should've put something warmer on.'

'You look fine as you are.'

'Maybe, but I'm cold. I should've worn my duffel coat.'

Tony laughed. 'No girlfriend of mine's going to walk around in a duffel coat.'

'And why's that?'

'Because I'll soon be earning enough to keep her in style. Stick around, you'll see.'

She snuggled further into him. He couldn't see her face, but he knew she was smiling.

'Shall we go for a walk?' Tony said when they reached the corner of Grey Street.

'Shouldn't you have an early night? Don't you have to be up for training in the morning?'

'Yeah, but that's tomorrow.'

'I don't want my future life of luxury wrecked before it's even started.'

Tony grinned. 'It won't be. Trust me.'

Louise looked in his eyes, liked what she saw, returned his smile. 'OK, then.'

They walked along Dean Street, down the Side, on to the Quayside. Above them, the massive floodlit supports of the Tyne Bridge; opposite, the multicoloured fairy lights of the Tuxedo Princess, the floating nightclub. Along the front, bars and cars, old warehouses, a few flats. And the Tyne below them lapping the sides, catching the light, glinting like ephemeral diamonds bobbing on dark spilled oil, too quick to grasp, then gone, borne out to the open sea.

They leaned on the railings, looked out at the river.

'This is my favourite part of Newcastle,' said Tony.

'Mine too.'

They huddled closer together.

'You know what you said before?' asked Louise. 'About me sticking around?'

'Yeah.'

'Well, how long did you have in mind?'

Tony turned to her. The lights caught Louise's eyes. Made them glint like diamonds.

'As long as you like,' he said.

Tony took a deep breath, looked at her. Those eyes. Those diamonds. But not the unreachable ones of the river. They were here. Real and attainable. Not hard or cold, just beautiful and precious.

'Look, I'm ... I'm not very good at this sort of thing. I haven't ... haven't done it before. But look, Louise, I just...'

He sighed. She waited.

'I love you. I've never felt like this about anyone before. I don't think I ever will again. I love you and never want to be without you. Ever.'

He sighed again. He was shaking. Despite the cold, he was sweating.

Louise smiled.

'It means a lot to hear you say that. And I know how difficult it was for you to say it. And I love you. I feel exactly the same. And I hope we're never apart. Ever.'

They grabbed each other, pulling together, wanting flesh to join, to meld. They kissed, mouths devouring, demanding more than touch, wanting the other's life, their soul.

Love.

Consuming, rebirthing love.

Holding on. For ever.

Keith watched.

Parked inconspicuously behind several other cars on the Quayside. Looking like a predatory minicab waiting to shovel up the waterfront drunks expelled onto the pavement at closing time.

They hadn't seen him. That was a small triumph he could hold on to. Not when the new boyfriend picked her up. Not when they drove, parked and went to the restaurant. Not when they came out. And not now.

He watched them in the restaurant, anger welling. It was the kind of place he couldn't afford on his salary. So that was what she saw in him.

They hadn't seen him. No one had. He had melted into the shadows so perfectly it had been like he didn't exist: a shadow himself.

A young couple had come out of the pub with an urgent passion for each other. The boy had pushed his girl up against a wall right next to where Keith had been hiding. He had pushed up her skirt and pulled down her knickers while she had undone his jeans. They had fucked there and then, hard and fast. So close that Keith could have reached out of the darkness and touched them.

The sight had made his own cock hard. He had wanted to knock the boy out of the way and take the girl himself. But he hadn't. He had just watched. He would have settled for a wank but he hadn't dared. Because he might have lost his focus. And he had a job to do.

The episode had left him hungry, unfulfilled, and the sight before him, Louise and her new boyfriend devouring each other, made him feel even worse. At least that slut and her boyfriend had fucked in the dark away from watching eyes. Louise, Keith thought, was just turning into a whore.

They broke apart, walked away. Smiling. Like they had put on a show specially for Keith. A show that he could only watch and not take part in. Louise showing him how she paid for her rich boyfriend's attention.

He felt his anger twist and bubble up inside him.

He knew where they were going. Where the boyfriend had parked his car on Grey Street. They would drive back to Louise's flat. Sometimes the boyfriend would go in, sometimes not. He seemed to have a set pattern. Tuesday night. He wouldn't stay.

Keith started the car, drove to Louise's flat, parked in his usual spot in the alley. Soon, the boyfriend's car pulled up. Keith smiled to himself, taking pride in how accurately he had plotted their routine.

They kissed. He watched. Bile churning in his stomach.

Louise left the car, entered the house, closed the door behind her. The boyfriend sped off.

He watched as an upstairs light went on. Sighed.

'Now we're alone,' Keith said out loud. 'Just you and me together...'

He watched.

The earlier couple came back to him. Fucking hard against the wall. Rough urgency as they took each other.

He could do that with Louise. Just walk over there now. There was nothing stopping him. He could just walk over the road, go straight in, throw her on the bed. Push up her skirt, pull down her knickers. Rough urgency. That would make her see the error of her ways. Soon he would have her begging, pleading with him to take her back.

Yes. Throwing her on the floor. Teaching her a lesson. He liked that idea. His cock stiffened at the thought of it. He got it out, started to stroke it.

He could do it. Just walk over there. Right now. Show her who was boss...

'You're mine, you bitch, you slut...'

Throw her on the floor...

'Bitch... Cunt...'

Slap her if she gave him any lip...

'Whore... Whore...'

Hit her, punch her if he had to...

'Bitch...'

Boss. He'd show her who was boss...

He came.

Spurting over the steering wheel, over the front of his trousers.

He opened his eyes, looked quickly around. No one there, no one had witnessed him.

Good.

The light went out in the flat.

Keith found a handkerchief in his pocket, wiped himself down.

He sighed, composed himself. He waited for the guilt to come. Expected some kind of post-ejaculatory shame for his thoughts.

But none came. In fact it was the opposite. He felt quite pleased with himself.

He settled back for the night.

Watching.

Waiting.

Biding his time.

For the right time.

## 12. Now

Tommy parked the Daimler in the visitors' car park, turned off the engine, sat listening to the CD player.

Diana Krall: *Boulevard of Broken Dreams*.

A blues voice of smoke and seduction, of loss and late-night loneliness wrapped in a body of blonde beauty. A slice of darkness in daylight.

The perfect Cathy.

He checked his watch: two p.m.

Visiting time.

The stone lodged in his chest fell all the way to the pit of his stomach.

He took a deep breath, locked the car, walked to the entrance, concrete and plaster concealing century-old red brick, and began the procedure.

The visiting order checked, the duty desk officer asked: 'Relation?'

Tommy looked him in the eyes.

'Son.'

The officer nodded, let him through the first door.

He joined the queue, was patted down, had a metal detector run over him, had his mobile taken, a receipt issued, was smelled by a sniffer dog.

Then another door, this one not opening until the previous one was firmly closed.

And finally through. Up a corridor, round the corner, a wait while the officer unlocked the door, locked it behind them. Into a room of Formica-topped tables and orange plastic chairs, men sitting at them wearing matching orange bibs.

Durham prison. Visits.

Tommy scoped the room. The men were physically different, racially mixed, various ages, but they all shared something in common. It wasn't something they had, rather something they lacked; an absence rather than a presence. A wilful deadening to outside stimuli, the reconfiguring of shrunken horizons and expectations, the recalibration of time.

The look of the lifer.

Clive Fairbairn sat at his table, hands together, back straight, a desk-bound CEO awaiting an underling's report or a headmaster awaiting a pupil's excuses.

The boss was fronting it, performing the

illusion of empire, but he was looking old, tired. Prison, although Mr Fairbairn wouldn't admit it, Tommy thought, was being tough on him.

Tommy sat down.

'Hello, Tommy.' It was an old man's voice. Still shot through with steel, but corroded.

'Huh-hello, Mr Fairbairn.'

Tommy swallowed hard. In moments of stress his voice still gave him away. It was a reminder of where he had come from, of what he still was underneath the expensive cars and fine suits. He willed himself to relax, mentally speed-ran the exercises the speech therapist had given him.

'How are you doing?'

That was better. Back in control.

Fairbairn looked around, gestured. 'I'm in prison. How d'you think I'm doing?'

Tommy nodded. 'They treating you all right?'

Fairbairn sighed, softened his attitude slightly. 'It's not too bad, I suppose. You get used to it. You ride it.'

Tommy nodded. 'Thanks for sorting the invite.'

Fairbairn nodded.

'Son.' Tommy smiled. 'Nice.'

'Yeah, well, there was a time.'

'What d'you mean?'

Fairbairn leaned forward. The movement caught the eye of a prison officer. Fairbairn sat back.

'I've been hearing things, Tommy. Word gets to me.'

'Wh-what d'you mean, things?'

'That you've taken your eye off the ball. You're going soft.'

318

Tommy stared at him. His eyes flint, his face stone. Like Fairbairn had taught him.

'I don't know who said that,' said Tommy, 'but they told you wrong.'

'I hope so, son. Because I don't want to get out of here and find nothing left for me. Know what I'm saying? And I will get out, you mark my words. I'm not paying good money to that bunch of overpaid briefs for nothing, you know.'

Tommy swallowed.

'Don't worry, Mr Fairbairn. Everything is in good hands. You know that. You can trust me.' Tommy smiled. 'Like family, you used to say.'

Fairbairn stared at him. Flint and stone. 'No smoke without fire.'

Tommy sighed. 'Listen. Everything is being run exactly as if you were there. There's no trouble.'

'So why am I hearing things?'

'Because with you in here all the chancers come out of the woodwork. They all see it as their time has come, you know? They make sure you hear things because they know they'll prey on your mind. Especially in here. Set you wondering, set us at each other's throats. So we destroy ourselves and you've got nothing to come out to. And they take over.'

Fairbairn kept his eyes on Tommy. The words were absorbed, like a stolen car sinking slowly to the bottom of a deep lake.

And in that moment, eyes unguarded, defences stripped down, worry marking his face, Tommy saw Fairbairn as he really was.

Not the feared/revered head of the biggest firm in the north-east, but an old man: scared, alone,

319

deluding himself about being released again, knowing in his heart he was here to die.

'Well...'

'Don't worry, Mr Fairbairn, everything'll be fine for when you come out.'

Fairbairn sighed, nodded. 'Yeah. You just... In here...'

'I know.' Tommy's voice had softened.

'No, you don't.' Fairbairn's eyes were suddenly ablaze. Like a spark of life animating a clay golem. Activated. Ready to rip out hearts. 'Don't you ever tell me what it's like in here. Ever. You have no idea.'

'Suh-sorry, Mr Fairbairn. You're right,' Tommy said quickly.

Fairbairn subsided, nodded.

They sat silently, looking at anything but each other.

Some of the other prisoners had wives and children meeting them. The younger children played in a play area in the corner, content. The older ones sat at the tables, sullen for the most part, unable or unwilling to equate the person opposite them with the word father. The wives looked at their husbands. Representatives of two different worlds looking for common ground conversations, hardly speaking, communicating through silence and near silence, or chatting volubly and incessantly, thin smiles papering over deep and, in most cases, irreparable cracks and chasms.

'How's Caroline?' said Fairbairn, eventually.

Tommy's eyes aimed for flint, missed. 'Fine,' he said. 'She sent her love.'

Fairbairn's eyes glittered. A smile that most

320

people would have missed appeared at the corners of his mouth. Cold. Mirthless.

'Tell her I send it back.'

Tommy swallowed hard. He tasted bitterness in his mouth. 'I will.'

They then set sail on a sea of silence for the remainder of the visit, making only occasional forced landings on to islands of words. Fairbairn began to reminisce, relive old triumphs. The action of a man whose best was in the past, whose future was grey and small. Tommy joined in, indulged him, played straight man.

Then time to go.

'Good to see you, Mr Fairbairn. Glad you're well. Thanks for inviting me.'

Fairbairn smiled. 'Call me Clive. After all this time.'

Tommy smiled. 'Clive.' The name seemed strange coming from his mouth. It fitted like a glove two sizes too small.

'But listen.' Fairbairn's smile disappeared. His eyes were suddenly hard and bright again. 'Whatever's going on, sort it. And quickly.'

'Yes, Mr Fairbairn.'

Time was up. Fairbairn was escorted, along with the other prisoners, back to his eight-by-four world. The visitors, patted down, mobiles returned, were free to go.

Back in the car park, Tommy checked the Daimler for signs of vandalism, found none, got in. Diana Krall was soon back in his ears, his mind.

He started the engine, changed the CD. He wanted something different.

He flicked around the five installed discs.

Sinatra. Dino. Billie Holiday. Dino. Back to Diana.

He switched it off, drove out of Durham and back home in silence.

He wanted something different.

But he didn't have it. And he didn't know what it was.

Karl supplied, Davva and Skegs sold. The system was simple and good. It worked.

Their territory was now the whole of the T. Dan. They had regulars. Clients, Karl called them. They worked their market, got to know their customers' needs, who wanted what. Blow. Skunk. Crack. E. Horse. Got stuff on demand. Uppers. Downers. Speed. Tried not to miss an opportunity to sell.

They stashed stuff all over the estate. Merchandise. Money. Behind loose bricks, buried in secret places. The golden rule: carry as little money or product as possible at any time. Karl had wised them up, trained them well: don't get caught. If you do get caught, don't get done as dealers. And don't give up names.

They cycled the length and breadth of the estate, sorting clients out. Strictly cash. No cash, no hash. Karl took his share of the wedge, left them with their wages. When they weren't working, they were having fun. In the arcades, on the video games, the bandits, the pool tables. Feeding themselves on burgers, kebabs, chicken. Chips with everything. Lifting, or occasionally buying, designer gear and CDs.

They were living it, larging it, loving it.

Skegs drew all the mucus from the tubes in his

face into his mouth, rolled it, and let it fly. It landed square in the middle of the lamppost.

'Beat that,' he said, triumph lighting up his face.

Davva, sitting next to him on the wall, looked at his friend. Skegs had beaten him in everything today. He had stunt-ridden his mountain bike without falling off. Davva had fallen off. He had got a higher score on Quake in the arcade. Davva kept dying. And now the spitting contest.

Davva got down off the wall. No point in even taking part.

'Wassamatter?' said Skegs.

'I'm goin' home.'

'What for?'

Davva shrugged. 'Just am.'

'But we've still got stuff to do. We've got to go to your Tanya's.'

'You do it. I'm goin' home.'

Davva started to walk off.

'See you later.'

He left Skegs sitting alone on the wall, confused by Davva, but proud of his spit.

Davva walked through the T. Dan dragging his feet, in no hurry to reach his destination. He hated going home. Only went there when he had nowhere else to go. Best thing about it: his stuff was there. Worst thing about it: his parents were there.

He reached the house. A small square box terraced to a row of identical small square boxes. An occasional burned-out or boarded-up one broke the monotony Davva's house was neither well nor badly maintained. It was just there.

His footsteps slowed further. Legs dragged as he walked round the back, opened the gate, let himself into the postage-stamp-sized strip of blasted barren earth described by his parents as a garden.

He opened the kitchen door and entered. His mother was there unloading carrier bags, putting pans on the gas. She stopped what she was doing, looked at him.

'Oh. So you're back, then.'

She didn't smile.

Davva nodded, grunted.

'I suppose you want feedin', then.'

'Aye.'

'Where've you been, then?'

Davva shrugged, started to rummage in a carrier bag for something to eat. His mother grabbed the bag off him.

'Get yer thievin' fingers out of there.'

He got his thieving fingers out of there.

'We're havin' chips, sausages and fried eggs if you want to eat with us.'

'Smashin'.'

Davva's mother: big to start with, getting bigger. He saw she had a packet of biscuits open on the worktop, saw her help herself to one. A new packet, straight from the shopping. Davva noticed it was nearly half-empty She crunched the biscuit round in her mouth, absently, as if she was just giving her jaws something to do. Her face was fat: piggy big, but hard. Davva could never remember her laughing or even smiling much when he was around. Less when Tanya had been at home. All he had got from her was questions. Judgements. It was all he had ever got from her.

The emotions Davva felt for his mother had full titles. They had been named and documented. But not by him. So he didn't know what he felt for his mother. He couldn't name it.

And he had no idea what she felt for him.

'Where's me fatha?'

'Front room,' she said through a mouthful of biscuit.

Davva wandered into the front room. His father was sitting in an armchair, *Mirror* on his knee, *Neighbours* on the box, rolling a fag.

'Hello, bonny lad.' He smiled at Davva.

'Hiya.'

Davva sat on the settee, stared absently at the prancing Aussie bimbos and himbos.

'Had a good day?'

Davva shrugged.

'All right.'

'Where you been?'

'Round.'

Davva didn't take his eyes off the TV. He knew there were questions his father wanted to ask, answers he didn't want to hear. But his father wouldn't ask them. He was too weak. So if he stared at the screen long enough, the questions would go away.

'Hey,' said Davva's dad, deliberately changing the subject, 'did I tell you about the football match on Sunday. You shoulda been there, man. Hey, it was crackin'.'

'Aye.'

'I played, y'kna. Second half.'

Davva nodded.

'Helped set up the goal.'

Davva watched TV.

'You know, that's what you should do. Play football. Give you an interest. Somethin' to do. You'd like it.'

*Neighbours* finished. The air in the house was thick with more than frying: a kind of squandered energy that started with his parents and radiated outwards. Like they'd given up and you could feel it. Davva noticed it every time he set foot in the house. He thought of it as an airborne disease, something he could catch if he sat there long enough. He got up, went upstairs.

His room had a padlock nailed to it. He had done it himself. He took the key from the back pocket of his D&G jeans and opened it.

Inside, it was a teenage boy's Aladdin's cave. PS2. Games. DVDs. CDs: Garage and RnB. Portable CD player, bass-heavy.

Clothes in the wardrobe, label-heavy.

In a slit in the bed base: stashed notes. A small supply of pills. Draw. Es. Personal use only. Not for sale.

He slid the bolt into place on the door and relaxed.

This was his space. The only place he felt safe in the whole word. He could lock everyone and everything else out, forget about them. Just be himself. His parents' disease couldn't touch him in here.

He didn't know what he had been feeling when he left Skegs. Some sort of sadness. He couldn't name it. All he knew was when he felt it he wanted to be home, in his room, surrounded by his own things. Things he'd bought with his own money or lifted with his own skill. He drew comfort from them. Found solace in them.

He crossed to the CD player, stuck in a CD.

UK garage. The best.

He whacked up the volume, rolled a spliff, opened the window.

He lay on the bed, beats thumping their way into his brain, draw easing its way into his mind. Soothing him, stopping the sad thoughts. Stopping any thoughts.

He took another drag, held the smoke in his chest until it burned, exhaled. Felt the numbness rush to his head.

He smiled. Not happy, but near to it.

Angela threw the sausages into the pan, ignoring the hot fat pin-spitting at her, and sighed. She made her way into the front room, stood hands on hips, looking down at Mick.

'Listen to that,' she said, pointing up at the ceiling. 'Do we have to put up with that?'

'Boy's got to do somethin',' said Mick, not meeting her eyes. 'You were a teenager once.'

'Not like that. Not like him. Those locks on his room...'

'He needs privacy. Boy his age. It's natural.' Mick's hands were shaking as he placed the roll-up between his lips.

'It's not natural. No shuttin' us out like that. And where does all that stuff he's got come from, eh? You never ask him about it.'

Mick cleared his throat, swallowed.

'Neither do you.'

'I wash me hands of the whole thing. He's like

327

his sister. Just as bad. He has to learn, like her, that you either toe the line in this house or you get out.'

Mick said nothing. He held the match with both hands as he lit his roll-up. He looked at the TV. Tried to be interested in the election coverage.

'Are you listenin' to me?'

He looked up.

'Aye, pet. Aye.'

Angela looked at him, her eyes hard, unreadable.

'You're his father. You say somethin' to him.'

'Aye. Aye.'

Mick smoked, watched TV.

She left the room, went back to the kitchen.

The tea was soon ready and dished up. Mick was instructed to shout upstairs for their son. The music went off, the door was re-padlocked. Down he came. Davva took his seat at the kitchen table.

They ate in silence.

The occasion felt uncomfortable, unfamiliar. They weren't a family who sat down together at mealtimes. Or hadn't been for a long time. Davva's presence made them regard each other as strangers.

'Your father has somethin' to say to you,' said Angela through a mouthful of sausage.

Mick looked up.

'Now?'

'Yes. Now.'

Mick swallowed, looked thoughtful.

'Listen, son. Wh-where you been today?'

'Around.'

328

'It's just that … me an' your mother, we get, you know, we think you should be at school or somethin'. Learnin'.'

'No point, is there? No jobs.'

Mick's voice sounded hollow in his own ears. 'But you have to go to school–'

'Why? So I can spend all me life on the dole? Like you?'

Mick put his knife and fork down, stopped eating.

'Don't speak like that to your father,' said Angela. 'You with all that stuff in your room. Where did all that come from, eh? Where's the money? Here's us haven't got two pennies to rub together and there's you with all that stuff up there. Well?'

Davva stood up.

'Is that it, is it?'

He thrust his hand into his jeans pocket, gathered up whatever notes were in there and flung them down on the table.

'There,' he said. 'If that's what you want, take it.' He walked away, leaving his tea half-eaten, and went straight out the back door, slamming it as he went. Mick and Angela sat still, not looking at each other, Mick not eating. Angela absently forking in mouthfuls, the money lying on the table between them. They sat like that for a long time. Eventually Angela finished, placed her knife and fork on the plate, sighed.

'Well,' said Mick, his voice small, hesitant, 'least he's helpin' out with money If he's got it comin' in, he should be doin' that.'

Angela looked at the notes lying there, then

slowly reached across the table and picked them up. She counted them, pocketed them. She nodded, stood up.

They didn't know what they were feeling. They couldn't name it.

'I'll get the puddin',' Angela said.

Her voice was rich with the disease Davva believed she had.

Coldwell Colliery was opened in 1901. The seam was expected to last for nearly two hundred years. It was owned by the Northumbrian Colliery Company. Hartsdean House was where the NCC had its headquarters. An imposing Edwardian structure, heavy with red brick and soot. It lay to the north of Coldwell colliery, and from the top floor the three businessmen who owned it could look out over the mine, watching the winding tower wheels turn, calculate how much coal could be turned into profit.

In 1947, when the industry was nationalized, the house was sold off. For years it was a nursing home then, when the owners went bankrupt, the building was allowed to become derelict. In 2001 a brewery bought the land and razed it.

The Hartsdean pub was new, themed and chained. It smelled not of ale and smoke but of fragrance and polish. Faux Victoriana-facaded CD jukeboxes pumped out bland and palatable background noise. Computerized tills beeped. Electric gas flickering on the wall, dimmer controlled from behind the bar, bounced a warm glow off the factory-produced stained-glass windows.

The pub had a bar and a dining area. Waiting

staff costumed as Victorian maids and man-servants could be glimpsed going about their duties. There were outdoor and indoor children's play areas. Trestle tables bordered an artificial lake built on the site of the deepest seam of the old mine, where twelve men lost their lives in a gas explosion in 1919. All around the lake, new trees and shrubs were planted, encased in white plastic sleeves, like grave markers for dead soldiers. A large gravelled car park was sprinkled with luxury saloons. Beyond was the roof of the leisure centre. Beyond that sprawled the T. Dan.

'So what d'you want to know, exactly?'

Dave Wilkinson sat in a Liberty-print chair, a glass of orange juice on the dark wood table in front of him. He was again tracksuited, gym bag at his side.

Larkin sat in the chair opposite him. Stubbled, dishevelled, with a bottle of lager and a dicta-phone beside him. He had performed the obliga-tories: thanked Wilkinson for meeting at short notice, allowed Wilkinson to pick the venue, assured him his work would be seen in nothing but a good light and that anything remotely contentious would be quoted anonymously.

Larkin switched on the dictaphone: the red light glowed.

'We'll start with just an overview. How d'you see the role of the police today in Coldwell?'

'Well, Stephen, my area, and therefore the only one I can really comment on with any kind of authority, is community policing. I'm based on the T. Dan. You'll have seen our mobile police station, the Portakabin?'

Larkin hadn't but nodded that he had.

'Well, that's where my team is based. As you know, the T. Dan is an area with a lot of problems. Crimes against the person and property. Street crime. Theft, burglary. Very common. The majority of them drug-related. What we're there to do is give residents a reassuring presence, let them drop in for a cup of tea if they want, share their concerns with us, show them they haven't been forgotten. And act as a deterrent, of course. It's policing based on the needs of the community. A set of initiatives implemented after consultation with local residents themselves.'

It wasn't an answer; it was a recitation. Management-speak bullshitters r us. He'll go far, thought Larkin.

'Which means what, in real terms?'

'It means a more holistic approach to policing. People who commit crimes do so for many different sociological and psychological reasons. We have to balance that alongside the victim's view. We have to make people feel safe within their own homes and on their own streets. Bottom line.'

Wilkinson sipped his orange juice. Smacked his lips as if he enjoyed it. Smiled.

Larkin smiled back.

'Far cry from the miners' strike, isn't it? Sounds more like you're social workers in uniform.'

It looked like the orange juice had soured in Wilkinson's mouth.

'As I said to you the other day, I wasn't here during the miners' strike. I was just starting university then. I can't speak for what happened then. Nor would I want to. The force has changed

332

since then. Moved on. Everything has. It's a different world now.'

Larkin took a pull from the neck of his beer bottle.

'So how d'you get on with Tony Woodhouse?'

Wilkinson thought before answering. Whether he was deciding to get up and leave or just formulating his thoughts on Tony Woodhouse, Larkin couldn't tell.

'He's a good man to work with.'

'I wouldn't have thought you two would agree on many things.'

'There's a common ground.'

Larkin nodded to encourage Wilkinson to continue. Instead he leaned across the table and switched off the dictaphone. Larkin looked startled. Wilkinson smiled.

'I know where you're going with this line of questioning. I've worked out how you operate. You want me to admit that I'm in favour of decriminalization. Perhaps even legalization. Well, I might be. But if I am, I wouldn't admit it to you.

'You said social workers in uniform before. Well, you're right. That's what we do. We pick them up, listen to their hard luck stories, try to sort them out with something or someone that'll keep them on the straight and narrow. We do everything but wipe their noses and arses. They tell us they're the victims. And yes, some of them have been through hell themselves. And some of them have had terrible lives, worse than we can imagine. And some of them are just plain bad. Plain nasty. And we try to work out which is which and we treat them accordingly.

'But for all that, they're all the same. There's one thing they've got in common. A victim. Some eighty-year-old granny's frightened to live in her own home. Some honest, hard-working bloke's had his car nicked and torched by joyriders and he can't afford the insurance any more. Some girl's terrified of going out now in case the boys who raped her are still out there. Victims. We've become a society of victims. We're all victims. It's my job to work out who are the real ones.'

Wilkinson looked at his watch, drained his glass.

'Now, if you'll excuse me, I've got to go. I've got a squash partner waiting.'

He stood up. Larkin did otherwise.

'Dave?'

Wilkinson turned.

'Thank you for your honesty. I appreciate it. I just wished you'd let me keep the tape on.'

Wilkinson searched Larkin's face for any trace of sarcasm. He found none. 'Thank you.'

'That's OK. There is one other thing.'

'Yes?'

'Tommy Jobson. D'you know him?'

'Know of him. Why?'

'I thought I saw him at the charity football match the other day. That's all.'

'I wouldn't know. Wouldn't be surprised, though. That type think that giving to charity makes up for everything else. Now, if you'll excuse me.'

Wilkinson walked out, bag in hand.

Larkin sat down again, pocketed the dictaphone. He got to work on his beer, looking around the pub as he did so.

334

Wilkinson's words: it's a different world now.

The minimum wage barstaff, dressed in their Victorian weeds, were serving families disgorged from the Beamers and Mercs in the car park.

Larkin drained his bottle, stood up to leave.

Not that different, he thought.

Skegs climbed the stairs. He didn't even bother with the lift.

Cold concrete underfoot, cold plastic handrail. The block the twin of the one he lived in. He kept his hands beside him, not touching the rails. He had heard the stories: junkies leaving old syringes sticking out, needles upright, waiting to catch people unaware, share their previous owner's bad blood.

The air was cold. Even in the summer the air in the stairwell was cold. It smelled of old piss, so ingrained that Skegs barely noticed. The walls were scrawled with graffiti. Tags and messages: lives recorded, registered, writ large. A small slice of fame, immortal until they faded or were covered over.

Skegs felt strange, nervous. He doubted anyone would attack him – everyone knew who he was, who he worked for. A lone nutter might have a go but no one else. The thing that troubled him was being alone.

Davva was moody and hated to come second in anything. He was often cruel to Skegs, sometimes even beating him up. But despite all that, he was still Skegs's best friend. He did everything with Davva, and now he was on his own.

Strange. Nervous.

He reached the landing, found the correct door, knocked.

A chill wind carried old tabloids and kebab wrappers past his feet. He looked over the walkway, saw only dark towers against dark skies. He shivered.

The door opened. Tanya stood, holding on to the scarred wooden door as if it was the only thing keeping her upright.

Skegs looked at her, shocked. Her hair was lank and unwashed, absorbing light rather than reflecting it, her eyes dark-ringed. She was wearing something long and shapeless: a T-shirt, a nightie or even a shroud. She was shaking. She looked ill.

'Are y'all right, Tanya?'

She looked at him, hard, as if trying to focus through frosted glass. She smiled, showing teeth that needed attention.

'Our Davva's mate.'

She opened the door wide.

'You got somethin' nice for me?'

'Aye.'

Skegs swallowed hard.

'Come in, then.'

He entered. She closed the door behind him, walked down the hall.

Skegs watched her move. Her arse and hips swayed side to side. She was naked under that shift.

He followed her into the living room. It looked even sparser than before. Darker. The overhead light in its dirty frilled shade cast everything in harsh illumination, like an ugly truth exposed.

There was less furniture, only an old sofa, a small table. Carpet just an absorbent repository for dirt and waste.

Off the main room he could see the kitchen and the bedroom. The kitchen looked and smelled awful. Dishes piled up and mouldering, overflowing bins, old food left to rot. The bedroom consisted of a mattress covered by a stained sheet. It looked like it had been well used.

'Where's the telly?'

Tanya looked to where the TV had stood. She shrugged.

'Sold it.'

Skegs noticed something else about the flat. It was silent.

'Is the baby asleep?'

Tanya looked puzzled. She frowned. Then her eyes slowly lit up, like a reflection of the light cast by the overhead bulb.

'Oh, yeah. Someone's ... lookin' after her.'

She nodded, confirming the words as truth to herself.

Skegs didn't want to be there any more. It was as if bad spirits were living in the flat. He felt depressed and scared. He wanted to conclude his business, then leave.

Tanya's eyes were now misty and distant. Lost.

'I've got your stuff.'

She came back, crossed to Skegs. Smiled.

'Mmm. Gimme. Gimme.'

He took a bag from his pocket. She grabbed for it, hungry. He held it out of her reach.

'Money first.'

She turned and ran to the bedroom. He heard

her scrambling around. She came running back out, tits wobbling as she ran, Skegs noticed, notes and coins clenched in her fist.

'Here.'

She dumped them in his palm, made a grab for the bag. He again moved it out of her reach while he counted the money.

'There's not enough.'

Panic crossed her features.

'What?'

'There's not enough. You know the price.'

Her eyes filled with desperation.

'How much is missin'?'

'Five pounds nearly.'

'I'll get you the money. I'll pay you next time.'

Skegs shook his head, pocketed the bag. Bad spirits. Conclude and leave.

'I'm sorry, Tanya. Karl says I can't do that. He says I need to get the money. I can't make any exceptions.'

'Karl…'

A fox-cunning smile spread over her features.

'Sometimes I didn't have the money for Karl. He used to let us off.'

'He says I can't do that, Tanya.'

'I used to give him somethin', though.'

She smiled. Her teeth yellow, her breath stale. Her mouth looked like a sucking wound. She licked her dry, cracked lips. She dropped to her knees, began pulling open Skegs' jeans.

'This is what I used to do for Karl…'

Skegs jumped back, away from her fingers.

'What you doin'?'

She followed him on her knees.

338

'Come on, don't be shy...'

He moved further back, felt his legs connect with the sofa. He lost his balance, fell on to it.

'D'you want us naked, is that what it is?'

She pulled the shift over her head. Skegs looked at her body Ribs poking through skin, breasts tired and droopy. Her skin was bone-white, marbled and blemished by dark needle tracks, picked scabs, infected ulcers. Her pubic hair was dirty and matted. He was repelled by her.

But, apart from his mother and a cousin when he was little, she was the first naked female he had ever seen. He had always fancied Davva's sister. When they were growing up and she started to develop tits, Skegs was always trying to see them. When she began going out with older boys, Skegs would try to imagine what they were doing together.

Despite everything, he felt himself getting hard. She opened his jeans, pulled out his cock.

'You're goin' to love this...'

He closed his eyes, tried not to think of that horrible mouth touching his skin. That awful diseased-looking body wrapped around his legs. He thought of how she used to look. When she used to give him glimpses of her tits when she bent over. When he used to stare at her arse in a tight skirt. When she used to smile and laugh.

He imagined sunlight and kisses and love. Lots of love. Bodies entwined, rolling and rolling together.

He came, thought of her and smiled.

Then he opened his eyes. Bad spirits.

Tanya was kneeling on the floor spitting into

the carpet, her scabbed and tracked body shining in the ugly light. She looked up at him. He smiled. She didn't return it. There was only fear and pleading in her eyes. Need in her voice.

'So you gonna let me off with the money, then?'

Skegs looked at her, clear-eyed. He saw her not as she was but as she had become. A junkie whore. Stinking and drug-ugly.

He stood up, fastened his trousers. He threw her the bag, opened his mouth to speak to her, but she was already away into the bedroom, her whole world shrunk to the size of a small polythene bag.

He let himself out, closed the door, stood on the landing. He saw only dark towers against dark skies.

He thought of what had just taken place. His heart sank, like a rock thrown down a deep, dark well.

He wanted to scream, cry, throw up, go home.

But he couldn't do any of them.

So he turned and walked downstairs, trudged to his next delivery.


This is my daughter Caroline, old Ken Norris had said, grinning.

The girl had smiled. Demure but confident.

Tommy remembered Clive Fairbairn's words: she's a looker. And I hear she likes you. If you like her, that could solve an awful lot of trouble between me and her old man. He had winked then. And give you an awful lot of fun an' all.

Tommy had been struck by her. Anyone would have been struck by her. Auburn haired. Beautifully figured.

I'll just leave you two to get acquainted. Old Ken Norris's grin widened. It swallowed him up. He disappeared.

Hello, I'm Tommy. He was testing out his new voice. Modulated. Speech therapied. It was working well. He smiled.

Can I get you a drink?

And that was the start of it.

Now Tommy lay on the bed and watched her dress.

She dropped the thick white towel on the floor and stood before the mirror. Her eyes checked for sags, wrinkles or cellulite on her expensively maintained, health-club-toned body. She nodded to herself, finding little to complain about.

The wedding had been a dream. No expense spared, fairytale stuff.

She had looked beautiful, he had looked handsome.

Old Ken Norris had beamed, Clive Fairbairn had treated it like the wedding of a favourite son. The two men were united, drinking together at the reception, laughing at each other's jokes, back slaps and hugs when they made their red-faced, tottering goodbyes.

Just like Romeo and Juliet, old Ken Norris had said several times.

And Tommy and Caroline had their beautiful new house filled with beautiful new things in a beautiful part of Northumberland and a beautiful new car to drive them there.

No expense spared, fairy-tale stuff.

Romeo and Juliet.

And that's when it started to go wrong.

The underwear was next: lacy, filmy, silky things, stroking her body like pastel gauze and scraps of mist. Then the stockings: shiny and sheer and sparkling in the light, held up by lace edges. Legs expensively giftwrapped, an exciting present to open.

She sat down to apply her make-up. It covered, it exposed, it heightened, it darkened. Like a gun in the hands of a killer or a computer to a hacker, she used clothes and make-up like a weapon. A smart bomb with pinpoint accuracy. She always hit her target.

Tommy knew that now. Tommy had once been her target.

And not just Tommy.

At the wedding, his business associates had joked: you'll not have to play around for a while. She'll keep you happy for a few years yet. Long time till she's forty and you'll have to exchange her for two twenties.

Tommy had laughed along. One of the lads.

But not inside. Because he wanted the fairy-tale stuff for himself. He believed in it. He wanted it for real.

Not long afterwards, she had put him right on a few things.

I only did this for my father, she said. I know this was all arranged. So I think we should just keep going as we were before and put on a brave face for them. It's for the best, don't you think?

Tommy wanted to scream and shout: you're my wife! I love you! I want this to last for ever!

But he didn't. As with so many things in his life,

he had just bottled it up. Stonewalled. Said OK.

And that was that. The end of the honeymoon.

Then came the dress. Short enough, tight enough, dark. Simultaneously concealing and revealing. Heeled shoes and one last tousle of the hair. Spray of Ghost. She was ready.

'I'll be late,' she said. 'You don't need to wait up.'

He nodded.

She left.

He looked around the bedroom. Cream, gold and off-white, pillows and duvets as soft as clouds in dreams. The rest of the house was the same. As opulent as a palace.

As constraining as a prison.

Just like a fairy tale.

He heard the rev of the engine, Caroline speeding away in her BMW roadster.

She was beautiful. He had to admit that. But cold and hard like a Rodin statue. Unyielding, flawless marble.

There was nothing between them now. Not even illusions.

He sighed, stretched. Thought of Caroline dressing. Something began to stir inside him.

He reached over to the bedside table, picked up the phone, dialled a number by heart. It answered on the third ring.

He said one word.

'Cathy.'

And waited. Eventually, the voice he wanted to hear came on the line.

'At the flat. One hour.'

He smiled. There was no humour in it. Just the

343

hollow smile of a hollow man.

'Come on, Rapunzel,' he said, 'time to let down your hair.'

Larkin dreamed.

He saw Charlotte again. It was the last time. The final time.

They were on the Swing Bridge. They were planning a new future together.

Then Torrington appeared with the shotgun.

And Larkin was again running towards him, trying to stop him from firing, legs weighted down with dream slowness as they had been in real life.

Then the blast. Shattering the night. Echoing down the years, the shockwaves still felt in the present.

And Charlotte was gone.

Larkin woke. Clutching for Charlotte, wanting to hold her, save her. Grasping only air. Ghosts.

He sighed, turned over.

Claire lay on her side, away from him. Naked, breathing deeply.

Lying on one arm, legs lightly crossed.

Etched in charcoal, white against dark.

He moved over, put his arm round her. She shifted slightly, eased her body back on to his.

He sighed, smiled. Felt the dream slip through his fingers like sand. Away.

He held her close, tried to go back to sleep.

It took a while, but it happened eventually.

## 13. Then

Larkin didn't care what he looked like. He only cared about where he was going.

Another day on and his injuries were in spring bloom. Bruises were a swirling Turner mix of purples, reds and blues, with spider webs of green and edges of yellow. They covered his body and face, mingled with scabbed-over gravel rash. He wore them all proudly, like a Pictish tribal warrior marked for battle against the invading hordes of Roman oppressors. His sense of purpose overrode his aching body.

The weather was unseasonably warm. The sun shines on the righteous, Larkin thought.

He had left Bolland's Jesmond flat wearing his cleaned clothes, proudly displaying the scuffs, rips and battlemarks. He had left late morning, timing his walk to the centre of the city. He could have taken the Metro and been there in a matter of minutes, but that didn't smack hard enough of struggle. He could have stayed in Jesmond, but it wasn't the right place for what he was going to do.

He had to walk into town. Motivate his injured body. It was important. Because:

He was going to buy a paper.

Sleep on Bolland's sofa had been fitful, tossing painfully and turning slowly, anxieties and excitements tumbling together. He had tried to compartmentalize. The anxieties: his relationship with Charlotte. His injuries. The direction of the miners' strike.

The excitements: seeing his report in print. Helping to turn public opinion. Shape a new future.

Down Sandyford Road, past the Civic Centre and the Playhouse, on to the Haymarket, down Northumberland Street. He stopped, stood watching a paper seller outside Eldon Square for several minutes. People approached, laid down their coins, walked away with a newspaper. Into their bags, under their arms.

Carrying Larkin's words away with them. He tingled at the thought.

He wrote, they read. So simple, so perfect. He could slip into their minds, put his ideas alongside theirs, let them fight it out for supremacy. Strongest wins. Which would be Larkin. Because his ideas were the strongest.

His words were the truth.

He stepped towards the seller, hand in pocket, but stopped himself.

Not this one. The moment wasn't right.

He continued his walk to Grey's Monument, stood beneath the column, looked around. Grey Street with its gentrified Georgian buildings and Theatre Royal stretched elegantly down to the river before him. Beside that stood Grainger Street, leading to the Grainger Market, the railway station and the lower-rent end of town. To his right, Blackett Street led to Gallowgate, St James' Park football ground and the west end of Newcastle. To the left, New Bridge Street bled away into the rougher environs of Byker. Behind him, Northumberland Street gave way to the rarefied surroundings of Jesmond.

Newcastle. Dead-centre. Rough and smooth, high and low coming together in democratic confluence.

This was where he would buy his paper.

He paid the man, smiling broadly, and placed the paper under his arm. He walked to the base of the monument, feeling the weight of importance contained within the newsprint, and sat down on the stone.

He opened the paper.

There he was on page four. Two-page spread.

His heart pumped blood faster round his body.

He read the title:

COLDWELL PICKET LINE VIOLENCE

Not the title he had given the piece, but he had expected them to change it.

Then he saw the byline:

By Stephen Larkin, Frontline Reporter

That was more like it. Frontline Reporter. That summed up his work. In the battle, at the front line. Sending missives as missiles, with words as incendiary and anything fired from a gun.

He nodded. Frontline Reporter.

Then in smaller letters underneath:

Additional Reporting by Doug Howe

A frisson of confusion. Who? Some staffer? What did that mean?

Then he looked at the photos chosen to accompany the piece:

Pickets pushing at a wall of plastic-shielded riot police. In the foreground an angry miner with crazed, hate-filled eyes clawing back one of the shields, looking as if he were about to rip the policeman's head off, the copper looking scared but stoical.

Pickets throwing makeshift missiles, some with faces covered by scarves and bandanas.

Police retreating along a debris-strewn street, firebombs nipping at their heels, pickets cheering their flight.

Library pictures. Not even from Coldwell.

He began to read.

By the second paragraph, he was stunned.

By the sixth paragraph, he was shaking with rage.

By the eighth paragraph, he was on his feet and walking quickly towards the editorial offices, the newspaper held tightly in his fist, his knuckles white.

Looking for answers.


'What the fuck have you done?'

Bob Carr was standing, elbow on the bar, pint at his fingertips, laughing at a joke he was telling two other journalists. It involved a typesetter replacing the word 'congenial' with 'congenital'. His audience had heard it before and were laughing out of politeness. Bob was laughing so much he didn't notice.

All three turned at the voice. So did the rest of the Groat Bar's lunchtime trade.

'Hello, Stephen.' Bob's tone was uncertain. Trepidation crept into his voice. 'Seen the article?'

Larkin slapped the angrily scrunched-up newspaper down on the bar.

'Yes, I've seen the fuckin' article.'

He looked about to explode.

'Oh.' Bob turned to the other two journalists. 'It's all right. Me and Stephen are going to have a chat.' The journalists moved away, already preparing an anecdote better than Bob's earlier one to tell on their return to work. He turned to the barman who was hovering, fists clenched, ready to wade in. 'It's all right,' said Bob again. 'He just needs a drink.'

'I don't need a fuckin' drink.'

'Get him a pint of lager.'

Larkin stared at Bob, eyes embers of anger. Bob, busying himself with paying, avoided returning the look.

The barman placed the lager down. Larkin ignored it.

'It's there if you want it,' said Bob.

'What I want,' said Larkin, his voice low and deep like underground lava looking for a fissure to erupt from, 'is to know what happened to my fuckin' article.'

Bob swallowed. When he spoke, his voice was small. 'We published it,' he said. 'We paid you for it and published it.'

'No, you didn't,' said Larkin. 'You published something with my name on but that wasn't what

349

I wrote.'

'Well, we subbed it, obviously. Gave it a polish.'

Larkin found the fissure. 'Subbed it? You fuckin' rewrote it! There's nothin' of mine in there, nothin'!'

'Keep your voice down. You'll get us thrown out.'

'I don't give a fuck!'

The barman appeared again.

'Keep your voice down, please, sir. If you don't, I'm gonna ask you to leave.'

He flexed and cracked his knuckles, showed which part of his anatomy would be doing the asking.

'He's all right,' said Bob. 'We're just talking.'

Unconvinced yet unable to intercede, the barman moved away, keeping an eye on the situation.

Bob turned back to Larkin. 'Your piece was good. Very good.'

'So why did you fuck about with it?'

Bob opened his mouth, furrowed his brow. He chose his next words carefully.

'You're a talented writer. An exceptionally talented one, I think. But you have some growing up to do still.'

'Don't patronize me.'

'I'm not patronizing you. I'm telling you the truth.' Larkin took a step closer. So did the barman. Bob flinched.

'I wrote about what was going on in Coldwell on Monday. What I saw. What I experienced. The truth. And what do I find when I open the paper? Propaganda, that's what. Poor me stories about injured policemen. Hate pieces about bullying, violent miners stopping honest folk from going to work. Nothing about what actually happened.'

Bob sighed.

'Stephen. What you wrote was brilliant. But unfortunately we couldn't publish it as it was.'

'Why not?'

'Up till now you've dealt with the small stuff. The free press. The left-wing magazines. And it's fine for them. But if you want to write in the mainstream, you have to be prepared to compromise.'

'Fuck off.'

'It's the truth, Stephen. We've got a readership that comprises all sections of society. All sides. Miners and police. And we don't want to alienate them.'

He took a sip of his beer. Larkin remained silent.

'Plus,' Bob continued, 'we've got to think of the legal perspective. You can't go throwing around unsubstantiated allegations about the police.'

'They're not unsubstantiated. I was there. I saw it happen.'

'So where's the evidence? Where's the pictures?'

'You know where they are.'

'There you go. With them, we'd have had our article. Without them...'

Bob shrugged.

Larkin stared mutely ahead. The lava flowed away.

'Your pint's there,' said Bob.

Larkin picked it up automatically, put it to his

lips, stopped.

'I don't want this.'

He placed it back on the bar.

'Suit yourself.'

Bob took a mouthful of beer, wiped his mouth with the back of his hand.

'You want some advice?' he said. 'Phone Pears. Accept his offer.'

Larkin just looked at him.

'Fuck you.'

'What are you going to do, Stephen? Go back to the magazines with six readers, that pay nothing and think they're changing the world? You've got talent. And ambition. I told you yesterday. There's nothing for you here.'

'Fuck you.'

'Listen, I know you're upset. But listen. I had chances like you once. But I didn't take them. And I've always wished I had.'

Larkin looked at Bob standing there in his threadbare cardigan, his greasy-collared shirt, his dirty, breakfast-stained tie as if seeing him for the first time. A sad, middle-aged man. Not even a has-been, just a never-was. And he understood. Bob couldn't do it himself so, like the man who discovered Jackie Milburn, he wanted Larkin to have success so he could experience it vicariously.

'Do yourself a favour. Phone Mike Pears.'

The barman had lost interest in them. The other two journalists were drinking up, ready to return to work.

Larkin turned and walked out.

Bob stood, watched him go. The other two

journalists put down their glasses, made their way to the door. Bob downed the remains of his beer, reached for his jacket. As he did so, he noticed Larkin's untouched pint on the bar top.

'Waste not, want not,' he said to himself.

He took a mouthful of beer and sat there alone.

A punter put a song on the jukebox:

Prince. 'When Doves Cry'.

Bob took another sip of his beer.

This is what it sounds like.

'Is that Dougie? Dougie Howden?'

'Aye.'

'It's Stephen. Stephen Larkin.'

Silence. Daytime TV rattled tinnily down the wire.

'Stephen Larkin. The journalist.'

A sigh.

'Oh, aye, bonny lad. Aye. Mind's wanderin'.'

The voice on the other end of the phone didn't sound like Dougie Howden. It belonged instead to an old man.

'Listen. Have you seen tonight's paper?'

Another silence, then:

'No, son, I haven't. Stopped gettin' the paper.'

'OK. Well, I just wanted to let you know, there's a piece in it. It's about the strike in Coldwell and it's got my name on it but it's not written by me. Those aren't my words. OK?'

'Aye, lad. I haven't seen it meself but I'll let people know.'

Dougie's voice: detached, somnolent.

It was Larkin's turn for silence.

'Dougie... You all right?'

'All right?' Dougie sighed. 'Aye, I suppose I'm all right.'

'Right. Well, I just wanted to let you know. About the article. I'm sorry, I had nothing to do with it.'

'Never mind, son, you tried your best. We've all done our best.' Another sigh. 'Aye, we've all done our best.'

Dougie's voice didn't just sound old, it sounded weary. Like he had put down a heavy weight he had been carrying for a very long time and was trying to find rest for his weary body.

'Brutality and propaganda, he said. Aye. That's how they do it.' Dougie spoke dreamily, his words like clouds, as if he wasn't sure who he was talking to and didn't care. 'They makin' the world over with brutality and propaganda. Well, let them, eh? Let them. Aye.'

A click and a burr and Larkin was left holding a dead phone.

He replaced the payphone receiver, stepped outside the box.

Late afternoon in Newcastle city centre, back at Grey's Monument.

Movement all around him as commuters began the first stages of their journeys home, shoppers, bags bulging, deciding on one more store before calling it a day. And the unemployed, walking more slowly, less purposefully, with no immediate direction or reachable goal in sight. With one thing in common:

They were stopping to buy a paper.

They would open it on the bus or on the Metro or at home. Maybe they would read the article

354

with his name on it – he couldn't call it his article – maybe they would only glance at it. They would see the headline, the photos. The opinion would be lodged. The message subliminally ingested, the side unconsciously chosen.

He wanted to rush up to the paper seller, knock over his stock, spill his money, shout: Don't read it! It's lies! It's not the truth, I know the truth! I'll tell you the truth!

But he didn't.

He just watched. People putting down coins, picking up newsprint.

He timed, he counted.

As it got busier, the stall averaged six or seven customers a minute. He calculated. Four hundred and twenty people an hour. For three or four hours. From just one seller.

That was what he was up against. That was what he was fighting.

At the other side of the monument were two miners rattling buckets, Coal, Not Dole stickers on both the bucket and them. They looked tired, badly dressed, sallow-skinned. Occasionally passers-by would throw in some coins. They would smile, thank them, hand out stickers in return.

They didn't have as many customers as the paper seller. They didn't make nearly as much money.

That was what they were up against. That was what they were fighting.

Larkin turned away.

He had to think.

He had to meet Charlotte.

The first picture showed a tower block. Empty, but standing. The area around it had been cleared in expectation. A concrete and brick anachronism, out of place with its surroundings, its frame of reference. Its world.

The second picture showed the detonation. Charges placed at the base, blowing out the lower floors, decimating the foundations. The explosive cloud at its base like the lift-off for an Apollo rocket. It looked surprised, if a building could possess such characteristics. It wondered why it was alone, why it was falling instead of others being built to join it.

The third and final picture in the sequence. No longer a building, just a reductive, sprawled mass of brick, mortar and concrete, a fast-billowing dust storm rising overhead. What it had stood for was now unwanted. It couldn't change, it couldn't adapt, so it had to be destroyed. Now it was gone. Unmourned. The world it was a part of gone.

The Side photographic gallery. An exhibition of collapsing buildings by German photographer Dietmar Hacker. Hacker quoted in the exhibition leaflet: The present destroys the past. Every generation creates its own Year Zero. History is never built upon or learned from.

He was talking about his generation's attitudes to the Second World War, but Larkin found something closer to home in the collapsing buildings. His own collapsing beliefs.

He was killing time before meeting Charlotte. He looked at his watch, made his way out.

The city was in crepuscular transition: day wear

356

to evening wear.

He walked to the Swing Bridge, wondering just how much worse his day could get.

He was the first one there. He stood against the old metal handrail of the bridge, watching the Tyne flow out and away from him. Lights were coming on along the quayside. It twinkled picture postcard: bars and restaurants with wish-you-were-here illumination, streets open and friendly. Behind the lights, pooled dark shadows, harsh and dangerous to step in.

Charlotte appeared, walking from the New-castle side, dressed for an evening out.

He looked up, smiled. Waited for her in the middle of the bridge. Waited to meet her halfway.

She attempted to return his smile. It flitted about on her face like a swallow trapped in a barn. As she approached, her eyes widened once she took in Larkin's appearance.

'Hello, Charlotte.'

He moved towards her, made to kiss her. She flinched away.

'What the hell happened to you?'

Her eyes were all over his face.

'I got attacked in Coldwell. Beaten up.'

'The miners?'

'The police.'

Her mouth opened incredulously.

'What did you do to provoke them? Did you get arrested?'

'No, I didn't get arrested. And all Dave and I did was take photos of them beating up miners.'

She shook her head, disbelieving, but trying to

avoid an argument. Her eyes travelled down his body.

'You look a state. We can't go anywhere tonight with you looking like that.'

Larkin felt a match being applied to something hot and glowing inside him. It kindled, flared.

'So, you don't want to be seen with me because my clothes are torn and I've got a few scratches, is that it?'

Charlotte responded. 'Well, look at you. No wonder you stayed at Dave's. I thought you just wanted to give us both time to think. I didn't realize it was because you'd gone twelve rounds with Frank Bruno.'

'Very fuckin' funny. Y'know, that's part of the reason I didn't come home. Because I knew you'd have a go. Have somethin' to say.'

'And why shouldn't I? Just look at you.'

Larkin's pointed finger was stuck in Charlotte's face.

'Don't start. I've had a fuckin' awful day.'

She stared him straight in the eye.

'Oh, diddums,' she said, her voice low, level. 'Poor fucking you.'

Larkin dropped his finger, turned away biting his tongue. He felt an angry retort building inside him but held it in. He allowed it to accumulate, bottled it up, then let it go: a huge sigh directed at the flowing water, the intensity of which left his body trembling.

He remained where he was, leaning on the railing, staring out. Avoiding looking at Charlotte.

Silently she joined him, assumed the same position.

Behind them, traffic passed. People going home, people coming out. Separate lives. Separate worlds.

'My article came out today.' Larkin spoke to the air in a small voice. 'Did you see it?'

Charlotte shook her head. Larkin felt the action more than saw it. 'I thought you'd show it to me tonight.'

He nodded. 'Don't bother. It's not worth it.'

She said nothing.

'They took my words away. They kept my name and took my words away.'

He felt suddenly tired. A huge wave of fatigue washed over him, bringing with it the long-subdued pain from his injuries. He wanted to sit down. He wanted to lie down.

He wanted to give in.

'What d'you mean?' Charlotte's voice softened. She inclined her head towards him slightly.

'They said it was too anti-police. Too pro-miner. So they rewrote it.'

'Well ... I suppose they felt ... they were being honest.'

He turned to face her, not bothering to disguise the pain and hurt in his voice, his eyes.

His heart.

'It was the truth. I told the truth. I wrote about what I saw. If they hadn't taken the photos off us, everyone would have seen.'

'But they did take the photos.' Her voice was not uncompassionate. 'So the article couldn't go ahead.' She shrugged. 'Welcome to the real world.'

The hot and glowing thing was rekindled inside him.

'Don't fuckin' patronize me!'

'I'm not patronizing you. But this is how things are. Why should you be in some way exempt from that? You've just got to accept it.'

He opened his mouth to argue, found he didn't have the strength. He sighed, looked back out at the flowing water. He shook his head.

'I remember when I was little, 1960 something. I remember my dad taking me to the Miners' Gala that year in Durham. Harold Wilson was Prime Minister then. He had come to make a speech. I remember him standing … I think it was on a balcony, an upstairs window... And I remember him smiling. He started talking. My dad sat me on his shoulders so I could see better. Who's that? I remember asking. Harold Wilson, my dad said. He's a great man. So I listened. I can't remember the words but at the end all the men cheered and clapped. And my dad joined in. So I joined in. Because if my dad thought he was a great man, I thought he was a great man.'

'And d'you still think he was a great man?'

Larkin gave a hard sigh.

'No.' His voice sounded as weary as he felt. 'He wasn't a great socialist hero. He was as bent as the rest of them.'

Charlotte turned to him. Looked at him.

'They're all the same, Stephen. All of them. That's why it's not worth it. Why you should just do the best for yourself. Not rely on anyone else.'

'You think so?'

'I do, Stephen.' Charlotte's voice was becoming heated. 'You can't look at the past like it was some golden age and the present just an aberration. It's always been the same. The rich have always been rich. The poor have always been poor. And I know which I'd rather be.'

'I'm sure you do.'

'Yes, I do, and so should you. Idealism's all very well, but you have to grow up some time and make something of yourself.'

That kindling again inside him.

'That's the second time today I've been told to grow up.'

'Well, it's about time, don't you think?'

'It's about time for something, all right. I've had enough.'

'Oh, really?'

'Yeah. I've had enough of your Thatcherite bullshit and your spineless yuppie cunt friends. I've had enough of you never taking me or my work seriously. I've had enough of being fucking patronized.'

Charlotte opened her mouth to speak, words to be guided by the hot anger building up inside, but nothing emerged. Instead, she brought her right hand up, balled it into a fist and crashed it into his face.

Larkin fell back against the railing, his injured state weakening his resistance. His fingers touched his jaw.

'You bitch.' His voice was low, breathy. 'You fucking bitch.'

'Did that hurt, Stephen? I fucking hope so.' Charlotte was breathing heavily, flexing and unflexing her fingers. 'I've wanted to do that for a long time.'

'Oh, have you now?'

Larkin straightened up, stared at her. Her eyes held love flipped to hate: his own eyes mirrored it back at her.

His left arm rose up. He slapped her across the face. Her head snapped sideways with the force.

'Bitch.'

'Bastard!'

And she was on him, hands thumping, nails raking skin, feet kicking. He grabbed her shoulders, hand still stinging, fingers digging through layers of clothes, trying to reach skin, aiming for bone.

They moved up and down the path, grappling, tussling, unchoreographed body movements locking them in a dance of despair. Locked together, fighting to be apart.

Pedestrians dodged them, pointed at them, walked round them.

Cars slowed down for drivers and passengers to get a better view.

Larkin and Charlotte were oblivious to all this, oblivious to everything but themselves.

Eventually they began to tire.

Danced out, Charlotte's feet slowed, her hands stopped. Larkin eased his grip on her. Her head fell on to his chest. They slowed to a standstill. Larkin looked down. Charlotte's shoulders were shaking. She was crying.

His grip altered. He put his arm round her, encircling her, drawing her to him. She allowed herself to be drawn.

Pedestrians began to ignore them. Cars sped by.

Charlotte took deep breaths, attempted to control her tears. She looked up.

'I can't do this any more.' Her voice was cracked, a porcelain vase broken many times and glued back together, its shape preserved, its original beauty tarnished. 'I'm not strong enough.'

They looked at each other, spent, as if by a bout of vigorous lovemaking.

'So what d'you want to do?'

She sighed, ran her fingers through her hair. 'It's not doing us any good,' she said. 'Either of us.'

Her head dropped. Her eyes couldn't meet his.

'I love you.'

Charlotte's body juddered as a fresh onslaught of tears threatened to well up and out of her. She struggled to keep them down.

'I love you probably more than I'll ever love anybody in my life,' she said, her voice strained. 'But this is killing me. Living like this...'

The tears came. She couldn't stop them.

Larkin held her close to him, clung on to her until she rode the crying out.

'What d'you want to do?'

Her voice sounded small, like it was retreating to the end of a long corridor. 'Stay at Dave's tonight. Move your stuff out tomorrow when I'm out.' She sighed, quivered. 'That's the way it's got to be. Sorry.'

She pulled away from him.

'I love you. But I can't bear to be with you.'

She began to walk away.

'I love you too, Charlotte.'

But she was gone. Into the pools of darkness behind the bright lights of the quayside.

And Larkin was alone.

He sat on a bench outside the cathedral, felt the city ebb and flow around him.

The wind struck up. It blew the night's debris over his feet.

Styrofoam kebab boxes. Waxed paper fast-food wrappers with ketchuped chips stuck to them like bloody, severed fingers. Newspapers.

Newspapers.

He looked down. There was today's paper. There were the pictures from his article.

There was his name.

He saw it briefly, then it was gone with the rest of the torn, soiled paper, blowing down the street, joining the rest of the day's effluence.

He sighed.

In the end, that was all it came down to.

He sat, saw the paper float away, watched while it disappeared from sight.

The building was demolished, just rubble and dust. When the paper had gone he stood up, made his way to a payphone, dug a card from his pocket, dialled a number.

Three rings and it was answered. Music tinkled in the background. Smooth and warm, like aural oil. Voices laughing.

'Mike Pears.'

The voice matched the music.

'Hello.' Larkin cleared his throat, tried to remove the hesitancy. 'It's Stephen Larkin here.'

'Stephen. Good to hear from you. How are you?'

It was like the greeting of a long-lost friend.

'Fine.'

'To what do I owe this pleasure?'

Larkin could almost see Pears grin as he spoke.

'The job. Is the offer still open?'

'Do you still want it?'

'Is it still going?'

'Do you still want it?'

Larkin sighed.

'Yes.'

'Then the offer stands. How soon can you get down here?'

Larkin looked around. He saw the city he had grown up in, the only one he had ever lived in. He saw familiar buildings, streets. Saw people on pavements whom he didn't know but who had that familiar north-east look. Stone and brick, concrete and glass. Flesh and blood. Roots and foundations solid. Impervious to change.

'There's nothing to keep me here. I'll be down tomorrow.'

'Good.'

Pears gave him directions and instructions.

'I look forward to seeing you. It's the right decision. You won't regret it. Now I must dash. Dinner guests to entertain. See you tomorrow.'

Larkin said goodbye, recradled the phone.

Then walked away.

# 14. Now

The voice was thrown upstairs, a vocal hand grenade. It landed harshly, exploding on un-appreciative ears.

'Get downstairs now. I won't tell you again.'

'Then don't,' Suzanne mumbled to herself, turned over.

She threw the duvet over her head, snuggled down within. She felt safe inside, cocooned, warm. Too warm, in fact. Hot. But better than being cold. Better than being outside, shivering on an anonymous street corner. Or lying stripped and cuffed to a hard bed in a shivery, antiseptic room.

She heard footsteps on the stairs, an angry bustle. She lay still, anticipating.

The duvet was pulled roughly from her body.

'Get up. Now. And get ready for school.'

Her mother's voice: tired, battle-weary, but still fighting.

'I'm not going. I don't want to.'

Suzanne's voice: flatlining in her own ears, toneless, dead.

'You're going to get up.'

'I feel sick. I'm not going.'

'There's nothing wrong with you. Get up.'

'I'm not going.'

A sigh from her mother, the bunched duvet thrown to the floor. Face-to-face close.

'You're in the last year of your GCSEs. You

need to go. And as long as you're living under my roof, young lady, and part of this family, you'll do what I tell you.'

Eye-to-eye contact. Louise held. Suzanne, eventually, dropped.

Her body felt like lead as she swung her legs over the side of the bed and on the floor.

Louise sighed, straightened up.

'Come on down. I'll get your breakfast ready.'

Her voice had softened, warmed. A truce in the battle.

Suzanne nodded.

'What's that?'

Louise's voice was sharp again. She grabbed Suzanne's right hand, examined the wrist.

'And that one.' She grabbed the other wrist. 'What's that? How'd you get these?'

Suzanne knew what her mother was staring at but looked anyway. Saw the circular bruises, new piled on old, fading through the skin spectrum from purple to yellow, that enclosed her wrists.

Kisses from the chain of love, Karl had called them. Then he had laughed.

She pulled her feet close to the bed, hoping her mother wouldn't see the matching marks there.

'Don't know,' said Suzanne.

'You must know,' her mother said, anger, panic and worry bubbling under her words.

'They're...' Suzanne sighed. 'Just leave me alone. I've got to get ready.'

'But–'

Suzanne stood up.

'Leave me alone. Get out of my room. Leave me alone!'

Her hands slapped against her mother's chest, pushing her out of the bedroom, pushing her away.

Louise, too surprised to speak or retaliate, found herself standing on the landing. The bedroom door slammed in front of her. She turned, made her way downstairs, her mind a whirlpool of emotions.

She reached the bottom. Held it in. Let no ripples disturb the surface.

Into the dining room where her son Ben sat at the table, dressed for school, silently spooning in mouthfuls of Cinnamon Grahams and milk.

He looked up when she entered, eyes skittering nervously about, then back to his cereal.

Louise looked at Ben. The opposite of his sister. Inward as she was outward. Quiet as she was loud. Down as she was up. The opposite, but just as difficult to talk to.

She screwed a smile to her face. A hard, shiny plaque, covering the cracks.

'All right?'

Ben, eating, nodded.

'Good.' She spoke in a calm, measured voice. 'When you've finished, get a wash.'

Ben nodded again.

Louise realized that was all she was going to get and left the room. She entered the kitchen, looked around.

Sometimes she found it hard to believe this was all hers. This house, this family. This life. She stretched her arms out in front of her, flexed her fingers. Clench, unclench. Clench, unclench. Even her skin, her bone, her own body. Like she was just looking after it until the proper owner returned.

She felt someone else in the room, turned. Ben stood there, bowl and spoon in hand, staring at her.

She dropped her arms, moved to one side. Reddened. Ben passed her, eyes down, deposited his dishes in the dishwasher, left the kitchen.

She watched him go. Why had she felt uncomfortable when he looked at her? Not just this time, she always did. But she knew why. Because the way he had looked at her, body posture, mouth set, eyes, was pure Keith. Distilled essence poured into a miniature bottle.

Ben abluted, packed his bag, left the house.

Louise sighed in relief.

She checked her watch, moved to the bottom of the stairs.

'Come on, Suzanne, you'll be late.'

A sullen clump on the stairs was the response. Suzanne slowly made her way down. Louise looked at her.

'You're not wearing that to go out in.'

'I'm going straight out after school.'

'Not dressed like that.'

Suzanne reached the bottom of the stairs, grabbed her bag.

'I said–'

Suzanne turned. 'Just leave me alone. You're always on at me! Leave me alone!'

'Suzanne–'

'Don't touch me! Get away from me!'

The doorbell rang.

They both looked at it, at the outline of the

369

figure behind the glass.

Suzanne opened the door, walked out. The figure in the doorway stepped aside.

'Suzanne!' Louise said.

Suzanne didn't look back, didn't break her stride. Louise sighed, shook her head. She looked to see who was at the door. Her brother.

'Morning,' he said and looked around. 'Haven't called at a bad time, have I?'

Louise sighed again. 'It always seems to be a bad time. Come in.'

Larkin entered, closed the door behind him.

Louise stomped towards the kitchen. Larkin followed her.

'Tea? Coffee?' she asked, her back to him.

'Whatever. Coffee's fine.'

Louise stood, unmoving, staring out of the window.

'Louise? You OK?'

Larkin crossed to her, looked at her. Tears were bunching in the corners of her eyes, beginning their descent down her cheeks. She closed her eyes. They fell.

Larkin took her in his arms, cradled her head against his chest. Her body convulsed, sobs and tears escaping it.

He held her. It was a strange experience for both of them. Family but not close. Intimate yet distant. Strangers, but there for each other. And with each tear that choked out of Louise, the more they held each other, the narrower the distance between them became.

Louise's tears peaked, subsided.

'Why don't you have a sit-down?' Larkin's voice

quiet, unobtrusive. 'Why don't I make us both a cup of tea?'

Louise nodded and, grabbing a couple of tissues from the box, made her way to the front room.

Larkin boiled water, navigated the unfamiliar kitchen, made a pot of tea. He found a tray, carried everything into the front room, set it down.

'I've probably done it all wrong and used all the wrong things,' he said.

'Doesn't matter.' Her voice quiet, cracked.

He poured her a mug of tea, handed it to her. Poured one for himself. They waited for them to cool, silently, then drank.

'That better?'

Louise nodded.

'You OK now?'

She nodded again, then stopped.

'No,' she said. 'No, I'm not.'

'You want to talk about it?' Larkin's voice again quiet, supportive.

She emitted a noise that, at a push, could have been a laugh but sounded more like a harsh bark.

'You just caught me at a bad time, that's all.' She sniffed, straightened up. 'Just feeling vulnerable. We all go through phases.'

Her words were like Perspex: cheap, see-through and easy to break down.

'Being in tears at nine o'clock in the morning doesn't sound like a phase.'

Louise looked into her mug as if expecting to find answers there.

'I suppose you're... I don't know...' She sighed. 'Where do I start?' she said into her tea.

371

'Wherever you like. Take all day if you have to.'

She took a mouthful of tea, sighed again.

'I'm not... Oh, I don't know. You don't want to hear this.'

'Louise, I'm family.'

She looked at him.

'Yeah, I know, we've been pretty shit where being family's concerned. Maybe it's about time that changed.' He smiled. 'So, I'm here now. Talk to me.'

She smiled, savouring the novel idea of supportive family. She looked again into her tea, searched for words that would encapsulate and articulate her emotions. She could find nothing definitive, so started as best she could.

'I'm not ... happy.'

Her head came up. Just hearing her voice admit that fact openly was something. Larkin didn't move, just listened. Emboldened, she continued.

'It's not recent. I haven't been happy for a long time, now that I think about it.'

Another mouthful of tea.

'Any reason in particular?'

'Well, you saw the way Suzanne behaved. Shouting and walking out like that. I just can't talk to her. Can't communicate with her.'

'Isn't that what teenagers are supposed to do with their parents?'

'Yes, I know, but this is something more. She's like a stranger to me. I don't know where she goes or who her friends are or what she's doing. She won't tell me. Won't let me in.'

Larkin remembered the car he'd seen on his previous visit. The boy racer noisebox on wheels.

'She's got a boyfriend, right?'

'Yes, but I only know that because he picks her up and drops her off. I don't know who he is, how old he is, what he does, anything. I ask her but she won't tell me.' Another sip of tea. 'And then this morning I found these bruises round her wrists.'

Larkin leaned forward. 'What kind of bruises?'

'Like...' Louise gestured. 'Like circles round her wrists. Some old, some more recent.'

'Restraint marks?'

'Yes. Oh, I don't know.'

'If that's what they are, she's young to be messing with that kind of stuff.'

'I know.' Louise sighed, put her tea down. 'You try to protect them from these things, give them a loving home, some grounding for the future... Oh, I don't know.'

'What about–' Larkin had to think of his name ' –Keith? Can't he talk to her?'

'No, he can't.'

'Why not?'

Louise picked up her mug again, started swirling the liquid around.

'Why can't he?' Larkin asked again.

'Because...' Louise stared hard at her tea, as if that would tell her whether or not to answer. 'Because ... Keith's never believed Suzanne is his daughter.'

Larkin sat back in his chair as if he'd been pushed.

'What?'

He looked at Louise. She kept her eyes on her tea.

'Who else could–'

'It's… I don't want to talk about it now.'

'So who does he think the father is? Not Tony?'

She looked up, straight in the eye.

'I wish.'

And that encapsulated everything. A lifetime of longing, the span of a fifteen-year-old girl's life, and the wish for change, for renewal.

'Imagine what that must do to you,' said Louise, rekindling interest in her tea. 'Being brought up, having your father making snide comments about who your real father is. Imagine what that would do to you.'

Imagine who that could send you into the arms of, Larkin thought.

'And is he her father?'

Louise sighed.

'He just won't accept his responsibility, that's all.' Her voice dripped bitterness.

'Have you talked to her?'

''Course I have. But the more I told her one thing, the more Keith told her another.' Another sigh. 'Poor little girl.'

'What about your son? Ben, is it?'

'Yes, Ben. Oh, he's his father's boy, no doubt. Sometimes it's like having a miniature version of Keith in the house.'

'Mini Me.'

They both laughed but it soon died away.

'And Keith?' asked Larkin.

'I hate him.'

Louise had spoken without thinking. Inadvertently, without searching for the right words to articulate her feelings, she had found them.

'Bit strong,' said Larkin. 'Don't mince words.'

She thought about what she had just said, searched her emotions for signs of guilt or even shame. She found none. Those words had been the right ones. Once acknowledged, she found she didn't regret them at all. She gave a small smile.

'No,' she said, 'those are the right words. That's how I feel. I hate him.'

She sat up straight in the chair, emboldened by her admission.

'If you feel that strongly, you should leave.'

'Yes, I should.' She sighed. An ice pick of uncertainty chipped away at her confidence. 'But I can't. Not until the kids are a bit older. When they'll need me less.'

'You should think of yourself, Louise.'

'I know that,' she said, as if in answer to an argument she had played in her head over and over again. 'But I keep thinking of our mam and dad. What they would say if they were still alive.'

'They'd probably want you to be happy.'

'Or they'd want me to finish what I started. Do my duty.'

'I doubt that.'

Louise shrugged. 'I don't know.'

'There'll never be a right time, you know.'

'I know. I'm just trying to pick the best time.'

'I always thought you had what you wanted, you know.'

'Really?'

'Yeah. The perfect little marriage. The perfect little family. It was all you ever seemed to want.'

Louise gave a hollow laugh.

'You never knew me well, did you? No, I don't

375

think there's such a thing as the perfect family. There's only people. And they're never perfect. Some are just better at hiding things from others, that's all.'

Larkin sipped his tea. It had gone cold.

'So,' he said, smiling, 'have you got anyone else lined up?'

She looked at him, frowned. 'What?'

'Are you seeing anyone else?'

She opened her mouth to reply but stopped herself.

'No. Well, yes. Sort of.' She felt herself reddening. 'It's hard to explain.'

Larkin smiled again. 'And none of my business.'

Louise joined in the smile. 'Something like that. Maybe some other time.'

Larkin put down his mug.

'Tea's gone cold,' said Louise. 'Want another?'

'That would be lovely, thanks.'

Louise looked at her watch. 'It'll be lunchtime soon. Would you like something to eat?'

'Why don't we go out somewhere? My treat.'

Louise smiled radiantly: it lit up her eyes.

'I'd like that a lot. Thank you. You know, I think we've got a lot of catching up to do.'

'We have.'

They both stood up, caught each other's eye.

'Thanks for listening.'

'That's OK. That's what brothers are for. Or supposed to be for.'

'It's nice to see you again.'

Larkin laughed.

'Again? We may as well say it's nice to meet you.'

They both laughed.

Then got ready and went out for lunch.

The warehouse was chocked: boxes and crates, sealed and bound, were shelved high to the cciling, stocked deep to the walls.

Tommy stood in the centre of the space. An emperor surveying his empire.

Knee-deep in filth.

The boxes were crammed full of magazines, videos, books, CD-ROMs, DVDs. All pornography. All tastes catered for.

The warehouse at a point midway down the line; where demand grabbed at supply, where sex became money.

What filled the boxes was initially cheap to make. Cut-price camcorder footage, the models paid in cash or comfort drugs, burned on to disk or copied on to tape. Photos taken and treated likewise, cheaply bound on coloured paper. Mainly from Europe, some home-grown, some American. The costs kept deliberately low.

Then Tommy became involved. The distributor. Bulk whittled down to singles and delivered to stores, which, follow the paper trail, his company also owned.

The customer was kept drained, happy and eager for more. And both Tommy and the whole operation were totally legit. He was a businessman. He had assumed Clive Fairbairn's mantle: King of the Middlemen. The thousand per cent mark-up man. Respected. But not openly so.

I hear you're going soft. Fairbairn's words.

And Tommy had allayed his fears as best he could.

But the truth: going legit costs. Especially in the porn industry. Profits were dipping.

The Internet. The DIYers. Cutting out the middleman. Anyone with a digicam and a computer could outmatch what he was doing. Sites with monthly subscription rates. Free sites accessed by premium-rate phone lines. Then there were the enthusiasts, amdrammers squeezing the pros out of the market. And the customers had never had it so good. Why pay for it when you can get it for free?

But Tommy couldn't tell Mr Fairbairn that. Couldn't make him see. This wasn't the old days. These weren't business rivals who would see sense after a visit from a hammer artist or a craftsman with the pliers. These e-porn barons weren't even in the same city, perhaps not even the same country. And they did it for fun. Not money, fun.

And Tommy didn't know how to fight that.

Tommy found a crate, sat down, sighed. His trips to the warehouse had become increasingly frequent. It was the only place offering tranquility. He would stand, sit, stare, think. Examine his life, what it was, what it had become.

Where it was going.

He looked around the warehouse again. It was big, like a cathedral. But for blood sacrifices, for the worship of false idols, of graven images.

He knew all about blood sacrifices: times when the floor had been a red river as the market competition had been forcibly removed. And Tommy, naked, hands and body covered in other men's blood, his hard-on from pain not porn, had been the high priest.

And he knew all about worshipping false idols. Putting his faith in the wrong things. Like his first idols: Frank. Dino. Even the half-blind, black Jew to an extent. Men who knew who they were. What they were about. His first role models, men who left footsteps for him to follow in. Lifestyles to emulate. Words to live up to.

And he had tried. Growing up, he had clung to their vision, made himself over in their image.

But now they were gone. Frank and his apostles had finished their last Vegas supper, checked out of the Sands for the last time. And no loungecore resurrection could ever bring them back. Their world had disappeared too. They had died clinging to a crumbling myth they had built around themselves: men out of time. Just men. Only men.

And Tommy had wanted more.

Like a son. Fairbairn's words. His next idol, his next role model.

And like a son he was. He worked hard at it, being a good son, a worthy heir, and for a time he thought he had made it, thought that families could be more than biology.

With the wedding, he had thought that was it, that was him for life.

But then Caroline had put him right on a few things. Told him where he stood. And where she stood.

Or rather lay.

He had come in one day and found her in bed with another man. In his house, in his bedroom. With Clive Fairbairn.

Tommy could remember that day, see it as clearly as if it was unfolding before him now. He had entered the room and stood there. Said nothing, done nothing. Just stood there, feeling like his heart had been ripped out, his balls cut off.

Fairbairn had sat up, looked at him. Grinned.

Hello, Tommy, he said. Here I am, you cuckolded cunt. What are you going to do about it? Are you going to be a man about it?

And Tommy had done nothing. There was nothing he could have done.

He went to another part of the house. Listened to Frank: 'In the Wee Small Hours of the Morning'. He wanted it to help him but it didn't touch him, didn't move him. He heard the voice but the words were empty.

Later, when Fairbairn had finished and left, Caroline had come to see Tommy. She had sat looking at him, smoking. Her dressing gown falling open. He didn't look. He didn't care.

I told you I wanted to see other people, she said. I'm sorry you found out this way, if it hurt you. But Clive and I have done this for a long time. I don't mind. It keeps him happy. And that keeps my dad happy. You should see someone else too.

Tommy said nothing. Waited for her to leave the room.

Then, after a long while, phoned Cathy.

Fairbairn and Tommy never spoke about the incident. Caroline and Tommy never spoke.

Tommy joined the golf club. And carried on with his life, his faith, his belief gone.

He began to see his situation for what it was. His knife work stopped bringing him joy. The euphoria became boredom and finally revulsion. His business dealings gave him no thrill. He needed a change. More than that, he wanted to make amends. He wanted more than faith. He wanted redemption.

Then out of the blue he had a visitation. One night, working late at the casino. Tony Woodhouse.

You owe me, he said, limping, wincing from the pain. You fuckin' owe me. Time you started payin'.

Tommy didn't even bother being tough with him. The fact that Tony had shown up at all showed he had balls.

I've got work to do, said Tony, and I need a partner. A silent one. And I thought of you. Come on, I'll give you the sales pitch.

Into Tony's Astra automatic and off down the coast road.

Where we going?

Home, said Tony. My home.

Coldwell. The 1992 version. The 'unprofitable' mine had closed in '86. It had been the heart of the town, now cut out. The rest of the town had been propped up, its health artificially maintained, but a replacement heart had not arrived. The town was dying.

They drove around the streets, slowly. Tony letting the images settle into Tommy's mind.

Long way from Ponteland, aren't you? No golf clubs here.

Tony turned the tape player on.

Bruce Springsteen: 'Lucky Town'.

Nothing lucky about it, he said.

They drove to a housing estate, pulled over, stopped. They looked at each other.

I could make one call on my mobile and you would vanish so quickly it would be like you'd never lived on this planet.

Yeah, I know. Tony sounded unimpressed. But you won't.

Why not?

Because if you were going to do that, you'd have done it by now. Look out of the window.

Tommy looked.

What d'you see?

A housing estate.

Describe it.

Is this part of your sales pitch?

Describe it.

Tommy sighed, playing along. Run down. Boarded up. Broken windows.

Tony nodded. Right. Broken windows. There's a theory about them. Want to hear it?

Tommy shrugged.

OK, then. Tony looked through the window. A window gets broken. It doesn't get repaired. Another one appears. And another. Then places get boarded up. And the weeds start to grow. And people stop fighting for things. Some of them move out. Others stay. And the ones who stay stop trying. They stop controlling their children. Then things are dumped in the street. Then cars are parked and stripped. Then there's no law.

Then drugs take a hold. Tony looked at Tommy. Broken windows.

Tommy looked back at him.

Why can't they get them repaired?

Oh, I'm sure they want to. But maybe they don't know how. Or can't afford it. Or aren't physically able. And the ones who should be repairing them, who've got the money and the know-how, can't. They think people who live there should take responsibility. And they won't help until they do. And in the meantime, more broken windows appear. And more.

Tony sighed.

I was brought up around here. And it didn't used to be like this.

He turned to face Tommy.

I'm going into business. And I want you to back me.

Tommy laughed. You're going into the double-glazing business?

Tony smiled. No. I'm setting up an addiction treatment centre. I've been promised some money but I need more. And that's where you come in.

Tommy laughed. Really?

Yes, really. Fairbairn's got this area of the coast sewn up tight. And that means you do too. This – he pointed to the estate – is where you're making your money from.

Tommy laughed again. Not so loud this time. So you want me, who does what I do for a living, to fund a centre for drug addicts?

Yes. I'm sure the irony won't escape you.

And I'm just going to hand this money over, am I?

Tony's voice dropped, became low and

dangerous. Yes, you fucking are. Because I used to work for you. I helped you get rich. And look what happened to me. You could say it's because of me you're where you are today. So yes, you owe me.

Tommy looked at the estate. Saw what Tony saw. And something else: above the clouds, a small white chink of light. A glimpse of sun through heavy clouds. A small, stirring epiphany.

The beginnings of redemption.

Tommy smiled.

Tony was still talking. And of course it's tax deductible. A charitable donation from a well-respected local businessman.

OK.

Tony smiled. Good. There is one other thing I want from you.

And he told him.

And Tommy laughed. And that irony topped them all.

And he was back in the warehouse. Back in the present.

The legitimate businessman, still buying his ticket on the road to redemption. In instalments.

Another look around. Stock that seemed to arrive more quickly, leave more slowly.

The cathedral, worshipping false gods, hot idols. Blood sacrifices a thing of the past.

Frank and Dino: useless saints. Failed him when he needed them.

Fairbairn: I hear you're going soft.

I wish I could care, he thought. I wish I could.

He turned the lights out, reset the alarms, bolted the door.

He got into the Daimler, drove away.

He said it out loud:

'I wish I could care.'

Lunchtime. And Suzanne sat alone.

She was in the café not far from her school nursing a latte. The café was small, box-like. It suited her perfectly. That was exactly how she felt. Boxed. On all sides.

Her friends: she couldn't talk to them any more. She found their concerns childish and petty, their lives and interests boring. She no longer had anything in common with them and knew they had little time for her.

Her teachers: all they could do was get on her case. How did she ever expect to pass her exams if she didn't apply herself? How did she hope to do A-levels, go to university, if she didn't work? What had happened to her? She used to be such a good student.

She wanted to scream and shout: fuck off, all of you! Leave me alone! You all want a part of me! Fuck off!

But she didn't. She kept it inside.

And then there was Karl. It was getting too much now. He scared her. She wanted out. But the thing was, the part of him that scared her had a flipside. It gave her butterflies of a different kind. It was what had attracted her to him in the first place. Thrilling. Dangerous. It was what kept her going back.

That and the fear of what would happen if she didn't.

She wanted to scream, she wanted to cry, beg

for help, let the tears run down her face, her voice echo round the room. She wanted someone to throw their arms round her and tell her they loved her. Tell her they weren't going to leave her alone.

But she knew that wouldn't happen.

So she just sat there, kept it all locked away inside.

Boxed in.

Her mobile trilled. She checked it. A text message from Karl, telling her when and where. She put the phone back in her bag. She would be there.

She checked her watch. Time to go back to school.

She picked her cup up, drained it, set it down.

Her hand was shaking.

She couldn't stop it.

Time fell away.

Larkin and Louise hadn't stopped talking, covering the years with words, pouring memories into the spaces in between.

The weather improved. Clouds moved away, the sun shone. They walked down the Tynemouth streets enjoying the weather, the sea, each other's company.

They found a café: pretty, genteel, with a view of the ruined abbey that put an extra few pounds on the price of their lunch.

They ate: wholemeal sandwiches and coffee. A fancy cake each.

They talked.

'So what happened to you?' Louise asked after

their plates had been cleared and coffee fill-ups poured. 'London and that. One minute you were here, the next you were gone. Then you were back.'

Larkin sipped his coffee. 'Long story. I just split up with Charlotte. Remember her?'

Louise nodded.

He replaced his cup in its saucer. He had been holding it before his face like a shield, hiding behind it.

'I got a good job offer and I went. It was good for a while, then it all turned to shit. And a lot of people got hurt.' He gave a grim laugh. 'The way the 80s ended.'

He drained his cup, signalled for a refill.

'Thirsty?'

'Not used to talking,' Larkin said. 'About myself, anyway.'

'When did you come back?'

'Four years ago. I came to cover a story for this tabloid I was working for then. Drugs war thing. And I decided not to go back to London. Stayed up here. Went freelance.'

'And what happened with–' Louise reddened, began to fall over her words '–Charlotte?'

Larkin looked at his coffee, the liquid swirling around, black and seemingly bottomless.

'It all ended badly,' he said. 'I started seeing her again. Bad idea. For one thing she was married, for another she wasn't the person she once was.'

'In what way?'

'Well...' He sighed, tried to find the right words. 'She'd ... chased her dreams a little too vigorously. Her dreams involved money. She'd got

387

involved with drugs. In a big way. And some very heavy people. And it–' he sighed again '–killed her.'

His dream flashed back: Charlotte on the Swing Bridge, a shotgun blast, himself unable to stop it. And Charlotte gone.

'You read all this, though. It was in the papers.'

'I remember. I wanted to contact you, but I didn't know how.'

Larkin gave a weak smile. 'Don't worry. I wasn't much company.'

Louise reddened again. 'No, you idiot. Just to let you know I was here if you wanted, you know.'

'Thanks.' He smiled. 'But don't worry, I'm OK now.'

She gave him a look that said she wasn't convinced.

'I am, honestly. I'm sorted. I'm working and I'm seeing someone else too.'

Louise smiled, her interest piqued. 'Really? Tell me about her.'

'Not that much to tell. Her name's Claire, she used to be an art student and she lives near here. That's why I was at your house so early this morning.'

'Age?'

'The Spanish Inquisition. Younger than me.'

'Serious?'

It was Larkin's turn to redden. 'I don't know. I've only just met her.'

'And how did you meet her?'

Larkin laughed.

'You going to keep this up all day?'

Louise smiled, nodded.

'I met her through Tony Woodhouse. She works with him.'

Louise's mood changed. Her smile quickly switched off. 'Oh. Claire.'

'D'you know her?'

'No,' she said quickly. 'No.' She looked at her watch. 'Shall we go for a walk?'

Larkin paid the bill and they set off along the seafront. Brightly painted Edwardian stone houses on one side, sand and the North Sea on the other. Seagulls swooped and whirled. People strolled, walked on the beach. It was a good day to be alive and under the sun.

'So how's the book going?' asked Louise.

'Fine, I think.'

'You think?'

'Yeah, it's just ... you know. You do so much, you start questioning your motive. Am I just looking at the miners' strike and its legacy, or am I trying to resurrect the past? Simplify the present? I don't know. Let's have an ice cream.'

They stopped at an ice cream van, had two Natriani's 99s.

'Is this about Charlotte, d'you think?' said Louise, pushing her flake into the tube of her cornet.

Larkin bit into his flake, chewed it thoughtfully.

'I don't know,' he said. 'Maybe it is Charlotte. But maybe it's something more. Everything seemed easier back then. The world seemed simpler. Black and white. No grey.'

She took a lick of ice cream, smiled.

'If you don't mind me saying so, it was you that was simpler, not the world.'

389

Larkin looked at her.

'I remember you then. You knew what was right and what was wrong. You know who your enemy was.'

He smiled. 'True. Maybe it was the last time for me. The last time it all made sense. 'Cause then I moved to London, got lost in everything that was happening there then—'

'The sex and drugs and rock 'n' roll?'

'Exactly.'

'So you come back here and try to relive the past. Your past. Or at least make sense of it.'

Larkin laughed. 'How come you haven't seen me in years and you've got all this stuff figured out?'

'Woman's intuition. Plus, I'm your sister. I know you better than you think.'

'Point taken.'

They walked further. Retired couples sat on benches, eating ice cream, looking at the sea. One particular couple were holding hands, talking and laughing. The joy they took in each other's company made it appear as if they'd just met, but the easy familiarity they had with each other showed they had been together for a long time.

'How do they do it?' asked Louise. 'How do they get to be that age and still be in love with each other?'

'Shall we ask them?'

'I doubt they'd know.'

They walked on.

'Anyway,' said Louise, popping the final piece of cornet into her mouth. 'The time you're writing about wasn't that good.' She shuddered despite the warmth. 'Memory is deceptive. Unreliable. I've never looked on the past in a rosy glow.'

Larkin nodded. 'Talking of Tony,' he said, 'something else came up regarding this book. D'you know Tommy Jobson?'

Louise stopped dead. 'What about him?'

'Just something in connection with Tony, that's all. You know him, then?'

'Let's just say, he and Tony go way back. I said it was a bad time back then. A lot of it was down to him.'

'In what way?'

Louise stopped walking, found a railing, leaned on it, watching the sea. She opened her mouth to speak, hesitated. Wondering what to tell Larkin. How much to tell him.

'Remember what I said about Keith?' she said eventually, her voice measured. 'How he doesn't think he's Suzanne's father?'

Larkin nodded.

'Well, it's a bit more complicated than that. I was raped.'

'What?'

She kept staring at the sea. 'My flat got broken into. Trashed. While I was in it. That's how Tony got his injured leg. That's how I got–' she stopped, staring hard at the horizon '–Suzanne.'

Larkin was stunned.

'Why... Nobody told me. Mam and Dad never mentioned it...'

'That's because you'd gone to London. No one knew how to get in touch with you. Where to find you.'

'D'you know who did it? Did they find him?'

Louise shook her head, said nothing.

'Louise, I'm sorry ... I had no idea...'

'S'OK. It's in the past. Tony and I split up after that. I just couldn't face seeing him. It reminded me of ... that night. Then Keith re-emerged. And he was so good to me, y'know? Flowers, chocolates, coming to see me all the time. They tried to make me have an abortion but I just couldn't go through with it. Couldn't kill what was inside me. Keith said he didn't mind. If I would have him back, he would marry me. Bring up the baby as his.'

'So why does he keep trying to tell Suzanne he's not her real father?'

'Because he's a bitter, sad little bastard.'

She looked at her watch, sighed. 'I'd better get back. The kids'll be home from school soon. Keith'll be wanting his tea.'

The way she said her husband's name, Larkin was glad it wasn't him.

They walked back to the car, clouds beginning to obscure the sun.

They drove back to Louise's house, the clouds thickening, matching Louise's mood.

'He sent his love, by the way.'

'Who?' she asked.

'Tony. Want me to send it back?'

She looked out of the window, away from Larkin.

'If you like.'

He pulled up in front of her house, stopped the engine.

'Oh, well,' Louise said. 'I've been out to play

and now it's time to be the dutiful mother and wife.'

'If you're not happy, get out,' said Larkin. 'Just leave.'

Louise sighed.

'I will. I'm just waiting for the right time.'

'There'll never be a right time.'

She opened the door. 'I've really enjoyed today. Let's not leave it so long next time.'

They exchanged a chaste, sibling kiss and Larkin drove off to meet Claire.

Louise opened the door, went in, closed it behind her. It slammed shut, reverberating like the clanging of a cell door.

That's what it feels like, she thought. A cell door. And here I sit, incarcerated.

Condemned.

She thought through her day out. Sunshine and laughter. A life lived on the other side.

She was still thinking of that when Ben let himself in. She smiled at him, said hello, asked if he had had a good day at school. He nodded and mumbled, then wordlessly went upstairs. She knew he would be in his room, sitting at his computer or at his play station, doing whatever it was that teenage boys did with their toys.

She smiled. Thought of the sun. Thought of life lived on the other side.

She was still doing that when the door opened again. Keith entered the living room, put his briefcase down, stopped.

'Why are you sitting in my chair?' he said by way of a greeting.

'Is this your chair?' Her voice was light,

drifting. 'Does it have your name on it?'

Keith stepped nearer to her. 'Now, don't set your lip up to me, or I'll–'

She looked at him, straight in the eye. 'What, Keith. Or you'll what?'

Her voice was like hard steel, ready to snap, ready to thrust its sharpness into him.

He backed off.

'What's for dinner?' he asked, his voice shrunken.

Louise stretched her arms above her head, her feet along the carpet. Like a cat uncoiling.

'Nothing. I'm having a day off.'

'What d'you mean you're having a day off? You can't. We have to eat.'

'Then you do it.'

'But you can't just–'

She stood up. Keith flinched. Louise smiled.

'Did I scare you?'

She walked to the door.

'Where are you going?'

Louise shrugged. 'Don't know. But I've had a good day today. The best for a long time. And I'm not going to let you spoil it.'

She left the room, made her way upstairs. She opened the wardrobe, looked at the clothes inside. Stylish clothes for going out in, a few years out of date, perhaps, but better than the dowdy shrouds she had taken to wearing recently. She pulled things out, began to change.

Began to admire herself.

Thinking of sunshine and laughter. Thinking of a life lived on the other side.

A cloud passed over the sun. Over her mood.

She held a dress against her body, looked in the mirror, smiled.

But not for much longer.

The CAT Centre was silent, the last client having left half an hour previously.

Claire Duffy was in the art studio, washing brushes, propping work on easels to help it dry, tidying round. Just filling in time until she went to meet Stephen Larkin.

Stephen Larkin. She liked him, he was complex. She liked that in a man. Complicated no, complex yes. There was a lot to him, many doors he kept closed. Perhaps in time he would open them for her. One day.

She dried her hands, gathered her things together.

And heard a noise.

Her heart skipped. She had thought she was the only one in the building.

Her heart began to pound, her legs to shake. She swallowed; her throat was dry. She made her way into the corridor, looking quickly around all the time. The noise had come from the office at the end of the hall. Tony's office. She slowly walked towards it.

And heard another noise.

Someone was in there. Someone was inside Tony's office.

She looked around for a weapon. Something – anything – she could use if she had to.

Found nothing.

Heart too big for her chest and blood moving at a furious pace round her body, she put a hand on the door knob, turned it, opened the door.

Cautiously, she stepped in.

And there was Tony sitting behind his desk.

Claire smiled, relief spreading through her body, face reddening at her own nervousness. She opened her mouth to speak, to let him know how stupid she had been.

But stopped. She looked at him again.

Her mouth fell open, feet rooted to the spot. She could only stare.

For there was Tony behind his desk, sleeves rolled up, arm tied off, works spread in front of him.

A needle in his vein.

Shooting heroin into his body.

# PART FOUR

# Reckoning

## 15. Then

Keith was still following.

The act was obsessing him, consuming him.

It was becoming his life.

He had started taking notes:

Times. Places. Days of the week. Goings. And comings.

The notes had become a book:

Searching for patterns, building a structure, a grid, a matrix to store this information. To cross-reference seemingly random events – meals at restaurants, walks in parks, shopping trips, pub visits, country drives – and find a sense, a logic behind it all.

Of course, she could have just been in love, but Keith didn't believe that. She was with the man for a reason. He had tried to find out what. And he thought he had.

He knew the boyfriend's name. Who he was, what he did. A trip to St James' Park to watch a football match had sent him back to his notes. That was totally out of character for Louise. She had always hated football. But he had watched. And gathered information.

Tony Woodhouse.

Keith discovered the fact by buying a programme and asking a scarf-clad fan to name the player seen in a photograph. That, he thought, was using research and detection techniques that would make any member of the CID proud.

Once he had the man's name and profession, it all fell into place. Louise wasn't in love. The attraction to Woodhouse was for two things: money and sex. Woodhouse would soon tire of that, get what he wanted from her, move on to the next one.

And Louise would fall straight back into Keith's arms.

Simple.

Keith had mixed feelings about that day coming. He wanted her back, obviously, but he also enjoyed the following. The stalking. The feeling of standing alone in the shadows, watching, seeing everything, but remaining undetected.

A ghost.

A living shadow.

It thrilled him, gave him an erotically charged power he had never felt before. It wasn't something he wanted to give up.

It wasn't something he was going to give up.

When Louise came back to him, he could still secretly follow her. Or better yet, keep Louise at home and find somebody new to follow. Somebody younger.

Yes.

He felt his cock stiffen at the thought and quickly looked around.

He was at work in the office. He felt sure someone must have known what he was thinking, seen what was happening to him.

But no. Everyone was going about their business, ignoring him.

Good. As long as they left him alone, he was happy.

He had become a model employee. Head down, work done. No trouble to anyone. If anything, an asset. He was sure his hard work was being noticed, but he didn't care. He lived through his job, not for it, detached himself during the day, lived for his evenings and weekends. His real work. His real life.

He looked around the office again. No one was looking. Good. He eased open the desk drawer, slid out a book.

The book.

His heart was pounding. He had to swallow hard. The book itself was such a thrill for him, much better than pornography had ever been.

He looked at the dates. Entries. Columns. Times.

Fragments of a life secretly recorded, secretly captured. Pieced together to form a whole.

By him. Only by him.

His cock was stone now. The longing was building within him; he wanted to relieve himself all over his girlfriend's secrets.

But he controlled himself. He used patience, letting the feeling build, enjoying the anticipation.

He put the book away, went back to his work.

Tonight.

Back in his car, down the alley, deep in the shadows. Watching.

Tonight.

Keith resumed work, willed the day away.

Tonight.

Mick opened the door, then moved aside to allow

Angela to enter first. She limped slightly as she walked, stitches not yet healed, pain reminding her of the birth. She sat down in an armchair, white and worn out.

Mick followed, a borrowed carrycot in both hands.

'Here she is,' he said, placing the cot on the floor.

He sat down in the other armchair, wincing from his own injuries.

He had tidied the house for Angela and Tanya's homecoming. Top to bottom. Every room. Inside and out. Acquainted himself with cleaning products he had never previously thought about. It had felt good to be working again, to be useful. Even if it was only housework.

He looked at Angela, smiled. She attempted a tentative one in return.

'The house looks nice,' she said. 'You've worked hard.'

'Aye,' he said. He took pride in hearing her words. 'Would you like a cup of tea?'

Angela thought that would be nice. Mick went into the kitchen.

Angela looked at the baby Tanya lying asleep in her cot, arms thrown out, hands up as if in surrender. She thought of the things she had whispered to her at night on the ward. How life was going to be different for her daughter. How she would give her things she herself had never had, go without if necessary. How she would make sure Tanya would do something with her life.

Angela looked around. At the house they couldn't afford to live in. At the furniture they couldn't afford to plan for.

A crash came from the kitchen. Something breaking on the floor.

'You all right in there?'

'Yes,' said Mick. 'I just... I broke ... a mug fell off, that's all. I'll clear it up.'

She looked at Tanya. The noise had made the baby stir but not wake. Angela smiled. Tanya was a good baby.

But Mick. She was worried about Mick. The strike, the police beating, it was all beginning to take its toll on him. He seemed to be breaking up, fragmenting before her eyes.

Mick re-entered, bearing a tray. Teapot, mugs, milk and biscuits. He placed them down, poured. He settled back, looked at the baby.

'She's beautiful, isn't she?' he said, smiling.

Angela nodded.

Mick looked at Tanya's face, her hands. Everything about her was so tiny, so delicate yet precise. Her fingernails. The ridges of her knuckles. The curve of her ears. Her eyelids. An amazing feat of human engineering. A life, a wondrous creation, perfection in miniature. He felt himself well up.

'You just want to ... to do everythin' right, don't you?'

Angela nodded again.

Mick blew his nose, sighed.

'I've, I've been thinkin',' he said. 'What to do. About, you know, the future.'

Angela listened, said nothing.

'This is only temporary, mind,' he said. 'Just till things get better. Why don't we sell the house. Get a council one instead. Then we'd have some money, you know, behind us. Get a car. Help with the baby. Help to retrain. Just temporary. Just to get us back on our feet again.'

He looked down at his mug of tea, drank from it.

'What d'you think?'

Angela didn't say no immediately. Instead, she ran the arguments through her head. The house they had was aspirational, a stepping stone to their future.

Then she looked at Mick. Sitting there, holding his mug with shaking hands. Bent out of shape but not yet broken. She felt a pang of anger at his ineffectualness. She wanted to hit him, shout at him to get on his feet again, be a man, provide for his family, give them the life they wanted. But she could clearly see his injuries, both physical and mental, so she refrained. Forced herself to feel compassion, sympathy and empathy for him.

Bent out of shape but not yet broken. If they stayed here, he would be.

She nodded.

'All right,' she said.

Mick nodded, felt a sad relief course through him.

'Just till we're back on our feet. Just temporarily.'

They drank their tea.

On the floor, Tanya began to stir. She opened her eyes and looked around.

Then she began to cry.

Dougie was coughing so hard he had moved off the chair on to his knees. He couldn't breathe,

404

couldn't find relief. His body racking, his ribs aching. Like his lungs were full of gravel and he had to spit it out through a too-small plastic tube. He put his handkerchief over his mouth, tried to catch whatever came out.

Gradually the coughing began to subside and Dougie struggled to get his breath back, gasping at air like a deep-sea diver. He felt calmer but his lungs were still burning, still full of gravel. He pulled himself back on to the seat, checked the handkerchief.

Blood.

He sighed, pocketed it. No panic about his movements, no shock, just a sense of weary inevitability.

Blood.

He knew what would happen next. It was how his father had gone.

Arthur Howden: miner and painter. Dougie still had one of his paintings framed on the wall.

Part of the Ashington Group in the 1930s. The Pitman Painters. Some moneyed, do-gooding society women had tried to encourage the miners to express themselves creatively through paint. Patronizing it may have been, but the results were very pleasing. The work was good, the men proud. The paintings were exhibited nationally and one, Oliver Kilbourn, went on to some acclaim in his own right. Dougie could remember the others, though: George Blessed, Arthur Whinnom, George and Leslie Brownrigg, Fred Laidler. And others. And his father.

He looked at the picture hanging in pride of place above his mantelpiece. Almost totally black, it showed a miner chipping away at a seam with his pickaxe. A big man wearing trousers, vest, boots and helmet. It had physicality, strength to it. It communicated hard graft, pride.

He thought of contemporary images of miners: shouting, fighting, attacking policemen.

Different world. He knew which one he preferred, which one he wanted to be in.

Which one he was part of.

He sat, too tired to move, the fight gone out of him. He braced himself as another coughing fit began to well up.

Let it come, he thought. Let it come.

The Fisherman's Wharf on the Newcastle quayside. Dark interior, old wood, old-world ambience. Where money dined with money. Where deals were made and things were taken care of. No price on the menu.

Tommy opened the door, entered. Suited, booted, he was nervous. He had to be. He was meeting Clive Fairbairn.

Fairbairn gave a small wave, a beckoning. Tommy crossed the floor. Fairbairn's table was away from the other diners. Intimate. Secluded. Tommy sat down. Immediately, a waiter flourished a menu before him. Tommy went to take it. Fairbairn waved it away.

'He's having the same as me. Monkfish. Aren't you?'

Tommy shrugged. He wouldn't have known a monkfish if it had bitten him.

'Yuh-yes.'

Fairbairn took a mouthful of white wine,

swooshed it round his mouth and swallowed, smacking his lips.

'Nice here,' he said. 'They know how to treat you. Help yourself to some wine.'

Tommy did so, filling his glass. He drank. Wine was wine to him.

'Guh-good.'

'Yeah. The best.'

Fairbairn leaned back. Tommy took him in: black double-breasted silk suit with an ivory silk shirt and bright red silk tie with matching pocket handkerchief. Tommy would have betted that the man's braces were red too. And silk. Gold glistened on his fingers, wrists and neck.

'So,' Fairbairn said, smiling, 'how you doing, Tommy?'

'Fuh-fine.'

'Any problems I should know about?'

'Nuh-nothing I can think of.'

Fairbairn smiled again. It made him look like something that should have been caught, landed and eaten at this restaurant.

'Good. Good. I'm hearing good things about you, Tommy. Good things from the people who matter.'

He took another sip of wine, smacked his lips again.

'This is good stuff.' He replaced his glass. 'Now, Tommy. To business.'

Fairbairn rested his arms on the table, steepled his fingers before his face. His captain-of-industry look. He spoke, voice low, murmuring, hiding the words from any hidden microphones.

'Times are changing in our business, Tommy,

and we have to change with them. Drugs are becoming socially acceptable. Take cocaine, for instance. It's now the drug of choice to a lot of people in the south. and I don't mean the usual crowd, the skaghead estate kids who'd try anything, I mean the middle classes. Moneyed, affluent. Professional people.'

Another mouthful of wine, another smack of the lips.

'Now, I've had people doing market research. And they tell me that just as those southern markets are very lucrative, the northern territories could be too. It's up to us to exploit them. Get it sewn up.'

The food arrived. They ate.

'Lovely, isn't it?' said Fairbairn. He ate slowly, cutting his fish into small chunks, popping them into his mouth, chewing leisurely.

'Something to savour, this.'

Tommy agreed that it was and kept eating, mimicking Fairbairn's actions. Learning all the time.

Fairbairn didn't talk business all through the meal. He told anecdotes, stories. He was in a good mood.

It looked to Tommy like Fairbairn enjoyed cultivating the high life image. Tommy liked it: it was how he had reckoned Frank had been in his prime, holding court at the Sands. He also imagined that a lot of it was put on for his benefit, an aspirational measure, a subtle glimpse of the high life that could be Tommy's if he played the game by Fairbairn's rules.

'Saw Cliff Richard in here once,' said Fairbairn

after another lip-smacking mouthful of white wine. 'I thought of sending someone over for his autograph. For the wife. But then thought again. I didn't think it would be something she would thank me for.'

He laughed. Tommy joined in, simultaneously trying to swallow a mouthful of monkfish.

'We're out of wine,' said Fairbairn. 'Let's have another bottle.'

The meal continued in that fashion until coffee and brandy were served. Then Fairbairn reverted to type. The warm bon viveur disappeared. The hard, cold businessman returned.

Enjoy the life, Tommy took as the message, but make sure you earn it.

And make sure you know how to earn it.

'Now,' said Fairbairn, granite-eyed, 'business. Cocaine. Lawyers. Businessmen. Rock stars. Actors. Sportsmen. They all take it. What we have to do is set up regular routes and customers for our area. And make sure that anyone visiting our fair region knows where to come for their Bolivian marching powder. D'you think you're up to the task?'

'Muh-me, Mr Fairbairn?'

'Yes, Tommy, you. I want you in charge of this. It's what you've been doing on a small scale and now it's time you stepped up. So, I'll ask again. D'you think you're up to the task?'

Tommy smiled. He couldn't help himself.

'Definitely, Mr Fairbairn.'

No hesitation, no trace of a stammer.

Fairbairn smiled.

Tommy felt like he'd grown another couple of

inches in height.

'Good. Start tomorrow. Move through the city. Any unclaimed area is yours. Create new areas. If you think you can, take areas from others.'

'What about the opposition?'

'That's up to you. But if I were you, I'd send a message. A clear warning about what'll happen if they don't co-operate with you.'

Fairbairn leaned forward.

'Know anybody who moves in those circles? Anybody who fits the bill?'

Tommy thought. Then smiled. 'One.'

'Is this our friend from before?'

'Could be.'

'Good. Give him a chance, get him to play ball–' Fairbairn chuckled at his own joke '–and if he won't – and let's be honest, we don't expect him to – do whatever you like with him.'

'Thank you, Mr Fairbairn.'

Fairbairn nodded benevolently.

'Now then, Tommy, how about another brandy?'

Keith watched. In the car, in the alley. In the shadows.

Straight there after work, only a large doner and his book for company.

Always his book.

Tonight.

The word had made him tingle with antici-pation all afternoon. But so far it had been something of a letdown. Louise had come in from college and stayed in. That was that. No flatmate, no boyfriend.

But she was in there. Alone. That gave him

some kind of *frisson*.

Alone.

What was she doing alone in the flat? He knew what he imagined her doing. Where he imagined her lying. Where he imagined her touching herself.

His cock stiffened once again. He remembered all the times she wouldn't let him watch her pleasure herself. The pleading he had done, how she had ignored it.

And she was probably up there right now, doing just that.

His hand trembled as he fed the cooling pink kebab meat into his mouth.

He had to know. He had to see.

He checked his watch. Ten thirty. Woodhouse wouldn't be coming for her now.

He had to know. He had to see.

He placed the half-eaten kebab on the passenger seat, locked the book in the glove compartment, got out and, shaking, locked the car.

There was no way he could see in from the front. The flats opened straight on to the street. The back door opened on to a set of wooden steps which led down to a shared back yard and a gate leading into an alley. That was his best bet.

Keith walked down the deserted street, trying not to draw attention to himself. He reached the alley, counted along to Louise's gate. He tried the latch, careful not to make any sound, and swung the gate slowly inward. His heart was beating salsa rhythms in his chest, legs turning to liquid as he stepped in, noiselessly moving over the concrete yard to the wooden steps.

He placed his foot gently on the first step. Then

the next one. And the next. The wood creaked. He stood stock-still, waited. Not breathing. Nothing happened. No one had heard. He continued his ascent. Soon he was standing outside the back door that led into the kitchen.

It wasn't enough. He needed to see into the back bedroom window. Louise's bedroom.

He swung his legs up to the wooden handrail and braced himself for his next move, tried not to look down.

Keith grabbed hold of the side of the building with one hand, then the other. He moved his right hand up the wall until it met a metal guttering support. He pulled on the support, testing to see whether it would hold his weight, decided to chance it.

He swung off the wooden platform, edged his left hand to the next support. He swung his legs forward. They landed on the bathroom windowsill. He looked along at the bedroom window. The curtains were drawn, but there was a chink of light showing through them. Encouraged and emboldened by this, Keith edged his way along until he could see in.

Half-hanging, half-crouching, he managed to peek through the thin sliver.

He was rewarded. There was Louise lying on the bed.

He was disappointed too. She wasn't doing any of the things he had imagined her doing. She was wearing her dressing gown over her pyjamas and her hair was turbaned into a towel. She was reading a magazine, mouthing the words to a song coming from her cassette player.

Nevertheless he watched. Thrilled to be privy to something secret, something no one else would ever see, a moment no one else would ever share.

It wasn't long before she took the towel from her head, gave her hair a final rub dry, turned off the tape player and the light and settled down to go to sleep.

Keith watched as her eyes closed, her breathing slowed and she drifted off.

And in that moment she had never looked more beautiful. He had never wanted her more.

Realizing nothing more was going to happen, Keith edged himself backwards along the window ledge until he reached the platform and swung on to it. His reverse journey seemed quicker and quieter, and it wasn't long before he was back in his car with his half-eaten kebab. And his book.

He smiled.

Tonight he had moved up a level. He hadn't seen what he wanted to see, but he had seen something.

And he hadn't been caught.

He wanted to write it all down, brag to his book about it. But first he had a more pressing matter to attend to.

He unzipped his trousers, took out his cock.

He thought of Louise lying there. Still. Alone.

He could have gone in and made her do anything.

Anything.

He came quickly, wiped himself off.

He smiled.

Tonight was good.

From now on, every night would be better.

# 16. Now

Claire stared. Rendered immobile. Struck dumb. Tony's vein was spiked. Eyes closed, head back. Unaware of her, unaware of anything but the deep, sensual velvet blackness coursing through his bloodstream, massaging his nervous system.

Through deafening white noise in her head, she found her voice.

'Tony...'

But stopped. She couldn't find the right words.

He had given in, was on a journey of personal rapture, of almost religious ecstasy. So internal, so exclusive, so at odds with the mundane surroundings: the desk, the chair, the office. Herself.

She couldn't articulate her emotions. There were too many: racing through her body, her mind, like the drug raced through Tony.

She crossed to him, took his face in her hand, moved his head side to side.

'Tony.'

He slowly opened his eyes, looking first through her, then, as he began to reground, at her.

'Claire...'

Her name spoken like a post-orgasmic sigh. It disappeared like an eight-mile-high vapour trail against a blue sky.

Tony smiled. Claire didn't recognize the man she knew in that smile. She turned, walked towards the door.

'Claire ... don't go...'

She placed a shaking palm on the handle, turned. The words were out of her mouth before she could stop them.

'Junkie. Fuckin' heroin junkie.'

Tony slowly shook his head.

'You don't understand...'

She went out, slamming the office door behind her. In the corridor she put her back against the wall to steady herself, took a deep breath, sucked as much air as she possibly could into her body, held it, exhaled in a tightly controlled stream.

From downstairs, the ring of the doorbell.

Her eyes opened with a start, her heart jumped. Then she remembered who it would be.

Stephen Larkin. Come to take her out for the night.

She pulled away from the wall, tried a couple of broad, experimental breaths. She stopped shaking. Good. Another breath. Better.

With a backward glance at Tony's office, she made her way downstairs, opened the main door.

'Hello,' said Stephen Larkin.

'Hi.'

He pulled her to him, kissed her. She kissed him back but didn't return his enthusiasm. He stopped, stepped back.

'You OK?'

'Yeah,' she said, her voice, her manner, distracted.

'What's up?'

She looked at Larkin, his brow furrowed, his eyes holding concern and compassion. She smiled, sighed.

'I'm OK.'

'Tough day at work?'

'You could say that.'

'Come on, I'll take you away from all this.'

She closed the door. They began to walk to his car.

'So,' he said, putting his arm round her, 'where d'you fancy going?'

'Anywhere,' she said. 'Just as far away from here as possible.'

They got into the Saab and drove off.

Lights flashed, tunes played. Virtual bullets hit their targets. Muscle-bound men's bodies were ripped apart, instantly resurrected on the insertion of a pound coin. The dark arcade, lit only by sparse neon and fruit machine holds and wins, sound-tracked by tinny techno bleeps, rapid fire and agonized wails, was a hall dedicated to death, money and bad driving.

Skegs saw Karl at the far end of a row of video violence. Quake. Codename: Assassin. Metal Gear Solid. Vicarious thrills for empty lives. Unreal death and painless injuries. Cartoon-violent role models for an abandoned, desensitized generation.

Karl was playing something different. He was a rebel in a galaxy far, far away, flying his X-Wing against the Death Star, fighting for a noble cause against tyranny and fascism.

Skegs approached him, stood at his side.

'Heh-hello, Karl.'

Karl ignored him, piloted his X-Wing through canyons, dodged Empire pursuit craft.

He twisted and turned, controlling the fighter, surprising his enemy with a burst of fire, pumping the joystick like a true flier.

But not quick enough for the Imperial fighter that appeared on the screen from nowhere. He fired. Too late. Dead.

The theme tune played, the roll call of honour appeared. Highest player positions: Karl was offered joint fourth. He entered his name, Han S., then turned to Skegs.

'That old shit's better than that new shit. Hello, Skegs.'

Skegs cleared his dry throat, said hello in return.

'What brings you here?'

The noble rebel was gone. Hard, cold Karl replaced him. 'You got money for me?'

Skegs dug into his pocket, forked over some notes. Karl positioned himself away from Skegs, other punters and any CCTV cameras that might have been watching, and counted it.

'Good,' he said, turning back. 'Need anythin'?'

Skegs shook his head. It wobbled as if it was loose.

'Right.'

Karl looked at Skegs, the look telling him their audience was at an end. Skegs didn't move.

'Was there somethin' else, Skegs?'

Karl sounded irritated, his voice sharp-edged.

'I nee ... need to talk to you, Karl.'

Skegs was beginning to shake.

Karl held up his hand, shrugged.

'So, talk.'

Skegs looked around, checked for listening

feds, the way Karl had taught him. He mumbled something.

'Speak up.'

'I said, I wuh-want out, Karl.' Skegs shuffled from foot to foot. 'I can't do this any more.'

Karl looked at him, his eyes flat, dead. Then he turned back to the video game, fed some coins into it.

'OK.'

Skegs couldn't hide his surprise. 'Really?'

Karl punched some buttons, gestured to the joystick.

'Here,' he said, 'have a go.'

Karl moved aside. Skegs moved in. The theme tune started and Skegs was now the noble rebel, fighting against tyranny.

The game began.

'You want out, Skegs, fine by me.'

Karl watched the screen, checked Skegs's progress.

'You ... you sure?' Skegs's voice distracted by heroics.

'Just return any unsold stuff an' walk away.' Karl's voice, focused, controlled.

'I thought you'd give us bare trouble.'

'No. Up to you, innit? I remember when I was your age.' Karl spoke with a wise, world-weary wisdom, the voice of someone forty years older than Skegs, not four. 'I was offered the chance to make money. Like you. So I weighed up the pros and cons. The risks an' benefits. An' I did it.'

They both flinched as Skegs narrowly avoided an attack by a concealed Imperial fighter.

'An' here I am. Rich an' successful. Shoot 'im.'

Skegs fired. The Imperial fighter exploded.

'You don't want that,' Karl continued, 'fine. I'll put you back on the street an' that's that. To your left.'

Another attack, another successful counter-attack.

'Yeah?' said Skegs.

'Yeah,' said Karl. 'But it'll be hard. You've had money. You'll have none. You've had a job. It won't be there any more. You've tasted my stuff. It won't be free any more. You'll have nothing to do.' Karl put his mouth to Skegs's ear. 'The street'll claim you.'

Skegs struggled to avoid an unexpected attack.

'You'll probably need somethin' to help cope with the days. So you'll come to me. An' you'll have to pay.'

One laser blast and Skegs was dead.

Game over.

Skegs watched the screen. The theme tune played. No high-scoring roll call came up. Skegs couldn't hide his disappointment. He stood still, head down.

'How d'ya know?' Skegs mumbled. 'How d'ya know I'll be on drugs?'

'Because I know.'

Skegs looked up, right at Karl. At his hardly blinking eyes. At the threat and authority in his body. At his creepy self-assurance. And Skegs was scared. He knew then that he would end up in a gutter somewhere on heroin or crack, dependent on Karl. Because he knew Karl would see to it.

Karl smiled.

'Off you go. If you're goin'.'

'I'll stay.'

Skegs's voice was quiet, dumbly acquiescent.

'Good.'

Karl could barely conceal the triumph in his voice.

Skegs turned and, shoulders slumped, began to walk away.

'Oh, Skegs.'

He turned. Karl beckoned him back. Karl put his arm round his shoulder, suddenly matey, and smiled.

'Just had an idea. To show that we're all in business together, to demonstrate solidarity, like, why don't you an' Davva come round to my flat tomorrow night?'

'Yeah?'

'Yeah. We'll get some booze, some blow, some skunk. Make a night of it.'

'Aye, Karl, that sounds champion.'

'An' I tell you what.' Karl's voice dropped, became conspirational. 'I've got this girl I'm workin' on at the moment. Primin' 'er up, gettin' 'er ready. You see, I'm thinkin' of diversifyin'. Gettin' a few girls workin' for me. I'll bring her along an' all. Let you two have a go on her. See if she's ready to be turned out. What d'you reckon? You up for it?'

Skegs could feel the erection beginning in his jeans.

'Aye, am I.'

'Off you go, then.'

Karl watched him go, proud of the way he had manipulated the boy. Knowing he had ensnared him for life.

Or for as long as Karl had use for him.

He turned back to the machine. He didn't want to be a noble rebel any more. He wanted something more visceral, more violently celebrational.

He found it, put his money in, unholstered his weapons and got to work.

As the body count increased and the on-screen blood and gore thickened, he found himself getting hard.

He began to think of Suzanne and what he had planned for her. It made him harder still.

He dodged bullets. He dispatched death without letting it touch him.

No longer noble or a rebel.

He was immortal.

The doorbell rang. Claire went to the door, opened it.

Despite the late hour, she wasn't in bed. She had been expecting the call.

'I think I owe you an explanation.'

Tony Woodhouse stood on her doorstep.

She left the door open, walked away. Tony entered, closing it behind him. He limped to the living room, found her sitting on the sofa. Arms crossed, legs clasped together. He stood, looked at her.

'Well?' she said.

'I suppose you had to find out sooner or later.'

She said nothing, waited for him to continue.

'It's heroin,' he said. 'You were right. I've been on it for years, ever since–' he gestured to his shattered leg '–this. It hooked me.'

'So how come no one's ... how come we never

421

found out?'

'Because it's a clean supply. It's a painkiller, that's all. Heroin. Diamorphine. Breaks down the morphine inside the body. And that takes away my pain. Like I've always said, it's the shit it's cut with that fucks you up. Unfortunately, it's very addictive.'

'You should know. You run a treatment centre for the stuff.'

'I know. Suppose you could say I practise what I preach.'

He smiled. Weakly.

'Why don't you try to come off it?'

He shook his head. 'How can I? What would happen to the Centre if word of this got out? And what if I did get off it? I'd just have to replace it with something else. The pain's not going to go away, you know. No, there are some things you can't get rid of, can't shake off. I'm stuck with it.'

She looked at him, eyes boring into him.

'It's OK. It's a clean supply.'

'Where from? No doctor round here would prescribe this.'

'A friend. Who deals in this kind of thing.'

Claire stared, unblinking. The penny dropped. 'That gangster. Tommy Jobson.'

Tony looked surprised. 'How d'you know about him?'

'Stephen. Stephen Larkin. The journalist. I'm seeing him. I was out with him tonight.'

Tony looked around. 'Is he here now?'

'No. I told him I didn't feel well. Wanted an early night. I thought you'd come round.'

'Just like old times.'

'Yeah.' Claire laughed mirthlessly. She realized she was shaking with emotion. 'Old times. You mean when you felt lonely and fancied a fuck you would turn up here.'

Tony sighed. 'It wasn't like that.'

'Not at first, not. But then I told you I loved you. And you backed off, told me there was somebody else. And because of her you couldn't get involved with anyone else.'

'There was. There is.'

'Didn't stop you coming round here for a fuck, though, did it? And creeping out before the morning. Letting me wake up alone.'

'Sorry.'

'And that makes it OK?'

Tony sighed again, shook his head. 'This other person. It's ... complicated. She's someone I've known for years. We used to be very close until I involved her in something I shouldn't have done. And I've always regretted it. We tried to keep each other at arm's length. But we couldn't. We're still close. But she's got responsibilities. So we just ... talk on the phone. Or one of us does. The other listens. But that doesn't take care of everything.'

'And I did? Thanks a lot.'

He tried to speak, but closed his mouth again. The correct words weren't there.

They remained that way, Claire sitting, pulling herself in close, Tony standing, feeling uncomfortable.

'So what happens next?' Tony said eventually.

'I don't know,' said Claire. 'I'll have to think about it.'

Tony nodded.

'I understand if you want to tell people about this. But I would ask you not to. Not for me, for the sake of the Centre.'

Claire looked straight ahead, over Tony's shoulder, at the picture on the wall. Charcoal etched on paper.

Black and white.

'I want you to leave now. I think you've said enough.'

Tony opened his mouth to speak, to say something that would resolve the situation. But Claire wasn't looking at him. Wasn't listening. He walked slowly towards the front door, let himself out. The door closed behind him, the click of the lock a small, final sigh of relief.

Claire stayed on the sofa, immobile. Looking at the picture, seeing beyond it.

A figure detached itself from the darkened bedroom, came over to the sofa, sat next to her.

'You OK?' asked Larkin.

Claire's eyes began to well, her lower lip to quiver. He put his arm gently round her and she yielded to him, burrowing her face into his shoulder.

She sobbed soundlessly. He held her.

'Take me to bed,' she said eventually. 'Take me to bed. And don't leave me in the morning.'

'OK.'

Larkin stood up, bringing her up with him. He walked towards the bedroom, not letting her go.

They went inside.

Closed the door behind them.

Tanya was hungry.

She knelt on the filthy floor of her flat, bare and balled up beneath the dust-covered light bulb. She was shivering. Hot. Cold. She clutched her stomach, felt the pain blading round her body.

Her stomach was a cavernous, convulsing space bordered with sharks' teeth gnashing angrily at her insides. It raged, it growled.

It hungered for something more than food.

She clutched herself, fingernails digging through flesh, rolled on her side. Gasped with pain.

Once, she had had needs to fulfil, desires, like other people. Normal people. Home. Family. Love. Happiness. Respect. Those things were long gone now, eaten up, subsumed: only the ghost of a memory remaining. A dusty image.

In their place was the hunger, the craving: a writhing black pit inside her, surrounded by pumping, blood-laden walls. Not a monkey on her back but an angry, empty void demanding to be filled; physically, spiritually, mentally.

She had money. She had worked for it. Hard. But the boys hadn't come. They hadn't left enough stuff. It was never enough. It hadn't lasted.

No good.

She searched round on the floor, through the carpet, looking for crumbs to pick up, specks to suck. Nothing. Just dirt. And dust. Everywhere dust. All around her. From dust she came, in dust she was.

No good. She would have to go out.

She stood up, slowly made her way to the bedroom, pulled on a sweatshirt, jeans, trainers – nothing was clean any more – raked together the money that men had given her to use her body, left the flat, stumbled downstairs into the darkness.

She knew where she was going. Which flat. She had vowed never to go there again after the men there had made her hurt inside, made her bleed for her smack. Took her pain as payment. But this time she had money. It would be different.

She crossed streets, clutching her stomach, blind to everyone and everything but her own need.

Tanya reached the flat. The door, battleship steel and bolted into place, had a reinforced slot through which money passed in, gear out. She rang the bell. The slot opened.

'Aye. What you want?'

Tanya pulled the wadded-up bills from her pocket, stuffed them into the slot. Her face contorted with pain, her eyes tearing over.

'Give us some gear.'

Her voice rasping and cracked.

'How much?'

'That much! That much! Just ... please...'

The money was taken, the flap closed. She heard voices, laughter seeping round the edges of the thick steel.

She shivered, stamped from foot to foot. No good. The pain moved when she moved.

The flap reopened. A small, tinfoil-wrapped bundle appeared.

'There you go, pet. 'S a good mixture, that. Somethin' special, just for you.'

Laughter behind the voice, the speaker joining in.

'Hey, pet, you wanna come in here? Have a

little party? Give you a good time.'

The laughter exploded. Tanya ignored it, snatched up the bundle, pocketed it. The flap closed. She turned, began to hurry back to the flat.

The pain was even more intense, tempered with the knowledge that it would soon be assuaged.

'Nearly there, nearly there, nearly there...' She repeated the phrase over and over again. A train-like mantra.

She reached the flat, let herself in.

Straight into the bedroom, works out. The bundle unwrapped. Looking for an uncollapsed vein, finding one between her fingers. Hands shaking, nearly too unstable to hold the spoon over the lighter.

That familiar fizz and bubble.

That smell.

She almost smiled in anticipation.

Breathing deeply, holding herself steady, concentrating.

Drawing it up into the hypo.

Looking at it through the plastic.

Her lover. Her life.

The colour looked different, but she couldn't think about that now She had to have it.

Had to.

The vein was pushed, tapped, made prominent.

The needle inserted.

In. Back. In. All the way.

And out.

She lay back on the mattress, waited. For that beautiful, exciting numbness to take over her body, to transport her away.

She waited.

But it never came.

Instead, her heart became an old, corroded battery pumping acid through her veins.

Her bones were being pipecleaned with barbed wire.

Razor-toed ballerinas danced furiously inside her muscles.

She rolled over, screamed. It came out as a muffled gag, a bleach gurgle.

*'Somethin' special, just for you.'*

*Laughter behind the voice.*

She clawed at her body, tried to rip the poison out.

Couldn't.

Sobbed tears of molten metal.

'Please ... please...'

The words more in her head than her mouth.

'Help me... I'm sorry, I'm sorry, please... Help me...'

Carly, that was her name, Carly.

'I'm sorry... Oh, God, I'm sorry...'

Tossing from side to side, vomiting and shitting her insides out.

A nuclear bomb detonated inside her head, her heart. The fallout poisoned her body. A final corruption.

She screamed. It was choked off, gurgled away.

And Tanya stopped fighting.

She lay still, the pain, the life bleached from her body.

Empty, lifeless eyes staring at a bare bulb sun.

No more sadness. No more happiness.

Just oblivion.

And dust.

## 17. Then

'Thuh-there's our boy.'

The BMW was parked opposite the gates of Newcastle United's Chester-le-Street training ground. The players were going through their paces. Bibbed and tracksuited, dodging cones, doing sprints, jogs and five-a-sides.

Nev grunted. 'Like a bunch a' puffs. Look at their hair.'

'Nuh-not a fu-fan, Nev?'

Nev shrugged. 'Not a man's game any more.'

Tommy smiled. 'When wuh-we've finished, our buh-boy won't be playin' eh-eh-eh-any games any more.'

Nev grunted, shrugged.

'Teach him a luh-lesson.'

Tony finished training, showered. He was feeling good, happy. Tingling from more than just exercise. He was no longer training with the reserves. Big Jack had him with the first team. That gave him a warm yet giddy feeling inside. The first team. His future: here and now. It was happening.

He dressed, threw his gear into his sports bag, made his way into the car park.

He unlocked his car, threw the bag on the back seat, looked up.

'Shit.'

The warm and giddy feeling disappeared,

replaced by something sour and shivering.

Tommy Jobson and Big Nev were crossing the car park towards him. Tommy was smiling his shark smile, Nev was his usual colossal self, as dangerous and threatening as an out-of-control petrol tanker.

'Hel-hello, Tony. How you duh-doin'.'

Tony stared at them, fronting it. Hoping the sudden shake in his limbs couldn't be seen.

'Hello, lads,' he said. His voice sounded high, tight and strangled in his own ears. 'What brings you here? Autograph hunting?'

'Nuh-not interested in the rest,' said Tommy. 'Juh-just you.'

Tony's stomach back-flipped. He attempted a smile.

'I can't get you a season ticket if that's what you want.'

Tommy laughed. It came out forced and harsh, dredged from within like a lump of toxic phlegm. 'No, it's yuh-you we want. Gu-got a proposition for you. Mr Fairbairn sent us.'

Tony shivered inwardly. 'No,' he said. 'Whatever it is, the answer's no.'

'Hear it fuh-first. Then say no.'

Tony sighed, wished he was somewhere else. Said nothing.

'We've found a way where you can still play football and work for us.'

'Not interested. Sorry.'

Tony shook his head, tried to get into his car. Nev placed his huge paw on the doorframe, stopped him. It looked like he could have ripped the door off with one hand.

'Hear us out.'

Tommy's voice sounded sharp and confident. He smiled again.

'There's a lot of new markets opening up. Lot of money to be made by a bright, ambitious, enterprisin' young lad such as yourself. Take your team, for instance. Young men about town earnin' a good livin'. Why not give them some good-time charlie?'

'Not interested.'

'Needn't interfere with your career. Could be a profitable luh-little sideline.'

Tony swallowed hard. 'How many times do I have to tell you? I'm not interested.'

'But, Tony—'

'Listen, Tommy. I thought we had a deal. I thought that what I did for you was in the past.'

Tommy shrugged, smiled. 'It's not.'

The words fired Tony. Adrenalin kicked in, a surge of strength. Fight or flight.

'As far as I'm concerned, it is. I don't owe you anythin'.'

He looked at Nev then back at Tommy.

'Tell your trained gorilla to take his hand off my car. And then both of you piss off. I've got a date. And I don't want to keep the lady waitin'.'

Nev lifted his arm, pulled it back, ready to strike Tony. But Tommy put his hand up, stopped him.

'Leave it, Nev. Let him go.'

Nev dropped his arm but didn't relax.

Tony looked between the two of them, saw no immediate threat. He climbed into his car, started it, drove away as fast as he could go.

Tommy and Nev watched him. Nev turned to Tommy, anger and violence in his eyes. 'You let him go.'

Tommy nodded, eyes on the receding car.

'What for? Whassamatter? You gettin' soft?'

Tommy turned to him, eyes like two hot coals. The blade Tommy kept up his sleeve had materialized in his hand. 'Don't you ever say that to me again. Ever. Y'understand?'

Nev looked into Tommy's eyes, saw that he was only seconds from death. He was scared. Despite his size and strength, he didn't have something that Tommy had. Or rather, he had something Tommy lacked.

'Yes, Tommy. Sorry, Tommy.'

The volcano inside Tommy subsided. The blade disappeared. 'Good,' he said. 'Good. I didn't let him go, Nev. I just gave him his last chance to save himself. What happens next is his own fault.'

'How d'you mean?'

'Mr Fairbairn suh-said he wanted me to make an example out of someone. Send out a message. Keep the others in line.'

'We gonna follow him, then?'

'No need, Nev. We know where he's goin' to be tonight.'

'Where?'

'He's got a date, he said. That'll be with his girlfriend. And I know where she lives.'

Nev looked at him. Tommy smiled.

'Let's get back to the car, Nev. We've got a ruh-rinky dink time ahead of us.'

Louise was out of the shower, towelling her hair

dry, listening to Bronski Beat on the tape player telling her to run away, get away, run away.

She wore no make-up and a white terrycloth robe. She felt relaxed, good about herself. She was alone. Rachel having gone straight out from college.

She was only expecting one person.

Tony.

He was the reason she felt so good. She was loving her life, loving the present. And she could see the future, her future, with him.

And she loved him all the more for it.

She put down the towel, sat before the mirror, shook a canister of hair mousse.

The doorbell rang.

Louise checked her watch. He was early.

She stood up, made for the stairs, started down. The last time he arrived early and she wasn't dressed, they had ended up being late out.

She smiled at the memory, opened the door.

'Well,' she said, 'you've caught me undressed again. So–'

She looked up, stopped.

This wasn't Tony. This was two men, one young and sharp-suited, one older and bulkier in a leather jacket. The younger one smiled.

'We huh-have indeed. Luh-Louise Lu-Larkin?'

She instinctively clutched her robe to her chest. 'Yes?'

'We're friends of Tony's. Cuh-can we come in and wait for him, please?'

The younger one was smiling, polite, but there was nothing warm about him. He was like ice.

She sensed trouble, tried to push the door

closed, stop them entering. They ignored her. The larger one grabbed her arm, twisted it behind her back, walked her upstairs. The younger one stepped inside, closed the door behind him.

The whole thing, from door opening to closing, took only a matter of seconds. Louise had not time to think, scream, or close the door.

Nev walked her into the living room, threw her on the sofa.

She sat, rubbing her sore arm, her eyes darting nervously between the two of them. Scared. Heart trying to escape from her body. 'Who are you? What d'you want?'

Her voice was tumbling into hysteria.

'I told you,' said Tommy. 'We're friends of Tony's. Business associates. I'm Tommy. This is Nev. We just want a word with him.'

Louise looked at the bigger one. Something was sticking out of his pocket.

'What's that?' she said.

Nev pulled the object out, showed it to her. 'A hammer,' he said.

At the sight of that, it felt as if the bones had been removed from Louise's body. Her flesh quivered like an electrified jellyfish.

'Muh-my flatmate's here,' she said. She was finding it hard to breathe.

'No, she's not,' said Tommy. 'We know she's not, so don't lie.'

'I'll scream.'

'No, you won't.'

She gave a desperate look towards the phone. Nev caught the look, crossed to the phone, ripped it out of the wall.

Louise pulled her robe tighter about her body. Her head dropped, eyes closed.

'Please. Just do what you're going to do, then go. Please.'

'I tuh-told you. We have to wait for Tony.'

'But what d'you want with him? He's a footballer.'

'Not always. He used to work for me.'

'Doing what?'

Tommy raised his hand to his nose, sniffed. Despite the fear, Louise was shocked.

'No.'

'Oh, yuh-yes.'

'Don't believe you.'

Tommy shrugged. 'I don't cuh-care.'

Louise looked around the room. She checked the doors: her distance from them, what obstacles were in the way, whether they were locked or unlocked.

Nev had sat down; Tommy was standing by the fireplace. If she ran for the front door, he would reach her. Her only chance was the back door. She could make a dash for that and hope Nev would be too slow to catch her. He was big. He must be slow.

She tried to look relaxed, hoped that would make her less of a sudden flight risk, more compliant. Her silence, she hoped, would cause them to relax too.

She slumped her shoulders, thinking that would make her look resigned. There seemed to be a relaxation of the men's posture when she did so. She took that as her chance.

She jumped up, went round the sofa, made it

through the kitchen to the back door. She got her hand on the lock, turned the key. She turned the handle.

A massive pair of arms encircled her body, crushing the air out of her like a huge boa constrictor.

She struggled, kicked blindly behind her. She felt her robe loosen, exposing her naked body. She ignored it. Even though the door was unlocked, she knew she wouldn't get another chance.

Nev swung her round, marched her back into the main room to face Tommy. He stood there grinning.

'That was a stupid thing to do, wasn't it?'

She opened her mouth to scream. Nev clamped one of his bear-like hands over it.

'D'you think we're jokin', eh?'

Tommy found the stereo, turned it up.

His eyes had flattened. They were cold, harder than ever.

Like a lizard from *V,* she thought.

'We're serious, you bitch. I'll have to show you how serious.' A knife appeared in Tommy's hand.

Louise's eyes widened in terror. She struggled, fought, but it was no good.

Tommy brought the knife closer.

Louise felt urine run down her leg. She struggled, desperate to be free. Her mouth latched on to Nev's hand. She bit it, hard.

'Bitch!'

Nev let her go. She tried to run again but Nev grabbed her arm, swung her round. He punched her in the face. Her head snapped back; she began to go down. Her temple connected with the fireplace as she fell. She collapsed on the floor.

Tommy sighed, put down the knife. 'Aw, shit,' he said.

'What?' said Nev.

'What did you do that for?'

'Bitch bit me hand.'

Tommy shook his head. He sounded angry with himself. 'I can't do them when they're unconscious.'

'Pissed herself an' all,' said Nev.

'Give us a hand.'

Nev helped Tommy to lay Louise on the sofa. Nev studied her. Ignored the bleeding gash on the side of her head, the swelling on her face. Concentrated on the undone terry robe and what was underneath. Good tits. Nice bush. His cock began to stir.

'You might not be able to do anythin',' he said, 'but I can.'

Nev pulled his zip down.

'Leave it,' said Tommy.

Nev looked at him, puzzled.

'Whassamatter with you, like? You were gonna cut 'er a minute ago.'

Tommy looked at the unconscious body of Louise. She was tempting. But he was right not to touch her, take advantage of her. Frank would have said so. Dino even. And that was good enough for him

'No, I wasn't. I was goin' to scu-scare her. Real men don't do that to women. Anyway, we're here for huh-him, not her.'

Nev gave a small snort of disgust that he hoped

437

Tommy didn't hear, then sat down in the armchair.

Tommy pulled Louise's robe around her. She had a beautiful body, no doubt. But without that spark of life, that animation, thought Tommy, it was nothing.

'What d'we do now, then?' said Nev.

Tommy sat down next to Louise.

'We wait.'

Keith was furiously flipping through the pages of his book, nearly ripping them out as he went, desperately searching for cross-referenced precedents.

There were none.

He had never seen the two men before. He was sure of that.

From the alley he had managed to see only the backs of their heads, but he knew they weren't familiar.

Their manner of entry was strange too. To a casual observer there would be nothing untoward, but Keith was more than that. He thought they bundled Louise in, forced her back into her own flat. He couldn't be a hundred per cent, but that was what it had looked like.

Perhaps they were burglars and she was in danger.

Or rapists.

Or perhaps Woodhouse had told his mates about her and they all wanted a piece.

Yes, he thought, cheeks burning, that would be it.

He continued flipping through the book, slower

now, knowing he would find nothing. He sighed, placed it on the passenger seat.

He watched.

And wondered.

Tapped a disco back beat on the steering wheel.

What was going on in there? Something he should be concerned about? Or taking part in? Or watching?

Watching.

It was getting dark, but not dark enough for him to go unseen. He would wait. Bide his time. See what happened.

Woodhouse's car pulled up to the kerb.

Keith wriggled in his seat, leaned forward.

This should be interesting.

Woodhouse locked the car, rang the bell. The door was opened by the bigger of the two men. Woodhouse looked shocked to see him, started arguing.

Keith concentrated, screwed up his eyes. But he couldn't hear what was said.

The big man gestured Woodhouse inside. Woodhouse went in, the door closing behind him.

Keith was breathing heavily.

This was throwing the logic of his book completely out of the window.

Keith watched.

And waited to see what would happen next.


'Hello, Tuh-Tony.'

'What the fuck have you done to her?'

Tony tried to run across the room, to Louise's unconscious body on the sofa. Nev grabbed him, held him in a bear hug, stopped him from moving.

439

'Let me go, you cunt!'

Tommy stood up. 'Stop shouting, Tuh-Tuh-Tony. We du-du-don't want the neighbours to hear.'

The blade appeared in Tommy's hand. He held it over Louise's face, smiled. 'Stop shu-shu-shu-shouting, Tony.'

Tony fell silent, stopped struggling.

'That's better.'

'You cunt.' Tony's voice was low, rich with anger. 'Pickin' on women now? You little piece of shit. What a hard man, fightin' girls–'

'She fainted, Tony. She hasn't been hurt.' Tommy twirled the knife. 'Yet.'

Tony was breathing heavily. If he had been able to, he would have killed both of them. Or tried to.

Tommy sat down, patted Louise's leg.

'What happens next, Tony, depends on you. I want to ask you some qu-qu-questions. You listenin'?'

Tony said nothing.

'I'll take that as a yes. Ruh-right. Now, I'm offerin' you the chance to make a lot of money. Cocaine. Next big thing. So–' he looked at his reflection in the blade '–you in or out?'

'Out.'

'Take your tuh-time. Thu-thu-think about it.'

'I've thought. Out. Now fuck off.'

Tommy shook his head.

'Sorry, Tuh-Tony. It doesn't work like that. Yes, we will leave. But, you see, Mr Fairbairn wanted an example made. Of anyone who didn't want to join our empire. Send a clear signal, he said. So, which will it be?'

440

Tommy gestured with his blade to Louise.

'Your lovely girlfriend?'

He pointed the blade at Tony.

'Or yourself?'

Tony stared at him. Pupils pinpoints of hatred. Heart exploding with fear. 'You bastard. You sick fuckin' bastard.'

Tommy's eyes narrowed. His voice hardened. 'I'm gu-givin' you a chance, you cu-cunt. It's more than I give most people.'

Tony said nothing.

'Tell you what,' said Tommy, reaching into his pocket, 'we'll toss for it.' He pulled out a ten pence piece, spun it in the air, caught it, slapped it down unseen on the back of his knife-wielding hand.

'Heads or tails?'

Tony just stared.

'I said heads or tails, you cunt.'

Tony gasped in pain as he felt Nev's arms squeeze his ribs harder. Any tighter and they would snap.

'Heads or tails?'

'Tails!'

Tommy looked at the coin, sighed.

'Oh, well,' he said and pocketed it.

He gave Nev a nod.

Tony felt a loosening on one side of his body. Nev's arm was free. He then felt a searing, sharp pain in his right kidney. Nev had punched him. He arched his back in agony. Nev released his arms and he fell to the floor. He couldn't move, the pain was indescribable. Nev landed a kick to his side to make sure.

He then felt a wad of cloth being roughly stuffed into the back of his mouth. He couldn't speak, could barely breathe.

'We've been so quiet. Shuh-shame to alarm the neighbours now.'

Tommy nodded again to Nev who drew the hammer from his jacket.

Tony tried to move, tried to scream. He could do neither.

'Cuh-consider our business relationsh-sh-ship over. Severance pay from the chairman of the board.'

Nev brought the hammer down on Tony's knee.

Fireworks.

Then freezing ice.

Then hellfire pain.

Then nothing.


Keith watched the two men leave.

They got into their BMW, drove away.

Keith had to know what was going on. Had to.

Woodhouse was still inside. With Louise.

Keith had to see.

He got out of the car, locked it, looked around.

Satisfied he was alone, he made his way to the back door, his previous night's behaviour now enshrined as ritual.

Counting down the back-yard doors.

Opening the latch with his right hand.

His left foot first over the threshold.

Ritual. Re-creating the conditions. Summoning up the success.

Walking across the yard, willing himself invisible from the eyes of the downstairs occupants.

Up the wooden staircase, filling his steps with lightness and stealth.

At the back door, ear against the half-glass, listening.

No conversation. No movements. Stereo on loud, the Smiths asking what difference it all made.

Keith looked along the windows to the bedroom. Saw open curtains and a made-up bed.

His heart was beating from more than his usual voyeuristic buzz.

Something was wrong in there. The visit from the two men had confirmed that.

Breath coming in thrill-gasps, he tried the handle.

It turned.

Legs shaking, chest palpitating, hands sweating, he pushed the door open, stepped inside.

The kitchen looked normal. Plates on the drainer, mugs and bowls in the sink. Just like he'd last seen it.

He walked into the living room.

And stopped dead.

The room had been wrecked. Like a bad, messy robbery. Woodhouse lay, leg twisted, jeans bloodied, in a still heap by the door at the top of the stairs. He looked as though he was foaming at the mouth until Keith realized it was some kind of gag.

Louise lay, robe untied, eyes closed, on the sofa. Unmoving. Unconscious. Or dead.

Keith stood in the centre of the room, tried to catalogue the emotions surging through his body.

Woodhouse, the man who had stolen Louise

away from him, now lying helpless or dead before him.

Robe untied. Eyes closed.

He crossed and knelt down beside her. Her chest was rising and falling. She was alive.

Keith smiled, so happy for her. Relief flooded through him. There she was, beautiful and breathing.

Beautiful.

He reached across, stroked the soft skin of her cheek with the back of his hand.

Beautiful.

Let his hand trail down her neck to her chest, fingers following the curve of her breasts. Her nipples.

Beautiful.

His cock was rising, straining to be released for his girlfriend. Keith put one hand on it, stroking his erection, as he let his other hand stroke down Louise's body, over her stomach, coming to rest on her dark, thick pubic hair.

He was gasping for breath now, rubbing himself furiously.

Behind him, Woodhouse let out a muffled moan.

Keith turned, shocked into rigidity. Woodhouse's eyes were still closed, his forehead knitted in pain. Keith didn't want this man, this intruder, in the same room as his girlfriend.

Anger rising in him, he crossed to the body and dragged it to the top of the stairs. Woodhouse was heavier than he thought and it took so much strength he began to lose his erection.

Keith reached the top of the stairs. He knelt down and pushed.

Woodhouse's body tumbled slowly down, getting wedged in the stairwell before reaching the bottom.

Keith stood up, smiled. Pleased with his work. Pleased at being a man who stood up to his enemy. Flushed with success, he turned to Louise, robe still untied, eyes still closed.

Beautiful.

His girlfriend. His woman. With his rival out of the way, there would be no contest.

Keith crossed to Louise. Heart bursting with love. Cock straining with lust.

He smiled. Whoever those two men were, he would have to thank them. For bringing the two of them back together.

He undid his belt, loosened his trousers, took his cock out.

He leaned over her, parted her legs, pushed his cock inside her.

She was dry, unyielding. He would soon change that. Soon have her in the mood.

He worked at her, pumping hard. Eyes closed.

You belong to me...

Thrust. Hard.

You should be with me. Not him...

Into her. And again.

I love you.

And again.

I love you.

And again.

He opened his eyes. And jumped in shock.

Louise's eyes were open, staring back at him.

He felt his face redden, tried to smile. Tried to find words to speak.

But he didn't need to. Her eyes closed again. She was gone.

Relief washed over him.

He resumed thrusting with renewed vigour.

Hard.

I love you.

Hard.

I love you.

Hard.

He came. Body twisting and buckling, almost blacking out from the sensation.

It was the best orgasm of his life.

He opened his eyes. Louise's were still closed. She was still unconscious.

Good.

He climbed off her, fastened himself up, looked around the room.

Looked down at Louise.

And was hit by sudden postcoital shame.

He tried to put those thoughts out of his head and concentrate on the positive ones.

It was love.

What he had just done was an act of love.

He pulled Louise's robe back around her, covered her up.

He looked at Tony Woodhouse's body lying bundled halfway down the stairs and felt a pang of anxiety. He might have killed the man.

Not that Keith cared, but he didn't want to go to prison for it.

He walked down the stairs, looked at the body. There was no way he could drag it back up again, but he could make it more comfortable.

He reached into Woodhouse's mouth, pulled

out the gag and let the head fall back gently.

He went back upstairs and looked around the room for a phone. Discovering it had been forcibly disconnected, he decided it was time to leave.

He found a phone box, dialled 999. Told them where and who. Put the phone down when they asked him for more.

Conscience clearing, he returned to his car in the alley to wait and watch.

He didn't have to wait long. An ambulance pulled up in less than ten minutes, disgorging running paramedics who entered the flat, came back out bearing two bodies on stretchers with masks clamped to their faces.

Alive. Both of them.

Keith breathed a sigh of relief.

The ambulance doors closed. It moved off, siren wailing.

Keith started the car, ready to follow. Ready to find out which hospital Louise was being taken to.

He smiled.

Wondered what kind of flowers to take his girlfriend when he visited her the next day.

## 18. Now

Election day.

Candidates and their teams had been patrolling the streets since daybreak, loud-hailing from balloon-festooned cars. Up and down the seafront, round shops, down suburban roads. Imploring the electorate, extolling their candidate. The polling booths were seeing small but steady streams of people coming in, marking crosses, leaving. Little joy, just a sense of duty, of continuity. A reluctant nod towards the lesser of several evils, a disconsolate hope that things would finally get better.

Suzanne walked out of school. Make-up in place, uniform bundled into her shoulder bag. Karl was waiting in his car by the kerb. She attempted to smile for him, tried to speed up her footsteps.

It was becoming harder for her. Everything was getting harder for her.

She had locked herself away in the girls' toilets at break time just to be alone. Just to think. She had closed her eyes, tried to find peace in the darkness, but had succeeded only in nodding off to sleep. If Karl hadn't phoned her, the shrill, insistent trilling of her mobile waking her up, she might have slept all day.

She had answered it. Karl had reminded her he was picking her up tonight. Had something special in mind. The encouraging responses she had made were the correct ones, but, on ending the call, her heart was heavy.

She reached Karl's car, got in. He leaned over and kissed her, his hands groping her breast, kneading her inner thighs. He pulled back.

'You're lookin' good, Suzy.'

She said nothing. He started the car.

'Where we going?'

'Bit o' business to do. Then it's back to mine.'

They drove off. He lit a spliff, took a pull,

handed it to her. She did the same, swallowing the urge to cough. She felt it working its way round her body, visualized her insides being clouded up by a sweet, narcotized fog, hiding her anxieties, her questions. She took another toke, passed it back.

Karl laughed. 'Get it down you, make you feel good.'

'So what's happening tonight, then?' her words slurred.

'Somethin' different. Got a couple of lads who work for me comin' round. We're gonna have a bit of a party.'

'They bringing their girlfriends?'

Karl smiled. 'No. Just us. They're young, these two. Just kids, really. What they need is an experienced, sexy woman to break them in. Show them what they're missing. Hey,' Karl said, as if struck by a sudden thought. 'You could do it.'

A sharp blade of clarity knifed through Suzanne's mental fog.

'What?'

'Yeah. After me an' you have fu–, made love, you can show them how it's done.'

'No way.'

'Go on, it'll be a laugh.'

'Karl–'

'Do it for me.' He smiled. 'Remember. We're not like other people. We're excitin' an' different. I wouldn't ask you if I didn't love you.'

She looked at him. There was no point arguing. She knew she would have to go through with it. She knew he would get his way. He always did.

'I'll need some more of that.'

She pointed to the spliff. He handed it to her.

'Have as much as you like.'

She took it, sucked it down into her lungs.

''Course when they've had their fun,' he said casually, 'we'll charge them for it. No sense missin' an opportunity to make money.'

The smoke caught in her throat and she coughed. A wave of nausea passed over her: she thought she was going to be sick. Her face became red, her chest sore. She tasted bile in her throat. Karl took the spliff from her fingers.

'Whoa, careful. If you're gonna puke, tell us an' I'll stop. Don't do it in the car.'

Between bouts of coughing, she shook her head.

'Better now?'

Suzanne nodded as she began to regain control of her body.

'Good.' He offered her the spliff. 'Wanna try again?'

She took it, sucking the smoke into her body, holding it down, hoping it would cloud her over and quickly.

She doubted there was enough hash in the world to do that.

Everything was getting harder for her.

It was time to stop.

Anne Robinson winked, said goodbye. *The Weakest Link* closing credits rolled up, alongside discussions of success and failure. Louise lay stretched out on the sofa, feet up, watching, thinking. Scaring and belittling members of the general public for thirty minutes a day had made

Anne Robinson hugely popular and a millionaire. Being strong, Louise thought, was the only way forward. Anne had proved it.

She took a drag from her cigarette. She had decided to take up smoking again, it was something she used to do when she was younger but had stopped because Keith hadn't approved. She was doing it again for the same reason. She was going to start doing other things too. For the same reason.

She had prepared the family meal: something microwavable from Sainsbury's. She didn't feel like putting herself out for them any more. She would match their lack of appreciation with a lack of effort.

The front door opened just as *The Simpsons* came on. Closed again. Keith entered the room.

'What are you doing?'

Louise didn't turn round.

'What does it look like? I'm watching the telly.'

'You're ... you're ... you're smoking.'

Louise took a long, deep drag.

'That's right.'

'I will not have smoking in this house.'

Louise expelled a jet of smoke into the air, ignored him. Homer was hatching a grand scheme involving beer.

The phone began to ring.

'The phone's ringing,' he said.

'Then answer it.'

She knew he was looking at her. She knew he would do nothing to her. He was impotent with rage.

Keith stormed off into the hall to pick up the

phone. He returned, threw it on to her stomach.

'It's your daughter.'

He walked away.

Louise reached for the phone, a burr of anger germinating inside her at his words.

'Hello, Suzanne.'

'Mum, listen.'

Suzanne's voice was echoing and hushed. She was whispering, talking as if she didn't want to be heard.

Louise listened.

'I'm . . . I'm scared. I...' She sighed. 'I want to come home. Will you come and get me? Will you and Dad come and get me?'

Louise sat up.

'What's up, pet? Where are you?'

'I'm in a flat in the Wills Building. On the coast road. D'you know it?'

''Course I do. What's the number?'

She told her.

'Please come and get me. And bring Dad. There might be some ... some trouble.'

'I will. But what—'

'He's coming. I've got to go. Please come and get me. Please.'

The connection was cut, the line silenced. Louise sat straight up, galvanized into action. She stubbed her cigarette out, went into the kitchen. Keith was looking at the instructions on a packet of pre-cooked microwave lasagne as if they were written in ancient Hebrew.

'That was Suzanne,' she said. 'Come on, she's in trouble and she needs us to go and pick her up.'

Keith snorted.

'What's she done this time? Got herself drunk? Or got herself pregnant?'

Louise felt the anger grow within her. Her legs began to shake. Tiny stars danced before her eyes as her head started to feel light with rage.

'She's your daughter. And she's in trouble. Now come on.'

Keith put down the lasagne, turned to her. Lips curled in a sneering smirk.

'But she's not my daughter, is she? We both know that.'

Louise could hold it in no longer.

'She is your daughter, you bastard, she is yours!'

She punched him.

Everything moved down to slo-mo: seventeen years to pull back her arm, seventeen years to let it fly, seventeen years for the punch to fall, her fist clenched hard, connecting with the side of his jaw.

The impact of the blow knocked Keith off balance. He fell to his knees, tried to speak.

'Don't say a word, you little shit! Of course you're her father. D'you think I don't remember? That night at my flat? You raped me, you bastard! You fucking bastard!'

He tried to stand, she pushed him back down.

'Stay there.'

'I didn't... I didn't...' he said weakly.

'Don't lie to me. No, I didn't know at first. I tried to block that night out. Thought it was that big bloke at first. But things started coming back to me over the years. Things I thought I'd imagined. And I put it all together. So don't lie. I saw you. I opened my eyes, remember?'

He attempted to climb to his feet. She allowed him to.

'It wasn't like that,' he said, his voice fearful and pleading. 'It wasn't r–' He couldn't say the word. 'Wasn't what you think it was. It was love. I did it out of love. I love you.'

'Really? Well, I fucking hate you...'

And she was on him. Punching, kicking, biting. Venting over a decade and a half of pent-up hatred. Repaying him for every insult, slight and degradation he had heaped on her during their marriage.

'You never loved me...' she said, panting, 'you just wanted to possess me...'

Punch after punch.

Year after year.

Insult after insult.

She was tiring but she wouldn't stop. Couldn't stop. The tap was turned on, she would let it run out of her until the tank was empty.

'Get off my dad! Leave my dad alone!'

Louise stopped, turned at the voice. Ben was standing in the kitchen doorway, face twisted in shock and horror. He ran along the floor, launched himself at her, began pummelling with his small fists.

'Get off him! Get off him!'

Louise backed off, stunned by the turn of events. She made her way over to the kitchen door.

'All right,' she said. 'All right.'

The pummelling stopped. Ben crossed to Keith, began helping him up off the floor.

Louise looked at them. Father and son. A chip off the old block. Mini me.

Ben was Keith in miniature. He would grow up to be just like his father.

Louise didn't want to hang around and watch it happen.

'I'm going to get my daughter,' she said. 'And I'm going to find someone to help me.'

She left the house, slamming the door behind her.

She got into her Ka, drove away.

The sky was darkening. The night would soon be hitting hard.

The polls were coming to the end, the nation having made up its collective mind.

Tony stood on the jetty by the Garden of Eden pub. He looked out over the river, watched the clouds scud slowly across the sky, their greyness deepening to purple then black as the day drained out of them.

'Thanks for coming,' he said.

The other person nodded.

'Odd place for a meeting.'

'You think so?' Tony leaned on the railing. He was thoughtful. Preoccupied. 'I don't.'

He moved his head slowly to the left.

'It's perfect here. Perfect. Look.'

He pointed. The redundant piers, the tall cranes old and rusted, sticking up like tottering spider webs, too feeble to trap anything. The jetty, all rust and wet wood. Past them the river curved away back to its source. On the bed on the far side stood the power station. Its four chimneys belched billow after billow of smoke into the air, a twenty-four-hour cloud factory, its buildings lit by night-time arc lamps.

'Look at the power station. Still coal-fired. They take hard, black coal and turn it into bright, white energy. Coal's all imported now, of course. But it's old. Old energy. Unrenewable energy. It's the past. Now look along that way.'

He pointed to the right. By the river's entrance to the sea, along the harbour wall, stood the wind turbines. Huge, white windmills turning slowly, picking up the slightest breeze.

'There's the future. Clean, bright, dazzling. Renewable. And in the middle?'

He turned, looked behind him. Coldwell. The leisure centre replacing the colliery. The T. Dan.

'Us. The present. In the middle. Always. We try to reach the future, follow the flow of the river down to where it's clean and bright. But we can't. 'Cause we've still got the past sitting there. We're afraid to cut loose from it. We can't turn it off – so we leave it there. Choking up the air. Holding us back. Impeding our progress.'

Tony fell silent, leaned on the railing.

'Interesting theory.'

Tommy Jobson stood next to him. Leaned alongside him.

Tony nodded.

'Claire caught me in the office. Taking my medication. Our little arrangement might be in jeopardy.'

'Oh, dear.'

Tony turned to him. 'More than fucking "oh, dear", isn't it? For me anyway.'

Tommy shrugged. 'She might not say anything.'

Tony sighed. 'No, she might not. I'll have to talk to her again.'

Tony's mobile trilled. He answered it. 'Hello?'

'Listen, Tony, it's me.' Louise. Her voice frantic. 'Don't hang up. Please. Please talk to me. This is important, please.'

'He-hello, Louise.'

His voice was hesitant, unused to dialogue.

'Oh, thank God. Listen, you've got to help me. I've tried Stephen and he's not answering. Please. You have to help.'

'OK, Louise, calm down. Just tell me what's wrong.'

She told him.

He listened.

'Right. I'll meet you at my house. Ten minutes. Don't worry. It's going to be all right.'

He ended the call.

'Trouble?'

'Yeah.'

'We'll take my car. I'll drive.'

Suzanne wanted out of there.

She hadn't spoken since Karl picked the two boys up in Coldwell and drove back to his flat. She knew what they were thinking, expecting of her. They had openly stared at her body, especially the odd-looking one in the glasses. The other had tried to be cooler, more reserved about it, as if it was all no big deal. Something about him unnerved her. She sensed anger within him, which, one day, would probably manifest itself in cruelty and violence.

457

She had felt their eyes on her from the back seat of the car, like spiders crawling all over her body.

Karl lit a spliff, handed it round. The two boys demolished their share, Suzanne declined.

'Take it.'

A command, not a request.

She took it.

They reached the Wills Building, parked, went up to Karl's flat.

'Help yourself, lads,' said Karl, throwing Davva a bottle of tequila.

Davva examined it as if he'd never seen tequila before.

'Ta,' he said, then looked again. 'What's that at the bottom? Looks like a worm, or somethin'.'

'It is,' said Karl, happy to impart knowledge. 'That's gold tequila. The best stuff. An' the worm's supposed to be like a drug. Eat that when you've reached the end of the bottle and you get like an acid trip.'

Davva looked again at the bottle, awe in his eyes. 'Fuckin' brilliant...'

'Get stuck in.'

Karl smiled, turned to Skegs on the other side of the room.

'Put some music on, Skegs. There's some UK garage collections there. One o' them'll do.'

Skegs did as he was told. Oxide and Neutrino kicked things off. The air in the flat became angular with beats, solid with lyrics and sampled harmonies.

Skegs's attention was caught by something lying next to the CD cabinet. He picked it up. 'Hey, looka this.'

The others turned, looked. Skegs had found Karl's automatic.

'Careful with that,' Karl said. He smiled. 'You don't know where it's been.'

Karl looked at Suzanne to see if she was smiling. She wasn't.

'Whassamatter with you?'

Suzanne sighed.

'I can't do this, Karl. I can't go through with it. I want to go home.'

Karl looked at her. There was no love in his eyes, no warmth. He looked like a farmer at auction appraising cattle, weighing up cost and profit.

'See how it goes.'

He turned to the boys.

'Lads, amuse yourselves for a bit.' He pointed to the coffee table. 'There's skunk, weed, coke. Some white widow, you'll like that. Help yourselves. Then make yourselves scarce. Me an' the lady got a bit o' business to attend to.'

Davva and Skegs rolled themselves skunk spliffs. Karl a white widow. He inhaled a couple of times, shaking his head from the buzz. Suzanne did nothing.

The boys left the room. Karl turned to her. He was red-faced, keyed up, breathing hard. He began to touch her.

'Wait,' said Suzanne.

'What?' Irritation bordering on anger in Karl's voice.

'Need to go to the toilet.'

She grabbed her bag, left the room.

Once in the toilet she took out her mobile

phone. Dialled a number in desperation. Hoped it would be answered.

Hoped it would be her mother.

The Daimler pulled up to the kerb in front of Tony's house.

'There she is,' Tony said.

He pointed to a Ka parked on the opposite side of the road. He hauled himself out of the Daimler as quickly as his shattered leg would allow, made his way over to her.

She saw him coming, got out of the car and ran to him. She reached him in the middle of the road, flung her arms around him.

'Tony...'

She clung to him.

He held on to her.

'We'd better move,' he said.

They walked to the pavement, still holding on to each other.

There was too much to be said in such a small space of time. Instead they said nothing.

They reached the pavement. Louise stopped dead, stared at the man in the light-coloured suit emerging from the driver's side of the Daimler.

'That's—'

'Tommy Jobson,' said Tony.

'What's he—'

'It's OK. He's with me. Times change.'

*The knife. Tommy grinning about what he was going to do with it.*

'Times don't change for me,' she said.

Tommy looked at her, his face impassive.

'Shouldn't we be going to get your daughter?'

460

he said. He opened the car door.

She looked at him. Physically he was the same. Older, a little greyer. But his eyes were different.

They looked pained.

Lost.

'Get in,' he said.

They got in. Tommy drove. He stayed just within the speed limit, police involvement being the last thing they wanted.

The Wills Building. Red-brick and grass-brick art deco. Spotlit in the darkness.

Tommy pulled the car up in a residents' parking bay.

'Wait here,' he said.

'Where are you going?' said Louise.

'To get your daughter.'

Louise was getting out of the car.

'No. No. You're not going in there. I won't let you–'

'You think you're going to get her? Just walk in, walk back out with her?' He shook his head. 'Stay here.'

Tommy walked off.

Louise started to go after him. Tony put a restraining arm on her.

'Let him go. He knows what he's doing. It's what he does for a living.'

She subsided, sighed.

Tommy walked to the front door.

And struck lucky. Someone was leaving as he was entering. They held the door for him. He smiled, nodded his thanks.

He took the lift up to the right floor. Alighted.

He didn't need to know the number. The noise

461

led him to it. He rang the bell, waited. It was soon opened by a youth clutching his jeans about his waist.

Karl. That was the name Suzanne had given.

Knowing subtlety wouldn't work, Tommy grabbed the youth by the throat, gripped hard. He squeezed off air, making him light-headed and disorientated. Feeling the youth weaken, Tommy pushed him backwards as hard as he could.

Karl caught the side of the sofa, upended it as he fell. He crashed on to a coffee table, scattering weed and charlie, then tumbled on to the floor, lay there.

He checked the youth, found no signs of immediate threat, looked round for Suzanne. He found her crouched on the floor, naked. Fear in her eyes, clothes in her hands.

She looked just like her mother, Tommy thought. 'I've come to take you home,' he said. 'Your mother sent me.'

She couldn't hear. His words were lost to the music.

He looked around, trying to find the source of the noise. Couldn't. Angered by this, he took a step towards her and tried again.

'Come on, we're leaving.'

Suzanne collapsed to the floor, tried to scuttle over to the corner of the room. Away from Tommy.

He crossed towards her.

She opened her mouth to scream.

He held up his hands to quieten her.

And felt a thud on the back of his neck.

Tommy turned. Karl was standing there, blood running from his nose and mouth, fists bunched. Face contorted with violence.

Tommy knew the look. He had experienced it himself enough times.

The youth looked like Tommy at that age. It was like looking into the past.

Karl bellowed something incomprehensible and swung his right fist at Tommy.

Tommy dodged, feinted, punched Karl in the face.

Karl's nose split and he went down again, face a mask of sudden, wet, red.

Tommy turned again to Suzanne. She looked terrified.

A sudden pain hit him in the centre of his back. He crumpled to his knees, gasped in agony.

Karl had grabbed a heavy metal ornament, got to his knees, thrown it.

Tommy painfully knelt up. The ornament had fallen by his feet. He picked it up and, gasping for breath, threw it back at the now-standing Karl.

Karl ducked. It hit the mirror over the fireplace, rained shards on to the carpet.

Tommy pulled himself slowly to his feet. Karl was coming at him again.

Karl swung. Tommy blocked.

Karl swung again. Tommy blocked again.

Tommy was tiring. Karl's pinprick pupils showed his body had become a cocaine-driven engine. Tommy couldn't compete with that. He needed an edge. A weapon.

The ornament was lying on the mantelpiece. Tommy grabbed it, swung it sharply at the side of

Karl's head.

It connected.

Tommy didn't let go, followed through with the swing.

Karl fell, hit the floor hard.

Tommy dropped the ornament on top of him. Looked down.

Like looking into the past.

Tommy hoped the past had been defeated.

He turned again to Suzanne. She was by the window, curtain clutched around her body, sliver of broken mirror held knife-like in one hand. Blood pooling and dripping around her fingers and palms.

'It's OK,' said Tommy, moving cautiously up to her, shouting. 'I'm not here to hurt you. Your mother sent me. Put it down. You're hurting yourself.'

She looked at him and for a split second he thought his words had reached her. Then her gaze shifted beyond him, over his shoulder, to the other side of the room.

Tommy turned, looked.

Two boys, one holding a gun.

'Put the gun down,' he shouted. His words were lost in the din.

'Put it down,' he said again and began to cross to them.

The two boys looked scared, fearful of what would happen next. They remained rooted to the spot.

'Come on,' said Tommy, pointing to the gun, 'don't play silly buggers. Put that thing down before someone gets hurt.'

Tommy held out his hands, showed he had no weapons.

Then spun round, landed on his knee.

Pain seared through Tommy's body. He closed his eyes. A blinding, white starburst. He put his hand to his right side, pressed, brought his fingers away.

Blood.

He had been shot.

By a boy.

He looked up. The shooter was sitting on the kitchen floor, clutching the automatic in his hand, his face full of surprise.

Tommy tried to stand but couldn't. The pain was too great. He slumped to the floor, managed to drag himself over to the wall.

A shrill, ringing sound. Hammering.

Tommy thought the noise was in his head but then noticed the other boy reacting to it: the doorbell. Someone pounding on the door.

The boy was shaking his head, crying.

Tommy couldn't move. His vision began to blur. He blinked.

He watched as Suzanne grabbed the discarded throw from the sofa to cover herself, opened the door.

Black snowflakes began to fall in front of him. Gather at the sides of his eyes.

Tony and Louise entered. Louise and Suzanne hugged. They were both crying.

Tony knelt down before him, spoke.

Tommy didn't hear it.

The black snowflakes began to pile up, drifting to the centre of his vision.

His legs, side, felt wet. He knew the blood, the life, was leaking out of him.

Karl on the floor. The past defeated.

Louise and Suzanne hugging. Reunited.

He closed his eyes.

Smiled.

Wondered what counted as redemption.

And was gone.

# EPILOGUE

## How Soon Is Now?

# Now

Morning.

The day starts. The night ends.

Dreams either forgotten and abandoned or dragged through to waking.

## The Modern Age: An Epilogue

*The modern age, as we know it, began on Friday 8 June 2001. This is not a date plucked at random for its Clarke/Kubrick futuristic connotations nor is it yet an officially recognized one. It was the first morning after the general election.*

*Tony Blair's New Labour government has been returned to power for a second term by an apathetic landslide. People voted for them because there was no credible alternative.*

*In the country that Blair's government now oversee, the gap between rich and poor has never been wider. A fatally dilapidated rail infrastructure. A crisis in education. In housing. In health. In social welfare. Funding withdrawn. Never returned.*

*Thatcher's legacy: time bombs exploding all over the country.*

*Seventeen years of deliberate Tory underfunding.*

*Five years of New Labour inertia.*

*A combined–*

'Here.'

A mug of tea was placed down beside Larkin's laptop.

'Thanks.'

'I've probably put everything back in the wrong place.'

'Impossible,' he said, reading over what he had just written. 'Nothing has its own place in here.'

'True,' said Claire, 'but we're getting there.'

Larkin stopped writing, stretched, looked around.

Order was being introduced to the room. Shelves contained books, CDs. The hi-fi had been wired up. Clothes had been wardrobed. Boxes were still on the floor, but they no longer dominated.

Getting there.

He walked over to Claire, stood beside her, placed his arm over her shoulder. She moved her neck into it.

'You want to get some furniture in here, mate,' she said. 'It's like you're waiting for a bus.'

'That's the next step.' He looked down at her. 'Wanna wait with me?'

Claire stood up. She was wearing Larkin's dressing gown. He was wearing a T-shirt and boxers. She turned to him, draped her arms round his shoulders. He placed his arms round her waist.

'Does it feel strange having a woman in your flat?'

'Feels strange having a woman in my life. But I'm getting used to it.'

Claire smiled.

'Y'know, when I woke up without you, I thought you'd–'

'Gone?'

Claire nodded.

'In my own flat?' Larkin smiled. 'No. I'm still here.'

'Good.'

She brought her face up to his. Kissed.

It was deep, involving. Eventually they finished, moved apart. Looked into each other's eyes. Smiled. And embraced. Just to feel each other's body close.

Larkin looked over Claire's shoulders around the corners of the room.

Ghosts rarely appeared in the morning light. They hid in the darkness, clung to the shadows. Claire's presence, he knew, was helping to throw light into those shadows.

Claire looked at her watch. 'Better get ready. Time to go soon.'

'OK.'

'That's a minus point about this place. Having to get up so early to travel in to work.'

'There are plus points.'

'I know. D'you mind if I have a shower?'

'Not at all. D'you mind if I join you?'

Claire smiled at him.

He smiled back.

They went into the bathroom together.

Louise woke slowly, stretched. She looked over to the right side of the bed. Tony was still sleeping.

She smiled to herself. She felt more relaxed than she had done in years.

Suzanne, she knew, was sleeping in another room. It was all her daughter had done for days, it seemed, sleep. Still, after what she had been through, that was a good thing.

Suzanne had told Louise everything. Broken down. Louise was helping to piece her back together again. Slowly, but they were getting there.

Tony had insisted they move in with him. It could have been a recipe for disaster, three damaged individuals living in close proximity to each other. But it had been a week now since the night in the Wills Building had changed everything for them. They were giving each other space. They were giving each other attention. They were allowing each other to heal.

Tony had agreed to accept treatment for his addiction. Louise had agreed to help him.

Louise looked at him lying there, eyes closed, peaceful. She loved him. She had always loved him. Even after that night in her flat with Tommy Jobson. She had been angry with him, not wanted to see him any more, but she had never stopped loving him. Loved him through all the years of living with Keith, the phone calls sustaining her, and finally lying with him in bed again. Loving him still.

The alarm rang.

Louise jumped up, shocked, then realized what it was. She settled back down again.

Tony's eyes opened. He smiled when he saw her.

'Mornin', you,' he said, sleep still in his voice.

She smiled at him.

'Sleep all right?' he asked.

'Like a log. Getting better all the time. What

about you?'

'Not too bad at all.'

He moved from his side on to his back, looked at the ceiling.

'Time to get up. Come on.'

Mick began his walk into town.

He hadn't slept. Or if he had, he couldn't remember it.

Days and nights were the same now. He was in darkness whether his eyes were closed or open. Waking or sleeping, he still moved through the same nightmare.

The police had visited him twice in the last week. The first time had been to inform him of his son's arrest and to ask him and Angela to join them at the station.

They had complied and found Davva in a terrible state, crying so much they couldn't understand him. The duty solicitor explained.

Drug dealing. Underage sex. Kidnapping. Actual bodily harm. Murder.

Mick was stunned. Angela had started on Davva. Screaming at him, shouting, telling him how stupid he had been. Mick had stepped in, calmed her down. Davva had started crying again. He needed a hug from his mother. It never came.

Davva was interviewed, charged, kept on remand. He and his friend, they were told, would be sent to a secure unit.

Mick and Angela had gone home.

Two days later, another policeman had called. The badly decomposed body of a teenage girl had been discovered in Wyn Davies House. They believed it was that of their daughter, Tanya. Dead from a heroin overdose.

Mick had slid into shock which in turn gave way to tears. Angela had just remained silent.

There was a baby, Mick said, Carly.

There was no baby found in the flat but they would make enquiries.

They had to identify the body. The bloated, corrupted corpse they saw bore no relation to the daughter they had once known.

Back home, Mick had cried. Angela had said, 'Well, that wasn't our daughter.'

'No,' said Mick sadly.

'She stopped bein' our daughter years ago.'

Mick looked at her, too stunned to reply.

'And as for our son, I just wash my hands of him.'

Mick could stay silent no longer.

'You wash your hands of him? You washed your hands of Tanya and look what happened to her!'

Angela turned to him, red cheeks wobbling with anger.

'You sayin' it's my fault, is it? Is that the thanks I get for everythin' I've done over the years? An' where were you in all this?'

'I was here. Right here. Lettin' you get away with everythin'.'

'That's right. Blame me.'

'Look at you! Just look at you! You've got no love in you, have you? No love at all.'

Mick grabbed his coat. He was shaking.

'Where you goin'?'

'Out.'

He slammed the door behind him.

He had gone out and stayed out.

Now, he reached the town centre. He checked the time on the clock. The supermarket would be open, but not for what he wanted.

He found a wall beside the rows of trolleys, checked the ground for pound coins, found none. Sat and waited.

Opposite was a fading poster, left up from the election. For the Labour Party:

GET OUT AND VOTE.
OR THEY GET IN AGAIN.

It showed Thatcher's hairdo on Hague's head.

Mick stared at the poster, squinted hard. The more he looked, the more he saw Blair's face beneath the hair, not Hague's. He laughed.

'Too late, mate,' he said out loud, 'they have got in again.'

Mick waited.

Tony sat behind his desk in the CAT Centre, nervous now the time had come. He could talk to other people about their problems, their addictions. That was his job, his talent. What he couldn't do was talk about his own.

'Thanks for coming.'

He looked around the room. Larkin, Claire and Louise. The door firmly shut.

'Thanks for saying you'll help. I appreciate it. I've taken advice, both medical and legal, to see where I stand. There's a doctor we do some work with here. We're going to come up with a treatment programme together. Got to do something to keep a clean supply.'

He smiled weakly. The others responded in kind.

'Are you still going to go public?' asked Claire.

'Stephen thinks it's the best thing to do. After everything that's happened recently there's going to be a lot of interest in us. I have to say I think he's right.'

'We make it pre-emptive,' said Larkin. 'If we don't come clean, so to speak, then word about Tony'll leak out. This way we control the interviews, the press. Make Tony come out of it in the best light possible.'

'And keep the Centre going,' said Claire.

'That's the important thing,' said Tony. 'We've got to keep this place running. Even if someone else has to take over.'

'It might not come to that,' said Louise.

Tony smiled at her. She smiled back, then looked out of the window.

The police had treated Tony, Suzanne and herself quite sympathetically, she thought. The only note of suspicion they had sounded was over Tommy's presence. Tony had explained that he had to take his charitable donations when and where he found them. He had also used his influence with local police and politicians to minimize the impact.

However, they knew word would get out. That was when Louise had suggested getting her brother to manage that end of things.

Tommy's funeral had been a media scrum. News cameras had fought for shots of celebs, crims or celeb crims, police cameras had quietly recorded the attendees, noting whose laugh was loudest, whose smile was widest, knowing they would try to make themselves in line for Tommy's vacant position.

Tony had been invited to attend Tommy's funeral. Louise had insisted he decline.

Karl was in hospital in a coma. Louise had attempted to be concerned over his condition but she couldn't manage it. She felt nothing but angry relief.

It was wonderful to be free of Keith, not to have her ideas, her thoughts constantly undermined. She was sad about Ben, though. She had given him the choice and he had opted to stay with his father. She had accepted it and hoped that he would come to understand her actions in time.

Keith wasn't fighting her demands for a divorce. She would get a very generous settlement too. He knew how much he had to lose.

She was pleased Suzanne was with her. They were trying with each other. It wasn't easy, but they would get there. Because they both wanted to.

And Tony. They would make it. They had survived this far.

She looked out at Coldwell.

One drinker sitting on the wall outside the public toilets. Smiling to himself.

She smiled. Even he matched her mood.

She looked back at Tony.

They would make it.

Mick, feeling the satisfying clink from within his

carrier bag, sat down on the low wall outside the public toilets in Coldwell's main square. He opened his first can of Carlsberg Special, tingled at the anticipatory pop of the ring pull, put it to his lips and drank it down.

Lovely. This first one of the morning was always the best.

He was alone. His friends would be joining him soon. He was looking forward to it. He had finally found a place he felt comfortable in, people whose company he liked. They didn't judge, they didn't ask anything of him. He asked nothing of them in return.

It was somewhere he could go to forget, to be himself.

He glanced up at the windows of the CAT Centre. Felt a pang of guilt. Tony had tried to help. He really had. But it was too difficult. This, on the other hand, was so much easier.

And much more comforting.

There was a face at Tony's window. A woman's face. Mick didn't know who she was but she was smiling. He smiled back.

Mick looked around the square. The day was slowly coming to life.

Getting going.

He took another drink.

Lovely.

Worry flitted across his mind: what would happen when the cans ran out? He told himself to calm down. He would deal with that when it happened. For now, he had what he wanted.

He took another drink.

Waited.

The publishers hope that this book has given you enjoyable reading. Large Print Books are especially designed to be as easy to see and hold as possible. If you wish a complete list of our books please ask at your local library or write directly to:

**Magna Large Print Books**
Magna House, Long Preston,
Skipton, North Yorkshire.
BD23 4ND

This Large Print Book for the partially sighted, who cannot read normal print, is published under the auspices of

## THE ULVERSCROFT FOUNDATION